WALK IN THE LIGHT

AND

TWENTY-THREE TALES

By LEO TOLSTOY

TRANSLATED BY LEO WIENER AND LOUISE AND AYLMER MAUDE

Walk in the Light and Twenty-Three Tales
By Leo Tolstoy
Translated by Leo Wiener and Louise and Aylmer Maude

Print ISBN 13: 978-1-4209-6709-8
eBook ISBN 13: 978-1-4209-6710-4

Cover Image: a detail of "At the Bear's Den", c. 19th Century (colour litho), by Alexei Steipanovitch Stepanov (1858-1923) / Look and Learn / Elgar Collection / Bridgeman Images.

Please visit *www.digireads.com*

CONTENTS

PART VI. ADAPTATIONS FROM THE FRENCH

PART VII. STORIES GIVEN TO AID THE PERSECUTED JEWS

WALK IN THE LIGHT WHILE YE HAVE LIGHT

Translated by Leo Wiener

Conversations between a Pagan and a Christian.
Story from the Time of the Ancient Christians

1890

INTRODUCTION

Guests were one day assembled in a wealthy house, and a serious conversation on life was started. They spoke of present and of absent people, and they could not find a single man who was satisfied with his life. Not only was there not one man who could boast of happiness, but there was not even one man who thought that he was living as was becoming for a Christian. All confessed that they were living only a worldly life in cares for themselves and for their families, and that not one of them was thinking of his neighbour, and much less of God. Thus the guests spoke among themselves, and all agreed in accusing themselves of a godless, non-Christian life.

"Why, then, do we live thus?" exclaimed a youth. "Why do we do what we do not approve of? Have we not the power to change our life? We know ourselves that what ruins us is our luxury, our effeminacy, our wealth, and, chiefly, our pride, our separation from our brothers. To be noble and rich, we have to deprive ourselves of everything which gives the joy of life to a man. We crowd into cities, make ourselves effeminate, ruin our health, and, in spite of all our amusements, die from ennui and from self-pity, because our life is not such as it ought to be. Why should we live thus? Why ruin our whole life,—all that good which is given us by God? I do not want to live as heretofore! I will abandon all the teaching which I have entered upon, for it will lead me to nothing but the same agonizing life of which we all now complain. I will renounce my property and will go to the country and live with the poor; I will work with them, will learn to work with my hands; if my education is of any use to the poor, I will communicate it to them, but not through institutions and books, but by living directly with them in a brotherly relation. Yes, I have made up my mind!" he said, looking interrogatively at his father, who was also present.

"Your desire is good," said the father, "but frivolous and thoughtless. Everything presents itself to you as easy, because you do not know life. There are things enough that seem good to us! But the point is that the execution of what is good is frequently difficult and complicated. It is hard to walk well on a beaten track, and harder still to lay out new paths. They are laid out only by men who have fully matured and who have completely grasped everything which is accessible to men. The new paths of life seem easy to you, because you do not yet understand life. All this is thoughtlessness and pride of youth. We old men are needed for the very purpose that we may moderate your transports and guide you by means of our experience, while you young people should obey us, in order that you may be able to make use of our experience. Your active life is still ahead,—now you are growing and developing. Educate yourself, form yourself completely, stand on your feet, have your firm convictions, and then begin the new life, if you feel the strength for it. But now you should obey those who guide you for your good, and not open new paths of life."

The youth grew silent, and the elder guests agreed to what the father had said.

"You are right," a middle-aged married man turned to the father of the youth, "you are right, when you say that a youth, who has not any experience in life, may make mistakes in looking for new paths of life, and that his decision cannot be firm; but we have all agreed to this, that our life is contrary to our conscience and does not give us the good; therefore we cannot help but recognize that the desire to get out of it is just. A youth may take his reverie to be a deduction of reason, but I am not a young man, and I will tell you about myself that, as I listened to the conversation of this evening, the same thought came to me. The life which I lead, obviously for myself, cannot give me any peace of mind and the good; this is also shown me by reason and by experience. So what am I waiting for? We struggle from morning until evening for our family, but in reality it turns out that my family and I myself do not live in godly fashion, but sink deeper and deeper in our sins. We do everything for our families, but our families are not better off, because what we do for them is not the good. And so I have frequently thought that it would be better if I changed my whole life and stopped caring for my wife and my children, and began to think of my soul. There is good reason in what Paul says, 'He that is married careth how he may please his wife, and he that is unmarried careth for God.'"

The married man had barely finished his words, when all the women present and his wife began to attack him.

"You ought to have thought of it before," said one of the middle-aged women. "You have put on the collar and so pull! It is easy enough for anybody to come and say that he wants to be saved, when it appears hard for him to keep up and support a family. This is a deception and a rascality! No, a man must be able to live in godly fashion with a family. Of course, it is so easy to be saved all by oneself. Besides, if you do so, you act contrary to Christ's teaching. God has commanded us to love others, while the way you do, you wish for the sake of God to offend others. No one has a right to do violence to his family!"

But the married man did not agree to this. He said:

"I do not want to abandon my family. I only say that the family and the children should not be kept in worldly fashion, so that they get used to living for their lust, as we have just said, but that we should live in such a way that the children should from the earliest time become accustomed to privation, to labour, to aiding others, and chiefly to a brotherly life in respect to all men. But, to attain this, we must renounce aristocracy and wealth."

"There is no need of curbing others, while you do not yourself live in godly fashion!" his wife retorted to this, with irritation. "You yourself lived for your pleasure when you were young, so why do you want to torment your children and your family? Let them grow up quietly, and then, let them do what they please, but do not force them!"

The married man kept silence, but an old man, who was present, took his part:

"Let us admit," he said, "that a married man, who has accustomed his family to certain comforts, cannot suddenly deprive them of them. It is true, if the education of the children has been begun, it is better to finish it than to break up everything, the more so, since the children will themselves choose the path which they will deem best. I admit that for a married man it is hard and even impossible without sinning to change his life. But we old men have been commanded to do so by God. I will tell you about myself: I am living now without any obligations,—I must confess, I am living for my belly only,—I eat, drink, rest,—and I am ashamed and disgusted with myself. It is time for me to give up this life, to distribute my property, and at least before death to live as God has commanded a Christian to live."

But they did not agree with the old man either. Here was his niece and godchild, all of whose children he had christened and given presents to on holidays, and here was also his son. They all retorted to him.

"No," said his son, "you have worked enough in your life,—it is time for you to take a rest, and not to torture yourself. You have lived for sixty years with your habits, and you cannot stop them. You will only torture yourself in vain."

"Yes, yes," confirmed his niece, "you will be in want, and you will be out of sorts, and you will grumble and sin more than ever. God is merciful and pardons all the sinners, and not only you, such a dear uncle."

"And why should we?" added another old man, who was of the same age as the uncle. "You and I have, perhaps, two days left to live. Why should we begin anew?"

"How wonderful!" said one of the guests, who had been silent during the conversation, "how wonderful! All say that it is good to live in godly fashion, and that we live badly, and that we torment ourselves in body and soul; but the moment it comes to business, it turns out, that the children ought not to be broken in, but that they ought to be brought up, not in godly fashion, but as of old. The young people must not get out from under their parents' will, and they must not live in godly fashion, but as of old; married men must not change the life of their wives and children, and must not live in godly fashion, but as of old; and there is no reason why old men should begin anew,—they are not accustomed to it, and they have but two days to live, and all such things. It turns out that nobody can live well, but that we may only talk about it."

WALK IN THE LIGHT WHILE YE HAVE LIGHT

I.

This happened in the reign of the Roman Emperor Trajan, 100 Anno Domini. It was at a time when the disciples of Christ's disciples were still alive, and the Christians held firmly to the law of the teachers, as it says in the Acts.

The multitude of them that believed were of one heart and of one soul: and none of them said that aught of the things which he possessed was his own; but they had all things common. And with great power the apostles gave witness of the resurrection of the Lord Jesus Christ, and great grace was upon their faith. Neither was there any among them that lacked: for as many as were possessors of lands or houses sold them, and brought the prices of the things that were sold, and laid them down at the apostles' feet, and distribution was made unto every man according as he had need. (Acts, Chap. IV., 32-35.)

In these first times there lived in the country of Cilicia, in the city of Tarsus, a rich merchant, a Syrian, a dealer in precious stones, Juvenalis by name. He came from simple and poor people, but through labour and skill in his business he gained wealth and the respect of his fellow citizens. He had travelled much in foreign countries and, though he was not learned, had come to know and understand many things, and the inhabitants of the city respected him for his intellect and justice. He professed the same Roman, pagan faith which was professed by all the respected men of the Roman empire; that faith, the fulfillment of whose ceremonies they had begun strictly to demand from the time of Emperor Augustus and which the present Emperor Trajan himself strictly observed. The country of Cilicia is far from Rome, but it was governed by a Roman supreme officer, and what was done in Rome found its echo in Cilicia, and the governors imitated their emperors.

Juvenalis remembered from his childhood the stories of what Nero had done in Rome, had later seen how the emperors had perished one after another, and, being a clever man, understood that there was nothing sacred in the Roman religion, but that it all was the work of human hands. The senselessness of all the life surrounding him, especially of what was taking place in Rome, where he often went on business, had frequently disturbed him. He had doubts; he could not grasp it all, and he referred it all to his lack of education.

He was married, and he had had four children, but three of them had died in their youth, and there was only one son left, and his name was Julius.

In this Julius Juvenalis centered all his love and all his cares. Juvenalis was particularly anxious to have his son educated in such a way that his son should not be tormented by those doubts concerning life, by which he himself had been troubled. When Julius passed his fifteenth year, his father gave him to be instructed by a philosopher who had settled in their city, and who took youths to instruct them. The father gave him to the philosopher together with his comrade Pamphylius, the son of one of Juvenalis's deceased manumitted slaves. The youths were of the same age, both handsome, and they were friends.

Both youths studied diligently, and both were of good morals. Julius excelled more in the study of the poets and of mathematics, while Pamphylius excelled in the study of philosophy. A year previous to the end of their instruction, Pamphylius came to school and informed his teacher that his mother, a widow, was going to the city of Daphne, and that he would have to stop studying. The teacher was sorry to lose a pupil who was doing him honour; and so was Juvenalis, but most of all Julius. To all admonitions to stay and continue his instruction, Pamphylius remained imperturbable and, thanking his friends for their love and their cares of him, he parted from them.

Two years passed; Julius finished his studies, and during all that time he had not seen his friend.

Once he met him in the street; he invited him to his house and began to ask him how and where he was living. Pamphylius told him that he was living with his mother in the same place.

"We do not live alone," he said, "but there are many friends with us, and we have everything in common with them."

"How in common?" asked Julius.

"So that none of us considers anything his own."

"Why do you do so?"

"We are Christians," said Pamphylius.

"Is it possible?" exclaimed Julius. "But I was told that the Christians killed children and ate them. Is it possible you take part in this?"

"Come and see," replied Pamphylius. "We do not do anything in particular; we live simply, trying to do nothing bad."

"But how can one live without considering anything one's own?"

"We manage to live. If we give our brothers our labour, they give us theirs."

"Well, and if your brothers take your labour, and do not give it back, what then?"

"There are no such," said Pamphylius. "Such people like to live in luxury and will not come to us: our life is simple and not luxurious."

"But are there not many lazy people who will be glad to be fed for nothing?"

"There are such, and we receive them cheerfully. Lately there came to us such a man, a fugitive slave; at first, it is true, he was lazy and lived badly, but he soon changed his manner of life, and is now a good brother."

"But suppose he had not mended his ways?"

"There are such, too. Elder Cyril has said that such we must treat like the dearest brothers, and love even better."

"Is it possible to love good-for-nothing people?"

"One cannot help but love a man!"

"But how can you give to all everything which they ask for?" inquired Julius. "If my father gave to all who ask him for something, he would soon be left without anything."

"I do not know," replied Pamphylius, "but we have enough left for our needs; and if it happens that we have nothing to eat or to cover ourselves with, we ask of others and they give to us. Yes, this happens rarely. It happened but once that I had to go to bed without a supper, and that, too, was so because I was very tired and did not wish to go to a brother to ask him for it."

"I do not know how you do it," said Julius, "only, as my father has told me, if you do not guard what is yours, and if, besides, you give everything to those who ask it, you will yourself starve to death."

"We do not starve. Come and see. We live, and not only do not suffer want, but have enough to spare"

"How is this?"

"It is like this: We all confess the same law, but the force of execution varies in us: one has more, another less of it. One has already perfected himself in the good life, another is only beginning it. At the head of all of us stands Christ with his life, and we all try to emulate him, and in this alone do we see our good. Some, like Elder Cyril and his wife Pelagea, stand ahead of us; others stand behind us; others again are far behind, but all walk on the same path. The leaders are already near to Christ's law,—the renunciation of self,—and have lost their souls, in order to find them. They need nothing; they have no thought of themselves, and the last thing they have they, according to Christ's law, give to him who asks for it. There are others who are weaker, who cannot give up everything; they weaken and have still a thought of themselves; they weaken without the customary food and raiment, and do not give up everything. There are others, who are weaker still,— those who have but lately entered upon the path; they continue to live as of old, retain much for themselves, and give up only what is superfluous. And it is these hindmost people who come to the aid of those in front. We are, besides, all of us by relationship intermingled with the pagans. One has a father who is a pagan and holds property and gives it to his son. The son gives it to those who ask him for it, but the father gives him some again. Another has a pagan mother who pities her son and helps him. A third has pagan children, and their mother is a Christian, and the children solace their mother and give her things, asking her not to distribute them; and she takes them out of love for them, and none the less gives them to others. A fourth has a pagan wife. A fifth has a pagan husband. Thus are all intermingled, and the foremost would be glad to give their last, but are not able to do so. It is this which supports the weak in their faith, and from this a great superfluity is collected."

To this Julius said:

"But if it is so, you evidently depart from Christ's teaching and only make believe. If you do not give up everything, there is no difference between you and us. As I take it, if one is a Christian, he ought to fulfill everything,—give up everything and become a beggar."

"That is best of all," said Pamphylius. "Do so."

"Yes, I will, when I see that you do so."

"We do not wish to show anything, and I advise you not to come to us and not to abandon your life for the sake of appearances; what we do, we do, not for appearances, but according to faith."

"What is meant by according to faith?"

"By according to faith is meant that salvation from the evils of the world, from death, is only in a life according to Christ's teaching. It is all the same to us what people will say of us. We do not do anything for the sake of people, but because in this alone do we see life and the good."

"It is impossible not to live for oneself," said Julius. "The gods themselves have implanted this in us, that we love ourselves more than others and seek pleasures for ourselves. And you do the same. You say yourself that there are some among you who have a thought for themselves. They will be preparing more and more pleasures for themselves and will more and more abandon your faith and will do precisely as we do."

"No," replied Pamphylius, "our people walk along another path and never weaken, but keep growing stronger, just as the fire will never go out so long as wood is put on it. In this does our faith consist."

"I cannot make out in what this faith does consist."

"Our faith consists in this, that we understand life as Christ has explained it to us."

"How has he?"

"Christ told the following parable: Husbandmen were living in another man's garden and had to pay tribute to their master. It is we, the people, who are living in the world and must pay tribute to God,— to do His will. But those men with their worldly faith thought that the garden was theirs, that they did not need to pay for it, and that all they had to do was to enjoy its fruits. The master sent a messenger to the husbandmen to receive the tribute, but they drove him away. The master sent his son for the tribute, and they killed him, thinking that after that no one would disturb them. This is the worldly faith by which all the men of the world live, when they do not recognize the fact that life is given for the purpose of serving God. But Christ has taught us that the worldly faith, that it is better for a man if he drives the master's messenger and the son out of the garden and does not pay tribute, is a false faith, because one result or the other cannot be avoided, either you pay tribute, or you are driven out of the garden. He has taught us that all the joys, those which we call joys,—eating, drinking, merriment,— can be no joys if life is placed in them; that they are joys only when we seek something else,—the fulfillment of God's will; that only then these joys follow the fulfillment as a true reward. To wish to take the joys without the labour of fulfilling God's will, to tear the joys away from labour, is the same as to tear the stalks of flowers and plant them without roots. We believe in this, and so cannot seek the deception instead of the truth. Our faith consists in this, that the good of life is not in joys, but in the fulfillment of God's will without any thought as to joys or any hope respecting them. And thus we live, and the longer we live, the more we see that the joys and the good, like a wheel following the shaft, come in the wake of the fulfillment of God's will. Our teacher has said, 'Come unto me, all ye that labour and are heavy laden, and I will give you rest. Take my yoke upon you, and learn of me; for I am meek and lowly of heart, and ye shall find rest unto your souls. For my yoke is easy, and my burden is light.'"

Thus spoke Pamphylius. Julius listened and his heart was touched, but what Pamphylius had said was not clear to him; it seemed to him that Pamphylius was deceiving him; and he looked again into Pamphylius's good eyes, and it seemed to him that Pamphylius was deceiving himself. Pamphylius invited Julius to come to see him, to inspect their life, and, if he was pleased with it, to remain to live with them.

Julius promised he would come, but he did not go to see Pamphylius; he was carried away by his own manner of life, and forgot Pamphylius.

II.

Julius's father was rich, loved his only son, was proud of him, and spared no money on him. Julius's life passed like that of rich young men: in idleness, luxury, and the amusements of dissipation, which have always been the same,—wine, gaming, and fast women.

But the enjoyments to which Julius abandoned himself demanded more and more money, and Julius began to feel a lack of it. Once he asked his father for more than his father was in the habit of giving to him. The father gave it to him, but also reprimanded him. Feeling himself guilty and not wishing to confess his guilt, his son grew angry and insulted his father, as those always grow angry who know their guilt and do not wish to confess it. The money taken from his father was very soon spent, and, besides, Julius happened at that time to get into a brawl with a companion of his and to kill a man. The chief of the city learned of this and wanted to take Julius under guard, but his father obtained his pardon. Just then Julius needed more money for his dissipations. He borrowed money from a friend, promising to return it to him. Besides, his mistress demanded a present from him: she took a liking for a pearl necklace, and he knew that if he did not fulfill her prayer, she would abandon him and go to live with a rich man who had long been trying to get her away from Julius. Julius went to his mother, and told her that he was in need of money, and that he would kill himself if he did not get as much as he needed.

He did not blame himself, but his father, for the condition he was in. He said: "My father accustomed me to a life of luxury, and then began to begrudge me the money. If he had given me in the beginning without rebukes what he later gave me, I should have arranged my life and should have had no need; but as he never gave me any sufficiency, I was compelled to turn to usurers, and they squeezed everything out of me; and there was nothing left for me to live on, as is proper for a rich young man, and I am ashamed in the presence of my companions, while my father does not wish to understand anything. He has forgotten that he himself was once a young man. It is he who brought me to this state, and if he does not give me now what I am asking for, I shall kill myself."

The mother, who spoiled her son, went to his father. The father sent for his son, and began to scold him and his mother. The son answered insultingly to his father. The father struck him. The son grasped his father's hands. The father called the slaves and commanded them to bind his son and lock him up.

When Julius was left alone, he began to curse his father and his own life.

His death or the death of his father presented itself to him as the only way out from the condition in which he was.

Julius's mother suffered more than he. She did not try to make out who was to blame for all this. She only was sorry for her beloved child. She went to her husband to implore his pardon. Her husband would not listen to her, rebuked her for having spoiled her son; she rebuked him, and it all ended in the husband beating his wife. But the mother paid no attention to the blows, and went to her son to admonish him to beg his father's pardon and submit to him. For this she promised her son secretly that she would give him the money which he was in need of. Her son agreed, and then the mother went to her husband and begged him to forgive his son. The father for a long time scolded his wife and his son, but finally decided that he would forgive his son, but only on condition that he would abandon his life of dissipation and would marry a rich merchant's daughter, whom his father wanted to get as a wife for his son.

"He will get money from me and the wife's dowry," said the father, "and then let him begin a regular life. If he promises to do my will, I shall forgive him. But now I will not give him anything, and the first time he transgresses, I will turn him over to the chief."

Julius agreed to everything, and was released. He promised to get married and to abandon his bad life, but he did not have the intention of doing so.

His life at home became a hell for him: his father did not speak to him and quarreled with his mother on account of him, and his mother cried.

On the following day his mother called him to her apartments and secretly handed him a precious stone which she had carried off from her husband.

"Go and sell it, not here, but in another city, and do what you have to do. I shall know how for a time to conceal this loss, and if it is discovered, I will put the blame on one of the slaves."

The mother's words touched Julius's heart. He was terrified at what she had done and, without taking the precious stone, left the house.

He did not know himself whither he was going, and for what purpose. He walked on and on, away from the city, feeling the necessity of being left alone and reflecting on what had happened to him and on what was awaiting him. As he kept marching on and on, he left the city behind and entered a holy grove of the Goddess Diana. Upon reaching a solitary spot, he began to think. The first thought that came to him was to ask the goddess's aid, but he no longer believed in his gods and so knew that no aid was to be expected from them. And if not from them, from whom? It seemed too strange to him to reflect on his own situation. In his soul there was chaos and darkness. But there was nothing to be done: it was necessary for him to turn to his conscience, and he began before it to consider his life and his acts; and both seemed bad to him and, above all, foolish. Why had he been tormenting himself so much? Why had he been ruining his youthful years? There were few joys, and much sorrow and unhappiness! But the main thing was, he felt himself alone. Before this he had had a loving mother, a father, and even friends,—now there was nothing. No one loved him! He was a burden to all. He had managed to cross everybody's life: for his mother he was the cause of her discord with his father; for his father he was a spendthrift of his money, which had been collected by the labour of a whole life; for his friends he was a dangerous, disagreeable rival. For all of them it was desirable that he should die.

Passing his life in review, he recalled Pamphylius, and his last meeting with him, and how Pamphylius had invited him to come to them, the Christians. And it passed through his head that he would not return home, but would go to the Christians and would remain with them.

"But is my situation so desperate?" he thought, and he again recalled everything which had happened to him, and again he was frightened at this, that, as he thought, no one loved him and he loved no one. His mother, father, friends did not love him, could not help but desire his death; but did he himself love any one? His friends? He felt that he did not love any one. They were all his antagonists; all were pitiless to him now that he was in misfortune.

"My father?" he asked himself, and he was seized by terror, when, at this question, he looked into his own heart. He not only did not love him, but even hated him for the oppressions, for the insults. He hated him and, besides, he saw clearly that for his, Julius's happiness, he needed his father's death.

"Yes," he said to himself, "if I knew that no one would ever see or find out,—what would I do, if I could with one stroke, at once, deprive him of life and free myself?"

And Julius answered himself:

"Yes, I should kill him!"

He gave this answer to himself, and he was frightened at himself.

"My mother? Yes, I pity her, but I do not love her; it is all the same to me what will become of her,—all I need is her aid. Yes, I am a beast! and a hunted-down, a baited beast, and I differ from a beast only in this, that I can, by my will, go away from the deceptive, evil life; I can do what a beast cannot,—I can kill myself. I hate my father, I love no one—neither my mother, nor my friends—unless, perhaps, Pamphylius alone."

And he again thought of him. He began to recall the last meeting, and their conversation, and Pamphylius's words as to what Christ said, according to their teaching: "Come unto me, all ye that labour and are heavy laden, and I will give you rest." Is it true?

He began to think, to recall the meek, fearless, and joyful face of Pamphylius, and he wanted to believe what Pamphylius had said.

"What am I indeed?" he said to himself. "Who am I? A man searching after the good. I have searched after it in lustful desires and have not found it. And all those who live like me find it as little. All are evil and suffer. But there is a man who is always full of joy, because he is not searching after anything. He says that there are many such, and that all will be such, if they shall follow what their Teacher says. What if this is the truth? Truth or untruth,—I am drawn toward it, and I shall go."

Thus Julius said to himself, and he left the grove, having decided not to return home, and went toward the village in which the Christians lived.

III.

Julius walked cheerfully and joyously, and the farther he walked and the more vividly he presented to himself the life of the Christians, recalling everything which Pamphylius had said, the more happy he felt. The sun was declining toward evening, and he wanted to rest, when he met a man on the road, who was resting and eating his supper. The man was of middle age, with a bright face. He was sitting, and eating olives and a flat cake. When he saw Julius, he smiled, and said:

"Good evening, young man! The road is still far. Sit down and rest thyself."

Julius thanked him, and sat down.

"Whither dost thou go?" asked the stranger.

"To the Christians," said Julius, and, by degrees, he told the stranger his whole life and his determination.

The stranger listened attentively, asked him about the details, and himself did not express his opinion; but when Julius had ended, the stranger put the remaining food into his wallet, adjusted his clothes, and said:

"Young man, do not carry out thy intention! Thou art in error. I know life, but thou dost not know it. I know the Christians, but thou dost not know them. Listen: I will analyze all thy life and thy thoughts, and after thou hast heard them from me, thou wilt make that decision which will appear to thee most correct. Thou art young, rich, handsome, strong, and the passions are boiling in thee. Thou desirest to find a quiet harbour, where the passions shall not agitate thee and thou wilt not suffer from their consequences, and it seems to thee that thou wilt find such a harbour among the Christians. There is no such place, dear youth, because what is troubling thee is not to be found in Cilicia, nor in Home, but in thyself. In the quiet of the country solitude the same passions will torment thee, only a hundred times more powerfully. The deception of the Christians, or their error (I do not want to condemn them), consists in this, that they do not wish to recognize human nature. Only an old man, who has outlived all his passions, may be a complete executor of their teaching. But a man in possession of his strength, or a youth like thee, who has not experienced life and tried himself, cannot submit to their law, because this law has for its basis, not human nature, but the idle speculation of their founder, Christ. If thou shalt go to them, thou wilt suffer what thou sufferest now, only to a far greater extent. Now thy passions lead thee on false paths, but, having once made a mistake in the direction, thou art able to correct thyself; now thou hast at least the satisfaction of liberated passion, that is, life. But among them, thou, violently repressing thy passions, wilt err just as much, even worse, and besides this suffering wilt have the unceasing suffering of man's unsatisfied needs. Let the water out over a dam, and it will water the earth and the meadows, and animals; but hold it back, and it will tear up the earth and run out with dirt. The same is true of the passions. The teaching of the Christians, their teaching in regard to life, consists, besides the beliefs with which they console themselves, and of which I shall not speak, also in the following: they do not recognize violence, wars, courts, or property, or the sciences, arts,—all that which makes life easy and joyous. All this would be well, if all men were such as they describe their teacher to have been. But this is not the case, and this cannot be. Men are evil and are subject to their passions. This play of the passions and the conflicts which result from them hold men back in those conditions of life in which they live. Barbarians (savages) know no repression, and one savage would, for the gratification of his desires, destroy the whole world, if all men should submit as easily as the Christians do. If the gods have implanted the sentiment of anger in men, they have done so because these sentiments are necessary for the life of men. The Christians teach that these sentiments are evil, and that without them men would be happy; there would be no murders, capital punishments, wars. This is true, but it resembles the proposition that for their welfare they must not receive nourishment. Indeed, there would be no greed and hunger and all the calamities which result from them. But still this proposition would not change human nature. And if two or three dozens of men, believing this and actually not taking any food, should starve to death, this would not change human nature. The same is true of the other passions,—indignation, anger, revenge, even love of women, of luxury, of splendour, and of grandeur, are characteristic of the gods also, and so are man's unchangeable properties. Destroy man's nutrition, and man will be destroyed; similarly destroy man's characteristic passions, and humanity will be destroyed. The same is true of ownership, which the Christians are supposed to deny. Look

about thee: every vineyard, every enclosure, every house, every she-
ass,—all this has been produced by men only under the condition of
ownership. Reject the right of ownership, and not one vineyard will be
dug up, not one animal will be raised and trained. The Christians assert
that they have no property, but they enjoy its fruits. They say that they
have everything in common, and that everything is brought together.
But what they bring together, they have received from people who own
property. They only deceive men and, at best, deceive themselves.
Thou sayest that they work themselves, in order to support themselves;
but what they get by work would not support them, if they did not
make use of what men who recognize ownership have produced. Even
if they could support themselves, they only could sustain their lives,
and there would be no place among them for the sciences, nor for the
arts. They do not recognize the use of our sciences and arts. Nor can
they act differently. All their teaching tends only to bring them back to
the primitive state, to savagery, to the animal. They cannot serve
humanity by means of the sciences and arts, and, since they do not
know them, they deny them. They cannot serve by those means which
form man's exclusive property and bring him near to the gods. They
will have no temples, no statues, no theatres, no museums. They say
that they do not need them. The easiest way not to be ashamed of their
baseness is to despise altitude, and this they are doing. Their teacher is
an ignoramus and cheat. And they emulate him. Besides, they are
godless. They do not recognize the gods and their intervention in
human affairs. For them exists only the father of their teacher, whom
they also call their own father, and the teacher himself, who, according
to their conception, has revealed all the mysteries of life to them. Their
teaching is a miserable deception. Consider this: our teaching says that
the world exists through the gods and that the gods protect men. But
men, to live well, must worship the gods and themselves seek and
think,—and so we are guided in our life, on the one hand, by the will of
the gods, on the other, by the combined wisdom of all humanity. We
live, think, and seek, and so move toward truth. But they have no gods,
nor their will, nor human wisdom, but only one thing, the blind belief
in their crucified teacher, and in everything which he has said to them.
Weigh which guide is more reliable, the will of the gods and the
combined, free activity of human wisdom, or the compulsory, blind
belief in the words of one man."

Julius was struck by what the stranger had told him, especially by
his last words.

His intention of going among the Christians was not only shaken,
but it now even seemed strange to him how, under the influence of his
troubles, he could have decided upon such madness. But there was still
the question open for him what he was to do now and how to get out of
those difficult conditions in which he now was, and he told the stranger

about his situation and asked his advice.

"I wanted to speak of this very thing," continued the stranger. "What art thou to do? Thy path, in so far as human wisdom is accessible to me, is clear to me. All thy troubles arise from the passions which are characteristic of man. Thou hast been carried away by passion, which took thee so far that thou didst suffer. Such are the usual lessons of life. These lessons must be used to advantage. Thou hast experienced much, and thou knowest where it is bitter and where sweet: thou canst no longer repeat those blunders. Take advantage of thy experience. What grieves thee more than anything else is thy enmity toward thy father. This enmity is due to thy situation; choose another, and it will be destroyed, or, at least, it will no longer manifest itself so painfully. All thy troubles are due to the irregularity of thy situation. Thou hast abandoned thyself to the amusements of youth; this is natural and good. But it was good only so long as it corresponded to thy age. But the time passed and thou didst abandon thyself with the powers of a man to the wantonness of youth, and that was bad. Thou hast reached a time when thou oughtest to become a man, a citizen, and serve thy country, work in its behalf. Thy father proposes to thee that thou shouldst get married. His advice is wise. Thou hast outlived one period of life, youth, and hast entered upon another. All thy tribulations are symptoms of a transitional condition. Recognize that the time of youth has passed and, boldly rejecting what was proper for it, but not proper for a man, enter upon the new path. Get married, give up the enjoyments of youth, busy thyself with commerce, public affairs, the sciences, and the arts, and thou wilt not only make thy peace with thy father and thy friends, but thou wilt also find peace and joy. The main thing that agitated thee is the unnaturalness of thy situation. Thou hast become a man, and thou shouldst enter into matrimony and be a man. And so my chief counsel is: Do thy father's bidding, get married. If thou art attracted to solitude, which thou hadst intended to find among the Christians, if thou art inclined toward philosophy, and not toward the activity of life, thou canst usefully abandon thyself to this activity only after thou hast learned life in its true significance. This thou wilt know only as an independent citizen and head of a family. If after that thou shalt be attracted to solitude, abandon thyself to it, and then it will be a true attraction, and not an outburst of dissatisfaction, such as it is at present. Then go!"

The last words more than any others convinced Julius. He thanked the stranger and returned home.

His mother received him with joy. His father, too, when he learned of his readiness to submit to his will and to marry the maiden which had been proposed to him, was reconciled with his son.

IV.

Three months later they celebrated the wedding with beautiful Eulampia, and Julius, having changed his manner of life, began to manage a separate house with his wife, and himself attended to part of the business which his father had turned over to him.

Once he went for his business house to a near-by town, and while he was sitting there in a merchant's shop, saw Pamphylius pass by with a maiden, who was a stranger to him. Both were walking with heavy burdens of grapes, which they were selling. When Julius recognized his friend, he went up to him and asked him to step into the shop, in order to have a chat with him. When the maiden saw Pamphylius's desire to go with his friend and his misgiving about leaving her alone, she hastened to say that she did not need him and would sit alone with the grapes, waiting for purchasers. Pamphylius thanked her and went with Julius into the shop. Julius asked permission of the merchant, his friend, to go into his living-room, and when he had received the permission, retired with Pamphylius to the rooms in the back.

The friends asked one another for the details of their lives. Pamphylius's life had not changed since they had met the last time: he continued to live in the Christian commune, was not married, and assured his friend that his life was getting more and more joyous with every year, day, and hour. Julius told his friend what had happened with him, and how he had been on his way to the Christians, when his meeting with the stranger elucidated to him the errors of the Christians, and his own duty to get married, and how he had followed the advice and had married.

"Well, art thou happy now?" Pamphylius asked. "Hast thou found in marriage what the stranger promised thee?"

"Happy?" said Julius. "What do you mean by happy? If we are to understand by it a full gratification of my desires, I am naturally unhappy. So far I have been carrying on my business with success, and people begin to respect me; and in either of these things I find a certain satisfaction. Though I see many men who are richer and more honoured than I, I foresee the possibility of coming up to them and even surpassing them. This side of my life is full, but my wedded state, I will say outright, does not satisfy me. I will say more: I feel that this very matrimony, which ought to give me joy, has not given it to me, and that the joy, which I experienced at first, kept diminishing and finally was destroyed; and in the place where there was joy there has grown up sorrow. My wife is beautiful, clever, learned, and good. At first I was entirely happy. But now,—you do not know this, because you have no wife,—there occur causes for discord, because she seeks my love, when I am indifferent to her, and vice versa. Besides, for love we need novelty. A less attractive woman than my wife attracts me more at first, but later becomes less attractive to me than my wife; I have already experienced this. No, I have not found any satisfaction in my married state. Yes, my friend," concluded Julius, "the philosophers are right: life does not give what the soul wishes for. I have experienced this now in matrimony. But the fact that life does not give the good which the soul wishes for does not prove that your deception may give it," he added, smiling.

"In what dost thou see our deception?" asked Pamphylius.

"Your deception consists in this, that you, to liberate a man from the calamities which are connected with the affairs of life, deny all affairs of life,—life itself. To free yourselves from disenchantments you deny the enchantment, marriage itself."

"We do not deny marriage," said Pamphylius.

"If not marriage, you deny love."

"On the contrary, we deny everything but love. It serves us as the first foundation of everything."

"I do not understand thee," said Julius. "From what I have heard from others and from thee, and from the fact that thou art not yet married, though we are of the same age, I conclude that you do not have marriage. Your people continue in the married state, if they entered into it before, but they do not enter anew into wedlock. You do not trouble yourselves about the continuation of the human race. If you were alone, the human race would have long ago come to an end," said Julius, repeating what he had heard many times.

"That is not true," said Pamphylius. "It is true that we do not make it our aim to continue the human race and do not trouble ourselves about it as much as I have many a time heard your sages trouble themselves. We assume that our Father has already taken care of this: our aim consists only in living according to His will. If in His will is the continuation of the human race, it will be continued; if not, it will come to an end; this is not our affair, not our care; our care is to live according to His will. But His will is expressed both in our sermon and in our revelation, where it says that a man should unite with his wife, and there should not be two bodies, but one. Marriage is not only not prohibited among us, but is even encouraged by our old teachers. The difference between our marriage and yours consists in this, that our law has revealed to us that every lustful looking at a woman is a sin, and so we and our women, instead of adorning ourselves and provoking lust, try to remove ourselves from it so far that the sentiment of love between us, as between brothers and sisters, should be stronger than the sensation of lust for one woman, which you call love."

"But you can still not suppress the love of the beautiful," said Julius. "I am convinced, for example, that that beauty, the maiden with whom thou didst carry the grapes, in spite of her attire, which conceals her charms, evokes in thee the feeling of love for a woman."

"I do not yet know," Pamphylius said, blushing. "I have not thought of her beauty. Thou art the first who has told me of it. She is for me only a sister. But I shall go on with what I wanted to tell thee about the difference between our marriage and yours. The difference originates even from this, that with you lust, under the name of beauty and love and serving Goddess Venus, is sustained, provoked in men. But with us it is the very opposite: lust is not considered an evil (God has not created any evil), but a good, which becomes an evil when it is not in its place,—an offence, as we call it. And this is the reason why I am not yet married, though I may possibly be to-morrow."

"But what will decide it?"

"God's will."

"How dost thou recognize it?"

"If we never look for indications of it, we never find it; but if we look for them constantly, they become clear, as clear as are for you your divinations from sacrifices and birds. And as you have your own sages, who according to their wisdom, and according to the entrails of sacrificial animals, and according to the flight of the birds expound to you the will of the gods, so we have sages who explain to us the will of the Father, according to Christ's revelation, according to the feeling of their hearts and the thoughts of other men, and, chiefly, according to their love of them."

"But all this is very indefinite," retorted Julius. "What, for example, will show thee when to marry, and whom? When I was about to many, I had the choice among three maidens: these three were chosen from among others, because they were beautiful and rich, and my father was satisfied if I married any one of them. Of these three I chose Eulampia, because she was to me more beautiful and attractive than the rest; this is natural. But what will guide thee in thy choice?"

"To answer thee," said Pamphylius, "I must tell thee first of all that, since by our teaching all men are equal before their Father, they are just as equal before us, according to their position and to their spiritual and bodily qualities; and so our choice (if this word, which is incomprehensible to us, be used) cannot be limited to anything. A Christian's wife or husband may be chosen among any men or women of the world."

"This makes it even less possible to make up one's mind," said Julius.

"I will tell thee what our elder has said about the difference that exists between the marriage of a Christian and that of a pagan. A pagan, like thee, chooses a wife, who, in his opinion, will afford him, him personally, the greatest amount of enjoyment. But the eyes stray with this, and it is hard to decide, the more so since the enjoyment is ahead. But for a Christian there is no choice for himself, or rather, the choice for his personal enjoyment occupies a secondary, and not the first, place. For a Christian the question is, not to violate God's will by his marriage."

"But where can there be a violation of God's will in the marriage?"

"I might have forgotten the Iliad, which we studied and read together, but thou, who art living among sages and poets, canst not forget it. What is the whole Iliad? It is a story of the violation of God's will in relation to marriage. And Menelaus, and Paris, and Helen, and Achilles, and Agamemnon, and Chryseis,—all that is a description of all the strange calamities which arise for men and even now take place from this violation."

"But wherein does the violation consist?"

"The violation consists in this, that a man loves in woman his enjoyment from being near her, and not the human being like himself, and so enters into matrimony for the sake of his enjoyment. Christian marriage is possible only when a man has love for men and when the object of his carnal love is first of all an object of this brotherly love of man for man. Just as it is rational and safe to build a house only when there is a foundation, to paint a picture when everything on which it is to be painted is prepared,—so carnal love is legitimate only when it has respect and love of one man for another at its base. On this foundation alone can a rational Christian family life be reared."

"But I still fail to see why such a Christian marriage, as thou callest it," said Julius, "excludes the love for a woman, which Paris experienced."

"I do not say that the Christian marriage does not admit the exclusive love of woman; on the contrary, only then is it rational and sacred; but the exclusive love of woman can arise only when the formerly existing love toward all men has not been violated. But the exclusive love for one woman, which the poets extol, recognized as good in itself, without being based on the love of men, has no right to be called love. It is an animal lust and frequently passes over into hatred. The best examples of this, that the so-called love (eros), if it is not based on brotherly love for all men, becomes bestiality, are the cases of violence committed against the very woman, whom he who violates her makes suffer and whose ruin he causes. In violence there is evidently no love for a man, if he tortures him whom he loves. But with the non-Christian marriage there is frequently concealed violence, when he who marries a maiden, who does not love him, or who loves another, makes her suffer and has no compassion on her, only that he may be able to satisfy his love."

"Let us say that this is so," said Julius, "but if the maiden loves him, there is no injustice, and I do not see any difference between a Christian and a pagan marriage."

"I do not know the details of thy marriage," answered Pamphylius, "but I know that every marriage, which has for its basis nothing but the personal good, cannot help but be the cause of discord; even as the simple taking of food, among animals and among men who differ little from animals, cannot take place without quarrelling and fighting. Everybody wants a dainty morsel, but as there are not enough dainty morsels to go around, discord results from this. If there is no open discord, there is one which is concealed. The weak individual wants a dainty morsel, but he knows that the strong one will not give it to him, and, although he knows the impossibility of taking it away directly from the strong individual, he looks with concealed, envious malice upon the strong man and uses the first opportunity to take it away from him. The same is true of pagan marriage, only it is twice as bad, because the object of hatred is man, so that there arises discord between the married pair."

"But how can this be effected, that the married pair should love no one but one another? There will always be found a man or a maiden who loves some one else. And so, according to your opinion, marriage is impossible. And so I see that they say rightly of you that you do not marry at all. That is the reason why thou art not married and, probably, wilt not be. It cannot be that a man should marry a woman without having first roused the feeling of love for himself in another woman; or that a girl should live to maturity without having roused a feeling in a man. How was Helen to have acted?"

"Elder Cyril says of this as follows: in the pagan world, men, without thinking of the love of their brothers, without cultivating this sentiment, think only of one thing, of the provocation of a love of passion for woman, and they cultivate this passion. And so in their world every Helen, or one like her, arouses love in many. Rivals fight with one another, try to surpass one another, like animals, in order to get possession of a female. And in a greater or lesser degree, their marriage is an act of violence. In our community we not only do not think of the personal enjoyment of beauty, but we avoid all offences which lead to this, and which in the pagan world are made a merit and a subject of worship. We, on the contrary, think of those obligations of respect and love of our neighbour, which we have without distinction for all men, for the greatest beauty and for the greatest ugliness. We cultivate this feeling with all our strength, and so the feeling of love has for me the upper hand in us over the temptation of beauty and vanquishes it and destroys the discord, which results from the sexual relations. A Christian marries only when he knows that his union with the woman causes no one any harm."

"But is this possible?" retorted Julius. "Can we control our infatuations?"

"We cannot, if we give them full sway, but we can prevent their awakening and getting up. Take as an example the relation of father and daughter, mother and son, brother and sister. The mother is for her son, the daughter for her father, the sister for her brother, no matter how beautiful they may be, not an object of personal enjoyment, but of love, and no sensations are awakened. They would awaken, if the father should find out that the one he considered to be his daughter is not his daughter, and the same in the relation of mother and son, brother and sister; but even then this sensation would be very feeble and submissive, and it would be in man's power to control it. The feeling of lust would be weak, because at the base of it is the sentiment of love for mother, daughter, sister. Why dost thou not wish to admit that the same sentiment may be educated and confirmed in man in relation to all women, just as in the case of the mothers, sisters, daughters, and that on the basis of this sentiment there may grow up the sentiment of conjugal love? The moment a brother has discovered that the one whom he regarded as his sister is not his sister, he allows in himself the feeling of love, as for a woman; even so a Christian, feeling that his love is not offending any one, allows this sentiment to rise in his soul."

"Well, and if two men fall in love with the same maiden?"

"Then one sacrifices his happiness for the happiness of another."

"But if she loves one of them?"

"Then he whom she loves less sacrifices his sentiment, for her happiness."

"Well, and if she loves both alike, and both sacrifice themselves, she does not marry at all?"

"No, then the elders will look into the matter, and counsel in such a way that there shall be the greatest good for all, with the greatest love."

"But this is never done, and it is not done because it is contrary to human nature."

"Contrary to human nature? What human nature? Man, besides being an animal, is also a man, and it is true that such a relation to woman is not in accord with man's animal nature, but it is with his rational nature. And when he uses his reason in order to serve his animal nature, he does worse than an animal,—he rises to violence, to incest,—which no animal would do. But when he uses his rational nature for the restraint of the animal, when his animal nature serves his reason, he attains that good which satisfies him."

V.

"But tell me about thyself personally," said Julius. "I see thee with this beauty; thou evidently livest near her and servest her; dost thou really not wish to become her husband?"

"I have not thought of it," said Pamphylius. "She is the daughter of a Christian widow. I serve them just as others do. Thou didst ask me whether I love her so much as to wish to be united with her. This question is hard for me; but I shall answer it frankly. This thought has come to me, but there is a youth who loves her, and so I do not yet dare to think of it. This youth is a Christian and loves us both, and I cannot commit an act which would grieve him. I live without thinking about it. I seek but for this, to fulfill the law of love of men,—this is all that is needed. I shall marry when I see that that is necessary."

"But the acquisition of a good, industrious son-in-law cannot be a matter of indifference to her mother. She will wish for you, and not for others."

"No, it makes no difference to her, because she knows that, besides me, all our people are ready to serve her, as they would any one else, and I shall serve her neither more nor less, no matter whether I shall be her son-in-law or not. If from this shall result my marriage with her daughter, I shall accept it with joy, as I shall accept her marriage to some one else."

"That cannot be!" exclaimed Julius. "What is so terrible among you is, that you deceive yourselves. And thus you deceive others. That stranger told me correctly about you. As I listen to thee, I involuntarily submit myself to the beauty of the life which thou describest to me; but when I reflect, I see that all this is a deception, which leads to savagery, to coarseness which approaches that of animals."

"In what dost thou see this savagery?"

"In this, that supporting yourselves by work, you have no leisure or chance to busy yourselves with the sciences or the arts. Here thou art in a ragged garment, with coarsened hands and feet; thy companion, who might be a goddess of beauty, resembles a slave. You have neither any songs to Apollo, nor temples, nor poetry, nor games,—nothing which the gods have given for the adornment of human life. To work, to work like slaves or like oxen, only in order to feed coarsely, is this not a voluntary and godless renunciation of will and of human nature?"

"Again human nature!" said Pamphylius. "But in what does this nature consist? In torturing slaves by giving them work beyond their strength, in killing our brothers and making them slaves, in making of women a subject of amusement? All this is needed for that beauty of life, which thou considerest proper to human nature. Does man's nature consist in this, or in living in love and concord with all men, feeling himself a member of one universal brotherhood? Thou art very much mistaken, if thou thinkest that we do not recognize the sciences and art. We value highly all the abilities with which human nature is endowed; but we look upon all of man's inherent abilities as upon means for the attainment of one and the same end, to which we devote all our life, namely, the fulfillment of God's will. In science and in art we do not see an amusement, of use only as a pleasure for idle people; we demand from science and art the same that we demand from all human occupations,—that in them should be realized the same activity of love of God and our neighbour, by which all the acts of a Christian are permeated. We recognize as true science only such knowledge as helps us to live better, and we respect art only when it purities our designs, elevates our souls, strengthens our powers, which are necessary for a life of labour and of love. Such knowledge we, in proportion as we are able, do not fail to develop in ourselves and in our children, and to such art we gladly devote ourselves in our time of leisure. We read and study the writings bequeathed to us by the wisdom of men who have lived before us; we sing psalms, paint pictures, and our poems and pictures brace our spirit and console us in moments of grief. It is for this reason that we cannot approve of those applications which you make of the sciences and arts. Your learned men use their ability of imagination to invent new means for causing evil to men; they perfect the methods of war, that is, of murder; they invent new methods for gain, that is, for getting rich at the expense of others. Your art serves you for the erection and adornment of temples in honour of the gods, in whom the most advanced among you have long ago ceased believing, but you encourage this faith in them in other people, assuming that with this deception you will best retain them in your power. You erect statues in honour of the most powerful and cruel of your tyrants, whom nobody respects, but all fear. In your theatres you give representations of criminal love. Your music serves for the enjoyment of your rich, who glut themselves with food and drink at their feasts. And your painting, which adorns houses of debauchery, is such that a man who is not intoxicated by animal passion cannot even look upon without blushing. No, not for this have those higher abilities, which distinguish him from the animal, been given to man. It is not right to make of them an enjoyment for our bodies. In devoting all our lives to the fulfillment of God's will, we so much the more employ our highest abilities in the same service."

"Yes," said Julius, "all that would be beautiful, if life under such conditions were possible; but it is not possible to live thus. You deceive yourselves. You do not recognize the defense we provide. But if the Roman legions did not exist, would it be possible to live calmly? You make use of the defense, without acknowledging it. Even some of your people, so thou didst tell me thyself, have defended themselves. You do not recognize property, but you make use of it: our people have it, and give it to you. Thou wilt not thyself give thy grapes away, but sellest them and wilt buy them. All this is deception! If you did what you say, it would be all right; but as it is, you deceive others and yourselves."

Julius grew excited and said everything which he had on his mind. Pamphylius waited in silence. When Julius had ended, Pamphylius began to retort:

"In vain dost thou think that, though we do not recognize your defenses, we make use of them. We do not need the Roman legions, because we do not ascribe any value to what demands a defense by means of violence. Our good consists in what does not demand any defense, and this no one can take from us. Though material things, which in your eyes represent property, pass through our hands, we do not regard them as our own, and give them to those who need them for their sustenance. We sell the grapes to those who will buy them, not for the sake of personal gain, but with the one purpose of acquiring what the needy want. If any one should wish to take these grapes away from us, we should give them up without resistance. For the same reason we are not afraid of the incursion of savages. If they should begin to take from us the products of our labour, we should let them have them; if they should demand that we should work for them, we should do so with pleasure, and they would not only have no cause, but would even find it unprofitable, to kill and torture us. The savages would soon comprehend, and would love us, and we should have less to suffer from them than from those enlightened men of yours, who are about us now and who persecute us. It is said that only thanks to the right of ownership are all those products obtained, by which men subsist and live; but, reflect thyself, by whom are all the necessary articles of life produced? Thanks to whose labour do you accumulate that wealth, on which you pride yourselves? Is it produced by those who, folding their hands, command their slaves and hirelings, and are the only ones who enjoy the property? or by those poor slaves who, for the sake of bread, fulfill the commands of their master and themselves enjoy no property, receiving as their share barely enough for their daily sustenance? And why do you think that these men will stop working, when they shall have the possibility of doing rational labour, useful to themselves, for themselves and for those whom they love and pity? Thy accusations against us consist in this, that we do not fully attain what we strive after, that we do not even recognize violence and ownership, and yet make use of them. If we are cheats, there is no sense in talking with us, and we deserve neither anger nor arraignment, but only contempt, and this we gladly accept, because one of our rules is the recognition of our insignificance. But if we sincerely strive after what we profess, then thy accusations about our deception would be unjust. If we strive as do my brothers and I, in order to fulfill the law of our teacher, after living without violence and the ownership which results from it, we strive after it, not for external purposes, wealth, power, honours,—we recognize none of these things,—but for the sake of something else. We seek the good just as you do; the only difference is, that we see the good in something different. You believe that the good is in wealth and honours, but we believe differently. Our faith shows us that our good is not in violence, but in obedience; not in wealth, but in giving everything up. And, like plants striving after the light, we cannot help but strive after that where our good is. We do not fulfill everything we wish for our good, that is true. But can this be otherwise? Thou strivest after having the most beautiful wife, after having the largest possessions,—hast thou, or has any one else, ever reached it? If a marksman does not strike the target, does he stop aiming at it, because he has many times missed his aim? The same is true of us. Our good, according to Christ's teaching, is in love. We seek our good, but each one of us attains it variously and far from completely."

"Yes, but why do you not believe all human wisdom, and why have you turned away from it and believed only your crucified teacher? Your slavery, your submission to him, it is this that repels me."

"Again thou art mistaken, and he is mistaken who thinks that we, in professing our teaching, have our faith only because the man whom we believe has commanded us to have it. On the contrary, those who with their whole soul seek the knowledge of the truth, the communion with the Father, those who seek the good, involuntarily come to the path on which Christ walked, and so involuntarily stand behind Him, see Him in front of them. All those who love God will meet on this path, and thou, too. He is the son of God and a mediator between God and men, not because some one told us so and we believe in it blindly, but because all those who seek God find His son before them, and involuntarily, only through Him, understand, see, and know God."

Julius made no reply, and for a long time sat in silence.

"Art thou happy?" he asked.

"I wish for nothing better. But, more than this: I for the most part experience a feeling of perplexity, a consciousness of some injustice,— because I am so very happy," said Pamphylius, smiling.

"Yes," said Julius, "maybe I should be happier, if I had not met the stranger then, and had reached you."

"If thou thinkest so, what keeps thee back?"

"And my wife?"

"Thou sayest that she is inclined toward Christianity,—so she will go with thee."

"Yes, but the other life has been begun,—how is it to be broken up? It has been begun, it has to be finished," said Julius, presenting to himself the dissatisfaction of his father, mother, friends, but mainly those efforts which have to be made in order to make this change.

Just then the maiden, Pamphylius's companion, walked up to the door of the shop with a young man. Pamphylius went out to them, and the young man, in Julius's presence, told them that he had been sent by Cyril to buy hides. The grapes were all sold, and wheat was bought. Pamphylius proposed to the young man that he should go with Magdalene and take the wheat home, while he himself would buy and bring the hides.

"It will be better for thee," he said.

"No, Magdalene had better go with thee," said the young man, and departed.

Julius took Pamphylius into the shop of a merchant he knew. Pamphylius filled the wheat in bags and, having given Magdalene a small part, threw his heavy burden over his shoulder, bade Julius good-bye, and left the town with the maiden. At the turn of the street Pamphylius looked around and, smiling, shook his head to Julius and, smiling in the same way, and even more joyously, at Magdalene, he said something to her and they disappeared from view.

"Yes, I should have done better, if I had reached them then," thought Julius. And in his imagination, alternating, arose two pictures, that of powerful Pamphylius with the tall, strong maiden, carrying baskets on their heads and their good, bright faces, and now his domestic hearth, which he had left in the morning and to which he would return, and the pampered, beautiful, but wearisome and unpleasant wife, in fine raiment and bracelets, lying on rugs and pillows.

But Julius had not time to think: merchants, his companions, came up to him, and they began their habitual occupation, which ended with a dinner with drinking, and at night with women.

VI.

Ten years passed. Julius did not meet Pamphylius again, and the meetings with him slowly passed out of his mind, and the impressions of him and of the Christian life wore off.

Julius's life went its usual way. During this time his father died, and he had to take upon himself the whole business. The business was complicated: there were the usual purchasers; there were sellers in Africa, clerks, debts to be collected and to be paid. Julius was involuntarily drawn into his affairs, to which he devoted all his time. Besides, there appeared new cares. He was chosen to a public office, and this new occupation, which tickled his vanity, was attractive to him. Besides commercial affairs, he attended to public matters, and, as he possessed a good mind and the gift of words, he began to push to the front, so that he was able to attain a high public position. In the course of these ten years a significant and disagreeable change had taken place in his domestic affairs. Three children were born to him, and this birth of the children separated him from his wife. In the first place, his wife lost the greater part of her beauty and freshness; in the second, she busied herself less with her husband. All her tenderness and affection were concentrated on her children. Though the children, according to the custom of the pagans, were turned over to wet-nurses and attendants, Julius frequently found them with their mother, or did not find her in her apartments, but in those of her children, and the children generally annoyed Julius, affording him more displeasure than joy.

Being busy with his mercantile and public affairs, Julius abandoned his former life of dissipation, but he still needed, as he assumed, an elegant rest after his labours, and this he did not find with his wife, the more so since during this time his wife cultivated more and more the acquaintance of her Christian slave, and more and more was carried away by the new teaching, and rejected in her life everything external, pagan, which had formed her charm for Julius. As he did not find in his wife what he wanted, he cultivated the acquaintance of a woman of easy behaviour and with her passed those hours of leisure which he had left from his occupations.

If Julius had been asked whether he was happy or not, during these years of his life, he would have been unable to answer.

He was so busy! From one affair and pleasure he passed to another affair or pleasure, but not one of them was such that he was fully satisfied with it, or that he wished to continue it. Every affair was such that the quicker he could free himself from it, the better it was for him; and not one pleasure was such that it was not poisoned by something, that the tedium of satiety was not mixed in with it.

Thus Julius lived, when an event happened to him which almost changed the whole manner of his life. He took part in the races at the Olympian games, and, in bringing his chariot successfully to the goal, suddenly drove into another chariot, which he had overtaken. A wheel broke, and he fell down and broke two ribs and an arm. His injuries were severe, but not serious. Julius was carried home, and he had to lie in bed for three months.

During these three months, amidst severe physical sufferings, his mind began to work, and he had leisure to think about his life, looking upon it as that of an outsider. And his life presented itself to him in a gloomy light, the more so since at that time there happened three unpleasant events, which pained him sorely. The first was, that his slave, his father's trusted servant, having received some precious stones in Africa, had run away with them, thus causing a great loss and a disorganization in Julius's affairs. The second was, that Julius's concubine had left him and had chosen another protector. The third and the most disagreeable event for him was this, that during his illness took place the election to the governorship, a position which he had hoped to get, but to which his rival was chosen. All this, it seemed to Julius, had happened, because his chariot had gone one finger's breadth too much to the left.

As he was lying all alone on his bed, he began involuntarily to think of how his life depended on the most insignificant accidents, and these thoughts brought him to others, and to the recollection of his former misfortunes,—of his attempt to go to the Christians and of Pamphylius, whom he had not seen for ten years. These recollections were intensified by his conversations with his wife, who now stayed with him frequently during his illness and told him everything she knew about Christianity from her slave. This slave had at one time lived in the same community with Pamphylius, whom she knew. Julius wished to see this slave, and when she came to his couch, he asked her in detail about everything and especially about Pamphylius.

"Pamphylius," the slave told him, "was one of the best brothers, and was loved and respected by all." He was married to that same Magdalene, whom Julius had seen ten years before. They had already several children.

"Yes, the man who does not believe that God has created men for their good," concluded the slave, "needs only go and look at their life."

Julius dismissed the slave and, when left alone, buried himself in thought concerning everything which he had heard. He felt ashamed, when he compared his life with that of Pamphylius, and he wanted not to think of it.

To distract himself, he picked up a Greek manuscript, which his wife had laid down before him, and began to read. In the manuscript he read as follows:

"There are two ways,—one is the way of life, and the other the way of death. The way of life consists in this: In the first place, thou shalt love God, who has created thee; in the second place, thy neighbour as thyself; and what thou dost not wish to have done to thee, do not to another. The teaching which is included in these words is as follows: Bless those who curse you; pray for your enemies, and fast for your persecutors, for what reward is there, if ye love those who love you? Do not the pagans do likewise? Love those who hate you, and ye will have no enemies. Remove yourselves from carnal and from worldly lusts. If a man smite thee on the right cheek, turn to him the other also, and thou shalt be perfect. If a man compel thee to walk a mile, walk with him two; if a man take from thee what is thine, do not ask it back, for thou canst not; if a man take thy upper garment, give him also thy shirt. To all who ask, give, and demand not back, for the Father wishes that all should receive of His gifts of grace. Blessed is he who gives according to the commandment!

"The second commandment of the teaching: Thou shalt not kill, thou shalt not commit adultery, thou shalt not fornicate, nor steal, nor divine, nor poison, nor covet that which is thy neighbour's. Swear not, bear not false witness, speak not evil, remember not evil. Be not double in thought, nor double of tongue. Let not thy word be false, nor idle, but in conformity with the fact. Be not greedy, nor avaricious, nor hypocritical, nor evil-mannered, nor haughty. Have no evil intentions against thy neighbour. Have no hatred for any man, but arraign some, pray for others, and others again love more than thy soul.

"My child! Avoid every evil and everything like it. Be not angry, for anger leads to murder; nor jealous, nor quarrelsome, nor irritable, for from all this comes murder.

"My child! Be not lustful, for lust leads to fornication; be not foul of speech, for from this comes adultery.

"My child! Do not lie, for lying leads to stealing; be not greedy, nor vain, for from all this comes stealing.

"My child! Be no murmurer, for this leads to blasphemy; nor bold, nor evil-minded, for from all this comes blasphemy. But be meek, for the meek shall inherit the earth. Be long-suffering and merciful, and kindly, and humble, and good, and always tremble at the words which thou shall hear. Exalt not thyself in spirit, and give no boldness to thy soul. Let not thy soul cleave to the proud, but converse with the righteous, and with the humble. Accept everything which may happen with thee as good, knowing that nothing can be without God.

"My child! Cause no divisions, and reconcile those who quarrel. Extend not thy hand to receive, and close it not at giving. Waver not in giving and, giving, murmur not, for thou shalt find out who is a good giver of rewards. Turn not away from the needy, but in everything have communion with thy brother, and call nothing thine own property, for if ye are participants in the imperishable things, ye are so much the more in perishable things. From childhood teach thy children the fear of God. Command not thy slaves in anger, lest they cease to fear God, who is above both of you, for He comes not to call, judging by persons, but calls those whose spirit He has prepared.

"And the way of death is as follows: first of all it is evil and cursed,—here are murder, adultery, lust, fornication, stealing, idolatry, sorcery, poisoning, rape, false witness, hypocrisy, double-mindedness, cunning, pride, malice, haughtiness, avarice, foul speech, envy, impudence, conceit, vanity; here are the persecutors of the good, the haters of truth, the lovers of lying, who acknowledge no retribution for righteousness, nor cleave to good, nor to righteous judgment, watchful, not of the good, but of evil, from whom are removed humbleness and patience; here are also the lovers of vanity, the seekers of rewards, who have no compassion for their neighbours, who labour not for the oppressed, who know not their Creator; murderers of children, miners of God's image, who turn away from the needy, oppressors of the oppressed, defenders of the rich, unlawful judges of the poor, sinners in all things! Beware, children, of all such people."

Long before Julius had read the manuscript to the end, there happened with him, what happens with people who read a book, that is, another person's thoughts, with the sincere desire for the truth; he entered with his soul in communion with those who had inspired these thoughts. He read, guessing in advance what would be, and not only agreed with the thoughts of the book, but seemed himself to have expressed them.

With him happened that common, most mysterious, most

significant phenomenon in life, unnoticed by many, which consists in
this, that the so-called live man becomes alive, when he enters into
communion, unites into one, with the so-called dead, and lives one life
with them.

Julius's soul united with him who wrote and inspired these
thoughts, and after this communion he examined himself, his life. And
he himself and his whole life appeared to him as one terrifying mistake.
He did not live, but with all his cares about his life and with the
temptations only ruined in himself the possibility of the true life.

"I do not want to ruin my life,—I want to live, to walk on the path
of life," he said to himself.

He recalled everything Pamphylius had told him in their former
conversations, and all that now appeared to him so clear and so
indubitable that he was surprised how he could have believed the
stranger at that time and been kept from fulfilling his intention,—of
going to the Christians. He recalled also what the stranger had told him:

"Go there, when thou hast experienced life."

"Well, I have experienced life and have found nothing in it."

He also recalled the words of Pamphylius, that, no matter when he
would come to them, they would be glad to receive him.

"Yes, I have erred and suffered enough!" he said to himself. "I
shall give up everything, and I shall go and live with them, as it says
here."

He told his thought to his wife, and she was delighted at his
intention. His wife was ready for everything. The only question was
how to carry it out. What was to be done with the children? Were they
to be taken along, or to be left with their grandmother? How were they
to be taken? How could they, after the tenderness of their bringing up,
be subjected to all the difficulties of a stern life? The slave proposed to
go with them. But the mother was afraid for her children, and said that
it would be better to leave them with their grandmother and go alone.
And to this they agreed.

Everything was decided upon, and only Julius's sickness retarded
the execution of their plans.

VII.

Is this mood Julius fell asleep. Next morning he was told that a
skilful physician, who was passing through the city, wished to see him,
promising to cure him soon. Julius gladly received the physician. The
physician was no other than the same stranger whom Julius had met as
he was on his way to the Christians. The physician examined his
wounds, and prescribed to him potions of herbs to strengthen him.

"Shall I be able to work with my hand?" asked Julius.

"Oh, yes! Direct the chariot, write, yes."

"But hard work,—digging?"

"I have not thought of it," said the physician, "because this will not be needed in thy position."

"On the contrary, I shall need it very much," said Julius; and he told the physician that since he had seen him he had followed his advice and had experienced life; but life had not given him what it had promised, but, on the contrary, had disenchanted him, and that now he wished to carry out the intention of which he had spoken then.

"Yes, they have evidently put their whole deception into practice, and have enchanted thee in such a way that in thy position, with those obligations which lie upon thee, especially in relation to the children, thou dost none the less not see their error."

"Read this," was all Julius said, handing him the manuscript which he had read.

The physician took the manuscript and looked at it.

"I know this," he said, "I know this deception, and I marvel how such a learned man as thou art can fall into such a trap."

"I do not understand thee. In what does the trap consist?"

"The whole question is in the life, and they, these sophists and rioters against men and gods, offer a happy way of life, in which all men shall be happy; there will be no wars, no capital punishment, no poverty, no quarrels, no malice. And they assert that such a condition of men will exist when all men shall fulfill Christ's commandments,— when they shall not quarrel, nor fornicate, nor swear, nor offer violence, nor wage war upon one another. But they deceive us in that they take the aim for the means. The aim is not to quarrel, not to swear, not to fornicate, and so forth, and this aim is attained only by means of the public life. But they say very nearly what a teacher of shooting might say: 'Thou wilt hit the target, if thy arrow shall fly in a straight line to the target.' But the problem is, how to do so that it may fly in a straight line. And this problem is attained in shooting by the stringing of the string, the flexibility of the bow, the straightness of the arrow. The same is true of the life of men. The best life of men, in which there is no need for quarrelling, fornicating, killing, is attained by having a string,—the rulers,—the flexibility of the bow,—the strength of power,—and a straight arrow,—the justice of the law. But they, under the pretext of a better life, destroy everything which has improved life. They recognize neither government, nor power, nor laws."

"But they assert that without rulers, power, or laws we can live better, if men shall fulfill Christ's law."

"Yes; but what guarantees that men will fulfill it? Nothing. They say, 'You have experienced life with power and laws, and life did not become perfect; now experience the absence of power and of laws, and life will become perfect; you have no right to deny this, because you have not experienced it.' But it is here that the sophistry of the godless people becomes obvious. Saying this, do they not say the same that a man would say to a farmer? 'Thou sowest in the ground and coverest the seed, and yet the crop is not such as thou desirest; I advise thee, sow in the sea, and it will be better; and thou hast no right to deny my proposition, because thou hast not tried it.'"

"Yes, that is true," said Julius, who was beginning to waver.

"But this is not enough," continued the physician. "Let us assume what is insipid and impossible: let us assume that the foundations of the Christian teaching can be communicated to all men by the taking of certain drops, and that suddenly all men will fulfill Christ's teaching, loving God and their neighbours and fulfilling the commandments. Let us assume this, and yet the path of life according to their teaching will not stand scrutinizing. There will be no life, and life will come to an end. Their teacher was a young vagabond, and such will be his followers, and, according to our supposition, the whole world. Those who live now will continue living, but their children will not, or only one in ten will remain living. According to their teaching, all children must be equal to every mother and to every father, both one's own children and those of strangers. How will these children be saved, when we see that the whole passion, the whole love, for these children, which is implanted in the mothers, will scarcely keep the children from destruction; what will happen when this passion passes into compassion, which is equal for all children? Who is to be taken, and what child is to be saved? Who will sit up nights with a sick, ill-smelling child, if not its mother? Nature has made a protection for the child in the love of its mother; they take it away and put nothing in its place. Who will teach the son? Who will comprehend his soul, if it is not his father? Who will ward off danger from him? All this is done away with! The whole life, that is, the continuation of the human race, is done away with."

"This too is true," said Julius, carried away by the physician's eloquence.

"Yes, my friend, leave thy raving and live rationally, especially now, when upon thee lie such great, important, and real obligations. It is a matter of honour that you carry them out. Thou hast lived up to the second period of thy doubts, but go on, and there will be no more doubts. Thy first and most indubitable duty is the education of thy children, whom thou hast neglected: thy duty toward them consists in making of them most worthy servants of thy country. The existing political structure has given thee everything thou hast, and thou shouldst serve it thyself and give it worthy servants in the persons of thy children. Thy second duty is to serve society. Thy failure has grieved and disenchanted thee,—this is a temporary accident. Nothing is given without struggle, and the joy of the triumph is strong only when the victory has been difficult. Leave it to thy wife to amuse herself with the prattling of Christian writers; but be thyself a man and educate thy children to be men. Begin thy life with the consciousness of duty, and all thy doubts will fall off by themselves. They have come to thee anyway from your morbid state. Fulfill thy duty in relation to thy country by serving it and by preparing thy children for this service. Put them on their feet, that they may be able to take thy place, and then peacefully abandon thyself to the life which attracts thee, but until then thou hast no right to it; and if thou didst devote thyself to it, thou wouldst find nothing but suffering."

VIII.

Either the medicinal herbs or the counsels of the wise physician acted upon Julius, and he soon braced up, and his thoughts about the Christian life appeared to him wild ravings.

The physician remained a few days, and then went away. Julius got up soon after, and, taking advantage of his counsels, began a new life. He engaged teachers for his children and himself watched their studies. He passed his own time in public affairs, and soon attained great importance in the city.

Thus Julius lived a year, and during this time he did not even think of the Christians. But, at the expiration of a year, a court was held in his city to judge the Christians.

A lieutenant had arrived in Cilicia from the Roman emperor for the purpose of crushing the Christian propaganda. Julius had heard of the measures taken against the Christians, and, assuming that this had no reference to the Christian community in which Pamphylius was living, did not give it any thought. But once, as he was walking over the forum to the place of his business, he was accosted by a middle-aged, poorly clad man, whom he did not recognize at first: this was Pamphylius. He walked up to Julius, leading a boy by his hand.

"Good morning, friend," Pamphylius said to him. "I have a great request to make of thee, but I do not know whether thou wilt, during the present persecutions of the Christians, recognize me as thy friend, and whether thou art not afraid to lose thy place by keeping company with me."

"I am not afraid of any one," replied Julius, "and in proof of it, I beg thee to go with me to my house. I shall even miss my business at the forum in order to speak with thee and be useful to thee. Come with me! Whose child is this?"

"He is my son."

"Really, I ought not to have asked thee. I recognize thy face in him, and I recognize these blue eyes, and I need not ask who thy wife is: it is that beauty whom I saw several years ago with thee."

"Thou hast guessed it," replied Pamphylius. "Soon after thou sawest her with me, she became my wife."

The friends entered Julius's house. Julius called out his wife and gave her the boy, and himself led Pamphylius into his luxurious, secluded room.

"Here thou mayest say everything,—no one will hear us," said Julius.

"I am not afraid if I am heard," replied Pamphylius. "My request even does not consist in this, that the Christians who have been taken should not be judged and executed, but only that they should be permitted openly to confess their faith."

And Pamphylius told him that the Christians who had been seized by the authorities had sent word about their condition to their community. Elder Cyril, knowing of Pamphylius's relations to Julius, had commissioned Pamphylius to go and intercede for the Christians. The Christians were not asking to be pardoned: they regarded the witnessing to the truth of Christ's teaching as their calling. They could bear witness to this by a long life of eighty years, or prove it even by their martyrdom. Either was a matter of indifference to them, and carnal death, which was inevitable, was equally devoid of terror and full of joy for them, whether now or in fifty years; but they wished their life to be useful to men, and so sent Pamphylius to beg that the judgment and the execution should be public.

Julius was surprised at Pamphylius's request, but promised that he would do everything in his power.

"I have promised thee my aid," said Julius, "but I promise it to thee in consideration of my friendship for thee and that especial, good feeling of meekness which thou hast always evoked in me; but I must confess that I consider your teaching senseless and harmful. I can judge of this, because I myself lately, in a moment of disenchantment and sickness, during my dejection of spirit, shared your views and came very near abandoning everything and joining you. I know whereon your error is based, because I have myself passed through it,—on the love of self, on the weakness of spirit, and on morbid feebleness; it is a faith for women, and not for men."

"But why?"

"Because, while you recognize that in human nature lies dissension and violence, which results from dissension, you do not wish to take part in them and to teach them to others, and, by not doing your share, you do not wish to make use of the structure of the world, which is based on violence. Is this just? The world has always existed with rulers. These rulers have taken upon themselves the whole labour and the whole responsibility, and have protected us against external and internal enemies. And in return for this, we, the subjects, have submitted to these rulers, have bestowed honours upon them, or have aided them in their service. But you, instead of participating with your labours in the affairs of state, and in the measure of your deserts rising higher and higher in the estimation of men, have, in your pride, at once recognized all men to be equal, in order that you may not consider any one higher than yourselves, but may consider yourselves equal to Caesar. You think so yourselves and you teach others so. And for feeble-minded and lazy people this offence is great! Instead of labouring, every slave will at once regard himself as equal to Caesar. But more than that: you deny the tribute, and slavery, and the courts, and executions, and war,—everything which holds men together. If men obeyed you, society would fall to pieces and we should return to the time of savagery. You preach in the state the destruction of the state. But your very existence is conditioned by the state. If that did not exist, neither would you. You would all be the slaves of the Scythians or of wild men, the first that should know of your existence. You are like an ulcer which destroys the body, but which can appear and feed only on the body. And the living body struggles with it and crushes it! It is this that we are doing with you, and we cannot help but do so. And in spite of my promise to help thee in the fulfillment of your desire, I look upon your teaching as very harmful and base: base, because I consider it dishonest and unjust to gnaw the breast which feeds thee! It is base to make use of the benefits of the structure of the state and, without taking part in this structure, by which the state is supported, to destroy it!"

"In thy words," said Pamphylius, "there would be much that is just, if we really lived as thou thinkest. But thou dost not know our life, and hast formed a wrong impression about it. Those means for subsistence, which we employ for ourselves, are obtainable without the aid of violence. It is hard for you, with your habits of luxury, to form an idea how little a man needs in order to exist without privations. A man is so constructed that in a healthy state he can with his hands earn much more than what he needs for his own subsistence. But by living together, we are able, with the work in common, without any effort to sustain our children, and our old men, and the sick, and the feeble. Thou sayest of the rulers that they defend men against outer and inner enemies,—but we love our enemies, and so we have none. Thou affirmest that we, the Christians, provoke in the slave the desire to be a Caesar; we, on the contrary, both in word and in deed preach one thing,—patient humility and labour, the lowest kind of labour,—the labour of the working man. We know nothing and understand nothing about affairs of state; we know this much, and this we know indubitably, that our good is only there where the good of other men is, and we seek this good; the good of all men is in union, but union is not obtained through violence, but through love. The violence of a robber against a passer-by is as provoking to us as the violence exerted by an army over captives, by judges over those who are to be punished, and we cannot consciously take part in either. We cannot without labour make use of violence. Violence is reflected in us, but our participation in violence does not consist in applying it, but in bearing it humbly, when exerted against us."

"But tell me, Pamphylius, why are people hostile to you, and why do they persecute, drive, and kill you? Why does your teaching of love lead to dissension?"

"The cause is not in us, but in you. We put above everything else the divine law, which governs our conscience and reason. We can comply only with those laws of state which are not contrary to the divine laws: 'To Caesar the things which are Caesar's and to God the things which are God's.' And it is for this that men persecute us. We are not able to stop this hostility against us, because we cannot forget the truth, which we have come to comprehend; we cannot begin to live contrary to our conscience and to our reason. Of this hostility which our faith provokes in others against us, our teacher has said: 'Think not that I am come to send peace on earth; I came not to send peace, but a sword! 'Christ has experienced this hostility Himself, and he has warned us, His disciples, more than once of it: 'The world hateth me,' He said, 'because the works thereof are evil. If ye were of the world, the world would love you; but because ye are not of the world, but I have freed you from the world, therefore the world hateth you. The time Cometh, that whosoever killeth you will think that he doeth God service.' But, like Christ, we are not afraid of those who kill the body, and so they can do nothing more with us. 'And this is their condemnation, that light is come into the world, and men loved darkness rather than light, because their deeds were evil.' There is no reason for losing courage on account of this, because the truth prevails. The sheep hear the shepherd's voice and follow him, because they know his voice. And Christ's flock does not perish, but grows, drawing new sheep toward itself from all the countries of the earth, for, 'The wind bloweth where it listeth, and thou hearest the sound thereof, but canst not tell whence it cometh, and whither it goeth.'"

"Yes," Julius interrupted him, "but are there many among you who are sincere? You are frequently accused of pretending that you are martyrs, and that you are glad to perish for the truth, but the truth is not on your side. You are proud madmen, who destroy all the foundations of social life!"

Pamphylius made no reply, and looked sadly at Julius.

IX.

While Julius was saying this, Pamphylius's little son came running into the room and pressed close to his father's side.

In spite of all the affection of Julius's wife, he ran away from her and came to his father's side. Pamphylius drew a sigh, patted his son, and rose up, but Julius held him back, asking him to stay for dinner and talk with him longer.

"I am surprised," said Julius, "at your having married and had children. I cannot understand in what way you Christians can, in the absence of property, educate your children. How can your mothers live calmly, knowing that your children are not provided for?"

"Why are our children provided for less than yours?"

"Because you have no slaves and no property. My wife is very much inclined toward Christianity, and at one time she even wanted to abandon this life,—this was six years ago. I wanted to go with her: but first of all she was frightened by that uncertainty, that want, which presented itself for her children, and I could not help but agree with her. That was during my sickness. At that time all my life was loathsome to me and I wanted to give everything up. But my wife's fears and, on the other hand, the elucidations by my physician, who cured me, persuaded me that the Christian life, as you lead it, is possible and good for those who have no families, but that there is no place in it for married people, for mothers with children, and that with life as you understand it, life, that is, the human race, must come to an end. And this is quite true. Therefore thy appearance with thy child is particularly surprising to me."

"Not only one child; at home are left a suckling babe and a three-year-old girl."

"Explain to me how this is done. I do not understand it. Five years ago I was ready to give everything up and to join you; but I had children, and I understood that, no matter how well it would be for me, I had no right to sacrifice my children, and so I remained living as before, in order to bring them up under the conditions in which I myself grew up and lived."

"It is strange," said Pamphylius, "how differently we judge! We say, If grown persons live in a worldly fashion, this may be forgiven, because they are already spoiled, but for children,—that would be terrible! To live with them in the world and to offend them! 'Woe unto the world because of offences! for it must needs be that offences come; but woe to that man by whom the offence cometh!' Thus says our teacher, and I do not say this for a retort, but because it is really so. The chief need of living in such a way as we all live results for us from this, that among us there are children, those beings of whom it is said,

'Unless ye be as children, ye shall not enter the kingdom of God.'"

"But how can a Christian family be without any definite means?"

"According to our faith, there is but one means, the work of love for men, while yours is violence. It may be destroyed, as wealth is destroyed, and then only work and the love of men is left. We consider that what is the foundation of everything, that we must hold on to, and that we ought to increase. And when this exists, the family lives and even prospers. Yes," continued Pamphylius, "if I had any doubts as to the veracity of Christ's teaching and wavered in its execution, these doubts and waverings of mine would have ended at once, if I thought of the lot of the children who are brought up by the pagans under conditions in which thou hast grown up and bringest up thy children. No matter how we may arrange life with palaces, slaves, and the imported productions of foreign countries, the life of the majority of men remains what it ought to be. The only provision for life will always be the love of men and labour; We want to free ourselves and our children from these conditions, and not by means of violence, but with love, do we make men serve us, and, strange to say, the more we think we secure ourselves in this manner, the more we deprive ourselves of the true, natural, and safe provision, of love. The greater the power of the ruler, the less love there is for him. The same is true of the other provision, of labour. The more a man frees himself from labour and becomes accustomed to luxury, the less able he becomes to labour, the more he is deprived of the true and eternal provision. And these conditions, under which men place their children, they call provisions! Take thy son and mine, and send them both to find the way, to give an order, to do what is necessary, and thou wilt see which of the two will do better; and try to have the two educated by others: whom will they take more readily? No, do not say those terrible words, that the Christian life is possible only for the childless. On the contrary, it may be said: it is pardonable only for the childless to live a pagan life. But woe unto him that shall offend one of these little ones!"

Julius was silent.

"Yes," he said, "maybe thou art right, but the education of the children has been begun, and the best teachers teach them. Let them learn everything we know,—no harm can come from it. There is still time for me and for them. They can come to you, when they shall have strength and shall find it necessary. But I can do so later after I have put my children on their feet and am left free."

"Know the truth, and ye shall be free," said Pamphylius. "Christ gives full liberty at once; the worldly teaching will never give it."

And Pamphylius went away with his son.

The execution was public: Julius saw there Pamphylius, as he, with other Christians, was taking away the bodies of the martyrs.

He saw him; but, fearing the higher authorities, he did not go up to him and did not call him up.

X.

Another twenty years passed. Julius's wife had died. His life proceeded in the cares of a public activity, in the search after power, which now was given him, and now escaped from him. His fortune was great and kept increasing.

His sons were grown up: his second son more especially began to lead life on a broad scale. He made holes in the bottom of the bucket in which the fortune accumulated and, in proportion as the fortune grew, the leaks also were increased. Here began Julius's struggle with his sons, precisely such as had been his with his father: there were malice, hatred, jealousy.

At that time a new chief deprived Julius of favour. Julius was abandoned by his former flatterers, and exile awaited him. He went to Rome, to make explanations; he was not admitted, and was ordered to return home.

Upon returning he found his son with dissipated youths. The rumour had spread in Cilicia that Julius had died, and the son was celebrating the death of his father. Julius was beside himself, and struck his son so hard that he fell down as one dead. Then Julius went to his wife's apartments. There he found the Gospel, in which he read: "Come unto me, all ye that labour and are heavy laden, and I will give you rest. Take my yoke upon you, and learn of me; for I am meek and lowly in heart; and ye shall find rest unto your souls. For my yoke is easy, and my burden light."

"Yes," thought Julius, "He has been calling me for a long time. I did not believe Him and was not submissive and evil, and my yoke was heavy and my burden evil."

Julius sat for a long time with the open Gospel on his knees, reflecting on his whole past life, and recalling everything which Pamphylius had told him at different times. Then Julius arose and went to his son, whom, to his surprise, he found on his legs, and he was inexpressibly happy, because he had not injured him by his blow.

Without saying a word to his son, Julius went out into the street and walked in the direction of the Christian community. He walked the whole day and in the evening stopped for the night at the house of a peasant. In the room which he entered lay a man. At the noise of steps the man arose. It was the physician.

"No, now thou shalt no longer dissuade me," exclaimed Julius. "I am now going there for the third time, and I know that only there shall I find rest."

"Where?" asked the physician.

"With the Christians."

"Yes, maybe thou wilt find rest, but thou hast not fulfilled thy duty. There is no manliness in thee: thy misfortunes vanquish thee. Not thus do real philosophers act. Misfortune is only a fire in which the gold is tested. Thou hast passed through the crucible. Now thou art wanting, and now thou fleest! It is now that thou oughtest to test men and thyself. Thou hast acquired true wisdom, and this thou oughtest to use for the good of thy country. What would happen to the citizens, if those who have come to know men, their passions and conditions of life, instead of sharing their knowledge, their experience, in behalf of society, should bury it in their search after peace? Thy wisdom of life has been acquired in society, and thou oughtest to give it to the same society."

"But I have no wisdom! I am all in error! Though my errors are old, they have not on that account been changed to wisdom, just as water, no matter how old and foul it may be, will not be changed to wine."

Thus spoke Julius, and, seizing his cloak, he hurriedly left the house and without rest continued his journey. At the end of the next day he arrived at the community of the Christians.

He was welcomed by them, though they did not know that he was a friend of Pamphylius, who was beloved and respected by all. At the table Pamphylius saw his friend, and he ran up to him with joy and embraced him.

"Here I have come," said Julius. "Tell me what to do, and I shall obey thee."

"Have no thought of it," said Pamphylius. "Come with me."

And Pamphylius took Julius to the house where the newcomers stopped, and, pointing a bed out to him, he said:

"Thou wilt see thyself wherewith thou canst serve people, when thou hast had a chance to see our life; but, that thou mayest know how to dispose of thy leisure, I shall appoint thee some work for to-morrow. They are now gathering the grapes in our vineyards: go and help them. Thou wilt thyself find out where thy place is."

On the next morning Julius went into the vineyard. The first was a young vineyard, which was laden with clusters of grapes. Young people were gathering them. All the places were occupied, and Julius could not find any place there for himself, though he walked up and down the vineyard for a long time. He went farther, where there was an older vineyard, and where there was less of the fruit; but even here Julius found nothing to do: all worked in pairs, and there was no place for him. He went farther still, and entered an overgrown vineyard. It was all empty. The vines were blasted and crooked, and, as Julius thought, barren.

"So this is my life," he said to himself.

"If I had come the first time, it would have been as the fruit of the first vineyard. If I had come when I started for the second time, it would have been like the fruit of the second vineyard; but here is my life now: it is like these useless, overgrown vines, which are good for fuel only."

And Julius was frightened at what he had done; he was frightened at the punishment which awaited him for having wasted his lift; to no purpose. And Julius was grieved, and he said aloud:

"I am not good for anything and cannot do anything now."

And he did not rise from the spot, and wept because he had lost what could no longer be returned. And suddenly he heard an old man's voice, which called him:

"Labour, my brother!"

Julius looked back, and he saw an old man, bent with years, white as snow, who with difficulty moved his feet. He was standing at a vine and collecting the sweet clusters which were left here and there. Julius walked over to him.

"Labour, dear brother! Labour is joyful!"

And he showed him how to look for the clusters which were left here and there. Julius went to look for them and he brought some and deposited them in the old man's basket. And the old man said to him in reply:

"See whether these clusters are worse than those collected in the other vineyards! 'Walk in the light, while ye have light,' our master has said. 'It is the will of Him that sent me that every man who seeth the son and believeth on Him should have everlasting life, and I will bring him to life at the last day. For God sent not His son into the world to condemn the world: but that the world through Him might be saved. He that believeth on Him is not condemned: but he that believeth not is condemned already, because he hath not believed in the name of the only begotten son of God. And this is the condemnation, that light is come into the world, and men loved darkness rather than light, because their deeds were evil. For every one that doeth evil hateth the light, neither cometh to the light, lest his deeds should be reproved. But he that doeth truth cometh to the light, that his deeds may be made manifest, that they are wrought in God.' Grieve not, my son! We are all sons of God and His servants! We are all His army! Dost thou think he has no other servants but thee? And what if thou hadst, in thy full strength, devoted thyself to His service,—shouldst thou have done everything He wants, everything that ought to be done to men in order to establish His kingdom? Thou sayest that thou shouldst have done twice, ten times, a hundred times as much. But if you did a million times as much as all other men, what would this be in God's work? Nothing. There is no limit and no end to God's work, as there is not to God. Come to Him, and be not a labourer, but a son, and thou shalt become a participator of infinite God and His work. There is no great and no small with God, but there is what is straight and what is crooked. Enter the straight path of life and thou shalt be with God, and thy work will be neither small nor great, but the work of God. Remember that in heaven there is more joy on account of one sinner than of a hundred righteous. The worldly affairs, all that which thou hast missed, have only shown thee thy sin,—and thou hast repented. And since thou hast repented, thou hast found the straight path; walk on it with God, and think not of the past, of what is greater and what lesser. For God all the living are equal! There is one God and one life!"

And Julius calmed down, and began to live and to work for his brothers according to his strength and the best he knew how. And thus he lived in joy for another twenty years, and did not see how he died a carnal death.

Yásnaya Polyána, October, 1890.

TWENTY-THREE TALES

Translated by Louise and Aylmer Maude

PREFACE

This volume is divided into seven parts.

First we have Tales for Children, published about the year 1872, and reminding us of the time when Tolstoy was absorbed in efforts to educate the peasant children. This section of the book contains the two stories which of all that he has written Tolstoy likes best. In What is Art? he claims no place among examples of good art for any of his own productions 'except for the story God sees the Truth, but Waits, which seeks a place in the first class (religious art), and A Prisoner in the Caucasus, which belongs to the second (universal art).' In the first of these the subject (a favourite one with Tolstoy) is the forgiveness of injuries. The second deals with the simplest feelings common to all men: fear and courage, pity, endurance, &c.' expressed with that individuality, clearness, and sincerity, which Tolstoy says are the signs of true art.

Part II contains a series of stories written for the people; and among them What Men Live By, probably the most widely circulated of all Tolstoy's tales. It is founded on the oft-repeated legend of an angel sent by God to live for a while among men.

Part III consists of a Fairy Tale, Iván the Fool, which contains in popular form Tolstoy's indictment of militarism and commercialism.

Part IV contains three short stories written to help the sale of cheap reproductions of some good drawings; Tolstoy having for many years been anxious by all means in his power to further the circulation, at a cheap price, of good works of pictorial as well as literary art.

In Part V we have a series of Russian Folk-Tales. The gems of this collection are the temperance story, The Imp and the Crust, the anti-war story, The Empty Drum, and another story, How Much Land does a Man Need? which deals with a peasant's greed for land. A Grain as big as a Hen's Egg and The Godson are highly characteristic of the spirit of the Russian peasantry, and supply a glimpse of the sources from whence Tolstoy imbibed many of his own spiritual sympathies and antipathies.

Part VI gives two adaptations from the French which have appeared in no previous English edition of Tolstoy's works. They are not merely translations, for to some extent Tolstoy when translating them, modified them and made them his own.

Part VII consists of stories Tolstoy contributed in aid of the Jews left destitute after the massacres and outrages in Kishinéf and elsewhere in Russia in 1903,—outrages which were forerunners of the yet more terrible Jewish massacres of 1905.

The importance Tolstoy attributes to literature of the kind contained in this volume, is shown by the following passage in What is Art?—

'The artist of the future will understand that to compose a fairy tale, a little song which will touch, a lullaby or a riddle which will entertain, a jest which will amuse, or to draw a sketch such as will delight dozens of generations or millions of children and adults, is incomparably more important and more fruitful than to compose a novel, or a symphony, or paint a picture, of the kind which diverts some members of the wealthy classes for a short time and is then for ever forgotten. The region of this art of the simplest feelings accessible to all is enormous, and it is as yet almost untouched.'

The sections of the book have been arranged in chronological order. The date when each story was published is given. The translations are new ones, and for the footnotes I am responsible.

AYLMER MAUDE.

GREAT BADDOW
    CHELMSFORD.
        February 1, 1906.

PART I. TALES FOR CHILDREN: PUBLISHED ABOUT 1872.

GOD SEES THE TRUTH, BUT WAITS

In the town of Vladímir lived a young merchant named Iván Dmítritch Aksyónof. He had two shops and a house of his own.

Aksyónof was a handsome, fair-haired, curly-headed fellow, full of fun, and very fond of singing. When quite a young man he had been given to drink, and was riotous when he had had too much, but after he married he gave up drinking, except now and then.

One summer Aksyónof was going to the Nízhny Fair, and as he bade good-bye to his family his wife said to him, 'Iván Dmítritch, do not start to-day; I have had a bad dream about you.'

Aksyónof laughed, and said, 'You are afraid that when I get to the fair I shall go on the spree.'

His wife replied: 'I do not know what I am afraid of; all I know is that I had a bad dream. I dreamt you returned from the town, and when you took off your cap I saw that your hair was quite grey.'

Aksyónof laughed. 'That's a lucky sign,' said he. 'See if I don't sell out all my goods, and bring you some presents from the fair.'

So he said good-bye to his family, and drove away.

When he had travelled half-way, he met a merchant whom he

knew, and they put up at the same inn for the night. They had some tea together, and then went to bed in adjoining rooms.

It was not Aksyónof's habit to sleep late, and, wishing to travel while it was still cool, he aroused his driver before dawn, and told him to put in the horses.

Then he made his way across to the landlord of the inn (who lived in a cottage at the back), paid his bill, and continued his journey.

When he had gone about twenty-five miles, he stopped for the horses to be fed. Aksyónof rested awhile in the passage of the inn, then he stepped out into the porch and, ordering a samovár to be heated got out his guitar and began to play.

Suddenly a tróyka drove up with tinkling bells, and an official alighted, followed by two soldiers. He came to Aksyónof and began to question him, asking him who he was and whence he came. Aksyónof answered him fully, and said, 'Won't you have some tea with me?' But the official went on cross-questioning him and asking him, 'Where did you spend last night? Were you alone, or with a fellow-merchant? Did you see the other merchant this morning? Why did you leave the inn before dawn?'

Aksyónof wondered why he was asked all these questions, but he described all that had happened, and then added, 'Why do you cross-question me as if I were a thief or a robber? I am travelling on business of my own, and there is no need to question me.'

Then the official, calling the soldiers, said, 'I am the police-officer of this district, and I question you because the merchant with whom you spent last night has been found with his throat cut. We must search your things.'

They entered the house. The soldiers and the police-officer unstrapped Aksyónof's luggage and searched it. Suddenly the officer drew a knife out of a bag, crying, 'Whose knife is this?'

Aksyónof looked, and seeing a blood-stained knife taken from his bag, he was frightened.

'How is it there is blood on this knife?'

Aksyónof tried to answer, but could hardly utter a word, and only stammered: 'I—I don't know—not mine.'

Then the police-officer said, 'This morning the merchant was found in bed with his throat cut. You are the only person who could have done it. The house was locked from inside, and no one else was there. Here is this bloodstained knife in your bag, and your face and manner betray you! Tell me how you killed him, and how much money you stole?'

Aksyónof swore he had not done it; that he had not seen the merchant after they had had tea together; that he had no money except eight thousand roubles of his own, and that the knife was not his. But his voice was broken, his face pale, and he trembled with fear as though he were guilty.

The police-officer ordered the soldiers to bind Aksyónof and to put him in the cart. As they tied his feet together and flung him into the cart, Aksyónof crossed himself and wept. His money and goods were taken from him, and he was sent to the nearest town and imprisoned there. Enquiries as to his character were made in Vladímir. The merchants and other inhabitants of that town said that in former days he used to drink and waste his time, but that he was a good man. Then the trial came on: he was charged with murdering a merchant from Ryazán, and robbing him of twenty thousand roubles.

His wife was in despair, and did not know what to believe. Her children were all quite small; one was a baby at her breast. Taking them all with her, she went to the town where her husband was in gaol. At first she was not allowed to see him; but, after much begging, she obtained permission from the officials, and was taken to him. When she saw her husband in prison-dress and in chains, shut up with thieves and criminals, she fell down, and did not come to her senses for a long time. Then she drew her children to her, and sat down near him. She told him of things at home, and asked about what had happened to him. He told her all, and she asked, 'What can we do now?'

'We must petition the Tsar not to let an innocent man perish.'

His wife told him that she had sent a petition to the Tsar, but that it had not been accepted.

Aksyónof did not reply, but only looked downcast.

Then his wife said, 'It was not for nothing I dreamt your hair had turned grey. You remember? You should not have started that day.' And passing her fingers through his hair, she said: 'Ványa dearest, tell your wife the truth; was it not you who did it?'

'So you, too, suspect me!' said Aksyónof, and hiding his face in his hands, he began to weep. Then a soldier came to say that the wife and children must go away; and Aksyónof said good-bye to his family for the last time.

When they were gone, Aksyónof recalled what had been said, and when he remembered that his wife also had suspected him, he said to himself, 'It seems that only God can know the truth, it is to Him alone we must appeal, and from Him alone expect mercy.'

And Aksyónof wrote no more petitions; gave up all hope, and only prayed to God.

Aksyónof was condemned to be flogged and sent to the mines. So he was flogged with a knout, and when the wounds made by the knout were healed, he was driven to Siberia with other convicts.

For twenty-six years Aksyónof lived as a convict in Siberia. His hair turned white as snow and his beard grew long, thin, and grey. All his mirth went; he stooped; he walked slowly, spoke little, and never laughed, but he often prayed.

In prison Aksyónof learnt to make boots, and earned a little money, with which he bought *The Lives of the Saints*. He read this book when there was light enough in the prison; and on Sundays in the prison-church he read the lessons and sang in the choir; for his voice was still good.

The prison authorities liked Aksyónof for his meekness, and his fellow-prisoners respected him: they called him 'Grandfather,' and 'The Saint.' When they wanted to petition the prison authorities about anything, they always made Aksyónof their spokesman, and when there were quarrels among the prisoners they came to him to put things right, and to judge the matter.

No news reached Aksyónof from his home, and he did not even know if his wife and children were still alive.

One day a fresh gang of convicts came to the prison. In the evening the old prisoners collected round the new ones and asked them what towns or villages they came from, and what they were sentenced for. Among the rest Aksyónof sat down near the new-comers, and listened with downcast air to what was said.

One of the new convicts, a tall, strong man of sixty, with a closely-cropped grey beard, was telling the others what he had been arrested for.

'Well, friends,' he said, 'I only took a horse that was tied to a sledge, and I was arrested and accused of stealing. I said I had only taken it to get home quicker, and had then let it go; besides, the driver was a personal friend of mine. So I said, "It's all right." "No," said they, "you stole it." But how or where I stole it they could not say. I once really did something wrong, and ought by rights to have come here long ago, but that time I was not found out. Now I have been sent here for nothing at all... Eh, but it's lies I'm telling you; I've been to Siberia before, but I did not stay long.'

'Where are you from?' asked some one.

'From Vladímir. My family are of that town. My name is Makár, and they also call me Semyónitch.'

Aksyónof raised his head and said: 'Tell me, Semyónitch, do you know anything of the merchants Aksyónof, of Vladímir? Are they still alive?'

'Know them? Of course I do. The Aksyónofs are rich, though their father is in Siberia: a sinner like ourselves, it seems! As for you, Gran'dad, how did you come here?'

Aksyónof did not like to speak of his misfortune. He only sighed, and said, 'For my sins I have been in prison these twenty-six years.'

'What sins?' asked Makár Semyónitch.

But Aksyónof only said, 'Well, well—I must have deserved it!' He would have said no more, but his companions told the new-comer how Aksyónof came to be in Siberia: how some one had killed a merchant and had put a knife among Aksyónof's things, and Aksyónof had been unjustly condemned.

When Makár Semyónitch heard this, he looked at Aksyónof, slapped his own knee, and exclaimed, 'Well this is wonderful! Really wonderful! But how old you've grown, Gran'dad!'

The others asked him why he was so surprised, and where he had seen Aksyónof before; but Makár Semyónitch did not reply. He only said: 'It's wonderful that we should meet here, lads!'

These words made Aksyónof wonder whether this man knew who had killed the merchant; so he said 'Perhaps, Semyónitch, you have heard of that affair or maybe you've seen me before?'

'How could I help hearing? The world's full of rumors. But it's long ago, and I've forgotten what I heard.'

'Perhaps you heard who killed the merchant?' asked Aksyónof.

Makár Semyónitch laughed, and replied, 'It must have been him in whose bag the knife was found! If some one else hid the knife there, "He's not a thief till he's caught," as the saying is. How could any one put a knife into your bag while it was under your head? It would surely have woke you up?'

When Aksyónof heard these words, he felt sure this was the man who had killed the merchant. He rose and went away. All that night Aksyónof lay awake. He felt terribly unhappy, and all sorts of images rose in his mind. There was the image of his wife as she was when he parted from her to go to the fair. He saw her as if she were present; her face and her eyes rose before him; he heard her speak and laugh. Then he saw his children, quite little, as they were at that time: one with a little cloak on, another at his mother's breast. And then he remembered himself as he used to be—young and merry. He remembered how he sat playing the guitar in the porch of the inn where he was arrested, and how free from care he had been. He saw, in his mind, the place where he was flogged, the executioner, and the people standing around; the chains, the convicts, all the twenty-six years of his prison life, and his premature old age. The thought of it all made him so wretched that he was ready to kill himself.

'And it's all that villain's doing!' thought Aksyónof. And his anger was so great against Makár Semyónitch that he longed for vengeance, even if he himself should perish for it. He kept repeating prayers all night, but could get no peace. During the day he did not go near Makár Semyónitch, nor even look at him.

A fortnight passed in this way. Aksyónof could not sleep at nights, and was so miserable that he did not know what to do.

One night as he was walking about the prison he noticed some earth that came rolling out from under one of the shelves on which the prisoners slept. He stopped to see what it was. Suddenly Makár Semyónitch crept out from under the shelf, and looked up at Aksyónof with frightened face. Aksyónof tried to pass without looking at him, but Makár seized his hand and told him that he had dug a hole under the wall, getting rid of the earth by putting it into his high-boots, and emptying it out every day on the road when the prisoners were driven to their work.

'Just you keep quiet, old man, and you shall get out too. If you blab they'll flog the life out of me, but I will kill you first.'

Aksyónof trembled with anger as he looked at his enemy. He drew his hand away, saying, 'I have no wish to escape, and you have no need to kill me; you killed me long ago! As to telling of you—I may do so or not, as God shall direct.'

Next day, when the convicts were led out to work, the convoy soldiers noticed that one or other of the prisoners emptied some earth out of his boots. The prison was searched, and the tunnel found. The Governor came and questioned all the prisoners to find out who had dug the hole. They all denied any knowledge of it. Those who knew, would not betray Makár Semyónitch, knowing he would be flogged almost to death. At last the Governor turned to Aksyónof, whom he knew to be a just man, and said:

'You are a truthful old man; tell me, before God, who dug the hole?'

Makár Semyónitch stood as if he were quite unconcerned, looking at the Governor and not so much as glancing at Aksyónof. Aksyónof's lips and hands trembled, and for a long time he could not utter a word. He thought, 'Why should I screen him who ruined my life? Let him pay for what I have suffered. But if I tell, they will probably flog the life out of him and maybe I suspect him wrongly. And, after all, what good would it be to me?'

'Well, old man,' repeated the Governor, 'tell us the truth: who has been digging under the wall?'

Aksyónof glanced at Makár Semyónitch, and said 'I cannot say, your honour. It is not God's will that I should tell! Do what you like with me; I am in your hands.'

However much the Governor tried, Aksyónof would say no more, and so the matter had to be left.

That night, when Aksyónof was lying on his bed and just beginning to doze, some one came quietly and sat down on his bed. He peered through the darkness and recognized Makár.

'What more do you want of me?' asked Aksyónof. 'Why have you come here?'

Makár Semyónitch was silent. So Aksyónof sat up and said, 'What do you want? Go away, or I will call the guard!'

Makár Semyónitch bent close over Aksyónof, and whispered, 'Iván Dmítritch, forgive me!'

'What for?' asked Aksyónof.

'It was I who killed the merchant and hid the knife among your things. I meant to kill you too, but I heard a noise outside; so I hid the knife in your bag and escaped out of the window.'

Aksyónof was silent, and did not know what to say. Makár Semyónitch slid off the bed-shelf and knelt upon the ground. 'Iván Dmítritch,' said he, 'forgive me! For the love of God, forgive me! I will confess that it was I who killed the merchant, and you will be released and can go to your home.'

'It is easy for you to talk,' said Aksyónof, 'but I have suffered for you these twenty-six years. Where could I go to now?...My wife is dead, and my children have forgotten me. I have nowhere to go...'

Makár Semyónitch did not rise, but beat his head on the floor. 'Iván Dmítritch, forgive me!' he cried. 'When they flogged me with the knout it was not so hard to bear as it is to see you now...yet you had pity on me, and did not tell. For Christ's sake forgive me, wretch that I am!' And he began to sob.

When Aksyónof heard him sobbing he, too, began to weep.

'God will forgive you!' said he. 'Maybe I am a hundred times worse than you.' And at these words his heart grew light, and the longing for home left him. He no longer had any desire to leave the prison, but only hoped for his last hour to come.

In spite of what Aksyónof had said, Maker Semyónitch confessed his guilt. But when the order for his release came, Aksyónof was already dead.

1872

A PRISONER IN THE CAUCASUS

I

An officer named Zhílin was serving in the army in the Caucasus.

One day he received a letter from home. It was from his mother, who wrote: 'I am getting old, and should like to see my dear son once more before I die. Come and say good-bye to me and bury me, and then, if God pleases, return to service again with my blessing. But I have found a girl for you, who is sensible and good and has some property. If you can love her, you might marry her and remain at home.'

Zhílin thought it over. It was quite true, the old lady was failing fast and he might not have another chance to see her alive. He had better go, and, if the girl was nice, why not marry her?

So he went to his Colonel, obtained leave of absence, said good-bye to his comrades, stood the soldiers four pailfuls of vódka as a farewell treat, and got ready to go.

It was a time of war in the Caucasus. The roads were not safe by night or day. If ever a Russian ventured to ride or walk any distance away from his fort, the Tartars killed him or carried him off to the hills. So it had been arranged that twice every week a body of soldiers should march from one fortress to the next to convoy travellers from point to point.

It was summer. At daybreak the baggage-train got ready under shelter of the fortress; the soldiers marched out; and all started along the road. Zhílin was on horseback, and a cart with his things went with the baggage-train. They had sixteen miles to go. The baggage-train moved slowly; sometimes the soldiers stopped, or perhaps a wheel would come off one of the carts, or a horse refuse to go on, and then everybody had to wait.

When by the sun it was already past noon, they had not gone half the way. It was dusty and hot, the sun was scorching and there was no shelter anywhere: a bare plain all round—not a tree, not a bush, by the road.

Zhílin rode on in front, and stopped, waiting for the baggage to overtake him. Then he heard the signal-horn sounded behind him: the company had again stopped. So he began to think: 'Hadn't I better ride on by myself? My horse is a good one: if the Tartars do attack me, I can gallop away. Perhaps, however, it would be wiser to wait.'

As he sat considering, Kostílin, an officer carrying a gun, rode up to him and said:

'Come along, Zhílin, let's go on by ourselves. It's dreadful; I am famished, and the heat is terrible. My shirt is wringing wet.'

Kostílin was a stout, heavy man, and the perspiration was running down his red face. Zhílin thought awhile, and then asked: 'Is your gun loaded?'

'Yes it is.'

'Well, then, let's go, but on condition that we keep together.'

So they rode forward along the road across the plain, talking, but keeping a look-out on both sides. They could see afar all round. But after crossing the plain the road ran through a valley between two hills, and Zhílin said: 'We had better climb that hill and have a look round, or the Tartars may be on us before we know it.'

But Kostílin answered: 'What's the use? Let us go on.'

Zhílin, however, would not agree.

'No,' he said; 'you can wait here if you like, but I'll go and look round.' And he turned his horse to the left, up the hill. Zhílin's horse was a hunter, and carried him up the hillside as if it had wings. (He had bought it for a hundred roubles as a colt out of a herd, and had broken it in himself.) Hardly had he reached the top of the hill, when he saw some thirty Tartars not much more than a hundred yards ahead of him. As soon as he caught sight of them he turned round but the Tartars had also seen him, and rushed after him at full gallop, getting their guns out as they went. Down galloped Zhílin as fast as the horse's legs could go, shouting to Kostílin: 'Get your gun ready!'

And, in thought, he said to his horse: 'Get me well out of this, my pet; don't stumble, for if you do it's all up. Once I reach the gun, they shan't take me prisoner.'

But, instead of waiting, Kostílin, as soon as he caught sight of the Tartars, turned back towards the fortress at full speed, whipping his horse now on one side now on the other, and its switching tail was all that could be seen of him in the dust.

Zhílin saw it was a bad look-out; the gun was gone, and what could he do with nothing but his sword? He turned his horse towards the escort, thinking to escape, but there were six Tartars rushing to cut him off. His horse was a good one, but theirs were still better; and besides, they were across his path. He tried to rein in his horse and to turn another way, but it was going so fast it could not stop, and dashed on straight towards the Tartars. He saw a red-bearded Tartar on a grey horse, with his gun raised, come at him, yelling and showing his teeth.

'Ah,' thought Zhílin, 'I know you, devils that you are. If you take me alive, you'll put me in a pit and flog me. I will not be taken alive!'

Zhílin, though not a big fellow, was brave. He drew his sword and dashed at the red-bearded Tartar thinking: 'Either I'll ride him down, or disable him with my sword.'

He was still a horse's length away from him, when he was fired at from behind, and his horse was hit. It fell to the ground with all its weight, pinning Zhílin to the earth.

He tried to rise, but two ill-savored Tartars were already sitting on him and binding his hands behind his back. He made an effort and flung them off, but three others jumped from their horses and began beating his head with the butts of their guns. His eyes grew dim, and he fell back. The Tartars seized him, and, taking spare girths from their saddles, twisted his hands behind him and tied them with a Tartar knot. They knocked his cap off, pulled off his boots, searched him all over, tore his clothes, and took his money and his watch.

Zhílin looked round at his horse. There it lay on its side, poor thing, just as it had fallen; struggling, its legs in the air, unable to touch the ground. There was a hole in its head, and black blood was pouring out, turning the dust to mud for a couple of feet around.

One of the Tartars went up to the horse and began taking the saddle off, it still kicked, so he drew a dagger and cut its windpipe. A whistling sound came from its throat, the horse gave one plunge, and all was over.

The Tartars took the saddle and trappings. The red-bearded Tartar mounted his horse, and the others lifted Zhílin into the saddle behind him. To prevent his falling off, they strapped him to the Tartar's girdle;

and then they all rode away to the hills.

So there sat Zhílin, swaying from side to side, his head striking against the Tartar's stinking back. He could see nothing but that muscular back and sinewy neck, with its closely shaven, bluish nape. Zhílin's head was wounded: the blood had dried over his eyes, and he could neither shift his position on the saddle nor wipe the blood off. His arms were bound so tightly that his collar-bones ached.

They rode up and down hills for a long way. Then they reached a river which they forded, and came to a hard road leading across a valley.

Zhílin tried to see where they were going, but his eyelids were stuck together with blood, and he could not turn.

Twilight began to fall; they crossed another river and rode up a stony hillside. There was a smell of smoke here, and dogs were barking. They had reached an Aoul (a Tartar village). The Tartars got off their horses; Tartar children came and stood round Zhílin, shrieking with pleasure and throwing stones at him.

The Tartar drove the children away, took Zhílin off the horse, and called his man. A Nogáy with high cheek-bones, and nothing on but a shirt (and that so torn that his breast was all bare), answered the call. The Tartar gave him an order. He went and fetched shackles: two blocks of oak with iron rings attached, and a clasp and lock fixed to one of the rings.

They untied Zhílin's arms, fastened the shackles on his leg, and dragged him to a barn, where they pushed him in and locked the door.

Zhílin fell on a heap of manure. He lay still awhile then groped about to find a soft place, and settled down.

II

That night Zhílin hardly slept at all. It was the time of year when the nights are short, and daylight soon showed itself through a chink in the wall. He rose, scratched to make the chink bigger, and peeped out.

Through the hole he saw a road leading down-hill; to the right was a Tartar hut with two trees near it, a black dog lay on the threshold, and a goat and kids were moving about wagging their tails. Then he saw a young Tartar woman in a long, loose, bright-coloured gown, with trousers and high boots showing from under it. She had a coat thrown over her head, on which she carried a large metal jug filled with water. She was leading by the hand a small, closely-shaven Tartar boy, who wore nothing but a shirt; and as she went along balancing herself, the muscles of her back quivered. This woman carried the water into the hut, and, soon after, the red-bearded Tartar of yesterday came out dressed in a silk tunic, with a silver-hilted dagger hanging by his side, shoes on his bare feet, and a tall black sheepskin cap set far back on his head. He came out, stretched himself, and stroked his red beard. He stood awhile, gave an order to his servant, and went away.

Then two lads rode past from watering their horses. The horses' noses were wet. Some other closely-shaven boys ran out, without any trousers, and wearing nothing but their shirts. They crowded together, came to the barn, picked up a twig, and began pushing it in at the chink. Zhílin gave a shout, and the boys shrieked and scampered off, their little bare knees gleaming as they ran.

Zhílin was very thirsty: his throat was parched, and he thought: 'If only they would come and so much as look at me!'

Then he heard some one unlocking the barn. The red-bearded Tartar entered, and with him was another a smaller man, dark, with bright black eyes, red cheeks and a short beard. He had a merry face, and was always laughing. This man was even more richly dressed than the other. He wore a blue silk tunic trimmed with gold, a large silver dagger in his belt, red morocco slippers worked with silver, and over these a pair of thick shoes, and he had a white sheepskin cap on his head.

The red-bearded Tartar entered, muttered something as if he were annoyed, and stood leaning against the doorpost, playing with his dagger, and glaring askance at Zhílin, like a wolf. The dark one, quick and lively and moving as if on springs, came straight up to Zhílin, squatted down in front of him, slapped him on the shoulder, and began to talk very fast in his own language. His teeth showed, and he kept winking, clicking his tongue, and repeating, 'Good Russ, good Russ.'

Zhílin could not understand a word, but said, 'Drink! give me water to drink!'

The dark man only laughed. 'Good Russ,' he said, and went on talking in his own tongue.

Zhílin made signs with lips and hands that he wanted something to drink.

The dark man understood, and laughed. Then he looked out of the door, and called to some one: 'Dina!'

A little girl came running in: she was about thirteen, slight, thin, and like the dark Tartar in face. Evidently she was his daughter. She, too, had clear black eyes, and her face was good-looking. She had on a long blue gown with wide sleeves, and no girdle. The hem of her gown, the front, and the sleeves, were trimmed with red. She wore trousers and slippers, and over the slippers stouter shoes with high heels. Round her neck she had a necklace made of Russian silver coins. She was bareheaded, and her black hair was plaited with a ribbon and ornamented with gilt braid and silver coins.

Her father gave an order, and she ran away and returned with a metal jug. She handed the water to Zhílin and sat down, crouching so that her knees were as high as her head, and there she sat with wide open eyes watching Zhílin drink, as though he were a wild animal.

When Zhílin handed the empty jug back to her, she gave such a sudden jump back, like a wild goat, that it made her father laugh. He sent her away for something else. She took the jug, ran out, and brought back some unleavened bread on a round board, and once more sat down, crouching, and looking on with staring eyes.

Then the Tartars went away and again locked the door.

After a while the Nogáy came and said: 'Ayda, the master, Ayda!'

He, too, knew no Russian. All Zhílin could make out was that he was told to go somewhere.

Zhílin followed the Nógay, but limped, for the shackles dragged his feet so that he could hardly step at all. On getting out of the barn he saw a Tartar village of about ten houses, and a Tartar church with a small tower. Three horses stood saddled before one of the houses; little boys were holding them by the reins. The dark Tartar came out of this house, beckoning with his hand for Zhílin to follow him. Then he laughed, said something in his own language, and returned into the house.

Zhílin entered. The room was a good one: the walls smoothly plastered with clay. Near the front wall lay a pile of bright-coloured feather beds; the side walls were covered with rich carpets used as hangings, and on these were fastened guns, pistols and swords, all inlaid with silver. Close to one of the walls was a small stove on a level with the earthen floor. The floor itself was as clean as a thrashing-ground. A large space in one corner was spread over with felt, on which were rugs, and on these rugs were cushions stuffed with down. And on these cushions sat five Tartars, the dark one, the red-haired one, and three guests. They were wearing their indoor slippers, and each had a cushion behind his back. Before them were standing millet cakes on a round board, melted butter in a bowl and a jug of buza, or Tartar beer. They ate both cakes and butter with their hands.

The dark man jumped up and ordered Zhílin to be placed on one side, not on the carpet but on the bare ground, then he sat down on the carpet again, and offered millet cakes and buza to his guests. The servant made Zhílin sit down, after which he took off his own overshoes, put them by the door where the other shoes were standing, and sat down nearer to his masters on the felt, watching them as they ate, and licking his lips.

The Tartars ate as much as they wanted, and a woman dressed in the same way as the girl—in a long gown and trousers, with a kerchief on her head—came and took away what was left, and brought a handsome basin, and an ewer with a narrow spout. The Tartars washed their hands, folded them, went down on their knees, blew to the four quarters, and said their prayers. After they had talked for a while, one of the guests turned to Zhílin and began to speak in Russian.

'You were captured by Kazi-Mohammed,' he said, and pointed at the red-bearded Tartar. 'And Kazi-Mohammed has given you to Abdul Murat,' pointing at the dark one. 'Abdul Murat is now your master.'

Zhílin was silent. Then Abdul Murat began to talk, laughing, pointing to Zhílin, and repeating, 'Soldier Russ, good Russ.'

The interpreter said, 'He orders you to write home and tell them to send a ransom, and as soon as the money comes he will set you free.'

Zhílin thought for a moment, and said, 'How much ransom does he want?'

The Tartars talked awhile, and then the interpreter said, 'Three thousand roubles.'

'No,' said Zhílin,' I can't pay so much.'

Abdul jumped up and, waving his arms, talked to Zhílin' thinking, as before, that he would understand. The interpreter translated: 'How much will you give?'

Zhílin considered, and said, 'Five hundred roubles.' At this the Tartars began speaking very quickly, all together. Abdul began to shout at the red-bearded one, and jabbered so fast that the spittle spurted out of his mouth. The red-bearded one only screwed up his eyes and clicked his tongue.

They quietened down after a while, and the interpreter said, 'Five hundred roubles is not enough for the master. He paid two hundred for you himself. Kazi-Mohammed was in debt to him, and he took you in payment. Three thousand roubles! Less than that won't do. If you refuse to write, you will be put into a pit and flogged with a whip!'

'Eh!' thought Zhílin, 'the more one fears them the worse it will be.'

So he sprang to his feet, and said, 'You tell that dog that if he tries to frighten me I will not write at all, and he will get nothing. I never was afraid of you dogs, and never will be!'

The interpreter translated, and again they all began to talk at once.

They jabbered for a long time, and then the dark man jumped up, came to Zhílin, and said: 'Dzhigit Russ, dzhigit Russ!' (Dzhigit in their language means 'brave.') And he laughed, and said something to the interpreter, who translated: 'One thousand roubles will satisfy him.'

Zhílin stuck to it: 'I will not give more than five hundred. And if you kill me you'll get nothing at all.'

The Tartars talked awhile, then sent the servant out to fetch something, and kept looking, now at Zhílin, now at the door. The servant returned, followed by a stout, bare-footed, tattered man, who also had his leg shackled.

Zhílin gasped with surprise: it was Kostílin. He, too, had been taken. They were put side by side, and began to tell each other what had occurred. While they talked, the Tartars looked on in silence. Zhílin related what had happened to him; and Kostílin told how his horse had stopped, his gun missed fire, and this same Abdul had overtaken and captured him.

Abdul jumped up, pointed to Kostílin, and said something. The interpreter translated that they both now belonged to one master, and the one who first paid the ransom would be set free first.

'There now,' he said to Zhílin, 'you get angry, but your comrade here is gentle; he has written home, and they will send five thousand roubles. So he will be well fed and well treated.'

Zhílin replied: 'My comrade can do as he likes; maybe he is rich, I am not. It must be as I said. Kill me, if you like—you will gain nothing by it; but I will not write for more than five hundred roubles.'

They were silent. Suddenly up sprang Abdul, brought a little box, took out a pen, ink, and a bit of paper, gave them to Zhílin, slapped him on the shoulder, and made a sign that he should write. He had agreed to take five hundred roubles.

'Wait a bit!' said Zhílin to the interpreter; 'tell him that he must feed us properly, give us proper clothes and boots, and let us be together. It will be more cheerful for us. And he must have these shackles taken off our feet,' and Zhílin looked at his master and laughed.

The master also laughed, heard the interpreter, and said: 'I will give them the best of clothes: a cloak and boots fit to be married in. I will feed them like princes; and if they like they can live together in the barn. But I can't take off the shackles, or they will run away. They shall be taken off, however, at night.' And he jumped up and slapped Zhílin on the shoulder, exclaiming: 'You good, I good!'

Zhílin wrote the letter, but addressed it wrongly, so that it should not reach its destination, thinking to himself: 'I'll run away!'

Zhílin and Kostílin were taken back to the barn and given some maize straw, a jug of water, some bread, two old cloaks, and some worn-out military boots—evidently taken from the corpses of Russian soldiers. At night their shackles were taken off their feet, and they were locked up in the barn.

III

Zhílin and his friend lived in this way for a whole month. The master always laughed and said: 'You, Iván, good! I, Abdul, good!' But he fed them badly giving them nothing but unleavened bread of millet-flour baked into flat cakes, or sometimes only unbaked dough.

Kostílin wrote home a second time, and did nothing but mope and wait for the money to arrive. He would sit for days together in the barn sleeping, or counting the days till a letter could come.

Zhílin knew his letter would reach no one, and he did not write another. He thought: 'Where could my mother get enough money to ransom me? As it is she lived chiefly on what I sent her. If she had to raise five hundred roubles, she would be quite ruined. With God's help I'll manage to escape!'

So he kept on the look-out, planning how to run away.

He would walk about the Aoul whistling; or would sit working, modelling dolls of clay, or weaving baskets out of twigs: for Zhílin was clever with his hands.

Once he modelled a doll with a nose and hands and feet and with a Tartar gown on, and put it up on the roof. When the Tartar women came out to fetch water, the master's daughter, Dina, saw the doll and called the women, who put down their jugs and stood looking and laughing. Zhílin took down the doll and held it out to them. They laughed, but dared not take it. He put down the doll and went into the barn, waiting to see what would happen.

Dina ran up to the doll, looked round, seized it, and ran away.

In the morning, at daybreak, he looked out. Dina came out of the house and sat down on the threshold with the doll, which she had dressed up in bits of red stuff, and she rocked it like a baby, singing a Tartar lullaby. An old woman came out and scolded her, and snatching the doll away she broke it to bits, and sent Dina about her business.

But Zhílin made another doll, better than the first, and gave it to Dina. Once Dina brought a little jug, put it on the ground, sat down gazing at him, and laughed, pointing to the jug.

'What pleases her so?' wondered Zhílin. He took the jug thinking it was water, but it turned out to be milk. He drank the milk and said: 'That's good!'

How pleased Dina was! 'Good, Iván, good!' said she, and she jumped up and clapped her hands. Then, seizing the jug, she ran away. After that, she stealthily brought him some milk every day.

The Tartars make a kind of cheese out of goat's milk, which they dry on the roofs of their houses; and sometimes, on the sly, she brought him some of this cheese. And once, when Abdul had killed a sheep she brought Zhílin a bit of mutton in her sleeve. She would just throw the things down and run away.

One day there was a heavy storm, and the rain fell in torrents for a whole hour. All the streams became turbid. At the ford, the water rose till it was seven feet high, and the current was so strong that it rolled the stones about. Rivulets flowed everywhere, and the rumbling in the hills never ceased. When the storm was over, the water ran in streams down the village street. Zhílin got his master to lend him a knife, and with it he shaped a small cylinder, and cutting some little boards, he made a wheel to which he fixed two dolls, one on each side. The little girls brought him some bits of stuff, and he dressed the dolls, one as a peasant, the other as a peasant woman. Then he fastened them in their places, and set the wheel so that the stream should work it. The wheel began to turn and the dolls danced.

The whole village collected round. Little boys and girls, Tartar men and women, all came and clicked their tongues.

'Ah, Russ! Ah, Iván!'

Abdul had a Russian clock, which was broken. He called Zhílin and showed it to him, clicking his tongue.

'Give it me, I'll mend it for you,' said Zhílin.

He took it to pieces with the knife, sorted the pieces, and put them together again, so that the clock went all right.

The master was delighted, and made him a present of one of his old tunics which was all in holes. Zhílin had to accept it. He could, at any rate, use it as a coverlet at night.

After that Zhílin's fame spread; and Tartars came from distant villages, bringing him now the lock of a gun or of a pistol, now a watch, to mend. His master gave him some tools—pincers, gimlets, and a file.

One day a Tartar fell ill, and they came to Zhílin saying, 'Come and heal him!' Zhílin knew nothing about doctoring, but he went to look, and thought to himself, 'Perhaps he will get well anyway.'

He returned to the barn, mixed some water with sand, and then in the presence of the Tartars whispered some words over it and gave it to the sick man to drink. Luckily for him, the Tartar recovered.

Zhílin began to pick up their language a little, and some of the Tartars grew familiar with him. When they wanted him, they would call: 'Iván! Iván!' Others, however, still looked at him askance, as at a wild beast.

The red-bearded Tartar disliked Zhílin. Whenever he saw him he frowned and turned away, or swore at him. There was also an old man there who did not live in the Aoul, but used to come up from the foot of the hill. Zhílin only saw him when he passed on his way to the Mosque. He was short, and had a white cloth wound round his hat. His beard and moustaches were clipped, and white as snow; and his face was wrinkled and brick-red. His nose was hooked like a hawk's, his grey eyes looked cruel, and he had no teeth except two tusks. He would pass, with his turban on his head, leaning on his staff, and glaring round him like a wolf. If he saw Zhílin he would snort with anger and turn away.

Once Zhílin descended the hill to see where the old man lived. He went down along the pathway and came to a little garden surrounded by a stone wall; and behind the wall he saw cherry and apricot trees, and a hut with a flat roof. He came closer, and saw hives made of plaited straw, and bees flying about and humming. The old man was kneeling, busy doing something with a hive. Zhílin stretched to look, and his shackles rattled. The old man turned round, and, giving a yell, snatched a pistol from his belt and shot at Zhílin, who just managed to shelter himself behind the stone wall.

The old man went to Zhílin's master to complain. The master called Zhílin, and said with a laugh, 'Why did you go to the old man's house?'

'I did him no harm,' replied Zhílin. 'I only wanted to see how he lived.'

The master repeated what Zhílin said.

But the old man was in a rage; he hissed and jabbered, showing his tusks, and shaking his fists at Zhílin.

Zhílin could not understand all, but he gathered that the old man was telling Abdul he ought not to keep Russians in the Aoul, but ought to kill them. At last the old man went away.

Zhílin asked the master who the old man was.

'He is a great man!' said the master. 'He was the bravest of our fellows; he killed many Russians and was at one time very rich. He had three wives and eight sons, and they all lived in one village. Then the Russians came and destroyed the village, and killed seven of his sons. Only one son was left, and he gave himself up to the Russians. The old man also went and gave himself up, and lived among the Russians for three months. At the end of that time he found his son, killed him with his own hands, and then escaped. After that he left off fighting, and went to Mecca to pray to God; that is why he wears a turban. One who has been to Mecca is called "Hadji," and wears a turban. He does not like you fellows. He tells me to kill you. But I can't kill you. I have paid money for you and, besides, I have grown fond of you, Iván. Far from killing you, I would not even let you go if I had not promised.' And he laughed, saying in Russian, 'You, Iván, good; I, Abdul, good!'

IV

Zhílin lived in this way for a month. During the day he sauntered about the Aoul or busied himself with some handicraft, but at night, when all was silent in the Aoul, he dug at the floor of the barn. It was no easy task digging, because of the stones; but he worked away at them with his file, and at last had made a hole under the wall large enough to get through.

'If only I could get to know the lay of the land,' thought he, 'and which way to go! But none of the Tartars will tell me.'

So he chose a day when the master was away from home, and set off after dinner to climb the hill beyond the village, and to look around. But before leaving home the master always gave orders to his son to watch Zhílin, and not to lose sight of him. So the lad ran after Zhílin, shouting: 'Don't go! Father does not allow it. I'll call the neighbours if you won't come back.'

Zhílin tried to persuade him, and said: 'I'm not going far; I only want to climb that hill. I want to find a herb—to cure sick people with. You come with me if you like. How can I run away with these shackles on? To-morrow I'll make a bow and arrows for you.'

So he persuaded the lad, and they went. To look at the hill, it did not seem far to the top; but it was hard walking with shackles on his leg. Zhílin went on and on, but it was all he could do to reach the top. There he sat down and noted how the land lay. To the south, beyond the barn, was a valley in which a herd of horses was pasturing and at the bottom of the valley one could see another Aoul. Beyond that was a still steeper hill, and another hill beyond that. Between the hills, in the blue distance, were forests, and still further off were mountains, rising higher and higher. The highest of them were covered with snow, white as sugar; and one snowy peak towered above all the rest. To the east and to the west were other such hills, and here and there smoke rose from Aouls in the ravines. 'Ah,' thought he, 'all that is Tartar country.' And he turned towards the Russian side. At his feet he saw a river, and the Aoul he lived in, surrounded by little gardens. He could see women, like tiny dolls, sitting by the river rinsing clothes. Beyond the Aoul was a hill, lower than the one to the south, and beyond it two other hills well wooded; and between these, a smooth bluish plain, and far, far across the plain something that looked like a cloud of smoke. Zhílin tried to remember where the sun used to rise and set when he was living in the fort, and he saw that there was no mistake: the Russian fort must be in that plain. Between those two hills he would have to make his way when he escaped.

The sun was beginning to set. The white, snowy mountains turned red, and the dark hills turned darker; mists rose from the ravine, and the valley, where he supposed the Russian fort to be, seemed on fire with the sunset glow. Zhílin looked carefully. Something seemed to be quivering in the valley like smoke from a chimney, and he felt sure the Russian fortress was there.

It had grown late. The Mullah's cry was heard. The herds were being driven home, the cows were lowing, and the lad kept saying, 'Come home!' But Zhílin did not feel inclined to go away.

At last, however, they went back. 'Well,' thought Zhílin, 'now that I know the way, it is time to escape.' He thought of running away that night. The nights were dark—the moon had waned. But as ill-luck would have it, the Tartars returned home that evening. They generally came back driving cattle before them and in good spirits. But this time they had no cattle. All they brought home was the dead body of a Tartar—the red one's brother—who had been killed. They came back looking sullen, and they all gathered together for the burial. Zhílin also came out to see it.

They wrapped the body in a piece of linen, without any coffin, and carried it out of the village, and laid it on the grass under some plane-trees. The Mullah and the old men came. They wound clothes round their caps, took off their shoes, and squatted on their heels, side by side, near the corpse.

The Mullah was in front: behind him in a row were three old men in turbans, and behind them again the other Tartars. All cast down their eyes and sat in silence. This continued a long time, until the Mullah raised his head and said: 'Allah!' (which means God). He said that one word, and they all cast down their eyes again, and were again silent for a long time. They sat quite still, not moving or making any sound.

Again the Mullah lifted his head and said, 'Allah!' and they all repeated: 'Allah! Allah!' and were again silent.

The dead body lay immovable on the grass, and they sat as still as if they too were dead. Not one of them moved. There was no sound but that of the leaves of the plane-trees stirring in the breeze. Then the Mullah repeated a prayer, and they all rose. They lifted the body and carried it in their arms to a hole in the ground. It was not an ordinary hole, but was hollowed out under the ground like a vault. They took the body under the arms and by the legs, bent it, and let it gently down, pushing it under the earth in a sitting posture, with the hands folded in front.

The Nogáy brought some green rushes, which they stuffed into the hole, and, quickly covering it with earth, they smoothed the ground, and set an upright stone at the head of the grave. Then they trod the earth down, and again sat in a row before the grave, keeping silence for a long time.

At last they rose, said 'Allah! Allah! Allah!' and sighed.

The red-bearded Tartar gave money to the old men; then he too rose, took a whip, struck himself with it three times on the forehead, and went home.

The next morning Zhílin saw the red Tartar, followed by three others, leading a mare out of the village. When they were beyond the village, the red-bearded Tartar took off his tunic and turned up his sleeves, showing his stout arms. Then he drew a dagger and sharpened it on a whetstone. The other Tartars raised the mare's head, and he cut her throat, threw her down and began skinning her, loosening the hide with his big hands. Women and girls came and began to wash the entrails and the inwards. The mare was cut up, the pieces taken into the hut, and the whole village collected at the red Tartar's hut for a funeral feast.

For three days they went on eating the flesh of the mare, drinking buza, and praying for the dead man. All the Tartars were at home. On the fourth day at dinner-time Zhílin saw them preparing to go away. Horses were brought out, they got ready, and some ten of them (the red one among them) rode away; but Abdul stayed at home. It was new moon, and the nights were still dark.

'Ah!' thought Zhílin, 'to-night is the time to escape.' And he told Kostílin; but Kostílin's heart failed him.

'How can we escape?' he said. 'We don't even know the way.'

'I know the way,' said Zhílin.

'Even if you do'' said Kostílin, 'we can't reach the fort in one night.'

'If we can't,' said Zhílin, 'we'll sleep in the forest. See here, I have saved some cheeses. What's the good of sitting and moping here? If they send your ransom—well and good; but suppose they don't manage to collect it? The Tartars are angry now, because the Russians have killed one of their men. They are talking of killing us.'

Kostílin thought it over.

'Well, let's go,' said he.

V

Zhílin crept into the hole, widened it so that Kostílin might also get through, and then they both sat waiting till all should be quiet in the Aoul.

As soon as all was quiet, Zhílin crept under the wall, got out, and whispered to Kostílin, 'Come!' Kostílin crept out, but in so doing he caught a stone with his foot and made a noise. The master had a very vicious watch-dog, a spotted one called Oulyashin. Zhílin had been careful to feed him for some time before. Oulyashin heard the noise and began to bark and jump, and the other dogs did the same. Zhílin gave a slight whistle, and threw him a bit of cheese. Oulyashin knew Zhílin, wagged his tail, and stopped barking.

But the master had heard the dog, and shouted to him from his hut, 'Hayt, hayt, Oulyashin!'

Zhílin, however, scratched Oulyashin behind the ears, and the dog was quiet, and rubbed against his legs, wagging his tail

They sat hidden behind a corner for awhile. All became silent again, only a sheep coughed inside a shed, and the water rippled over the stones in the hollow. It was dark, the stars were high overhead, and the new moon showed red as it set, horns upward, behind the hill. In the valleys the fog was white as milk.

Zhílin rose and said to his companion, 'Well, friend, come along!'

They started; but they had only gone a few steps when they heard the Mullah crying from the roof, 'Allah, Beshmillah! Ilrahman!' That meant that the people would be going to the Mosque. So they sat down again, hiding behind a wall, and waited a long time till the people had passed. At last all was quiet again.

'Now then! May God be with us!' They crossed themselves, and started once more. They passed through a yard and went down the hillside to the river, crossed the river, and went along the valley.

The mist was thick, but only near the ground; overhead the stars shone quite brightly. Zhílin directed their course by the stars. It was cool in the mist, and easy walking, only their boots were uncomfortable, being worn out and trodden down. Zhílin took his off, threw them away, and went barefoot, jumping from stone to stone, and guiding his course by the stars. Kostílin began to lag behind.

'Walk slower,' he said, 'these confounded boots have quite blistered my feet.'

'Take them off!' said Zhílin. 'It will be easier walking without them.'

Kostílin went barefoot, but got on still worse. The stones cut his feet and he kept lagging behind. Zhílin said: 'If your feet get cut, they'll heal again; but if the Tartars catch us and kill us, it will be worse!'

Kostílin did not reply, but went on, groaning all the time.

Their way lay through the valley for a long time. Then, to the right, they heard dogs barking. Zhílin stopped, looked about, and began climbing the hill feeling with his hands.

'Ah!' said he, 'we have gone wrong, and have come too far to the right. Here is another Aoul, one I saw from the hill. We must turn back and go up that hill to the left. There must be a wood there.'

But Kostílin said: 'Wait a minute! Let me get breath. My feet are all cut and bleeding.'

'Never mind, friend! They'll heal again. You should spring more lightly. Like this!'

And Zhílin ran back and turned to the left up the hill towards the wood.

Kostílin still lagged behind, and groaned. Zhílin only said 'Hush!' and went on and on.

They went up the hill and found a wood as Zhílin had said. They entered the wood and forced their way through the brambles, which tore their clothes. At last they came to a path and followed it.

'Stop!' They heard the tramp of hoofs on the path, and waited, listening. It sounded like the tramping of a horse's feet, but then ceased. They moved on, and again they heard the tramping. When they paused, it also stopped. Zhílin crept nearer to it, and saw something standing on the path where it was not quite so dark. It looked like a horse, and yet not quite like one, and on it was something queer, not like a man. He heard it snorting. 'What can it be?' Zhílin gave a low whistle, and off it dashed from the path into the thicket, and the woods were filled with the noise of crackling, as if a hurricane were sweeping through, breaking the branches.

Kostílin was so frightened that he sank to the ground. But Zhílin laughed and said: 'It's a stag. Don't you hear him breaking the branches with his antlers? We were afraid of him, and he is afraid of us.'

They went on. The Great Bear was already setting. It was near morning, and they did not know whether they were going the right way or not. Zhílin thought it was the way he had been brought by the Tartars, and that they were still some seven miles from the Russian fort; but he had nothing certain to go by, and at night one easily mistakes the way. After a time they came to a clearing. Kostílin sat down and said: 'Do as you like, I can go no farther! My feet won't carry me.'

Zhílin tried to persuade him.

'No I shall never get there, I can't!'

Zhílin grew angry, and spoke roughly to him.

'Well, then, I shall go on alone. Good-bye!'

Kostílin jumped up and followed. They went another three miles. The mist in the wood had settled down still more densely; they could not see a yard before them, and the stars had grown dim.

Suddenly they heard the sound of a horse's hoofs in front of them. They heard its shoes strike the stones. Zhílin lay down flat, and listened with his ear to the ground.

'Yes, so it is! A horseman is coming towards us.'

They ran off the path, crouched among the bushes and waited. Zhílin crept to the road, looked, and saw a Tartar on horseback driving a cow and humming to himself. The Tartar rode past. Zhílin returned to Kostílin.

'God has led him past us; get up and let's go on!'

Kostílin tried to rise, but fell back again.

'I can't; on my word I can't! I have no strength left.'

He was heavy and stout, and had been perspiring freely. Chilled by the mist, and with his feet all bleeding, he had grown quite limp.

Zhílin tried to lift him, when suddenly Kostílin screamed out: 'Oh, how it hurts!'

Zhílin's heart sank.

'What are you shouting for? The Tartar is still near; he'll have heard you!' And he thought to himself, 'He is really quite done up. What am I to do with him? It won't do to desert a comrade.'

'Well, then, get up, and climb up on my back. I'll carry you if you really can't walk.'

He helped Kostílin up, and put his arms under his thighs. Then he went out on to the path, carrying him.

'Only, for the love of heaven,' said Zhílin, 'don't throttle me with your hands! Hold on to my shoulders.'

Zhílin found his load heavy; his feet, too, were bleeding, and he was tired out. Now and then he stooped to balance Kostílin better, jerking him up so that he should sit higher, and then went on again.

The Tartar must, however, really have heard Kostílin scream. Zhílin suddenly heard some one galloping behind and shouting in the Tartar tongue. He darted in among the bushes. The Tartar seized his gun and fired, but did not hit them, shouted in his own language, and galloped off along the road.

'Well, now we are lost, friend!' said Zhílin. 'That dog will gather the Tartars together to hunt us down. Unless we can get a couple of miles away from here we are lost!' And he thought to himself, 'Why the devil did I saddle myself with this block? I should have got away long ago had I been alone.'

'Go on alone,' said Kostílin. 'Why should you perish because of me?'

'No I won't go. It won't do to desert a comrade.'

Again he took Kostílin on his shoulders and staggered on. They went on in that way for another half-mile or more. They were still in the forest, and could not see the end of it. But the mist was already dispersing, and clouds seemed to be gathering, the stars were no longer to be seen. Zhílin was quite done up. They came to a spring walled in with stones by the side of the path. Zhílin stopped and set Kostílin down.

'Let me have a rest and a drink,' said he, 'and let us eat some of the cheese. It can't be much farther now.'

But hardly had he lain down to get a drink, when he heard the sound of horses' feet behind him. Again they darted to the right among the bushes, and lay down under a steep slope.

They heard Tartar voices. The Tartars stopped at the very spot where they had turned off the path. The Tartars talked a bit, and then seemed to be setting a dog on the scent. There was a sound of crackling twigs, and a strange dog appeared from behind the bushes. It stopped, and began to bark.

Then the Tartars, also strangers, came climbing down, seized Zhílin and Kostílin, bound them, put them on horses, and rode away with them.

When they had ridden about two miles, they met Abdul, their owner, with two other Tartars following him. After talking with the strangers, he put Zhílin and Kostílin on two of his own horses and took them back to the Aoul.

Abdul did not laugh now, and did not say a word to them.

They were back at the Aoul by daybreak, and were set down in the street. The children came crowding round, throwing stones, shrieking, and beating them with whips.

The Tartars gathered together in a circle, and the old man from the foot of the hill was also there. They began discussing, and Zhílin heard them considering what should be done with him and Kostílin. Some said they ought to be sent farther into the mountains; but the old man said: 'They must be killed!'

Abdul disputed with him, saying: 'I gave money for them, and I must get ransom for them.' But the old man said: 'They will pay you nothing, but will only bring misfortune. It is a sin to feed Russians. Kill them, and have done with it!'

They dispersed. When they had gone, the master came up to Zhílin and said: 'If the money for your ransom is not sent within a fortnight, I will flog you; and if you try to run away again, I'll kill you like a dog! Write a letter, and write properly!'

Paper was brought to them, and they wrote the letters. Shackles were put on their feet, and they were taken behind the Mosque to a deep pit about twelve feet square, into which they were let down.

VI

Life was now very hard for them. Their shackles were never taken off, and they were not let out into the fresh air. Unbaked dough was thrown to them as if they were dogs, and water was let down in a can.

It was wet and close in the pit, and there was a horrible stench. Kostílin grew quite ill, his body became swollen and he ached all over, and moaned or slept all the time. Zhílin, too, grew downcast; he saw it was a bad look-out, and could think of no way of escape.

He tried to make a tunnel, but there was nowhere to put the earth. His master noticed it, and threatened to kill him.

He was sitting on the floor of the pit one day, thinking of freedom and feeling very downhearted, when suddenly a cake fell into his lap, then another, and then a shower of cherries. He looked up, and there was Dina. She looked at him, laughed, and ran away. And Zhílin thought: 'Might not Dina help me?'

He cleared out a little place in the pit, scraped up some clay, and began modelling toys. He made men, horses, and dogs, thinking, 'When Dina comes I'll throw them up to her.'

But Dina did not come next day. Zhílin heard the tramp of horses; some men rode past, and the Tartars gathered in council near the Mosque. They shouted and argued; the word 'Russians' was repeated several times. He could hear the voice of the old man. Though he could not distinguish what was said, he guessed that Russian troops were somewhere near, and that the Tartars, afraid they might come into the Aoul, did not know what to do with their prisoners.

After talking awhile, they went away. Suddenly he heard a rustling overhead, and saw Dina crouching at the edge of the pit, her knees higher than her head, and bending over so that the coins of her plait dangled above the pit. Her eyes gleamed like stars. She drew two cheeses out of her sleeve and threw them to him. Zhílin took them and said, 'Why did you not come before? I have made some toys for you. Here, catch!' And he began throwing the toys up, one by one.

But she shook her head and would not look at them.

'I don't want any,' she said. She sat silent for awhile, and then went on, 'Iván, they want to kill you!' And she pointed to her own throat.

'Who wants to kill me?'

'Father; the old men say he must. But I am sorry for you!'

Zhílin answered: 'Well, if you are sorry for me, bring me a long pole.'

She shook her head, as much as to say, 'I can't!'

He clasped his hands and prayed her: 'Dina, please do! Dear Dina, I beg of you!'

'I can't!' she said, 'they would see me bringing it. They're all at home.' And she went away.

So when evening came Zhílin still sat looking up now and then, and wondering what would happen. The stars were there, but the moon had not yet risen. The Mullah's voice was heard; then all was silent. Zhílin was beginning to doze, thinking: 'The girl will be afraid to do it!'

Suddenly he felt clay falling on his head. He looked up, and saw a long pole poking into the opposite wall of the pit. It kept poking about for a time, and then it came down, sliding into the pit. Zhílin was glad indeed. He took hold of it and lowered it. It was a strong pole, one that he had seen before on the roof of his master's hut.

He looked up. The stars were shining high in the sky, and just above the pit Dina's eyes gleamed in the dark like a cat's. She stooped with her face close to the edge of the pit, and whispered, 'Iván! Iván!' waving her hand in front of her face to show that he should speak low.

'What?' said Zhílin.

'All but two have gone away.'

Then Zhílin said, 'Well, Kostílin, come; let us have one last try; I'll help you up.'

But Kostílin would not hear of it.

'No,' said he, 'It's clear I can't get away from here. How can I go, when I have hardly strength to turn round?'

'Well, good-bye, then! Don't think ill of me!' and they kissed each other. Zhílin seized the pole, told Dina to hold on, and began to climb. He slipped once or twice; the shackles hindered him. Kostílin helped him, and he managed to get to the top. Dina with her little hands, pulled with all her might at his shirt, laughing.

Zhílin drew out the pole and said, 'Put it back in its place, Dina, or they'll notice, and you will be beaten.'

She dragged the pole away, and Zhílin went down the hill. When he had gone down the steep incline, he took a sharp stone and tried to wrench the lock off the shackles. But it was a strong lock and he could not manage to break it, and besides, it was difficult to get at. Then he heard some one running down the hill, springing lightly. He thought: 'Surely, that's Dina again.'

Dina came, took a stone and said, 'Let me try.'

She knelt down and tried to wrench the lock off, but her little hands were as slender as little twigs, and she had not the strength. She threw the stone away and began to cry. Then Zhílin set to work again at the lock, and Dina squatted beside him with her hand on his shoulder.

Zhílin looked round and saw a red light to the left behind the hill. The moon was just rising. 'Ah!' he thought, 'before the moon has risen I must have passed the valley and be in the forest.' So he rose and threw away the stone. Shackles or no, he must go on.

'Good-bye, Dina dear!' he said. 'I shall never forget you!'

Dina seized hold of him and felt about with her hands for a place to put some cheeses she had brought. He took them from her.

'Thank you, my little one. Who will make dolls for you when I am gone?' And he stroked her head.

Dina burst into tears hiding her face in her hands. Then she ran up the hill like a young goat, the coins in her plait clinking against her back.

Zhílin crossed himself took the lock of his shackles in his hand to prevent its clattering, and went along the road, dragging his shackled leg, and looking towards the place where the moon was about to rise. He now knew the way. If he went straight he would have to walk nearly six miles. If only he could reach the wood before the moon had quite risen! He crossed the river; the light behind the hill was growing whiter. Still looking at it, he went along the valley. The moon was not yet visible. The light became brighter, and one side of the valley was growing lighter and lighter, and shadows were drawing in towards the foot of the hill, creeping nearer and nearer to him.

Zhílin went on, keeping in the shade. He was hurrying, but the moon was moving still faster; the tops of the hills on the right were already lit up. As he got near the wood the white moon appeared from behind the hills, and it became light as day. One could see all the leaves on the trees. It was light on the hill, but silent, as if nothing were alive; no sound could be heard but the gurgling of the river below.

Zhílin reached the wood without meeting any one, chose a dark spot, and sat down to rest.

He rested and ate one of the cheeses. Then he found a stone and set to work again to knock off the shackles. He knocked his hands sore, but could not break the lock. He rose and went along the road. After walking the greater part of a mile he was quite done up, and his feet were aching. He had to stop every ten steps.

'There is nothing else for it,' thought he. 'I must drag on as long as I have any strength left. If I sit down, I shan't be able to rise again. I can't reach the fortress; but when day breaks I'll lie down in the forest, remain there all day, and go on again at night.'

He went on all night. Two Tartars on horseback passed him; but he heard them a long way off, and hid behind a tree.

The moon began to grow paler, the dew to fall. It was getting near dawn, and Zhílin had not reached the end of the forest. 'Well,' thought he, 'I'll walk another thirty steps, and then turn in among the trees and sit down.'

He walked another thirty steps, and saw that he was at the end of the forest. He went to the edge; it was now quite light, and straight before him was the plain and the fortress. To the left, quite close at the foot of the slope, a fire was dying out, and the smoke from it spread round. There were men gathered about the fire.

He looked intently, and saw guns glistening. They were soldiers— Cossacks!

Zhílin was filled with joy. He collected his remaining strength and set off down the hill, saying to himself: 'God forbid that any mounted Tartar should see me now, in the open field! Near as I am, I could not get there in time.'

Hardly had he said this when, a couple of hundred yards off, on a hillock to the left, he saw three Tartars.

They saw him also and made a rush. His heart sank. He waved his hands, and shouted with all his might, 'Brothers, brothers! Help!'

The Cossacks heard him, and a party of them on horseback darted to cut across the Tartars' path. The Cossacks were far and the Tartars were near; but Zhílin, too, made a last effort. Lifting the shackles with his hand, he ran towards the Cossacks, hardly knowing what he was doing, crossing himself and shouting, 'Brothers! Brothers! Brothers!'

There were some fifteen Cossacks. The Tartars were frightened, and stopped before reaching him. Zhílin staggered up to the Cossacks.

They surrounded him and began questioning him. 'Who are you? What are you? Where from?'

But Zhílin was quite beside himself, and could only weep and repeat, 'Brothers! Brothers!'

Then the soldiers came running up and crowded round Zhílin—one giving him bread, another buckwheat, a third vódka: one wrapping a cloak round him, another breaking his shackles.

The officers recognized him, and rode with him to the fortress. The soldiers were glad to see him back, and his comrades all gathered round him.

Zhílin told them all that had happened to him.

'That's the way I went home and got married!' said he. 'No. It seems plain that fate was against it!'

So he went on serving in the Caucasus. A month passed before Kostílin was released, after paying five thousand roubles ransom. He was almost dead when they brought him back.

1870

THE BEAR-HUNT

The adventure here narrated is one that happened to
Tolstoy himself in 1858. More than twenty years later
he gave up hunting, on humanitarian grounds.

We were out on a bear-hunting expedition. My comrade had shot
at a bear, but only gave him a flesh-wound. There were traces of blood
on the snow, but the bear had got away.

We all collected in a group in the forest, to decide whether we
ought to go after the bear at once, or wait two or three days till he
should settle down again. We asked the peasant bear-drivers whether it
would be possible to get round the bear that day.

'No. It's impossible,' said an old bear-driver. 'You must let the
bear quiet down. In five days' time it will be possible to surround him;
but if you followed him now, you would only frighten him away, and
he would not settle down.'

But a young bear-driver began disputing with the old man, saying
that it was quite possible to get round the bear now.

'On such snow as this,' said he, 'he won't go far, for he is a fat
bear. He will settle down before evening; or, if not, I can overtake him
on snowshoes.'

The comrade I was with was against following up the bear, and
advised waiting. But I said:

'We need not argue. You do as you like, but I will follow up the
track with Damian. If we get round the bear, all right. If not, we lose
nothing. It is still early, and there is nothing else for us to do to-day.'

So it was arranged.

The others went back to the sledges, and returned to the village.
Damian and I took some bread, and remained behind in the forest.

When they had all left us, Damian and I examined our guns, and
after tucking the skirts of our warm coats into our belts, we started off,
following the bear's tracks.

The weather was fine, frosty and calm; but it was hard work snow-
shoeing. The snow was deep and soft: it had not caked together at all in
the forest, and fresh snow had fallen the day before, so that our snow-
shoes sank six inches deep in the snow, and sometimes more.

The bear's tracks were visible from a distance, and we could see
how he had been going; sometimes sinking in up to his belly and
ploughing up the snow as he went. At first, while under large trees, we
kept in sight of his track; but when it turned into a thicket of small firs,
Damian stopped.

'We must leave the trail now,' said he. 'He has probably settled
somewhere here. You can see by the snow that he has been squatting

down. Let us leave the track and go round; but we must go quietly. Don't shout or cough, or we shall frighten him away.'

Leaving the track, therefore, we turned off to the left. But when we had gone about five hundred yards, there were the bear's traces again right before us. We followed them, and they brought us out on to the road. There we stopped, examining the road to see which way the bear had gone. Here and there in the snow were prints of the bear's paw, claws and all, and here and there the marks of a peasant's bark shoes. The bear had evidently gone towards the village.

As we followed the road, Damian said:

'It's no use watching the road now. We shall see where he has turned off, to right or left, by the marks in the soft snow at the side. He must have turned off somewhere; for he won't have gone on to the village.'

We went along the road for nearly a mile, and then saw, ahead of us, the bear's track turning off the road. We examined it. How strange! It was a bear's track right enough, only not going from the road into the forest, but from the forest on to the road! The toes were pointing towards the road.

'This must be another bear,' I said.

Damian looked at it, and considered a while.

'No,' said he. 'It's the same one. He's been playing tricks, and walked backwards when he left the road.'

We followed the track, and found it really was so! The bear had gone some ten steps backwards, and then, behind a fir tree, had turned round and gone straight ahead. Damian stopped and said:

'Now, we are sure to get round him. There is a marsh ahead of us, and he must have settled down there. Let us go round it.'

We began to make our way round, through a fir thicket. I was tired out by this time, and it had become still more difficult to get along. Now I glided on to juniper bushes and caught my snow-shoes in them, now a tiny fir tree appeared between my feet, or, from want of practise, my snow-shoes slipped off; and now I came upon a stump or a log hidden by the snow. I was getting very tired, and was drenched with perspiration; and I took off my fur cloak. And there was Damian all the time, gliding along as if in a boat, his snowshoes moving as if of their own accord, never catching against anything, nor slipping off. He even took my fur and slung it over his shoulder, and still kept urging me on.

We went on for two more miles, and came out on the other side of the marsh. I was lagging behind. My snow-shoes kept slipping off, and my feet stumbled. Suddenly Damian, who was ahead of me, stopped and waved his arm. When I came up to him, he bent down, pointing with his hand, and whispered:

'Do you see the magpie chattering above that undergrowth? It scents the bear from afar. That is where he must be.'

We turned off and went on for more than another half-mile, and presently we came on to the old track again. We had, therefore, been right round the bear who was now within the track we had left. We stopped, and I took off my cap and loosened all my clothes. I was as hot as in a steam bath, and as wet as a drowned rat. Damian too was flushed, and wiped his face with his sleeve.

'Well, sir,' he said, 'we have done our job, and now we must have a rest.'

The evening glow already showed red through the forest. We took off our snow-shoes and sat down on them, and got some bread and salt out of our bags. First I ate some snow, and then some bread; and the bread tasted so good, that I thought I had never in my life had any like it before. We sat there resting until it began to grow dusk, and then I asked Damian if it was far to the village.

'Yes,' he said. 'It must be about eight miles. We will go on there to-night, but now we must rest. Put on your fur coat, sir, or you'll be catching cold.'

Damian flattened down the snow, and breaking off some fir branches made a bed of them. We lay down side by side, resting our heads on our arms. I do not remember how I fell asleep. Two hours later I woke up, hearing something crack.

I had slept so soundly that I did not know where I was. I looked around me. How wonderful! I was in some sort of a hall, all glittering and white with gleaming pillars, and when I looked up I saw, through delicate white tracery, a vault, raven black and studded with coloured lights. After a good look, I remembered that we were in the forest, and that what I took for a hall and pillars, were trees covered with snow and hoar-frost, and the coloured lights were stars twinkling between the branches.

Hoar-frost had settled in the night; all the twigs were thick with it, Damian was covered with it, it was on my fur coat, and it dropped down from the trees. I woke Damian, and we put on our snowshoes and started. It was very quiet in the forest. No sound was heard but that of our snow-shoes pushing through the soft snow; except when now and then a tree, cracked by the frost, made the forest resound. Only once we heard the sound of a living creature. Something rustled close to us, and then rushed away. I felt sure it was the bear, but when we went to the spot whence the sound had come, we found the footmarks of hares, and saw several young aspen trees with their bark gnawed. We had startled some hares while they were feeding.

We came out on the road, and followed it, dragging our snow-shoes behind us. It was easy walking now. Our snow-shoes clattered as they slid behind us from side to side of the hard-trodden road. The snow creaked under our boots, and the cold hoar-frost settled on our faces like down. Seen through the branches, the stars seemed to be running to meet us, now twinkling, now vanishing, as if the whole sky were on the move.

I found my comrade sleeping, but woke him up, and related how we had got round the bear. After telling our peasant host to collect beaters for the morning, we had supper and lay down to sleep.

I was so tired that I could have slept on till midday, if my comrade had not roused me. I jumped up, and saw that he was already dressed, and busy doing something to his gun.

'Where is Damian?' said I.

'In the forest, long ago. He has already been over the tracks you made, and been back here, and now he has gone to look after the beaters.'

I washed and dressed, and loaded my guns; and then we got into a sledge, and started.

The sharp frost still continued. It was quiet, and the sun could not be seen. There was a thick mist above us, and hoar-frost still covered everything.

After driving about two miles along the road, as we came near the forest, we saw a cloud of smoke rising from a hollow, and presently reached a group of peasants, both men and women, armed with cudgels.

We got out and went up to them. The men sat roasting potatoes, and laughing and talking with the women.

Damian was there too; and when we arrived the people got up, and Damian led them away to place them in the circle we had made the day before. They went along in single file, men and women, thirty in all. The snow was so deep that we could only see them from their waists upwards. They turned into the forest, and my friend and I followed in their track.

Though they had trodden a path, walking was difficult, but, on the other hand, it was impossible to fall: it was like walking between two walls of snow.

We went on in this way for nearly half a mile, when all at once we saw Damian coming from another direction—running towards us on his snowshoes, and beckoning us to join him. We went towards him, and he showed us where to stand. I took my place, and looked round me.

To my left were tall fir trees, between the trunks of which I could see a good way, and, like a black patch just visible behind the trees, I could see a beater. In front of me was a thicket of young firs, about as high as a man, their branches weighed down and stuck together with snow. Through this copse ran a path thickly covered with snow, and leading straight up to where I stood. The thicket stretched away to the right of me, and ended in a small glade, where I could see Damian placing my comrade.

I examined both my guns, and considered where I had better stand.

Three steps behind me was a tall fir.

'That's where I'll stand,' thought I, 'and then I can lean my second gun against the tree'; and I moved towards the tree, sinking up to my knees in the snow at each step. I trod the snow down, and made a clearance about a yard square, to stand on. One gun I kept in my hand; the other, ready cocked, I placed leaning up against the tree. Then I unsheathed and replaced my dagger, to make sure that I could draw it easily in case of need.

Just as I had finished these preparations, I heard Damian shouting in the forest:

'He's up! He's up!'

And as soon as Damian shouted, the peasants round the circle all replied in their different voices.

'Up, up, up! Ou! Ou! Ou!' shouted the men.

'Ay! Ay! Ay!' screamed the women in high. pitched tones.

The bear was inside the circle, and as Damian drove him on, the people all round kept shouting. Only my friend and I stood silent and motionless, waiting for the bear to come towards us. As I stood gazing and listening, my heart beat violently. I trembled, holding my gun fast.

'Now now,' I thought. 'He will come suddenly. I shall aim, fire, and he will drop—'

Suddenly, to my left, but at a distance, I heard something falling on the snow. I looked between the tall fir trees, and, some fifty paces off, behind the trunks, saw something big and black. I took aim and waited, thinking:

'Won't he come any nearer?'

As I waited I saw him move his ears, turn, and go back; and then I caught a glimpse of the whole of him in profile. He was an immense brute. In my excitement, I fired, and heard my bullet go 'flop' against a tree. Peering through the smoke, I saw my bear scampering back into the circle, and disappearing among the trees.

'Well,' thought I. 'My chance is lost. He won't come back to me. Either my comrade will shoot him, or he will escape through the line of beaters. In any case he won't give me another chance.'

I reloaded my gun, however, and again stood listening. The peasants were shouting all round, but to the right, not far from where my comrade stood, I heard a woman screaming in a frenzied voice: 'Here he is! Here he is! Come here, come here! Oh! Oh! Ay! Ay!'

Evidently she could see the bear. I had given up expecting him, and was looking to the right at my comrade. All at once I saw Damian with a stick in his hand, and without his snow-shoes, running along a footpath towards my friend. He crouched down beside him, pointing his stick as if aiming at something, and then I saw my friend raise his gun and aim in the same direction. Crack! He fired.

'There,' thought I. 'He has killed him.'

But I saw that my comrade did not run towards the bear. Evidently he had missed him, or the shot had not taken full effect.

'The bear will get away,' I thought. 'He will go back, but he won't come a second time towards me.—But what is that?'

Something was coming towards me like a whirlwind, snorting as it came; and I saw the snow flying up quite near me. I glanced straight before me, and there was the bear, rushing along the path through the thicket right at me, evidently beside himself with fear. He was hardly half a dozen paces off, and I could see the whole of him—his black chest and enormous head with a reddish patch. There he was, blundering straight at me, and scattering the snow about as he came. I could see by his eyes that he did not see me, but, mad with fear, was rushing blindly along; and his path led him straight at the tree under which I was standing. I raised my gun and fired. He was almost upon me now, and I saw that I had missed. My bullet had gone past him, and he did not even hear me fire, but still came headlong towards me. I lowered my gun, and fired again, almost touching his head. Crack! I had hit, but not killed him!

He raised his head, and laying his ears back, came at me, showing his teeth.

I snatched at my other gun, but almost before I had touched it, he had down at me and, knocking me over into the snow, had passed right over me.

'Thank goodness, he has left me,' thought I.

I tried to rise, but something pressed me down, and prevented my getting up. The bear's rush had carried him past me, but he had turned back, and had fallen on me with the whole weight of his body. I felt something heavy weighing me down, and something warm above my face, and I realized that he was drawing my whole face into his mouth. My nose was already in it, and I felt the heat of it, and smelt his blood. He was pressing my shoulders down with his paws so that I could not move: all I could do was to draw my head down towards my chest away from his mouth, trying to free my nose and eyes, while he tried to get his teeth into them. Then I felt that he had seized my forehead just under the hair with the teeth of his lower jaw, and the flesh below my eyes with his upper jaw, and was closing his teeth. It was as if my face were being cut with knives. I struggled to get away, while he made haste to close his jaws like a dog gnawing. I managed to twist my face away, but he began drawing it again into his mouth.

'Now,' thought I, 'my end has come!'

Then I felt the weight lifted, and looking up, I saw that he was no longer there. He had jumped off me and run away.

When my comrade and Damian had seen the bear knock me down and begin worrying me, they rushed to the rescue. My comrade, in his haste, blundered, and instead of following the trodden path, ran into the deep snow and fell down. While he was struggling out of the snow, the bear was gnawing at me. But Damian just as he was, without a gun, and with only a stick in his hand, rushed along the path shouting:

'He's eating the master! He's eating the master!'

And as he ran, he called to the bear:

'Oh you idiot! What are you doing? Leave off! Leave off!'

The bear obeyed him, and leaving me ran away. When I rose, there was as much blood on the snow as if a sheep had been killed, and the flesh hung in rags above my eyes, though in my excitement I felt no pain.

My comrade had come up by this time, and the other people collected round: they looked at my wound, and put snow on it. But I, forgetting about my wounds, only asked:

'Where's the bear? Which way has he gone?'

Suddenly I heard:

'Here he is! Here he is!'

And we saw the bear again running at us. We seized our guns, but before any one had time to fire he had run past. He had grown ferocious, and wanted to gnaw me again, but seeing so many people he took fright. We saw by his track that his head was bleeding and we wanted to follow him up; but, as my wounds had become very painful, we went, instead, to the town to find a doctor.

The doctor stitched up my wounds with silk, and they soon began to heal.

A month later we went to hunt that bear again, but I did not get a chance of finishing him. He would not come out of the circle, but went round and round growling in a terrible voice.

Damian killed him. The bear's lower jaw had been broken, and one of his teeth knocked out by my bullet.

He was a huge creature, and had splendid black fur.

I had him stuffed, and he now lies in my room. The wounds on my forehead healed up so that the scars can scarcely be seen.

1872

PART II. POPULAR STORIES

WHAT MEN LIVE BY (1881)

'We know that we have passed out of death into life, because we love the brethren. He that loveth not abideth in death.'—*I Epistle St. John iii. 14.*

'Whoso hath the world's goods, and beholdeth his brother in need, and shutteth up his compassion from him, how doth the love of God abide in him? My little children, let us not love in word, neither with the tongue; but in deed and truth.'—*iii. 17-18.*

'Love is of God; and every one that loveth is begotten of God, and knoweth God. He that loveth not knoweth not God; for God is love.'—*iv. 7-8.*

'No man hath beheld God at any time; if we love one another, God abideth in us.'—*iv. 12.*

'God is love; and he that abideth in love abideth in God, and God abideth in him.'—*iv. 16.*

'If a man say, I love God, and hateth his brother, he is a liar; for he that loveth not his brother whom he hath seen, how can he love God whom he hath not seen?'—*iv. 20.*

I

A shoemaker named Simon, who had neither house nor land of his own, lived with his wife and children in a peasant's hut, and earned his living by his work. Work was cheap but bread was dear, and what he earned he spent for food. The man and his wife had but one sheepskin coat between them for winter wear, and even that was worn to tatters, and this was the second year he had been wanting to buy sheep-skins for a new coat. Before winter Simon saved up a little money: a three-rouble note lay hidden in his wife's box, and five roubles and twenty kopeks were owed him by customers in the village.

So one morning he prepared to go to the village to buy the sheep-skins. He put on over his shirt his wife's wadded nankeen jacket, and over that he put his own cloth coat. He took the three-rouble note in his pocket, cut himself a stick to serve as a staff, and started off after breakfast. 'I'll collect the five roubles that are due to me,' thought he, 'add the three I have got, and that will be enough to buy sheep-skins for the winter coat.'

He came to the village and called at a peasant's hut, but the man was not at home. The peasant's wife promised that the money should be paid next week, but she would not pay it herself. Then Simon called on another peasant, but this one swore he had no money, and would only pay twenty kopeks which he owed for a pair of boots Simon had mended. Simon then tried to buy the sheep-skins on credit, but the deader would not trust him.

'Bring your money,' said he, 'then you may have your pick of the skins. We know what debt-collecting is like.'

So all the business the shoemaker did was to get the twenty kopeks for boots he had mended, and to take a pair of felt boots a peasant gave him to sole with leather.

Simon felt downhearted. He spent the twenty kopeks on vódka, and started homewards without having bought any skins. In the morning he had felt the frost; but now, after drinking the vódka, he felt warm even without a sheep-skin coat. He trudged along, striking his stick on the frozen earth with one hand, swinging the felt boots with the other, and talking to himself.

'I'm quite warm,' said he, 'though I have no sheepskin coat. I've had a drop, and it runs through all my veins. I need no sheepskins. I go along and don't worry about anything. That's the sort of man I am! What do I care? I can live without sheep skins. I don't need them. My wife will fret, to be sure. And, true enough, it's a shame; one works all day long, and then does not get paid. Stop a bit! If you don't bring that money along, sure enough I'll skin you, blessed if I don't. How's that? He pays twenty kopeks at a time! What can I do with twenty kopeks: Drink it—that's all one can do! Hard up, he says he is! So he may be— but what about me? You have house, and cattle, and everything; I've only what I stand up in! You have corn of your own growing; I have to buy every grain. Do what I will, I must spend three roubles every week for bread alone. I come home and find the bread all used up, and I have to fork out another rouble and a half. So just you pay up what you owe, and no nonsense about it!'

By this time he had nearly reached the shrine at the bend of the road. Looking up, he saw something whitish behind the shrine. The daylight was fading, and the shoemaker peered at the thing without being able to make out what it was. 'There was no white stone here before. Can it be an ox? It's not like an ox. It has a head like a man, but it's too white; and what could a man be doing there?'

He came closer, so that it was clearly visible. To his surprise it really was a man, alive or dead, sitting naked, leaning motionless against the shrine. Terror seized the shoemaker, and he thought, 'Some one has killed him, stripped him, and left him here. If I meddle I shall surely get into trouble.'

So the shoemaker went on. He passed in front of the shrine so that he could not see the man. When he had gone some way, he looked back, and saw that the man was no longer leaning against the shrine, but was moving as if looking towards him. The shoemaker felt more frightened than before, and thought, 'Shall I go back to him, or shall I go on? If I go near him something dreadful may happen. Who knows who the fellow is? He has not come here for any good. If I go near him he may jump up and throttle me, and there will be no getting away. Or if not, he'd still be a burden on one's hands. What could I do with a naked man? I couldn't give him my last clothes. Heaven only help me to get away!'

So the shoemaker hurried on, leaving the shrine behind him— when suddenly his conscience smote him and he stopped in the road.

'What are you doing, Simon?' said he to himself. 'The man may be dying of want, and you slip past afraid. Have you grown so rich as to be afraid of robbers? Ah, Simon, shame on you!'

So he turned back and went up to the man.

II

Simon approached the stranger, looked at him, and saw that he was a young man, fit, with no bruises on his body, only evidently freezing and frightened, and he sat there leaning back without looking up at Simon, as if too faint to lift his eyes. Simon went close to him, and then the man seemed to wake up. Turning his head, he opened his eyes and looked into Simon's face. That one look was enough to make Simon fond of the man. He threw the felt boots on the ground undid his sash, laid it on the boots, and took off his cloth coat.

'It's not a time for talking,' said he. 'Come, put this coat on at once!' And Simon took the man by the elbows and helped him to rise. As he stood there, Simon saw that his body was clean and in good condition, his hands and feet shapely, and his face good and kind. He threw his coat over the man's shoulders but the latter could not find the sleeves. Simon guided his arms into them, and drawing the coat well on trapped it closely about him, tying the sash round the man's waist.

Simon even took off his torn cap to put it on the man's head, but then his own head felt cold, and he thought: 'I'm quite bald, while he has long curly hair.' So he put his cap on his own head again. 'It will be better to give him something for his feet,' thought he; and he made the man sit down, and helped him to put on the felt boots, saying, 'There, friend, now move about and warm yourself. Other matters can be settled later on. Can you walk?'

The man stood up and looked kindly at Simon, but could not say a word.

'Why don't you speak?' said Simon. 'It's too cold to stay here; we must be getting home. There now, take my stick, and if you're feeling weak, lean on that. Now step out!'

The man started walking, and moved easily, not lagging behind.

As they went along, Simon asked him, 'And where do you belong to?'

'I'm not from these parts.'

'I thought as much. I know the folks hereabouts. But how did you come to be there by the shrine?'

'I cannot tell.'

'Has some one been ill-treating you?'

'No one has ill-treated me. God has punished me.

'Of course God rules all. Still, you'll have to find food and shelter somewhere. Where do you want to go to?'

'It is all the same to me.'

Simon was amazed. The man did not look like a rogue, and he spoke gently, but yet he gave no account of himself. Still Simon thought, 'Who knows what may have happened?' And he said to the stranger: 'Well then, come home with me, and at least warm yourself awhile.'

So Simon walked towards his home, and the stranger kept up with him, walking at his side. The wind had risen and Simon felt it cold under his shirt. He was getting over his tipsiness by now, and began to feel the frost. He went along sniffling and wrapping his wife's coat round him, and he thought to himself: 'There now—talk about sheepskins! I went out for sheepskins and come home without even a coat to my back and what is more, I'm bringing a naked man along with me. Matryóna won't be pleased!' And when he thought of his wife he felt sad; but when he looked at the stranger and remembered how he had looked up at him at the shrine, his heart was glad.

III

Simon's wife had everything ready early that day. She had cut wood, brought water, fed the children eaten her own meal, and now she sat thinking. She wondered when she ought to make bread: now or to-morrow? There was still a large piece left.

'If Simon has had some dinner in town,' thought she, and does not eat much for supper, the bread will last out another day.'

She weighed the piece of bread in her hand again and again, and thought: 'I won't make any more to-day. We have only enough flour left to bake one batch. We can manage to make this last out till Friday.'

So Matryóna put away the bread, and sat down at the table to patch her husband's shirt. While she worked she thought how her husband was buying skins for a winter coat.

'If only the dealer does not cheat him. My good man is much too simple; he cheats nobody, but any child can take him in. Eight roubles is a lot of money—he should get a good coat at that price. Not tanned skins, but still a proper winter coat. How difficult it was last winter to get on without a warm coat. I could neither get down to the river, nor go out anywhere. When he went out he put on all we had, and there was nothing left for me. He did not start very early to-day, but still it's time he was back. I only hope he has not gone on the spree!'

Hardly had Matryóna thought this, when steps were heard on the threshold, and some one entered. Matryóna stuck her needle into her work and went out into the passage. There she saw two men: Simon, and with him a man without a hat, and wearing felt boots.

Matryóna noticed at once that her husband smelt of spirits. 'There now, he has been drinking,' thought she. And when she saw that he was coatless, had only her jacket on, brought no parcel, stood there silent, and seemed ashamed, her heart was ready to break with disappointment. 'He has drunk the money,' thought she, 'and has been on the spree with some good-for-nothing fellow whom he has brought home with him.'

Matryóna let them pass into the hut, followed them in, and saw that the stranger was a young, slight man, wearing her husband's coat. There was no shirt to be seen under it, and he had no hat. Having entered, he stood neither moving, nor raising his eyes, and Matryóna thought: 'He must be a bad man—he's afraid.'

Matryóna frowned, and stood beside the oven looking to see what they would do.

Simon took off his cap and sat down on the bench as if things were all right.

'Come, Matryóna; if supper is ready, let us have some.'

Matryóna muttered something to herself and did not move, but stayed where she was, by the oven. She looked first at the one and then at the other of them, and only shook her head. Simon saw that his wife was annoyed, but tried to pass it off. Pretending not to notice anything, he took the stranger by the arm.

'Sit down, friend,' said he, 'and let us have some supper.'

The stranger sat down on the bench.

'Haven't you cooked anything for us?' said Simon.

Matryóna's anger boiled over. 'I've cooked, but not for you. It seems to me you have drunk your wits away. You went to buy a sheep-skin coat, but come home without so much as the coat you had on, and bring a naked vagabond home with you. I have no supper for drunkards like you.'

'That's enough, Matryóna. Don't wag your tongue without reason! You had better ask what sort of man—'

'And you tell me what you've done with the money?'

Simon found the pocket of the jacket, drew out the three-rouble note, and unfolded it.

'Here is the money. Trífonof did not pay, but promises to pay soon.'

Matryóna got still more angry; he had bought no sheep-skins, but had put his only coat on some naked fellow and had even brought him to their house.

She snatched up the note from the table, took it to put away in safety, and said: 'I have no supper for you. We can't feed all the naked drunkards in the world.'

'There now, Matryóna, hold your tongue a bit. First hear what a man has to say!'

'Much wisdom I shall hear from a drunken fool. I was right in not wanting to marry you—a drunkard. The linen my mother gave me you drank; and now you've been to buy a coat—and have drunk it too!'

Simon tried to explain to his wife that he had only spent twenty kopeks; tried to tell how he had found the man—but Matryóna would not let him get a word in. She talked nineteen to the dozen, and dragged in things that had happened ten years before.

Matryóna talked and talked, and at last she flew at Simon and seized him by the sleeve.

'Give me my jacket. It is the only one I have and you must needs take it from me and wear it yourself. Give it here, you mangy dog, and may the devil take you.'

Simon began to pull off the jacket, and turned a sleeve of it inside out; Matryóna seized the jacket and it burst its seams. She snatched it up, threw it over her head and went to the door. She meant to go out, but stopped undecided—she wanted to work off her anger, but she also wanted to learn what sort of a man the stranger was.

IV

Matryóna stopped and said: 'If he were a good man he would not be naked. Why, he hasn't even a shirt on him. If he were all right, you would say where you came across the fellow.'

'That's just what I am trying to tell you,' said Simon. 'As I came to the shrine I saw him sitting all naked and frozen. It isn't quite the weather to sit about naked! God sent me to him, or he would have perished. What was I to do? How do we know what may have happened to him? So I took him, clothed him, and brought him along. Don't be so angry, Matryóna. It is a sin. Remember, we all must die one day.'

Angry words rose to Matryóna's lips, but she looked at the stranger and was silent. He sat on the edge of the bench, motionless, his hands folded on his knees, his head drooping on his breast, his eyes closed, and his brows knit as if in pain. Matryóna was silent, and Simon said:

'Matryóna, have you no love of God?'

Matryóna heard these words, and as she looked at the stranger, suddenly her heart softened towards him. She came back from the door, and going to the oven she got out the supper. Setting a cup on the table, she poured out some kvas. Then she brought out the last piece of bread, and set out a knife and spoons.

'Eat, if you want to,' said she.

Simon drew the stranger to the table.

'Take your place, young man,' said he.

Simon cut the bread, crumbled it into the broth, and they began to eat. Matryóna sat at the corner of the table, resting her head on her hand and looking at the stranger.

And Matryóna was touched with pity for the stranger, and began to feel fond of him. And at once the stranger's face lit up; his brows were no longer bent, he raised his eyes and smiled at Matryóna.

When they had finished supper, the woman cleared away the things and began questioning the stranger. 'Where are you from?' said she.

'I am not from these parts.'

'But how did you come to be on the road?'

'I may not tell.'

'Did some one rob you?'

'God punished me.'

'And you were lying there naked?'

'Yes, naked and freezing. Simon saw me and had pity on me. He took off his coat, put it on me and brought me here. And you have fed me, given me drink, and shown pity on me. God will reward you!'

Matryóna rose, took from the window Simon's old shirt she had been patching, and gave it to the stranger. She also brought out a pair of trousers for him.

'There,' said she, 'I see you have no shirt. Put this on, and lie down where you please, in the loft or on the oven.'

The stranger took off the coat, put on the shirt, and lay down in the loft. Matryóna put out the candle, took the coat, and climbed to where her husband lay.

Matryóna drew the skirts of the coat over her and lay down, but could not sleep; she could not get the stranger out of her mind.

When she remembered that he had eaten their last piece of bread and that there was none for to-morrow and thought of the shirt and trousers she had given away, she felt grieved; but when she remembered how he had smiled, her heart was glad.

Long did Matryóna lie awake, and she noticed that Simon also was awake—he drew the coat towards him.

'Simon!'

'Well?'

'You have had the last of the bread, and I have not put any to rise. I don't know what we shall do tomorrow. Perhaps I can borrow some of neighbour Martha.'

'If we're alive we shall find something to eat.'

The woman lay still awhile, and then said, 'He seems a good man, but why does he not tell us who he is?'

'I suppose he has his reasons.'

'Simon!'

'Well?'

'We give; but why does nobody give us anything?'

Simon did not know what to say; so he only said, 'Let us stop talking,' and turned over and went to sleep.

V

In the morning Simon awoke. The children were still asleep; his wife had gone to the neighbour's to borrow some bread. The stranger alone was sitting on the bench, dressed in the old shirt and trousers, and looking upwards. His face was brighter than it had been the day before.

Simon said to him, 'Well, friend; the belly wants bread and the naked body clothes. One has to work for a living. What work do you know?'

'I do not know any.'

This surprised Simon, but he said, 'Men who want to learn can learn anything.'

'Men work, and I will work also.'

'What is your name?'

'Michael.'

'Well Michael, if you don't wish to talk about yourself that is your own affair; but you'll have to earn a living for yourself. If you will work as I tell you, I will give you food and shelter.'

'May God reward you! I will learn. Show me what to do.'

Simon took yarn, put it round his thumb and began to twist it.

'It is easy enough—see!'

Michael watched him, put some yarn round his own thumb in the same way, caught the knack, and twisted the yarn also.

Then Simon showed him how to wax the thread. This also Michael mastered. Next Simon showed him how to twist the bristle in, and how to sew, and this, too, Michael learned at once.

Whatever Simon showed him he understood at once, and after three days he worked as if he had sewn boots all his life. He worked without stopping, and ate little. When work was over he sat silently, looking upwards. He hardly went into the street, spoke only when necessary, and neither joked nor laughed. They never saw him smile, except that first evening when Matryóna gave them supper.

VI

Day by day and week by week the year went round. Michael lived and worked with Simon. His fame spread till people said that no one sewed boots so neatly and strongly as Simon's workman, Michael; and from all the district round people came to Simon for their boots, and he began to be well off.

One winter day, as Simon and Michael sat working a carriage on sledge-runners, with three horses and with bells, drove up to the hut. They looked out of the window; the carriage stopped at their door, a fine servant jumped down from the box and opened the door. A gentleman in a fur coat got out and walked up to Simon's hut. Up jumped Matryóna and opened the door wide. The gentleman stooped to enter the hut, and when he drew himself up again his head nearly reached the ceiling, and he seemed quite to fill his end of the room.

Simon rose, bowed, and looked at the gentleman with astonishment. He had never seen any one like him. Simon himself was lean, Michael was thin, and Matryóna was dry as a bone, but this man was like some one from another world: red-faced, burly, with a neck like a bull's, and looking altogether as if he were cast in iron.

The gentleman puffed, threw off his fur coat, sat down on the bench, and said, 'Which of you is the master bootmaker?'

'I am, your Excellency,' said Simon, coming forward.

Then the gentleman shouted to his lad, 'Hey, Fédka, bring the leather!'

The servant ran in, bringing a parcel. The gentleman took the parcel and put it on the table.

'Untie it' said he. The lad untied it.

The gentleman pointed to the leather.

'Look here, shoemaker,' said he, 'do you see this leather?'

'Yes, your honour.'

'But do you know what sort of leather it is?'

Simon felt the leather and said, 'It is good leather.'

'Good, indeed! Why, you fool, you never saw such leather before in your life. It's German, and cost twenty roubles.'

Simon was frightened, and said, 'Where should I ever see leather like that?'

'Just so! Now, can you make it into boots for me?'

'Yes, your Excellency, I can.'

Then the gentleman shouted at him: 'You can, can you? Well, remember whom you are to make them for, and what the leather is. You must make me boots that will wear for a year, neither losing shape nor coming unsewn. If you can do it, take the leather and cut it up; but if you can't, say so. I warn you now, if your boots come unsewn or lose shape within a year, I will have you put in prison. If they don't burst or lose shape for a year, I will pay you ten roubles for your work.'

Simon was frightened, and did not know what to say. He glanced at Michael and nudging him with his elbow, whispered: 'Shall I take the work?'

Michael nodded his head as if to say, 'Yes, take it.'

Simon did as Michael advised, and undertook to make boots that would not lose shape or split for a whole year.

Calling his servant, the gentleman told him to pull the boot off his left leg, which he stretched out.

'Take my measure!' said he.

Simon stitched a paper measure seventeen inches long, smoothed it out, knelt down, wiped his hands well on his apron so as not to soil the gentleman's sock, and began to measure. He measured the sole, and round the instep, and began to measure the calf of the leg, but the paper was too short. The calf of the leg was as thick as a beam.

'Mind you don't make it too tight in the leg.'

Simon stitched on another strip of paper. The gentleman twitched his toes about in his sock, looking round at those in the hut, and as he did so he noticed Michael.

'Whom have you there?' asked he

'That is my workman. He will sew the boots.'

'Mind,' said the gentleman to Michael, 'remember to make them so that they will last me a year.'

Simon also looked at Michael, and saw that Michael was not looking at the gentleman, but was gazing into the corner behind the gentleman, as if he saw some one there. Michael looked and looked, and suddenly he smiled, and his face became brighter.

'What are you grinning at, you fool?' thundered the gentleman. 'You had better look to it that the boots are ready in time.'

'They shall be ready in good time,' said Michael.

'Mind it is so,' said the gentleman, and he put on his boots and his fur coat, wrapped the latter round him, and went to the door. But he forgot to stoop and struck his head against the lintel.

He swore and rubbed his head. Then he took his seat in the carriage and drove away.

When he had gone, Simon said: 'There's a figure of a man for you! You could not kill him with a mallet. He almost knocked out the lintel, but little harm it did him.'

And Matryóna said: 'Living as he does, how should he not grow strong? Death itself can't touch such a rock as that.'

VII

Then Simon said to Michael: 'Well, we have taken the work, but we must see we don't get into trouble over it. The leather is dear, and the gentleman hot-tempered. We must make no mistakes. Come, your eye is truer and your hands have become nimbler than mine, so you take this measure and cut out the boots. I will finish off the sewing of the vamps.'

Michael did as he was told. He took the leather, spread it out on the table, folded it in two, took a knife and began to cut out.

Matryóna came and watched him cutting, and was surprised to see how he was doing it. Matryóna was accustomed to seeing boots made, and she looked and saw that Michael was not cutting the leather for boots, but was cutting it round.

She wished to say something, but she thought to herself: 'Perhaps I do not understand how gentlemen's boots should be made. I suppose Michael knows more about it—and I won't interfere.'

When Michael had cut up the leather, he took a thread and began to sew not with two ends, as boots are sewn, but with a single end, as for soft slippers.

Again Matryóna wondered, but again she did not interfere. Michael sewed on steadily till noon. Then Simon rose for dinner, looked around, and saw that Michael had made slippers out of the gentleman's leather.

'Ah!' groaned Simon, and he thought, 'How is it that Michael, who has been with me a whole year and never made a mistake before, should do such a dreadful thing? The gentleman ordered high boots, welted, with whole fronts, and Michael has made soft slippers with single soles, and has wasted the leather. What am I to say to the gentleman? I can never replace leather such as this.'

And he said to Michael, 'What are you doing friend? You have ruined me! You know the gentleman ordered high booth but see what you have made!'

Hardly had he begun to rebuke Michael, when 'rat-tat , went the iron ring that hung at the door. Some one was knocking. They looked out of the window; a man had come on horseback, and was fastening his horse. They opened the door, and the servant who had been with the gentleman came in.

'Good day,' said he.

'Good day,' replied Simon. 'What can we do for you?'

'My mistress has sent me about the boots.'

'What about the boots?'

'Why, my master no longer needs them. He is dead.'

'Is it possible?'

'He did not live to get home after leaving you, but died in the carriage. When we reached home and the servants came to help him alight he rolled over like a sack. He was dead already, and so stiff that he could hardly be got out of the carriage. My mistress sent me here, saying: "Tell the bootmaker that the gentleman who ordered boots of him and left the leather for them no longer needs the boots, but that he must quickly make soft slippers for the corpse. Wait till they are ready, and bring them back with you." That is why I have come.'

Michael gathered up the remnants of the leather; rolled them up, took the soft slippers he had made, slapped them together, wiped them down with his apron, and handed them and the roll of leather to the servant, who took them and said: 'Good-bye, masters and good day to you!'

VIII

Another year passed, and another, and Michael was now living his sixth year with Simon. He lived as before. He went nowhere, only spoke when necessary, and had only smiled twice in all those years— once when Matryóna gave him food, and a second time when the gentleman was in their hut. Simon was more than pleased with his workman. He never now asked him where he came from, and only feared lest Michael should go away.

They were all at home one day. Matryóna was putting iron pots in the oven, the children were running along the benches and looking out of the window; Simon was sewing at one window, and Michael was fastening on a heel at the other.

One of the boys ran along the bench to Michael, leant on his shoulder, and looked out of the window.

'Look, Uncle Michael! There is a lady with little girls! She seems to be coming here. And one of the girls is lame.'

When the boy said that, Michael dropped his work, turned to the window, and looked out into the street.

Simon was surprised. Michael never used to look out into the street, but now he pressed against the window, staring at something. Simon also looked out, and saw that a well-dressed woman was really coming to his hut, leading by the hand two little girls in fur coats and woollen shawls. The girls could hardly be told one from the other, except that one of them was crippled in her left leg and walked with a limp.

The woman stepped into the porch and entered the passage. Feeling about for the entrance she found the latch, which she lifted, and opened the door. She let the two girls go in first, and followed them into the hut.

'Good day, good folk!'

'Pray come in,' said Simon. 'What can we do for you?'

The woman sat down by the table. The two little girls pressed close to her knees, afraid of the people in the hut.

'I want leather shoes made for these two little girls, for spring.'

'We can do that. We never have made such small shoes, but we can make them; either welted or turnover shoes, linen lined. My man, Michael, is a master at the work.'

Simon glanced at Michael and saw that he had left his work and was sitting with his eyes fixed on the little girls. Simon was surprised. It was true the girls were pretty, with black eyes, plump, and rosy-cheeked, and they wore nice kerchiefs and fur coats, but still Simon could not understand why Michael should look at them like that—just as if he had known them before. He was puzzled, but went on talking with the woman, and arranging the price. Having fixed it, he prepared the measure. The woman lifted the lame girl on to her lap and said: 'Take two measures from this little girl. Make one shoe for the lame foot and three for the sound one. They both have the same sized feet. They are twins.'

Simon took the measure and, speaking of the lame girl, said: 'How did it happen to her? She is such a pretty girl. Was she born so?'

'No, her mother crushed her leg.'

Then Matryóna joined in. She wondered who this woman was, and whose the children were, so she said: 'Are not you their mother, then?'

'No, my good woman, I am neither their mother nor any relation to them. They were quite strangers to me, but I adopted them.'

'They are not your children and yet you are so fond of them?'

'How can I help being fond of them? I fed them both at my own breasts. I had a child of my own, but God took him. I was not so fond of him as I now am of them.'

'Then whose children are they?'

IX

The woman, having begun talking, told them the whole story.

'It is about six years since their parents died, both in one week: their father was buried on the Tuesday, and their mother died on the Friday. These orphans were born three days after their father's death, and their mother did not live another day. My husband and I were then living as peasants in the village. We were neighbours of theirs, our yard being next to theirs. Their father was a lonely man; a wood-cutter in the forest. When felling trees one day, they let one fall on him. It fell across his body and crushed his bowels out. They hardly got him home before his soul went to God; and that same week his wife gave birth to twins—these little girls. She was poor and alone; she had no one, young or old, with her. Alone she gave them birth, and alone she met her death.

'The next morning I went to see her, but when I entered the hut, she, poor thing, was already stark and cold. In dying she had rolled on to this child and crushed her leg. The village folk came to the hut washed the body, laid her out, made a coffin, and buried her. They were good folk. The babies were left alone. What was to be done with them? I was the only woman there who had a baby at the time. I was nursing my first-born—eight weeks old. So I took them for a time. The peasants came together, and thought and thought what to do with them, and at last they said to me: "For the present, Mary, you had better keep the girls, and later on we will arrange what to do for them." So I nursed the sound one at my breast, but at first I did not feed this crippled one. I did not suppose she would live. But then I thought to myself, why should the poor innocent suffer? I pitied her, and began to feed her. And so I fed my own boy and these two—the three of them—at my own breast. I was young and strong, and had good food, and God gave me so much milk that at times it even overflowed. I used sometimes to feed two at a time, while the third was waiting. When one had had enough I nursed the third. And God so ordered it that these grew up, while my own was buried before he was two years old. And I had no more children, though we prospered. Now my husband is working for the corn merchant at the mill. The pay is good and we are well off. But I have no children of my own, and how lonely I should be without these little girls! How can I help loving them! They are the joy of my life!'

She pressed the lame little girl to her with one hand while with the other she wiped the tears from her cheeks.

And Matryóna sighed, and said: 'The proverb is true that says, "One may live without father or mother, but one cannot live without God."'

So they talked together, when suddenly the whole hut was lighted up as though by summer lightning from the corner where Michael sat. They all looked towards him and saw him sitting, his hands folded on his knees, gazing upwards and smiling.

X

The woman went away with the girls. Michael rose from the bench, put down his work, and took off his apron. Then, bowing low to Simon and his wife, he said: 'Farewell, masters. God has forgiven me. I ask your forgiveness, too, for anything done amiss.'

And they saw that a light shone from Michael. And Simon rose, bowed down to Michael, and said: 'I see, Michael, that you are no common man, and I can neither keep you nor question you. Only tell me this: how is it that when I found you and brought you home, you were gloomy, and when my wife gave you food you smiled at her and became brighter? Then when the gentleman came to order the boots, you smiled again and became brighter still? And now, when this woman brought the little girls, you smiled a third time, and have become as bright as day? Tell me, Michael, why does your face shine so, and why did you smile those three times?'

And Michael answered: 'Light shines from me because I have been punished, but now God has pardoned me. And I smiled three times, because God sent me to learn three truths, and I have learnt them. One I learnt when your wife pitied me and that is why I smiled the first time. The second I learnt when the rich man ordered the boots and then I smiled again. And now, when I saw those little girls, I learnt the third and last truth, and I smiled the third time.'

And Simon said, 'Tell me, Michael, what did God punish you for? and what were the three truths? that I, too, may know them.'

And Michael answered: 'God punished me for disobeying Him. I was an angel in heaven and disobeyed God. God sent me to fetch a woman's soul. I flew to earth, and saw a sick woman lying alone, who had just given birth to twin girls. They moved feebly at their mother's side, but she could not lift them to her breast. When she saw me, she understood that God had sent me for her soul, and she wept and said: "Angel of God! My husband has just been buried, killed by a falling tree. I have neither sister, nor aunt, nor mother: no one to care for my orphans. Do not take my soul! Let me nurse my babes, feed them, and set them on their feet before I die. Children cannot live without father or mother." And I hearkened to her. I placed one child at her breast and gave the other into her arms, and returned to the Lord in heaven. I flew to the Lord, and said: "I could not take the soul of the mother. Her husband was killed by a tree; the woman has twins, and prays that her soul may not be taken. She says: 'Let me nurse and feed my children, and set them on their feet. Children cannot live without father or mother.' I have not taken her soul." And God said: "Go—take the mother's soul, and learn three truths: Learn What dwells in man, What is not given to man, and What men live by. When thou hast learnt these things, thou shalt return to heaven." So I flew again to earth and took the mother's soul. The babes dropped from her breasts. Her body rolled over on the bed and crushed one babe, twisting its leg. I rose above the village, wishing to take her soul to God; but a wind seized me, and my wings drooped and dropped off. Her soul rose alone to God, while I fell to earth by the roadside.'

XI

And Simon and Matryóna understood who it was that had lived with them, and whom they had clothed and fed. And they wept with awe and with joy. And the angel said: 'I was alone in the field, naked. I had never known human needs, cold and hunger, till I became a man. I was famished, frozen, and did not know what to do. I saw, near the field I was in, a shrine built for God, and I went to it hoping to find shelter. But the shrine was locked, and I could not enter. So I sat down behind the shrine to shelter myself at least from the wind. Evening drew on. I was hungry, frozen, and in pain. Suddenly I heard a man coming along the road. He carried a pair of boots, and was talking to himself. For the first time since I became a man I saw the mortal face of a man, and his face seemed terrible to me and I turned from it. And I heard the man talking to himself of how to cover his body from the cold in winter, and how to feed wife and children. And I thought: "I am perishing of cold and hunger, and here is a man thinking only of how to clothe himself and his wife, and how to get bread for themselves. He cannot help me. When the man saw me he frowned and became still more terrible, and passed me by on the other side. I despaired, but suddenly I heard him coming back. I looked up, and did not recognize the same man: before, I had seen death in his face; but now he was alive, and I recognized in him the presence of God. He came up to me, clothed me, took me with him and brought me to his home. I entered the house a woman came to meet us and began to speak. The woman was still more terrible than the man had been; the spirit of death came from her mouth; I could not breathe for the stench of death that spread around her. She wished to drive me out into the cold, and I knew that if she did so she would die. Suddenly her husband spoke to her of God, and the woman changed at once. And when she brought me food and looked at me, I glanced at her and saw that death no longer dwelt in her; she had become alive, and in her too I saw God.

'Then I remembered the first lesson God had set me: "Learn what dwells in man." And I understood that in man dwells Love! I was glad that God had already begun to show me what He had promised, and I smiled for the first time. But I had not yet learnt all. I did not yet know What is not given to man, and What men live by.

'I lived with you, and a year passed. A man came to order boots that should wear for a year without losing shape or cracking. I looked at him, and suddenly, behind his shoulder, I saw my comrade—the angel of death. None but me saw that angel; but I knew him, and knew that before the sun set he would take that rich man's soul. And I thought to myself, "The man is making preparations for a year, and does not know that he will die before evening." And I remembered God's second saying, "Learn what is not given to man."

'What dwells in man I already knew. Now I learnt what is not given him. It is not given to man to know his own needs. And I smiled for the second time. I was glad to have seen my comrade angel—glad also that God had revealed to me the second saying.

'But I still did not know all. I did not know What men live by. And I lived on, waiting till God should reveal to me the last lesson. In the sixth year came the girl-twins with the woman; and I recognized the girls, and heard how they had been kept alive. Having heard the story, I thought, "Their mother besought me for the children's sake, and I believed her when she said that children cannot live without father or mother; but a stranger has nursed them, and has brought them up." And when the woman showed her love for the children that were not her own, and wept over them, I saw in her the living God, and understood What men live by. And I knew that God had revealed to me the last lesson, and had forgiven my sin. And then I smiled for the third time.'

XII

And the angel's body was bared, and he was clothed in light so that eye could not look on him; and his voice grew louder, as though it came not from him but from heaven above. And the angel said:

'I have learnt that all men live not by care for themselves, but by love.

'It was not given to the mother to know what her children needed for their life. Nor was it given to the rich man to know what he himself needed. Nor is it given to any man to know whether, when evening comes, he will need boots for his body or slippers for his corpse.

'I remained alive when I was a man, not by care of myself, but because love was present in a passer-by, and because he and his wife pitied and loved me. The orphans remained alive, not because of their mother's care, but because there was love in the heart of a woman a stranger to them, who pitied and loved them. And all men live not by the thought they spend on their own welfare, but because love exists in man.

'I knew before that God gave life to men and desires that they should live; now I understood more than that.

'I understood that God does not wish men to live apart, and therefore he does not reveal to them what each one needs for himself; but he wishes them to live united, and therefore reveals to each of them what is necessary for all.

'I have now understood that though it seems to men that they live by care for themselves, in truth it is love alone by which they live. He who has love, is in God, and God is in him, for God is love.'

And the angel sang praise to God, so that the hut trembled at his voice. The roof opened, and a column of fire rose from earth to heaven. Simon and his wife and children fell to the ground. Wings appeared upon the angel's shoulders, and he rose into the heavens.

And when Simon came to himself the hut stood as before, and there was no one in it but his own family.

1881

A SPARK NEGLECTED BURNS THE HOUSE (1885)

'Then came Peter, and said to him, Lord, how oft shall my brother sin against me, and I forgive him? until seven times? Jesus saith unto him, I say not unto thee, Until seven times; but, Until seventy times seven. Therefore is the kingdom of heaven likened unto a certain king, which would make a reckoning with his servants. And when he had begun to reckon, one was brought unto him, which owed him ten thousand talents. But forasmuch as he had not wherewith to pay, his lord commanded him to be sold, and his wife, and children, and all that he had, and payment to be made. The servant therefore fell down and worshipped him, saying, Lord, have patience with me, and I will pay thee all. And the lord of that servant, being moved with compassion, released him, and forgave him the debt. But that servant went out, and found one of his fellow-servants, which owed him a hundred pence: and he laid hold on him, and took him by the throat saying, Pay what thou owest. So his fellow-servant fell down and besought him, saying, Have patience with me, and I will pay thee. And he would not: but went and cast him into prison, till he should pay that which was due. So when his fellow-servants saw what was done, they were exceeding sorry, and came and told unto their lord all that was done. Then his lord called him unto him, and saith to him, Thou wicked servant, I forgave thee all that debt, because thou besoughtest me: shouldest not thou also have had mercy on thy fellow-servant, even as I had mercy on thee? And his lord was wroth, and delivered him to the tormentors, till he should pay all that was due. So shall also my heavenly Father do unto you, if ye forgive not every one his brother from your hearts.'—*Matt. xviii. 21-35.*

There once lived in a village a peasant named Iván Stcherbakóf. He was comfortably off, in the prime of life, the best worker in the village, and had three sons all able to work. The eldest was married, the second about to marry, and the third was a big lad who could mind the horses and was already beginning to plough. Ivan's wife was an able and thrifty woman, and they were fortunate in having a quiet, hard-working daughter-in-law. There was nothing to prevent Iván and his family from living happily. They had only one idle mouth to feed; that was Iván's old father, who suffered from asthma and had been lying ill on the top of the brick oven for seven years. Iván had all he needed: three horses and a colt, a cow with a calf, and fifteen sheep. The women made all the clothing for the family, besides helping in the fields, and the men tilled the land. They always had grain enough of their own to last over beyond the next harvest and sold enough oats to pay the taxes and meet their other needs. So Iván and his children might have lived quite comfortably had it not been for a feud between him and his next-door neighbour, Limping Gabriel, the son of Gordéy Ivánof.

As long as old Gordéy was alive and Iván's father was still able to manage the household, the peasants lived as neighbours should. If the women of either house happened to want a sieve or a tub, or the men required a sack, or if a cart-wheel got broken and could not be mended at once, they used to send to the other house, and helped each other in neighbourly fashion. When a calf strayed into the neighbour's thrashing-ground they would just drive it out, and only say, 'Don't let it get in again; our grain is lying there.' And such things as locking up the barns and outhouses, hiding things from one another, or backbiting were never thought of in those days.

That was in the fathers' time. When the sons came to be at the head of the families, everything changed.

It all began about a trifle.

Iván's daughter-in-law had a hen that began laying rather early in the season, and she started collecting its eggs for Easter. Every day she went to the cart-shed, and found an egg in the cart; but one day the hen, probably frightened by the children, flew across the fence into the neighbour's yard and laid its egg there. The woman heard the cackling, but said to herself: 'I have no time now; I must tidy up for Sunday. I'll fetch the egg later on.' In the evening she went to the cart, but found no egg there. She went and asked her mother-in-law and brother-in-law whether they had taken the egg. 'No,' they had not; but her youngest brother-in-law, Tarás, said: 'Your Biddy laid its egg in the neighbour's yard. It was there she was cackling, and she flew back across the fence from there.'

The woman went and looked at the hen. There she was on the perch with the other birds, her eyes just closing ready to go to sleep. The woman wished she could have asked the hen and got an answer from her.

Then she went to the neighbour's, and Gabriel's mother came out to meet her.

'What do you want, young woman?'

'Why, Granny, you see, my hen flew across this morning. Did she not lay an egg here?'

'We never saw anything of it. The Lord be thanked, our own hens started laying long ago. We collect our own eggs and have no need of other people's! And we don't go looking for eggs in other people's yards, lass!'

The young woman was offended, and said more than she should have done. Her neighbour answered back with interest, and the women began abusing each other. Ivan's wife, who had been to fetch water, happening to pass just then, joined in too. Gabriel's wife rushed out, and began reproaching the young woman with things that had really happened and with other things that never had happened at all. Then a general uproar commenced, all shouting at once, trying to get out two words at a time, and not choice words either.

'You're this!' and 'You're that!' 'You're a thief!' and 'You're a slut!' and 'You're starving your old father-in-law to death!' and 'You're a good-for-nothing!' and so on.

'And you've made a hole in the sieve I lent you, you jade! And it's our yoke you're carrying your pails on—you just give back our yoke!'

Then they caught hold of the yoke, and spilt the water, snatched off one another's shawls, and began fighting. Gabriel, returning from the fields, stopped to take his wife's part. Out rushed Iván and his son and joined in with the rest. Iván was a strong fellow, he scattered the whole lot of them, and pulled a handful of hair out of Gabriel's beard. People came to see what was the matter, and the fighters were separated with difficulty.

That was how it all began.

Gabriel wrapped the hair torn from his beard in a paper, and went to the District Court to have the law of Iván. 'I didn't grow my beard,' said he, 'for pockmarked Iván to pull it out!' And his wife went bragging to the neighbours, saying they'd have Iván condemned and sent to Siberia. And so the feud grew.

The old man, from where he lay on the top of the oven, tried from the very first to persuade them to make peace, but they would not listen. He told them, 'It's a stupid thing you are after, children, picking quarrels about such a paltry matter. Just think! The whole thing began about an egg. The children may have taken it—well, what matter? What's the value of one egg? God sends enough for all! And suppose your neighbour did say an unkind word—put it right; show her how to say a better one! If there has been a fight—well, such things will happen; we're all sinners, but make it up, and let there be an end of it! If you nurse your anger it will be worse for you yourselves.'

But the younger folk would not listen to the old man. They thought his words were mere senseless dotage. Iván would not humble himself before his neighbour.

'I never pulled his beard,' he said, 'he pulled the hair out himself. But his son has burst all the fastenings on my shirt, and torn it... Look at it!'

And Iván also went to law. They were tried by the Justice of the Peace and by the District Court. While all this was going on, the coupling-pin of Gabriel's cart disappeared. Gabriel's womenfolk accused Ivan's son of having taken it. They said: 'We saw him in the night go past our window, towards the cart; and a neighbour says he saw him at the pub, offering the pin to the landlord.'

So they went to law about that. And at home not a day passed without a quarrel or even a fight. The children, too, abused one another, having learnt to do so from their elders; and when the women happened to meet by the river-side, where they went to rinse the clothes, their arms did not do as much wringing as their tongues did nagging, and every word was a bad one.

At first the peasants only slandered one another; but afterwards they began in real earnest to snatch anything that lay handy, and the children followed their example. Life became harder and harder for them. Iván Stcherbakóf and Limping Gabriel kept suing one another at the Village Assembly, and at the District Court, and before the Justice of the Peace until all the judges were tired of them. Now Gabriel got Iván fined or imprisoned; then Iván did as much to Gabriel; and the more they spited each other the angrier they grew—like dogs that attack one another and get more and more furious the longer they fight. You strike one dog from behind, and it thinks it's the other dog biting him, and gets still fiercer. So these peasants: they went to law, and one or other of them was fined or locked up, but that only made them more and more angry with each other. 'Wait a bit,' they said, 'and I'll make you pay for it.' And so it went on for six years. Only the old man lying on the top of the oven kept telling them again and again: 'Children, what are you doing? Stop all this paying back; keep to your work, and don't bear malice—it will be better for you. The more you bear malice, the worse it will be.'

But they would not listen to him.

In the seventh year, at a wedding, Ivan's daughter-in-law held Gabriel up to shame, accusing him of having been caught horse-stealing. Gabriel was tipsy, and unable to contain his anger, gave the woman such a blow that she was laid up for a week; and she was pregnant at the time. Iván was delighted. He went to the magistrate to lodge a complaint. 'Now I'll get rid of my neighbour! He won't escape imprisonment, or exile to Siberia.' But Ivan's wish was not fulfilled. The magistrate dismissed the case. The woman was examined, but she was up and about and showed no sign of any injury. Then Ivan went to the Justice of the Peace, but he referred the business to the District Court. Ivan bestirred himself: treated the clerk and the Elder of the District Court to a gallon of liquor and got Gabriel condemned to be flogged. The sentence was read out to Gabriel by the clerk: 'The Court decrees that the peasant Gabriel Gordéyef shall receive twenty lashes with a birch rod at the District Court.'

Ivan too heard the sentence read, and looked at Gabriel to see how he would take it. Gabriel grew as pale as a sheet, and turned round and went out into the passage. Ivan followed him, meaning to see to the horse, and he overheard Gabriel say, 'Very well! He will have my back flogged: that will make it burn; but something of his may burn worse than that!'

Hearing these words, Ivan at once went back into the Court, and said: 'Upright judges! He threatens to set my house on fire! Listen: he said it in the presence of witnesses!'

Gabriel was recalled. 'Is it true that you said this?'

'I haven't said anything. Flog me, since you have the power. It seems that I alone am to suffer, and all for being in the right, while he is allowed to do as he likes.'

Gabriel wished to say something more, but his lips and his cheeks quivered, and he turned towards the wall. Even the officials were frightened by his looks. 'He may do some mischief to himself or to his neighbour,' thought they.

Then the old Judge said: 'Look here, my men; you'd better be reasonable and make it up. Was it right of you, friend Gabriel, to strike a pregnant woman? It was lucky it passed off so well, but think what might have happened! Was it right? You had better confess and beg his pardon, and he will forgive you, and we will alter the sentence.'

The clerk heard these words, and remarked:' That's impossible under Statute 117. An agreement between the parties not having been arrived at, a decision of the Court has been pronounced and must be executed.'

But the Judge would not listen to the clerk.

'Keep your tongue still, my friend,' said he. 'The first of all laws is to obey God, Who loves peace.' And the Judge began again to persuade the peasants, but could not succeed. Gabriel would not listen to him.

'I shall be fifty next year,' said he, 'and have a married son, and have never been flogged in my life, and now that pockmarked Ivan has had me condemned to be flogged, and am I to go and ask his forgiveness? No; I've borne enough... Ivan shall have cause to remember me!'

Again Gabriel's voice quivered, and he could say no more, but turned round and went out.

It was seven miles from the Court to the village, and it was getting late when Ivan reached home. He unharnessed his horse, put it up for the night, and entered the cottage. No one was there. The women had already gone to drive the cattle in, and the young fellows were not yet back from the fields. Iván went in, and sat down, thinking. He remembered how Gabriel had listened to the sentence, and how pale he had become, and how he had turned to the wall; and Ivan's heart grew heavy. He thought how he himself would feel if he were sentenced, and he pitied Gabriel. Then he heard his old father up on the oven cough, and saw him sit up, lower his legs, and scramble down. The old man dragged himself slowly to a seat, and sat down. He was quite tired out with the exertion, and coughed a long time till he had cleared his throat. Then, leaning against the table, he said: 'Well, has he been condemned?'

'Yes, to twenty strokes with the rods,' answered Iván.

The old man shook his head.

'A bad business,' said he. 'You are doing wrong, Iván! Ah! it's very bad—not for him so much as for yourself!...Well, they'll flog him: but will that do you any good?'

'He'll not do it again,' said Iván.

'What is it he'll not do again? What has he done worse than you?'

'Why, think of the harm he has done me!' said Iván. 'He nearly killed my wife, and now he's threatening to burn us up. Am I to thank him for it?'

The old man sighed, and said: 'You go about the wide world, Iván, while I am lying on the oven all these years, so you think you see everything, and that I see nothing... Ah, lad! It's you that don't see; malice blinds you. Others' sins are before your eyes, but your own are behind your back. "He's acted badly!" What a thing to say! If he were the only one to act badly, how could strife exist? Is strife among men ever bred by one alone? Strife is always between two. His badness you see, but your own you don't. If he were bad, but you were good, there would be no strife. Who pulled the hair out of his beard? Who spoilt his haystack? Who dragged him to the law court? Yet you put it all on him! You live a bad life yourself, that's what is wrong! It's not the way I used to live, lad, and it's not the way I taught you. Is that the way his old father and I used to live? How did we live? Why, as neighbours should! If he happened to run out of flour, one of the women would come across: "Uncle Trol, we want some flour." "Go to the barn, dear," I'd say: "take what you need." If he'd no one to take his horses to pasture, "Go, Iván," I'd say, "and look after his horses." And if I was short of anything, I'd go to him. "Uncle Gordéy," I'd say, "I want so-and-so!" "Take it Uncle Trol!" That's how it was between us, and we had an easy time of it. But now?...That soldier the other day was telling us about the fight at Plevna. Why, there's war between you worse than at Plevna! Is that living?...What a sin it is! You are a man and master of the house; it's you who will have to answer. What are you teaching the women and the children? To snarl and snap? Why, the other day your Taráska—that greenhorn—was swearing at neighbour Irena, calling her names; and his mother listened and laughed. Is that right? It is you will have to answer. Think of your soul. Is this all as it should be? You throw a word at me, and I give you two in return; you give me a blow, and I give you two. No, lad! Christ, when He walked on earth, taught us fools something very different... If you get a hard word from any one, keep silent, and his own conscience will accuse him. That is what our Lord taught. If you get a slap, turn the other cheek. "Here, beat me, if that's what I deserve!" And his own conscience will rebuke him. He will soften, and will listen to you. That's the way He taught us, not to be proud!...Why don't you speak? Isn't it as I say?'

Iván sat silent and listened.

The old man coughed, and having with difficulty cleared his throat, began again: 'You think Christ taught us wrong? Why, it's all for our own good. Just think of your earthly life; are you better off, or worse, since this Plevna began among you? Just reckon up what you've spent on all this law business—what the driving backwards and forwards and your food on the way have cost you! What fine fellows your sons have grown; you might live and get on well; but now your means are lessening. And why? All because of this folly; because of your pride. You ought to be ploughing with your lads, and do the sowing yourself; but the fiend carries you off to the judge, or to some pettifogger or other. The ploughing is not done in time, nor the sowing, and mother earth can't bear properly. Why did the oats fail this year? When did you sow them? When you came back from town! And what did you gain? A burden for your own shoulders... Eh, lad, think of your own business! Work with your boys in the field and at home, and if some one offends you, forgive him, as God wished you to. Then life will be easy, and your heart will always be light.'

Iván remained silent.

'Iván, my boy, hear your old father! Go and harness the roan, and go at once to the Government office; put an end to all this affair there; and in the morning go and make it up with Gabriel in God's name, and invite him to your house for to-morrow's holiday' (it was the eve of the Virgin's Nativity). 'Have tea ready, and get a bottle of vódka and put an end to this wicked business, so that there should not be any more of it in future, and tell the women and children to do the same.'

Iván sighed, and thought, 'What he says is true,' and his heart grew lighter. Only he did not know how, now, to begin to put matters right.

But again the old man began, as if he had guessed what was in Ivan's mind.

'Go, Iván, don't put it off! Put out the fire before it spreads, or it will be too late.'

The old man was going to say more, but before he could do so the women came in, chattering like magpies. The news that Gabriel was sentenced to be flogged, and of his threat to set fire to the house, had already reached them. They had heard all about it and added to it something of their own, and had again had a row, in the pasture, with the women of Gabriel's household. They began telling how Gabriel's daughter-in-law threatened a fresh action: Gabriel had got the right side of the examining magistrate, who would now turn the whole affair upside down; and the schoolmaster was writing out another petition, to the Tsar himself this time, about Iván; and everything was in the petition—all about the coupling-pin and the kitchen-garden—so that half of Ivan's homestead would be theirs soon. Iván heard what they were saying, and his heart grew cold again, and he gave up the thought of making peace with Gabriel.

In a farmstead there is always plenty for the master to do. Iván did not stop to talk to the women, but went out to the threshing-floor and to the barn. By the time he had tidied up there, the sun had set and the young fellows had returned from the field. They had been ploughing the field for the winter crops with two horses. Iván met them, questioned them about their work, helped to put everything in its place, set a torn horse-collar aside to be mended, and was going to put away some stakes under the barn, but it had grown quite dusk, so he decided to leave them where they were till next day. Then he gave the cattle their food, opened the gate, let out the horses. Tarás was to take to pasture for the night, and again closed the gate and barred it. 'Now,' thought he, 'I'll have my supper, and then to bed.' He took the horse-collar and entered the hut. By this time he had forgotten about Gabriel and about what his old father had been saying to him. But, just as he took hold of the door-handle to enter the passage, he heard his neighbour on the other side of the fence cursing somebody in a hoarse voice: 'What the devil is he good for?' Gabriel was saying. 'He's only fit to be killed!' At these words all Ivan's former bitterness towards his neighbour re-awoke. He stood listening while Gabriel scolded, and, when he stopped, Iván went into the hut.

There was a light inside; his daughter-in-law sat spinning, his wife was getting supper ready, his eldest son was making straps for bark shoes, his second sat near the table with a book, and Tarás was getting ready to go out to pasture the horses for the night. Everything in the hut would have been pleasant and bright, but for that plague—a bad neighbour!

Iván entered, sullen and cross; threw the cat down from the bench, and scolded the women for putting the slop-pail in the wrong place. He felt despondent, and sat down, frowning, to mend the horse-collar. Gabriel's words kept ringing in his ears: his threat at the law court, and what he had just been shouting in a hoarse voice about some one who was 'only fit to be killed.'

His wife gave Tarás his supper, and, having eaten it, Tarás put on an old sheepskin and another coat, tied a sash round his waist, took some bread with him, and went out to the horses. His eldest brother was going to see him off, but Iván himself rose instead, and went out into the porch. It had grown quite dark outside, clouds had gathered, and the wind had risen. Iván went down the steps, helped his boy to mount, started the foal after him, and stood listening while Tarás rode down the village and was there joined by other lads with their horses. Iván waited until they were all out of hearing. As he stood there by the gate he could not get Gabriel's words out of his head: 'Mind that something of yours does not burn worse!'

'He is desperate,' thought Iván. 'Everything is dry, and it's windy weather besides. He'll come up at the back somewhere, set fire to something, and be off. He'll burn the place and escape scot free, the villain!...There now, if one could but catch him in the act, he'd not get off then!' And the thought fixed itself so firmly in his mind that he did not go up the steps but went out into the street and round the corner. I'll just walk round the buildings; who can tell what he's after?' And Iván, stepping softly, passed out of the gate. As soon as he reached the corner, he looked round along the fence, and seemed to see something suddenly move at the opposite corner, as if some one had come out and disappeared again. Iván stopped, and stood quietly, listening and looking. Everything was still; only the leaves of the willows fluttered in the wind, and the straws of the thatch rustled. At first it seemed pitch dark, but, when his eyes had grown used to the darkness, he could see the far corner, and a plough that lay there, and the eaves. He looked a while, but saw no one.

'I suppose it was a mistake,' thought Iván; 'but still I will go round,' and Iván went stealthily along by the shed. Iván stepped so softly in his bark shoes that he did not hear his own footsteps. As he reached the far corner, something seemed to flare up for a moment near the plough and to vanish again. Iván felt as if struck to the heart; and he stopped. Hardly had he stopped, when something flared up more brightly in the same place, and he clearly saw a man with a cap on his head, crouching down, with his back towards him, lighting a bunch of straw he held in his hand. Iván's heart fluttered within him like a bird. Straining every nerve, he approached with great strides, hardly feeling his legs under him. 'Ah,' thought Iván, 'now he won't escape! I'll catch him in the act!'

Iván was still some distance off, when suddenly he saw a bright light, but not in the same place as before, and not a small flame. The thatch had flared up at the eaves, the flames were reaching up to the roof, and, standing beneath it, Gabriel's whole figure was clearly visible.

Like a hawk swooping down on a lark, Iván rushed at Limping Gabriel. 'Now I'll have him; he shan't escape me!' thought Iván. But Gabriel must have heard his steps, and (however he managed it) glancing round, he scuttled away past the barn like a hare.

'You shan't escape!' shouted Iván, darting after him.

Just as he was going to seize Gabriel, the latter dodged him; but

Iván managed to catch the skirt of Gabriel's coat. It tore right off, and Iván fell down. He recovered his feet, and shouting, 'Help! Seize him! Thieves! Murder!' ran on again. But meanwhile Gabriel had reached his own gate. There Iván overtook him and was about to seize him, when something struck Iván a stunning blow, as though a stone had hit his temple, quite deafening him. It was Gabriel who, seizing an oak wedge that lay near the gate, had struck out with all his might.

Iván was stunned; sparks flew before his eyes, then all grew dark and he staggered. When he came to his senses Gabriel was no longer there: it was as light as day, and from the side where his homestead was something roared and crackled like an engine at work. Iván turned round and saw that his back shed was all ablaze, and the side shed had also caught fire, and flames and smoke and bits of burning straw mixed with the smoke, were being driven towards his hut.

'What is this, friends? . . .' cried Iván, lifting his arms and striking his thighs.' Why, all I had to do was just to snatch it out from under the eaves and trample on it! What is this, friends? . . .' he kept repeating. He wished to shout, but his breath failed him; his voice was gone. He wanted to run, but his legs would not obey him, and got in each other's way. He moved slowly, but again staggered and again his breath failed. He stood still till he had regained breath, and then went on. Before he had got round the back shed to reach the fire, the side shed was also all ablaze; and the corner of the hut and the covered gateway had caught fire as well. The flames were leaping out of the hut, and it was impossible to get into the yard. A large crowd had collected, but nothing could be done. The neighbours were carrying their belongings out of their own houses, and driving the cattle out of their own sheds. After Ivan's house, Gabriel's also caught fire, then, the wind rising, the flames spread to the other side of the street and half the village was burnt down.

At Ivan's house they barely managed to save his old father; and the family escaped in what they had on; everything else, except the horses that had been driven out to pasture for the night, was lost; all the cattle, the fowls on their perches, the carts, ploughs, and harrows, the women's trunks with their clothes, and the grain in the granaries—all were burnt up!

At Gabriel's, the cattle were driven out, and a few things saved from his house.

The fire lasted all night. Iván stood in front of his homestead and kept repeating, 'What is this?...Friends!...One need only have pulled it out and trampled on it!' But when the roof fell in, Iván rushed into the burning place, and seizing a charred beam, tried to drag it out. The women saw him, and called him back; but he pulled out the beam, and was going in again for another when he lost his footing and fell among the flames. Then his son made his way in after him and dragged him out. Iván had singed his hair and beard and burnt his clothes and scorched his hands, but he felt nothing. 'His grief has stupefied him,' said the people. The fire was burning itself out, but Iván still stood repeating: 'Friends!...What is this?...One need only have pulled it out!'

In the morning the village Elder's son came to fetch Iván.

'Daddy Iván, your father is dying! He has sent for you to say good-bye.'

Iván had forgotten about his father, and did not understand what was being said to him.

'What father?' he said. 'Whom has he sent for?'

'He sent for you, to say good-bye; he is dying in our cottage! Come along, daddy Iván,' said the Elder's son, pulling him by the arm; and Iván followed the lad.

When he was being carried out of the hut, some burning straw had fallen on to the old man and burnt him, and he had been taken to the village Elder's in the farther part of the village, which the fire did not reach.

When Iván came to his father, there was only the Elder's wife in the hut, besides some little children on the top of the oven. All the rest were still at the fire. The old man, who was lying on a bench holding a wax candle in his hand, kept turning his eyes towards the door. When his son entered, he moved a little. The old woman went up to him and told him that his son had come. He asked to have him brought nearer. Iván came closer.

'What did I tell you, Iván?' began the old man 'Who has burnt down the village?'

'It was he, father!' Iván answered. 'I caught him in the act. I saw him shove the firebrand into the thatch. I might have pulled away the burning straw and stamped it out, and then nothing would have happened.'

'Iván,' said the old man, 'I am dying, and you in your turn will have to face death. Whose is the sin?'

Iván gazed at his father in silence, unable to utter a word.

'Now, before God, say whose is the sin? What did I tell you?'

Only then Iván came to his senses and understood it all. He sniffed and said, 'Mine, father!' And he fell on his knees before his father, saying, 'Forgive me, father; I am guilty before you and before God.'

The old man moved his hands, changed the candle from his right hand to his left, and tried to lift his right hand to his forehead to cross himself, but could not do it, and stopped.

'Praise the Lord! Praise the Lord!' said he, and again he turned his eyes towards his son.

'Iván! I say, Iván!'

'What, father?'

'What must you do now?'

Iván was weeping.

'I don't know how we are to live now, father!' he said.

The old man closed his eyes, moved his lips as if to gather strength, and opening his eyes again, said: 'You'll manage. If you obey God's will, you'll manage!' He paused, then smiled, and said: 'Mind, Iván! Don't tell who started the fire! Hide another man's sin, and God will forgive two of yours!' And the old man took the candle in both hands and, folding them on his breast, sighed, stretched out, and died.

Iván did not say anything against Gabriel, and no one knew what had caused the fire.

And Ivan's anger against Gabriel passed away, and Gabriel wondered that Iván did not tell anybody. At first Gabriel felt afraid, but after awhile he got used to it. The men left off quarrelling, and then their families left off also. While rebuilding their huts, both families lived in one house; and when the village was rebuilt and they might have moved farther apart, Iván and Gabriel built next to each other, and remained neighbours as before.

They lived as good neighbours should. Iván Stcherbakóf remembered his old father's command to obey God's law, and quench a fire at the first spark; and if any one does him an injury he now tries not to revenge himself, but rather to set matters right again; and if any one gives him a bad word, instead of giving a worse in return, he tries to teach the other not to use evil words; and so he teaches his womenfolk and children. And Iván Stcherbakóf has got on his feet again, and now lives better even than he did before.

1885

TWO OLD MEN (1885)

I

'The woman saith unto him, Sir, I perceive that thou art a prophet. Our fathers worshipped in this mountain; and ye say, that in Jerusalem is the place where men ought to worship. Jesus saith unto her, Woman, believe me, the hour cometh when neither in this mountain, nor in Jerusalem, shall ye worship the Father... But the hour cometh, and now is, when the true worshippers shall worship the Father in spirit and truth: for such doth the Father seek to be his worshippers.'—*John iv. 19-21, 23.*

There were once two old men who decided to go on a pilgrimage to worship God at Jerusalem. One of them was a well-to-do peasant named Efím Tarásitch Shevélev. The other, Elisha Bódrof, was not so well off.

Efim was a staid man, serious and firm. He neither drank nor smoked nor took snuff, and had never used bad language in his life. He had twice served as village Elder, and when he left office his accounts were in good order. He had a large family: two sons and a married grandson, all living with him. He was hale, long-bearded and erect, and it was only when he was past sixty that a little grey began to show itself in his beard.

Elisha was neither rich nor poor. He had formerly gone out carpentering, but now that he was growing old he stayed at home and kept bees. One of his sons had gone away to find work, the other was living at home. Elisha was a kindly and cheerful old man. It is true he drank sometimes, and he took snuff, and was fond of singing, but he was a peaceable man, and lived on good terms with his family and with his neighbours. He was short and dark, with a curly beard, and, like his patron saint Elisha, he was quite bald-headed.

The two old men had taken a vow long since and had arranged to go on a pilgrimage to Jerusalem together: but Efim could never spare the time; he always had so much business on hand; as soon as one thing was finished he started another. First he had to arrange his grandson's marriage; then to wait for his youngest son's return from the army, and after that he began building a new hut.

One holiday the two old men met outside the hut and, sitting down on some timber, began to talk.

'Well,' asked Elisha, 'when are we to fulfil our vow?'

Efim made a wry face.

'We must wait,' he said. 'This year has turned out a hard one for me. I started building this hut thinking it would cost me something over a hundred roubles, but now it's getting on for three hundred and it's still not finished. We shall have to wait tin the summer. In summer, God willing, we will go without fail.'

'It seems to me we ought not to put it off, but should go at once,' said Elisha. 'Spring is the best time.'

'The time's right enough, but what about my building? How can I leave that?'

'As if you had no one to leave in charge! Your son can look after it.'

'But how? My eldest son is not trustworthy—he sometimes takes a glass too much.'

'Ah, neighbour, when we die they'll get on without us. Let your son begin now to get some experience.'

'That's true enough, but somehow when one begins a thing one likes to see it done.'

'Eh, friend, we can never get through all we have to do. The other day the women-folk at home were washing and house cleaning for Easter. Here something needed doing, there something else, and they could not get everything done. So my eldest daughter-in-law, who's a sensible woman, says: 'We may be thankful the holiday comes without waiting for us, or however hard we worked we should never be ready for it.'

Efím became thoughtful.

'I've spent a lot of money on this building,' he said 'and one can't start on the journey with empty pockets. We shall want a hundred roubles apiece—and it's no small sum.'

Elisha laughed.

'Now, come, come, old friend!' he said, 'you have ten times as much as I, and yet you talk about money. Only say when we are to start, and though I have nothing now I shall have enough by then.'

Efím also smiled.

'Dear me, I did not know you were so rich!' said he. 'Why, where will you get it from?'

'I can scrape some together at home, and if that's not enough, I'll sell half a score of hives to my neighbour. He's long been wanting to buy them.'

'If they swarm well this year, you'll regret it.'

'Regret it! Not I, neighbour! I never regretted anything in my life, except my sins. There's nothing more precious than the soul.'

'That's so; still it's not right to neglect things at home.'

'But what if our souls are neglected? That's worse. We took the vow, so let us go! Now, seriously, let us go!'

II

Elisha succeeded in persuading his comrade. In the morning, after thinking it well over, Efím came to Elisha.

'You are right,' said he, 'let us go. Life and death are in God's hands. We must go now, while we are still alive and have the strength.'

A week later the old men were ready to start. Efím had money enough at hand. He took a hundred roubles himself, and left two hundred with his wife.

Elisha, too, got ready. He sold ten hives to his neighbour, with any new swarms that might come from them before the summer. He took seventy roubles for the lot. The rest of the hundred roubles he scraped together from the other members of his household, fairly clearing them all out. His wife gave him all she had been saving up for her funeral; and his daughter-in-law also gave him what she had.

Efím gave his eldest son definite orders about every thing: when and how much grass to mow, where to cart the manure, and how to finish off and roof the cottage. He thought out everything, and gave his orders accordingly. Elisha, on the other hand, only explained to his wife that she was to keep separate the swarms from the hives he had sold, and to be sure to let the neighbour have them all, without any tricks. As to household affairs, he did not even mention them.

'You will see what to do and how to do it, as the needs arise,' he said. 'You are the masters, and will know how to do what's best for yourselves.'

So the old men got ready. Their people baked them cakes, and made bags for them, and cut them linen for leg-bands. They put on new leather shoes, and took with them spare shoes of platted bark. Their families went with them to the end of the village and there took leave of them, and the old men started on their pilgrimage.

Elisha left home in a cheerful mood, and as soon as he was out of the village forgot all his home affairs. His only care was how to please his comrade, how to avoid saying a rude word to any one, how to get to his destination and home again in peace and love. Walking along the road, Elisha would either whisper some prayer to himself or go over in his mind such of the lives of the saints as he was able to remember. When he came across any one on the road, or turned in anywhere for the night, he tried to behave as gently as possible and to say a godly word. So he journeyed on, rejoicing. One thing only he could not do, he could not give up taking snuff. Though he had left his snuff-box behind, he hankered after it. Then a man he met on the road gave him some snuff; and every now and then he would lag behind (not to lead his comrade into temptation) and would take a pinch of snuff.

Efim too walked well and firmly; doing no wrong and speaking no vain words, but his heart was not so light. Household cares weighed on his mind. He kept worrying about what was going on at home. Had he not forgotten to give his son this or that order? Would his son do things properly? If he happened to see potatoes being planted or manure carted, as he went along, he wondered if his son was doing as he had been told. And he almost wanted to turn back and show him how to do things, or even do them himself.

III

The old men had been walking for five weeks, they had worn out their home-made bark shoes, and had to begin buying new ones when they reached Little Russia. From the time they left home they had had to pay for their food and for their night's lodging, but when they reached Little Russia the people vied with one another in asking them into their huts. They took them in and fed them, and would accept no payment; and more than that, they put bread or even cakes into their bags for them to eat on the road.

The old men travelled some five hundred miles in this manner free of expense, but after they had crossed the next province, they came to a district where the harvest had failed. The peasants still gave them free lodging at night, but no longer fed them for nothing. Sometimes, even, they could get no bread: they offered to pay for it, but there was none to be had. The people said the harvest had completely failed the year before. Those who had been rich were ruined and had had to sell all they possessed; those of moderate means were left destitute, and those of the poor who had not left those parts, wandered about begging, or starved at home in utter want. In the winter they had had to eat husks and goosefoot.

One night the old men stopped in a small village; they bought fifteen pounds of bread, slept there, and started before sunrise, to get well on their way before the heat of the day. When they had gone some eight miles, on coming to a stream they sat down, and, filling a bowl with water, they steeped some bread in it, and ate it. Then they changed their leg-bands, and rested for a while. Elisha took out his snuff-box. Efím shook his head at him.

'How is it you don't give up that nasty habit?' said he.

Elisha waved his hand. 'The evil habit is stronger than I,' he said.

Presently they got up and went on. After walking for nearly another eight miles, they came to a large village and passed right through it. It had now grown hot. Elisha was tired out and wanted to rest and have a drink, but Efím did not stop. Efím was the better walker of the two, and Elisha found it hard to keep up with him.

'If I could only have a drink,' said he.

'Well, have a drink,' said Efím. 'I don't want any.'

Elisha stopped.

'You go on,' he said, 'but I'll just run in to the little hut there. I will catch you up in a moment.'

'All right,' said Efím, and he went on along the high road alone, while Elisha turned back to the hut.

It was a small hut plastered with clay, the bottom a dark colour, the top whitewashed; but the clay had crumbled away. Evidently it was long since it had been re-plastered, and the thatch was off the roof on one side. The entrance to the hut was through the yard. Elisha entered the yard, and saw, lying close to a bank of earth that ran round the hut, a gaunt, beardless man with his shirt tucked into his trousers, as is the custom in Little Russia. The man must have lain down in the shade, but the sun had come round and now shone full on him. Though not asleep, he still lay there. Elisha called to him, and asked for a drink, but the man gave no answer.

'He is either ill or unfriendly,' thought Elisha; and going to the door he heard a child crying in the hut. He took hold of the ring that served as a door-handle, and knocked with it.

'Hey, masters!' he called. No answer. He knocked again with his staff.

'Hey, Christians!' Nothing stirred.

'Hey, servants of God!' Still no reply.

Elisha was about to turn away, when he thought ho heard a groan the other side of the door.

'Dear me, some misfortune must have happened to the people? I had better have a look.'

And Elisha entered the hut.

IV

Elisha turned the ring; the door was not fastened. He opened it and went along up the narrow passage. The door into the dwelling-room was open. To the left was a brick oven; in front against the wall was an icon-stand and a table before it, by the table was a bench on which sat an old woman, bareheaded and wearing only a single garment. There she sat with her head resting on the table, and near her was a thin, wax-coloured boy, with a protruding stomach. He was asking for something, pulling at her sleeve, and crying bitterly. Elisha entered. The air in the hut was very foul. He looked round, and saw a woman lying on the floor behind the oven: she lay flat on the ground with her eyes closed and her throat rattling, now stretching out a leg, now dragging it in, tossing from side to side; and the foul smell came from her. Evidently she could do nothing for herself and no one had been attending to her needs. The old woman lifted her head, and saw the stranger.

'What do you want?' said she.' What do you want man? We have nothing.'

Elisha understood her, though she spoke in the Little-Russian dialect.

'I came in for a drink of water, servant of God,' he said.

'There's no one—no one—we have nothing to fetch it in. Go your way.'

Then Elisha asked:

'Is there no one among you, then, well enough to attend to that woman?'

'No, we have no one. My son is dying outside, and we are dying in here.'

The little boy had ceased crying when he saw the stranger, but when the old woman began to speak, he began again, and clutching hold of her sleeve cried:

'Bread, Granny, bread.'

Elisha was about to question the old woman, when the man staggered into the hut. He came along the passage, clinging to the wall, but as he was entering the dwelling-room he fell in the corner near the threshold, and without trying to get up again to reach the bench, he began to speak in broken words. He brought out a word at a time, stopping to draw breath, and gasping.

'Illness has seized us...,' said he, 'and famine. He is dying...of hunger.'

And he motioned towards the boy, and began to sob.

Elisha jerked up the sack behind his shoulder and pulling the straps off his arms, put it on the floor. Then he lifted it on to the bench, and untied the strings. Having opened the sack, he took out a loaf of bread, and, cutting off a piece with his knife, handed it to the man. The man would not take it, but pointed to the little boy and to a little girl crouching behind the oven, as if to say:

'Give it to them.'

Elisha held it out to the boy. When the boy smelt bread, he stretched out his arms, and seizing the slice with both his little hands, bit into it so that his nose disappeared in the chunk. The little girl came out from behind the oven and fixed her eyes on the bread. Elisha gave her also a slice. Then he cut off another piece and gave it to the old woman, and she too began munching it.

'If only some water could be brought,' she said, 'their mouths are parched. I tried to fetch some water yesterday—or was it to-day—I can't remember, but I fell down and could go no further, and the pail has remained there, unless some one has taken it.'

Elisha asked where the well was. The old woman told him. Elisha went out, found the pail, brought some water, and gave the people a drink. The children and the old woman ate some more bread with the water, but the man would not eat.

'I cannot eat,' he said.

All this time the younger woman did not show any consciousness, but continued to toss from side to side. Presently Elisha went to the village shop and bought some millet, salt, flour, and oil. He found an axe, chopped some wood, and made a fire. The little girl came and helped him. Then he boiled some soup, and gave the starving people a meal.

V

The man ate a little, the old woman had some too, and the little girl and boy licked the bowl clean, and then curled up and fell fast asleep in one another's arms.

The man and the old woman then began telling Elisha how they had sunk to their present state.

'We were poor enough before?' said they, 'but when the crops failed, what we gathered hardly lasted us through the autumn. We had nothing left by the time winter came, and had to beg from the neighbours and from any one we could. At first they gave, then they began to refuse. Some would have been glad enough to help us, but had nothing to give. And we were ashamed of asking: we were in debt all round, and owed money, and flour, and bread.'

'I went to look for work,' the man said, 'but could find none. Everywhere people were offering to work merely for their own keep. One day you'd get a short job, and then you might spend two days looking for work. Then the old woman and the girl went begging, further away. But they got very little; bread was so scarce. Still we scraped food together somehow, and hoped to struggle through till next harvest, but towards spring people ceased to give anything. And then this illness seized us. Things became worse and worse. One day we might have something to eat, and then nothing for two days. We began eating grass. Whether it was the grass, or what, made my wife ill, I don't know. She could not keep on her legs, and I had no strength left, and there was nothing to help us to recovery.'

'I struggled on alone for a while,' said the old woman, 'but at last I broke down too for want of food, and grew quite weak. The girl also grew weak and timid. I told her to go to the neighbours—she would not leave the hut, but crept into a corner and sat there. The day before yesterday a neighbour looked in, but seeing that we were ill and hungry she turned away and left us. Her husband has had to go away, and she has nothing for her own little ones to eat. And so we lay, waiting for death.'

Having heard their story, Elisha gave up the thought of overtaking his comrade that day, and remained with them all night. In the morning he got up and began doing the housework, just as if it were his own home. He kneaded the bread with the old woman's help, and lit the fire. Then he went with the little girl to the neighbours to get the most necessary things, for there was nothing in the hut: everything had been sold for bread—cooking utensils, clothing, and all. So Elisha began replacing what was necessary, making some things himself, and buying some. He remained there one day, then another, and then a third. The little boy picked up strength and, whenever Elisha sat down, crept along the bench and nestled up to him. The little girl brightened up and helped in all the work, running after Elisha and calling,

'Daddy, daddy.'

The old woman grew stronger, and managed to go out to see a neighbour. The man too improved, and was able to get about, holding on to the wall. Only the wife could not get up, but even she regained consciousness on the third day, and asked for food.

'Well,' thought Elisha, 'I never expected to waste so much time on the way. Now I must be getting on.'

VI

The fourth day was the feast day after the summer fast, and Elisha thought:

'I will stay and break the fast with these people. I'll go and buy them something, and keep the feast with them, and to-morrow evening I will start.'

So Elisha went into the village, bought milk, wheat-flour and dripping, and helped the old woman to boil and bake for the morrow. On the feast day Elisha went to church, and then broke the fast with his friends at the hut. That day the wife got up, and managed to move about a bit. The husband had shaved and put on a clean shirt, which the old woman had washed for him; and he went to beg for mercy of a rich peasant in the village to whom his plowland and meadow were mortgaged. He went to beg the rich peasant to grant him the use of the meadow and field till after the harvest; but in the evening he came back very sad, and began to weep. The rich peasant had shown no mercy, but had said: 'Bring me the money.'

Elisha again grew thoughtful. 'How are they to live now?' thought he to himself. 'Other people will go haymaking, but there will be nothing for these to mow, their grass land is mortgaged. The rye will ripen. Others will reap (and what a fine crop mother-earth is giving this year), but they have nothing to look forward to. Their three acres are pledged to the rich peasant. When I am gone, they'll drift back into the state I found them in.'

Elisha was in two minds, but finally decided not to leave that evening, but to wait until the morrow. He went out into the yard to sleep. He said his prayers, and lay down; but he could not sleep. On the one hand he felt he ought to be going, for he had spent too much time and money as it was; on the other hand he felt sorry for the people.

'There seems to be no end to it, he said. 'First I only meant to bring them a little water and give them each a slice of bread: and just see where it has landed me. It's a case of redeeming the meadow and the cornfield. And when I have done that, I shall have to buy a cow for them, and a horse for the man to cart his sheaves. A nice coil you've got yourself into, brother Elisha! You've slipped your cables and lost your reckoning!'

Elisha got up, lifted his coat which he had been using for a pillow, unfolded it, got out his snuff-box and took a pinch, thinking that it might perhaps clear his thoughts.

But no! He thought and thought, and came to no conclusion. He ought to be going; and yet pity held him back. He did not know what to do. He refolded his coat and put it under his head again. He lay thus for a long time, till the cocks had already crowed once: then he was quite drowsy. And suddenly it seemed as if some one had roused him. He saw that he was dressed for the journey, with the sack on his back and the staff in his hand, and the gate stood ajar so that he could just squeeze through. He was about to pass out, when his sack caught against the fence on one side: he tried to free it, but then his leg-band caught on the other side and came undone. He pulled at the sack, and saw that it had not caught on the fence, but that the little girl was holding it and crying,

'Bread, daddy, bread!'

He looked at his foot, and there was the tiny boy holding him by the leg-band, while the master of the hut and the old woman were looking at him through the window.

Elisha awoke, and said to himself in an audible voice:

'To-morrow I will redeem their cornfield, and will buy them a horse, and flour to last till the harvest, and a cow for the little ones; or else while I go to seek the Lord beyond the sea, I may lose Him in myself.'

Then Elisha fell asleep, and slept till morning. He awoke early, and going to the rich peasant, redeemed both the cornfield and the meadow land. He bought a scythe (for that also had been sold) and brought it back with him. Then he sent the man to mow, and himself went into the village. He heard that there was a horse and cart for sale at the public-house, and he struck a bargain with the owner, and bought them. Then he bought a sack of flour, put it in the cart, and went to see about a cow. As he was going along he overtook two women talking as they went. Though they spake the Little-Russian dialect, he understood what they were saying.

'At first, it seems, they did not know him; they thought he was just an ordinary man. He came in to ask for a drink of water, and then he remained. Just think of the things he has bought for them! Why they say he bought a horse and cart for them at the publican's, only this morning! There are not many such men in the world. It's worth while going to have a look at him.'

Elisha heard and understood that he was being praised, and he did not go to buy the cow, but returned to the inn, paid for the horse, harnessed it, drove up to the hut, and got out. The people in the hut were astonished when they saw the horse. They thought it might be for them, but dared not ask. The man came out to open the gate.

'Where did you get a horse from, grandfather,' he asked.

'Why, I bought it,' said Elisha. 'It was going cheap. Go and cut some grass and put it in the manger for it to eat during the night. And take in the sack.'

The man unharnessed the horse, and carried the sack into the barn. Then he mowed some grass and put it in the manger. Everybody lay down to sleep. Elisha went outside and lay by the roadside. That evening he took his bag out with him. When every one was asleep, he got up, packed and fastened his bag, wrapped the linen bands round his legs, put on his shoes and coat, and set off to follow Efím.

VII

When Elisha had walked rather more than three miles it began to grow light. He sat down under a tree, opened his bag, counted his money, and found he had only seventeen roubles and twenty kopeks left.

'Well,' thought he, 'it is no use trying to cross the sea with this. If I beg my way it may be worse than not going at all. Friend Efím will get to Jerusalem without me, and will place a candle at the shrines in my name. As for me, I'm afraid I shall never fulfil my vow in this life. I must be thankful it was made to a merciful Master, and to one who pardons sinners.'

Elisha rose, jerked his bag well up on his shoulders, and turned back. Not wishing to be recognized by any one, he made a circuit to avoid the village, and walked briskly homeward. Coming from home the way had seemed difficult to him, and he had found it hard to keep up with Efím, but now on his return journey, God helped him to get over the ground so that he hardly felt fatigue. Walking seemed like child's play. He went along swinging his staff, and did his forty to fifty miles a day.

When Elisha reached home the harvest was over. His family were delighted to see him again, and all wanted to know what had happened: Why and how he had been left behind? And why he had returned without reaching Jerusalem? But Elisha did not tell them.

'It was not God's will that I should get there,' said he. 'I lost my money on the way, and lagged behind my companion. Forgive me, for the Lord's sake!'

Elisha gave his old wife what money he had left. Then he questioned them about home affairs. Everything was going on well; all the work had been done, nothing neglected, and all were living in peace and concord.

Efím's family heard of his return the same day, and came for news of their old man; and to them Elisha gave the same answers.

'Efím is a fast walker. We parted three days before St. Peter's day, and I meant to catch him up again, but all sorts of things happened. I lost my money, and had no means to get any further, so I turned back.'

The folks were astonished that so sensible a man should have acted so foolishly: should have started and not got to his destination, and should have squandered all his money. They wondered at it for a while, and then forgot all about it, and Elisha forgot it too. He set to work again on his homestead. With his son's help he cut wood for fuel for the winter. He and the women threshed the corn. Then he mended the thatch on the outhouses, put the bees under cover, and handed over to his neighbour the ten hives he had sold him in spring, and all the swarms that had come from them. His wife tried not to tell how many swarms there had been from these hives, but Elisha knew well enough from which there had been swarms and from which not. And instead of ten, he handed over seventeen swarms to his neighbour. Having got everything ready for the winter, Elisha sent his son away to find work, while he himself took to platting shoes of bark, and hollowing out logs for hives.

VIII

All that day while Elisha stopped behind in the hut with the sick people, Efim waited for him. He only went on a little way before he sat down. He waited and waited, had a nap, woke up again, and again sat waiting; but his comrade did not come. He gazed till his eyes ached. The sun was already sinking behind a tree, and still no Elisha was to be seen.

'Perhaps he has passed me,' thought Efim, 'or perhaps some one gave him a lift and he drove by while I slept, and did not see me. But how could he help seeing me? One can see so far here in the steppe. Shall I go back? Suppose he is on in front, we shall then miss each other completely and it will be still worse. I had better go on, and we shall be sure to meet where we put up for the night.'

He came to a village, and told the watchman, if an old man of a certain description came along, to bring him to the hut where Efim stopped. But Elisha did not turn up that night. Efim went on, asking all he met whether they had not seen a little, bald-headed, old man? No one had seen such a traveller. Efim wondered, but went on alone, saying:

'We shall be sure to meet in Odessa, or on board the ship,' and he did not trouble more about it.

On the way, he came across a pilgrim wearing a priest's coat, with long hair and a skull-cap such as priests wear. This pilgrim had been to Mount Athos, and was now going to Jerusalem for the second time. They both stopped at the same place one night, and, having met, they travelled on together.

They got safely to Odessa, and there had to wait three days for a ship. Many pilgrims from many different parts were in the same case. Again Efim asked about Elisha, but no one had seen him.

Efim got himself a foreign passport, which cost him five roubles. He paid forty roubles for a return ticket to Jerusalem, and bought a supply of bread and herrings for the voyage.

The pilgrim began explaining to Efim how he might get on to the ship without paying his fare; but Efim would not listen. 'No, I came prepared to pay, and I shall pay,' said he.

The ship was freighted, and the pilgrims went on board, Efim and his new comrade among them. The anchors were weighed, and the ship put out to sea.

All day they sailed smoothly, but towards night a wind arose, rain came on, and the vessel tossed about and shipped water. The people were frightened: the women wailed and screamed, and some of the weaker men ran about the ship looking for shelter. Efim too was frightened, but he would not show it, and remained at the place on deck where he had settled down when first he came on board, beside some old men from Tambóf. There they sat silent, all night and all next day, holding on to their sacks. On the third day it grew calm, and on the fifth day they anchored at Constantinople. Some of the pilgrims went on shore to visit the Church of St. Sophia, now held by the Turks. Efim remained on the ship, and only bought some white bread. They lay there for twenty-four hours, and then put to sea again. At Smyrna they stopped again; and at Alexandria; but at last they arrived safely at Jaffa, where all the pilgrims had to disembark. From there still it was more than forty miles by road to Jerusalem. When disembarking the people were again much frightened. The ship was high, and the people were dropped into boats, which rocked so much that it was easy to miss them and fall into the water. A couple of men did get a wetting, but at last all were safely landed.

They went on on foot, and at noon on the third day reached Jerusalem. They stopped outside the town, at the Russian inn, where their passports were indorsed. Then, after dinner, Efim visited the Holy Places with his companion, the pilgrim. It was not the time when they could be admitted to the Holy Sepulchre, but they went to the Patriarchate. All the pilgrims assembled there. The women were separated from the men, who were all told to sit in a circle, barefoot. Then a monk came in with a towel to wash their feet. He washed, wiped, and then kissed their feet, and did this to every one in the circle. Efim's feet were washed and kissed, with the rest. He stood through vespers and matins, prayed, placed candles at the shrines, handed in booklets inscribed with his parents, names, that they might be mentioned in the church prayers. Here at the Patriarchate food and wine were given them. Next morning they went to the cell of Mary of Egypt, where she had lived doing penance. Here too they placed candles and had prayers read. From there they went to Abraham's Monastery, and saw the place where Abraham intended to slay his son as an offering to God. Then they visited the spot where Christ appeared to Mary Magdalene, and the Church of James, the Lord's brother. The pilgrim showed Efim all these places, and told him how much money to give at each place. At mid-day they returned to the inn and had dinner. As they were preparing to lie down and rest, the pilgrim cried out, and began to search his clothes, feeling them all over.

'My purse has been stolen, there were twenty-three roubles in it,' said he, 'two ten-rouble notes and the rest in change.'

He sighed and lamented a great deal, but as there was no help for it, they lay down to sleep.

IX

As Efim lay there, he was assailed by temptation.

'No one has stolen any money from this pilgrim,' thought he, 'I do not believe he had any. He gave none away anywhere, though he made me give, and even borrowed a rouble of me.'

This thought had no sooner crossed his mind, than Efim rebuked himself, saying: 'What right have I to judge a man? It is a sin. I will think no more about it.' But as soon as his thoughts began to wander, they turned again to the pilgrim: how interested he seemed to be in money, and how unlikely it sounded when he declared that his purse had been stolen.

'He never had any money,' thought Efim. 'It's all an invention.'

Towards evening they got up, and went to midnight Mass at the great Church of the Resurrection, where the Lord's Sepulchre is. The pilgrim kept close to Efim and went with him everywhere. They came to the Church; a great many pilgrims were there; some Russians and some of other nationalities: Greeks, Armenians, Turks, and Syrians. Efim entered the Holy Gates with the crowd. A monk led them past the Turkish sentinels, to the place where the Saviour was taken down from the cross and anointed, and where candles were burning in nine great candlesticks. The monk showed and explained everything. Efim offered a candle there. Then the monk led Efim to the right, up the steps to Golgotha, to the place where the cross had stood. Efim prayed there. Then they showed him the cleft where the ground had been rent asunder to its nethermost depths; then the place where Christ's hands and feet were nailed to the cross; then Adam's tomb, where the blood of Christ had dripped on to Adam's bones. Then they showed him the stone on which Christ sat when the crown of thorns was placed on His head; then the post to which Christ was bound when He was scourged. Then Efim saw the stone with two holes for Christ's feet. They were going to show him something else, but there was a stir in the crowd, and the people all hurried to the church of the Lord's Sepulchre itself. The Latin Mass had just finished there, and the Russian Mass was beginning. And Efim went with the crowd to the tomb cut in the rock.

He tried to get rid of the pilgrim, against whom he was still sinning in his mind, but the pilgrim would not leave him, but went with him to the Mass at the Holy Sepulchre. They tried to get to the front, but were too late. There was such a crowd that it was impossible to move either backwards or forwards. Efim stood looking in front of him, praying, and every now and then feeling for his purse. He was in two minds: sometimes he thought that the pilgrim was deceiving him, and then again he thought that if the pilgrim spoke the truth and his purse had really been stolen, the same thing might happen to himself.

X

Efim stood there gazing into the little chapel in which was the Holy Sepulchre itself with thirty-six lamps burning above it. As he stood looking over the people's heads, he saw something that surprised him. Just beneath the lamps in which the sacred fire burns and in front of every one, Efim saw an old man in a grey coat, whose bald, shining head was just like Elisha Bódrof.

'It is like him,' thought Efim, 'but it cannot be Elisha. He could not have got ahead of me. The ship before ours started a week sooner. He could not have caught that; and he was not on ours, for I saw every pilgrim on board.'

Hardly had Efim thought this, when the little old man began to pray, and bowed three times: once forwards to God, then once on each side—to the brethren. And as he turned his head to the right, Efim recognized him. It was Elisha Bódrof himself with his dark, curly beard turning grey at the cheeks, with his brows, his eyes and nose, and his expression of face. Yes, it was he!

Efim was very pleased to have found his comrade again, and wondered how Elisha had got ahead of him.

'Well done, Elisha!' thought he. 'See how he has pushed ahead. He must have come across some one who showed him the way. When we get out, I will find him, get rid of this fellow in the skull-cap, and keep to Elisha. Perhaps he will show me how to get to the front also.'

Efim kept looking out, so as not to lose sight of Elisha. But when the Mass was over, the crowd began to sway, pushing forward to kiss the tomb, and pushed Efim aside. He was again seized with fear lest his purse should be stolen. Pressing it with his hand, he began elbowing through the crowd, anxious only to get out. When he reached the open, he went about for a long time searching for Elisha both outside and in the Church itself. In the cells of the Church he saw many people of all kinds, eating, and drinking wine, and reading and sleeping there. But Elisha was nowhere to be seen. So Efim returned to the inn without having found his comrade. That evening the pilgrim in the skull-cap did not turn up. He had gone off without repaying the rouble, and Efim was left alone.

The next day Efim went to the Holy Sepulchre again, with an old man from Tambóf, whom he had met on the ship. He tried to get to the front, but was again pressed back; so he stood by a pillar and prayed. He looked before him, and there in the foremost place under the lamps, close to the very Sepulchre of the Lord, stood Elisha, with his arms spread out like a priest at the altar, and with his bald head all shining.

'Well, now,' thought Efim, 'I won't lose him!'

He pushed forward to the front, but when he got there, there was no Elisha: he had evidently gone away.

Again on the third day Efim looked, and saw at the Sepulchre, in the holiest place, Elisha standing in the sight of all men, his arms outspread, and his eyes gazing upwards as if he saw something above. And his bald head was all shining.

'Well, this time,' thought Efim, 'he shall not escape me! I will go and stand at the door, then we can't miss one another!'

Efim went out and stood by the door till past noon. Every one had passed out, but still Elisha did not appear.

Efim remained six weeks in Jerusalem, and went everywhere: to Bethlehem, and to Bethany, and to the Jordan. He had a new shirt sealed at the Holy Sepulchre for his burial, and he took a bottle of water from the Jordan, and some holy earth, and bought candles that had been lit at the sacred flame. In eight places he inscribed names to be prayed for, and he spent all his money, except just enough to get home with. Then he started homeward. He walked to Jaffa, sailed thence to Odessa, and walked home from there on foot.

XI

Efim travelled the same road he had come by; and as he drew nearer home his former anxiety returned as to how affairs were getting on in his absence. 'Much water flows away in a year,' the proverb says. It takes a lifetime to build up a homestead, but not long to ruin it, thought he. And he wondered how his son had managed without him, what sort of spring they were having, how the cattle had wintered, and whether the cottage was well finished. When Efim came to the district where he had parted from Elisha the summer before, he could hardly believe that the people living there were the same. The year before they had been starving, but now they were living in comfort. The harvest had been good, and the people had recovered and had forgotten their former misery.

One evening Efim reached the very place where Elisha had remained behind; and as he entered the village, a little girl in a white smock ran out of a hut.

Daddy, daddy, come to our house!'

Efim meant to pass on, but the little girl would not let him. She took hold of his coat, laughing, and pulled him towards the hut, where a woman with a small boy came out into the porch and beckoned to him.

'Come in, grandfather,' she said. 'Have supper and spend the night with us.'

So Efím went in.

'I may as well ask about Elisha,' he thought. 'I fancy this is the very hut he went to for a drink of water.'

The woman helped him off with the bag he carried, and gave him water to wash his face. Then she made him sit down to table, and set milk, curd-cakes and porridge before him. Efím thanked her, and praised her for her kindness to a pilgrim. The woman shook her head.

'We have good reason to welcome pilgrims,' she said. 'It was a pilgrim who showed us what life is. We were living forgetful of God, and God punished us almost to death. We reached such a pass last summer, that we all lay ill and helpless with nothing to eat. And we should have died, but that God sent an old man to help us—just such a one as you. He came in one day to ask for a drink of water, saw the state we were in, took pity on us, and remained with us. He gave us food and drink, and set us on our feet again; and he redeemed our land, and bought a cart and horse and gave them to us.'

Here the old woman entering the hut, interrupted the younger one and said:

'We don't know whether it was a man, or an angel from God. He loved us all, pitied us all, and went away without telling us his name, so that we don't even know whom to pray for. I can see it all before me now! There I lay waiting for death, when in comes a bald-headed old man. He was not anything much to look at, and he asked for a drink of water. I, sinner that I am, thought to myself: "What does he come prowling about here for?" And just think what he did! As soon as he saw us, he let down his bag, on this very spot, and untied it.'

Here the little girl joined in.

'No, Granny,' said she, 'first he put it down here in the middle of the hut, and then he lifted it on to the bench.'

And they began discussing and recalling all he had said and done, where he sat and slept, and what he had said to each of them.

At night the peasant himself came home on his horse, and he too began to tell about Elisha and how he had lived with them.

'Had he not come we should all have died in our sins. We were dying in despair, murmuring against God and man. But he set us on our feet again; and through him we learned to know God, and to believe that there is good in man. May the Lord bless him! We used to live like animals; he made human beings of us.

After giving Efím food and drink, they showed him where he was to sleep; and lay down to sleep themselves.

But though Efím lay down, he could not sleep. He could not get Elisha out of his mind, but remembered how he had seen him three times at Jerusalem, standing in the foremost place.

'So that is how he got ahead of me,' thought Efim. 'God may or may not have accepted my pilgrimage but He has certainly accepted his!'

Next morning Efim bade farewell to the people, who put some patties in his sack before they went to their work, and he continued his journey.

XII

Efim had been away just a year, and it was spring again when he reached home one evening. His son was not at home, but had gone to the public-house and when he came back, he had had a drop too much. Efim began questioning him. Everything showed that the young fellow had been unsteady during his father's absence. The money had all been wrongly spent, and the work had been neglected. The father began to upbraid the son; and the son answered rudely.

'Why didn't you stay and look after it yourself?' he said. 'You go off, taking the money with you and now you demand it of me!'

The old man grew angry, and struck his son.

In the morning Efim went to the village Elder to complain of his son's conduct. As he was passing Elisha's house, his friend's wife greeted him from the porch.

'How do you do, neighbour,' she said. 'How do you do, dear friend? Did you get to Jerusalem safely?'

Efim stopped.

'Yes, thank God,' he said. 'I have been there. I lost sight of your old man, but I hear he got home safely.'

The old woman was fond of talking:

'Yes, neighbour, he has come back,' said she. 'He's been back a long time. Soon after Assumption, I think it was, he returned. And we were glad the Lord had sent him back to us! We were dull without him. We can't expect much work from him any more, his years for work are past; but still he is the head of the household and it's more cheerful when he's at home. And how glad our lad was! He said, "It's like being without sunlight, when father's away!" It was dull without him, dear friend. We're fond of him, and take good care of him.'

'Is he at home now?'

'He is, dear friend. He is with his bees. He is hiving the swarms. He says they are swarming well this year. The Lord has given such strength to the bees that my husband doesn't remember the like. "The Lord is not rewarding us according to our sins," he says. Come in, dear neighbour, he will be so glad to see you again.'

Efim passed through the passage into the yard and to the apiary, to see Elisha. There was Elisha in his grey coat, without any face-net or gloves, standing, under the birch trees, looking upwards, his arms stretched out and his bald head shining, as Efim had seen him at the Holy Sepulchre in Jerusalem: and above him the sunlight shone through the birches as the flames of fire had done in the holy place, and the golden bees flew round his head like a halo, and did not sting him.

Efim stopped. The old woman called to her husband.

'Here's your friend come,' she cried.

Elisha looked round with a pleased face, and came towards Efim, gently picking bees out of his own beard.

'Good day, neighbour, good-day, dear friend. Did you get there safely?'

'My feet walked there, and I have brought you some water from the river Jordan. You must come to my house for it. But whether the Lord accepted my efforts...'

'Well the Lord be thanked! May Christ bless you!' said Elisha.

Efim was silent for a while, and then added:

'My feet have been there, but whether my soul, or another's, has been there more truly . . .'

'That's God's business, neighbour, God's business,' interrupted Elisha.

'On my return journey I stopped at the hut where you remained behind...'

Elisha was alarmed, and said hurriedly:

'God's business, neighbour, God's business! Come into the cottage, I'll give you some of our honey.' And Elisha changed the conversation, and talked of home affairs.

Efim sighed, and did not speak to Elisha of the people in the hut, nor of how he had seen him in Jerusalem. But he now understood that the best way to keep one's vows to God and to do His will, is for each man while he lives to show love and do good to others.

1885

WHERE LOVE IS, GOD IS (1885)

In a certain town there lived a cobbler, Martin Avdéitch by name. He had a tiny room in a basement, the one window of which looked out on to the street. Through it one could only see the feet of those who passed by, but Martin recognized the people by their boots. He had lived long in the place and had many acquaintances. There was hardly a pair of boots in the neighbourhood that had not been once or twice through his hands, so he often saw his own handiwork through the window. Some he had re-soled, some patched, some stitched up, and to some he had even put fresh uppers. He had plenty to do, for he worked well, used good material, did not charge too much, and could be relied on. If he could do a job by the day required, he undertook it; if not, he told the truth and gave no false promises; so he was well known and never short of work.

Martin had always been a good man; but in his old age he began to think more about his soul and to draw nearer to God. While he still worked for a master, before he set up on his own account, his wife had died, leaving him with a three-year old son. None of his elder children had lived, they had all died in infancy. At first Martin thought of sending his little son to his sister's in the country, but then he felt sorry to part with the boy, thinking: 'It would be hard for my little Kapitón to have to grow up in a strange family; I will keep him with me.'

Martin left his master and went into lodgings with his little son. But he had no luck with his children. No sooner had the boy reached an age when he could help his father and be a support as well as a joy to him, than he fell ill and, after being laid up for a week with a burning fever, died. Martin buried his son, and gave way to despair so great and overwhelming that he murmured against God. In his sorrow he prayed again and again that he too might die, reproaching God for having taken the son he loved, his only son while he, old as he was, remained alive. After that Martin left off going to church.

One day an old man from Martin's native village who had been a pilgrim for the last eight years, called in on his way from Tróitsa Monastery. Martin opened his heart to him, and told him of his sorrow.

'I no longer even wish to live, holy man,' he said. 'All I ask of God is that I soon may die. I am now quite without hope in the world.'

The old man replied: 'You have no right to say such things, Martin. We cannot judge God's ways. Not our reasoning, but God's will, decides. If God willed that your son should die and you should live, it must be best so. As to your despair—that comes because you wish to live for your own happiness.'

'What else should one live for?' asked Martin.

'For God, Martin,' said the old man. 'He gives you life, and you must live for Him. When you have learnt to live for Him, you will grieve no more, and all will seem easy to you.'

Martin was silent awhile, and then asked: 'But how is one to live for God?'

The old man answered: 'How one may live for God has been shown us by Christ. Can you read? Then buy the Gospels, and read them: there you will see how God would have you live. You have it all there.'

These words sank deep into Martin's heart, and that same day he went and bought himself a Testament in large print, and began to read.

At first he meant only to read on holidays, but having once begun he found it made his heart so light that he read every day. Sometimes he was so absorbed in his reading that the oil in his lamp burnt out before he could tear himself away from the book. He continued to read every night, and the more he read the more clearly he understood what God required of him, and how he might live for God. And his heart grew lighter and lighter. Before, when he went to bed he used to lie with a heavy heart, moaning as he thought of his little Kapitón; but now he only repeated again and again: 'Glory to Thee, glory to Thee, O Lord! Thy will be done!'

From that time Martin's whole life changed. Formerly, on holidays he used to go and have tea at the public house, and did not even refuse a glass or two of vódka. Sometimes, after having had a drop with a friend, he left the public house not drunk, but rather merry, and would say foolish things: shout at a man, or abuse him. Now, all that sort of thing passed away from him. His life became peaceful and joyful. He sat down to his work in the morning, and when he had finished his day's work he took the lamp down from the wall, stood it on the table, fetched his book from the shelf, opened it, and sat down to read. The more he read the better he understood, and the clearer and happier he felt in his mind.

It happened once that Martin sat up late, absorbed in his book. He was reading Luke's Gospel; and in the sixth chapter he came upon the verses:

'To him that smiteth thee on the one cheek offer also the other; and from him that taketh away thy cloak withhold not thy coat also. Give to every man that asketh thee; and of him that taketh away thy goods ask them not again. And as ye would that men should do to you, do ye also to them likewise.'

He also read the verses where our Lord says:

'And why call ye me, Lord, Lord, and do not the things which I say? Whosoever cometh to me, and heareth my sayings, and doeth them, I will shew you to whom he is like: He is like a man which built an house, and digged deep, and laid the foundation on a rock: and when the flood arose, the stream beat vehemently upon that house, and could not shake it: for it was founded upon a rock. But he that heareth and doeth not, is like a man that without a foundation built an house upon the earth, against which the stream did beat vehemently, and immediately it fell; and the ruin of that house was great.'

When Martin read these words his soul was glad within him. He took off his spectacles and laid them on the book, and leaning his elbows on the table pondered over what he had read. He tried his own life by the standard of those words, asking himself:

'Is my house built on the rock, or on sand? If it stands on the rock, it is well. It seems easy enough while one sits here alone, and one thinks one has done all that God commands; but as soon as I cease to be on my guard, I sin again. Still I will persevere. It brings such joy. Help me, O Lord!'

He thought all this, and was about to go to bed, but was loth to leave his book. So he went on reading the seventh chapter—about the centurion, the widow's son, and the answer to John's disciples—and he came to the part where a rich Pharisee invited the Lord to his house; and he read how the woman who was a sinner, anointed his feet and washed them with her tears, and how he justified her. Coming to the forty-fourth verse, he read:

'And turning to the woman, he said unto Simon, Seest thou this woman? I entered into thine house thou gavest me no water for my feet: but she hath wetted my feet with her tears, and wiped them with her hair. Thou gavest me no kiss; but she, since the time I came in, hath not ceased to kiss my feet. My head with oil thou didst not anoint: but she hath anointed my feet with ointment.'

He read these verses and thought: 'He gave no water for his feet, gave no kiss, his head with oil he did not anoint...' And Martin took off his spectacles once more, laid them on his book, and pondered.

'He must have been like me, that Pharisee. He too thought only of himself—how to get a cup of tea, how to keep warm and comfortable; never a thought of his guest. He took care of himself, but for his guest he cared nothing at all. Yet who was the guest? The Lord himself! If he came to me, should I behave like that?'

Then Martin laid his head upon both his arms and, before he was aware of it, he fell asleep.

'Martin!' he suddenly heard a voice, as if some one had breathed the word above his ear.

He started from his sleep. 'Who's there?' he asked.

He turned round and looked at the door; no one was there. He called again. Then he heard quite distinctly: 'Martin, Martin! Look out into the street to-morrow, for I shall come.'

Martin roused himself, rose from his chair and rubbed his eyes, but did not know whether he had heard these words in a dream or awake. He put out the lamp and lay down to sleep.

Next morning he rose before daylight, and after saying his prayers he lit the fire and prepared his cabbage soup and buckwheat porridge. Then he lit the samovár, put on his apron, and sat down by the window to his work. As he sat working Martin thought over what had happened the night before. At times it seemed to him like a dream, and at times he thought that he had really heard the voice. 'Such things have happened before now,' thought he.

So he sat by the window, looking out into the street more than he worked, and whenever any one passed in unfamiliar boots he would stoop and look up, so as to see not the feet only but the face of the passer-by as well. A house-porter passed in new felt boots; then a water-carrier. Presently an old soldier of Nicholas' reign came near the window spade in hand. Martin knew him by his boots, which were shabby old felt ones, goloshed with leather. The old man was called

Stepánitch: a neighbouring tradesman kept him in his house for charity, and his duty was to help the house-porter. He began to clear away the snow before Martin's window. Martin glanced at him and then went on with his work.

'I must be growing crazy with age,' said Martin, laughing at his fancy. 'Stepánitch comes to clear away the snow, and I must needs imagine it's Christ coming to visit me. Old dotard that I am!'

Yet after he had made a dozen stitches he felt drawn to look out of the window again. He saw that Stepánitch had leaned his spade against the wall, and was either resting himself or trying to get warm. The man was old and broken down, and had evidently not enough strength even to clear away the snow.

'What if I called him in and gave him some tea?' thought Martin. 'The samovár is just on the boil.'

He stuck his awl in its place, and rose; and putting the samovár on the table, made tea. Then he tapped the window with his fingers. Stepánitch turned and came to the window. Martin beckoned to him to come in, and went himself to open the door.

'Come in,' he said, 'and warm yourself a bit. I'm sure you must be cold.'

'May God bless you!' Stepánitch answered. 'My bones do ache to be sure.' He came in, first shaking off the snow, and lest he should leave marks on the floor he began wiping his feet; but as he did so he tottered and nearly fell.

'Don't trouble to wipe your feet,' said Martin 'I'll wipe up the floor—it's all in the day's work. Come, friend, sit down and have some tea.'

Filling two tumblers, he passed one to his visitor, and pouring his own out into the saucer, began to blow on it.

Stepánitch emptied his glass, and, turning it upside down, put the remains of his piece of sugar on the top. He began to express his thanks, but it was plain that he would be glad of some more.

'Have another glass,' said Martin, refilling the visitor's tumbler and his own. But while he drank his tea Martin kept looking out into the street.

'Are you expecting any one?' asked the visitor.

'Am I expecting any one? Well, now, I'm ashamed to tell you. It isn't that I really expect any one; but I heard something last night which I can't get out of my mind Whether it was a vision, or only a fancy, I can't tell. You see, friend, last night I was reading the Gospel, about Christ the Lord, how he suffered, and how he walked on earth. You have heard tell of it, I dare say.'

'I have heard tell of it,' answered Stepánitch; 'but I'm an ignorant man and not able to read.'

'Well, you see, I was reading of how he walked on earth. I came to that part, you know, where he went to a Pharisee who did not receive him well. Well, friend, as I read about it, I thought now that man did not receive Christ the Lord with proper honour. Suppose such a thing could happen to such a man as myself, I thought, what would I not do to receive him! But that man gave him no reception at all. Well, friend, as I was thinking of this, I began to doze, and as I dozed I heard some one call me by name. I got up, and thought I heard some one whispering, "Expect me; I will come to-morrow." This happened twice over. And to tell you the truth, it sank so into my mind that, though I am ashamed of it myself, I keep on expecting him, the dear Lord!'

Stepánitch shook his head in silence, finished his tumbler and laid it on its side; but Martin stood it up again and refilled it for him.

'Here drink another glass, bless you! And I was thinking too, how he walked on earth and despised no one, but went mostly among common folk. He went with plain people, and chose his disciples from among the likes of us, from workmen like us, sinners that we are. "He who raises himself," he said, "shall be humbled and he who humbles himself shall be raised." "You call me Lord," he said, "and I will wash your feet." "He who would be first," he said, "let him be the servant of all; because," he said, "blessed are the poor, the humble, the meek, and the merciful."'

Stepánitch forgot his tea. He was an old man easily moved to tears, and as he sat and listened the tears ran down his cheeks.

'Come, drink some more,' said Martin. But Stepánitch crossed himself, thanked him, moved away his tumbler, and rose.

'Thank you, Martin Avdéitch,' he said, 'you have given me food and comfort both for soul and body.'

'You're very welcome. Come again another time. I am glad to have a guest,' said Martin.

Stepánitch went away; and Martin poured out the last of the tea and drank it up. Then he put away the tea things and sat down to his work, stitching the back seam of a boot. And as he stitched he kept looking out of the window, waiting for Christ, and thinking about him and his doings. And his head was full of Christ's sayings.

Two soldiers went by: one in Government boots the other in boots of his own; then the master of a neighbouring house, in shining goloshes; then a baker carrying a basket. All these passed on. Then a woman came up in worsted stockings and peasant-made shoes. She passed the window, but stopped by the wall. Martin glanced up at her through the window, and saw that she was a stranger, poorly dressed, and with a baby in her arms. She stopped by the wall with her back to the wind, trying to wrap the baby up though she had hardly anything to wrap it in. The woman had only summer clothes on, and even they were shabby and worn. Through the window Martin heard the baby crying, and the woman trying to soothe it, but unable to do so. Martin rose and going out of the door and up the steps he called to her.

'My dear, I say, my dear!'

The woman heard, and turned round.

'Why do you stand out there with the baby in the cold? Come inside. You can wrap him up better in a warm place. Come this way!'

The woman was surprised to see an old man in an apron, with spectacles on his nose, calling to her, but she followed him in.

They went down the steps, entered the little room, and the old man led her to the bed.

'There, sit down, my dear, near the stove. Warm yourself, and feed the baby.'

'Haven't any milk. I have eaten nothing myself since early morning,' said the woman, but still she took the baby to her breast.

Martin shook his head. He brought out a basin and some bread. Then he opened the oven door and poured some cabbage soup into the basin. He took out the porridge pot also but the porridge was not yet ready, so he spread a cloth on the table and served only the soup and bread.

'Sit down and eat, my dear, and I'll mind the baby. Why, bless me, I've had children of my own; I know how to manage them.'

The woman crossed herself, and sitting down at the table began to eat, while Martin put the baby on the bed and sat down by it. He chucked and chucked, but having no teeth he could not do it well and the baby continued to cry. Then Martin tried poking at him with his finger; he drove his finger straight at the baby's mouth and then quickly drew it back, and did this again and again. He did not let the baby take his finger in its mouth, because it was all black with cobbler's wax. But the baby first grew quiet watching the finger, and then began to laugh. And Martin felt quite pleased.

The woman sat eating and talking, and told him who she was, and where she had been.

'I'm a soldier's wife,' said she. 'They sent my husband somewhere, far away, eight months ago, and I have heard nothing of him since. I had a place as cook till my baby was born, but then they would not keep me with a child. For three months now I have been struggling, unable to find a place, and I've had to sell all I had for food. I tried to go as a wet-nurse, but no one would have me; they said I was too starved-looking and thin. Now I have just been to see a tradesman's wife (a woman from our village is in service with her) and she has promised to take me. I thought it was all settled at last, but she tells me not to come till next week. It is far to her place, and I am fagged out, and baby is quite starved, poor mite. Fortunately our landlady has pity on us, and lets us lodge free, else I don't know what we should do.'

Martin sighed. 'Haven't you any warmer clothing?' he asked.

'How could I get warm clothing?' said she. 'Why I pawned my last shawl for sixpence yesterday.'

Then the woman came and took the child, and Martin got up. He went and looked among some things that were hanging on the wall, and brought back an old cloak.

'Here,' he said, 'though it's a worn-out old thing, it will do to wrap him up in.'

The woman looked at the cloak, then at the old man, and taking it, burst into tears. Martin turned away, and groping under the bed brought out a small trunk. He fumbled about in it, and again sat down opposite the woman. And the woman said:

'The Lord bless you, friend. Surely Christ must have sent me to your window, else the child would have frozen. It was mild when I started, but now see how cold it has turned. Surely it must have been Christ who made you look out of your window and take pity on me, poor wretch!'

Martin smiled and said; 'It is quite true; it was he made me do it. It was no mere chance made me look out.'

And he told the woman his dream, and how he had heard the Lord's voice promising to visit him that day.

'Who knows? All things are possible,' said the woman. And she got up and threw the cloak over her shoulders, wrapping it round herself and round the baby. Then she bowed, and thanked Martin once more.

'Take this for Christ's sake,' said Martin, and gave her sixpence to get her shawl out of pawn. The woman crossed herself, and Martin did the same, and then he saw her out.

After the woman had gone, Martin ate some cabbage soup, cleared the things away, and sat down to work again. He sat and worked, but did not forget the window, and every time a shadow fell on it he looked up at once to see who was passing. People he knew and strangers passed by, but no one remarkable.

After a while Martin saw an apple-woman stop just in front of his window. She had a large basket, but there did not seem to be many apples left in it; she had evidently sold most of her stock. On her back she had a sack full of chips, which she was taking home. No doubt she had gathered them at some place where building was going on. The sack evidently hurt her, and she wanted to shift it from one shoulder to the other, so she put it down on the footpath and, placing her basket on a post, began to shake down the chips in the sack. While she was doing this a boy in a tattered cap ran up, snatched an apple out of the basket, and tried to slip away; but the old woman noticed it, and turning, caught the boy by his sleeve. He began to struggle, trying to free himself, but the old woman held on with both hands, knocked his cap off his head, and seized hold of his hair. The boy screamed and the old woman scolded. Martin dropped his awl, not waiting to stick it in its place, and rushed out of the door. Stumbling up the steps, and dropping his spectacles in his hurry, he ran out into the street. The old woman was pulling the boy's hair and scolding him, and threatening to take him to the police. The lad was struggling and protesting, saying, 'I did not take it. What are you beating me for? Let me go!'

Martin separated them. He took the boy by the hand and said, 'Let him go, Granny. Forgive him for Christ's sake.'

'I'll pay him out, so that he won't forget it for a year! I'll take the rascal to the police!'

Martin began entreating the old woman.

'Let him go, Granny. He won't do it again. Let him go for Christ's sake!'

The old woman let go, and the boy wished to run away, but Martin stopped him

'Ask the Granny's forgiveness!' said he. 'And don't do it another time. I saw you take the apple.'

The boy began to cry and to beg pardon.

'That's right. And now here's an apple for you, and Martin took an apple from the basket and gave it to the boy, saying, 'I will pay you, Granny.'

'You will spoil them that way, the young rascals,' said the old woman. 'He ought to be whipped so that he should remember it for a week.'

'Oh, Granny, Granny,' said Martin, 'that's our way—but it's not God's way. If he should be whipped for stealing an apple, what should be done to us for our sins?'

The old woman was silent.

And Martin told her the parable of the lord who forgave his servant a large debt, and how the servant went out and seized his debtor by the throat. The old woman listened to it all, and the boy, too, stood by and listened.

'God bids us forgive,' said Martin, 'or else we shall not be forgiven. Forgive every one; and a thoughtless youngster most of all.'

The old woman wagged her head and sighed.

'It's true enough,' said she, 'but they are getting terribly spoilt.'

'Then we old ones must show them better ways,' Martin replied.

'That's just what I say,' said the old woman. 'I have had seven of them myself, and only one daughter is left.' And the old woman began to tell how and where she was living with her daughter, and how many grandchildren she had. 'There now,' she said, 'I have but little strength left, yet I work hard for the sake of my grandchildren; and nice children they are, too. No one comes out to meet me but the children. Little Annie, now, won't leave me for any one. "It's grandmother, dear grandmother, darling grandmother."' And the old woman completely softened at the thought.

'Of course, it was only his childishness, God help him,' said she, referring to the boy.

As the old woman was about to hoist her sack on her back, the lad sprang forward to her, saying, 'Let me carry it for you, Granny. I'm going that way.'

The old woman nodded her head, and put the sack on the boy's back, and they went down the street together, the old woman quite forgetting to ask Martin to pay for the apple. Martin stood and watched them as they went along talking to each other.

When they were out of sight Martin went back to the house. Having found his spectacles unbroken on the steps, he picked up his awl and sat down again to work. He worked a little, but could soon not see to pass the bristle through the holes in the leather; and presently he noticed the lamplighter passing on his way to light the street lamps.

'Seems it's time to light up,' thought he. So he trimmed his lamp, hung it up, and sat down again to work. He finished off one boot and, turning it about, examined it. It was all right. Then he gathered his tools together, swept up the cuttings, put away the bristles and the thread and the awls, and, taking down the lamp, placed it on the table. Then he took the Gospels from the shelf. He meant to open them at the place he had marked the day before with a bit of morocco, but the book opened at another place. As Martin opened it, his yesterday's dream came back to his mind, and no sooner had he thought of it than he seemed to hear footsteps, as though some one were moving behind him. Martin turned round, and it seemed to him as if people were standing in the dark corner, but he could not make out who they were. And a voice whispered in his ear: 'Martin, Martin, don't you know me?'

'Who is it?' muttered Martin.

'It is I,' said the voice. And out of the dark corner stepped Stepánitch, who smiled and vanishing like a cloud was seen no more.

'It is I,' said the voice again. And out of the darkness stepped the woman with the baby in her arms and the woman smiled and the baby laughed, and they too vanished.

'It is I,' said the voice once more. And the old woman and the boy with the apple stepped out and both smiled, and then they too vanished.

And Martin's soul grew glad. He crossed himself put on his spectacles, and began reading the Gospel just where it had opened; and at the top of the page he read

'I was an hungered, and ye gave me meat: I was thirsty, and ye gave me drink: I was a stranger, and ye took me in.'

And at the bottom of the page he read:

'Inasmuch as ye did it unto one of these my brethren even these least, ye did it unto me'

And Martin understood that his dream had come true; and that the Saviour had really come to him that day, and he had welcomed him.

PART III. A FAIRY TALE

THE STORY OF IVÁN THE FOOL (1885)

I

Once upon a time, in a certain province of a certain country, there lived a rich peasant, who had three sons: Simon the Soldier, Tarás the Stout, and Iván the Fool, besides an unmarried daughter, Martha, who was deaf and dumb. Simon the Soldier went to the wars to serve the king; Tarás the Stout went to a merchant's in town to trade, and Iván the Fool stayed at home with the lass, to till the ground till his back bent.

Simon the Soldier obtained high rank and an estate, and married a nobleman's daughter. His pay was large and his estate was large, but yet he could not make ends meet. What the husband earned his lady wife squandered, and they never had money enough.

So Simon the Soldier went to his estate to collect the income, but his steward said, 'where is any income to come from? We have neither cattle, nor tools, nor horse, nor plough, nor harrow. We must first get all these, and then the money will come.'

Then Simon the Soldier went to his father and said: 'You, father, are rich, but have given me nothing. Divide what you have, and give me a third part, that I may improve my estate.'

But the old man said: 'You brought nothing into my house; why should I give you a third part? It would be unfair to Iván and to the girl.'

But Simon answered, 'He is a fool; and she is an old maid, and deaf and dumb besides; what's the good of property to them?'

The old man said, 'We will see what Iván says about it.'

And Iván said, 'Let him take what he wants.'

So Simon the Soldier took his share of his father's goods and removed them to his estate, and went off again to serve the king.

Tarás the Stout also gathered much money, and married into a merchant's family, but still he wanted more. So he, also, came to his father and said, 'Give me my portion.'

But the old man did not wish to give Tarás a share either, and said, 'You brought nothing here. Iván has earned all we have in the house, and why should we wrong him and the girl?'

But Tarás said, 'What does he need? He is a fool! He cannot marry, no one would have him; and the dumb lass does not need anything either. Look here, Iván!' said he, 'give me half the corn; I don't want the tools, and of the live stock I will take only the grey stallion, which is of no use to you for the plough.'

Iván laughed and said, 'Take what you want. I will work to earn some more.'

So they gave a share to Tarás also, and he carted the corn away to town, and took the grey stallion. And Iván was left with one old mare, to lead his peasant life as before, and to support his father and mother.

II

Now the old Devil was vexed that the brothers had not quarrelled over the division, but had parted peacefully; and he summoned three imps.

'Look here,' said he, 'there are three brothers Simon the Soldier, Tarás the Stout, and Iván the Fool. They should have quarrelled, but are living peaceably and meet on friendly terms. The fool Iván has spoilt the whole business for me. Now you three go and tackle those three brothers, and worry them till they scratch each other's eyes out! Do you think you can do it?'

'Yes, we'll do it,' said they.

'How will you set about it?'

'Why,' said they, 'first we'll ruin them. And when they haven't a crust to eat we'll tie them up together, and then they'll fight each other, sure enough!'

'That's capital; I see you understand your business. Go, and don't come back till you've set them by the ears, or I'll skin you alive!'

The imps went off into a swamp, and began to consider how they should set to work. They disputed and disputed, each wanting the lightest job; but at last they decided to cast lots which of the brothers each imp should tackle. If one imp finished his task before the others, he was to come and help them. So the imps cast lots, and appointed a time to meet again in the swamp to learn who had succeeded and who needed help.

The appointed time came round, and the imps met again in the swamp as agreed. And each began to tell how matters stood. The first, who had undertaken Simon the Soldier, began: 'My business is going on well. To-morrow Simon will return to his father's house.'

His comrades asked, 'How did you manage it?'

'First,' says he, 'I made Simon so bold that he offered to conquer the whole world for his king; and the king made him his general and sent him to fight the King of India. They met for battle, but the night before, I damped all the powder in Simon's camp, and made more straw soldiers for the Indian King than you could count. And when Simon's soldiers saw the straw soldiers surrounding them, they grew frightened. Simon ordered them to fire; but their cannons and guns would not go off. Then Simon's soldiers were quite frightened, and ran like sheep, and the Indian King slaughtered them. Simon was disgraced. He has been deprived of his estate, and to-morrow they intend to execute him. There is only one day's work left for me to do; I have just to let him out of prison that he may escape home. To-morrow I shall be ready to help whichever of you needs me.

Then the second imp, who had Tarás in hand, began to tell how he had fared. 'I don't want any help,' said he, 'my job is going all right. Tarás can't hold out for more than a week. First I caused him to grow greedy and fat. His covetousness became so great that whatever he saw he wanted to buy. He has spent all his money in buying immense lots of goods, and still continues to buy. Already he has begun to use borrowed money. His debts hang like a weight round his neck, and he is so involved that he can never get clear. In a week his bills come due, and before then I will spoil all his stock. He will be unable to pay and will have to go home to his father.'

Then they asked the third imp (Ivan's), 'And how are you getting on?'

'Well,' said he, 'my affair goes badly. First I spat into his drink to make his stomach ache, and then I went into his field and hammered the ground hard as a stone that he should not be able to till it. I thought he wouldn't plough it, but like the fool that he is, he came with his plough and began to make a furrow. He groaned with the pain in his stomach, but went on ploughing. I broke his plough for him, but he went home, got out another, and again started ploughing. I crept under the earth and caught hold of the ploughshares, but there was no holding them; he leant heavily upon the plough, and the ploughshare was sharp and cut my hands. He has all but finished ploughing the field, only one little strip is left. Come brothers, and help me; for if we don't get the better of him, all our labour is lost. If the fool holds out and keeps on working the land, his brothers will never know want, for he will feed them both.'

Simon the Soldier's imp promised to come next day to help, and so they parted.

III

Iván had ploughed up the whole fallow, all but one little strip. He came to finish it. Though his stomach ached, the ploughing must be done. He freed the harness ropes, turned the plough, and began to work. He drove one furrow, but coming back the plough began to drag as if it had caught in a root. It was the imp, who had twisted his legs round the ploughshare and was holding it back.

'What a strange thing!' thought Iván. 'There were no roots here at all, and yet here's a root.'

Iván pushed his hand deep into the furrow, groped about, and, feeling something soft, seized hold of it and pulled it out. It was black like a root, but it wriggled. Why, it was a live imp!

'What a nasty thing!' said Iván, and he lifted his hand to dash it against the plough, but the imp squealed out:

'Don't hurt me, and I'll do anything you tell me to.'

'What can you do?'

'Anything you tell me to.'

Iván scratched his head.

'My stomach aches,' said he; 'can you cure that?'

'Certainly I can.'

'Well then, do so.'

The imp went down into the furrow, searched about scratched with his claws, and pulled out a bunch of three little roots, which he handed to Iván.

'Here,' says he, 'whoever swallows one of these will be cured of any illness.'

Iván took the roots, separated them, and swallowed one. The pain in his stomach was cured at once. The imp again begged to be let off; 'I will jump right into the earth, and never come back,' said he.

'All right,' said Iván; 'begone, and God be with you!'

And as soon as Iván mentioned God, the imp plunged into the earth like a stone thrown into the water. Only a hole was left.

Iván put the other two pieces of root into his cap and went on with his ploughing. He ploughed the strip to the end, turned his plough over, and went home. He unharnessed the horse, entered the hut, and there he saw his elder brother, Simon the Soldier and his wife, sitting at supper. Simon's estate had been confiscated, he himself had barely managed to escape from prison, and he had come back to live in his father's house.

Simon saw Iván, and said: 'I have come to live with you. Feed me and my wife till I get another appointment.'

'All right,' said Iván, 'you can stay with us.'

But when Iván was about to sit down on the bench the lady disliked the smell, and said to her husband. 'I cannot sup with a dirty peasant.'

So Simon the Soldier said, 'My lady says you don't smell nice. You'd better go and eat outside.'

'All right,' said Iván; 'any way I must spend the night outside, for I have to pasture the mare.'

So he took some bread, and his coat, and went with the mare into the fields.

IV

Having finished his work that night, Simon's imp came, as agreed, to find Iván's imp and help him to subdue the fool. He came to the field and searched and searched; but instead of his comrade he found only a hole.

'Clearly,' thought he, 'some evil has befallen my comrade. I must take his place. The field is ploughed up, so the fool must be tackled in the meadow.'

So the imp went to the meadows and flooded Iván's hayfield with water, which left the grass all covered with mud.

Iván returned from the pasture at dawn, sharpened his scythe, and went to mow the hayfield. He began to mow but had only swung the scythe once or twice when the edge turned so that it would not cut at all, but needed resharpening. Iván struggled on for awhile, and then said: 'It's no good. I must go home and bring a tool to straighten the scythe, and I'll get a chunk of bread at the same time. If I have to spend a week here, I won't leave till the mowing's done.'

The imp heard this and thought to himself, 'This fool is a tough 'un; I can't get round him this way. I must try some other dodge.'

Iván returned, sharpened his scythe, and began to mow. The imp crept into the grass and began to catch the scythe by the heel, sending the point into the earth. Iván found the work very hard, but he mowed the whole meadow, except one little bit which was in the swamp. The imp crept into the swamp and, thought he to himself, 'Though I cut my paws I will not let him mow.'

Iván reached the swamp. The grass didn't seem thick, but yet it resisted the scythe. Iván grew angry and began to swing the scythe with all his might. The imp had to give in; he could not keep up with the scythe, and, seeing it was a bad business, he scrambled into a bush. Iván swung the scythe, caught the bush, and cut off half the imp's tail. Then he finished mowing the grass, told his sister to rake it up, and went himself to mow the rye. He went with the scythe, but the dock-tailed imp was there first, and entangled the rye so that the scythe was of no use. But Iván went home and got his sickle, and began to reap with that and he reaped the whole of the rye.

'Now it's time,' said he, 'to start on the oats.'

The dock-tailed imp heard this, and thought, 'I couldn't get the better of him on the rye, but I shall on the oats. Only wait till the morning.'

In the morning the imp hurried to the oat field, but the oats were already mowed down! Iván had mowed them by night, in order that less grain should shake out. The imp grew angry.

'He has cut me all over and tired me out—the fool. It is worse than

war. The accursed fool never sleeps; one can't keep up with him. I will
get into his stacks now and rot them.'

So the imp entered the rye, and crept among the sheaves, and they
began to rot. He heated them, grew warm himself, and fell asleep.

Iván harnessed the mare, and went with the lass to cart the rye. He
came to the heaps, and began to pitch the rye into the cart. He tossed
two sheaves and again thrust his fork—right into the imp's back. He
lifts the fork and sees on the prongs a live imp; dock-tailed, struggling,
wriggling, and trying to jump.

'What, you nasty thing, are you here again?'

'I'm another,' said the imp. 'The first was my brother. I've been
with your brother Simon.'

'Well,' said Iván, whoever you are, you've met the same fate!'

He was about to dash him against the cart, but the imp cried out:
'Let me off, and I will not only let you alone, but I'll do anything you
tell me to do.'

'What can you do?'

'I can make soldiers out of anything you like.'

'But what use are they?'

'You can turn them to any use; they can do anything you please.'

'Can they sing?'

'Yes, if you want them to.'

'All right; you may make me some.'

And the imp said, 'Here, take a sheaf of rye, then bump it upright
on the ground, and simply say:

"O sheaf! my slave
This order gave:
Where a straw has been
Let a soldier be seen!"'

Iván took the sheaf, struck it on the ground, and said what the imp had
told him to. The sheaf fell asunder, and all the straws changed into
soldiers, with a trumpeter and a drummer playing in front, so that there
was a whole regiment.

Iván laughed.

'How clever!' said he. 'This is fine! How pleased the girls will be!'

'Now let me go,' said the imp.

'No,' said Iván, 'I must make my soldiers of thrashed straw,
otherwise good grain will be wasted. Teach me how to change them
back again into the sheaf. I want to thrash it.'

And the imp said, 'Repeat:

"Let each be a straw
Who was soldier before,
For my true slave
This order gave!"'

Iván said this, and the sheaf reappeared.

Again the imp began to beg, 'Now let me go!

'All right.' And Iván pressed him against the side of the cart, held him down with his hand, and pulled him off the fork.

'God be with you,' said he.

And as soon as he mentioned God, the imp plunged into the earth like a stone into water. Only a hole was left.

Iván returned home, and there was his other brother, Tarás with his wife, sitting at supper.

Tarás the Stout had failed to pay his debts, had run away from his creditors, and had come home to his father's house. When he saw Iván, 'Look here', said he, 'till I can start in business again, I want you to keep me and my wife.'

'All right,' said Iván, 'you can live here, if you like.'

Iván took off his coat and sat down to table, but the merchant's wife said: 'I cannot sit at table with this clown, he smells of perspiration.'

Then Tarás the Stout said, 'Iván, you smell too strong. Go and eat outside.'

'All right,' said Iván, taking some bread and going into the yard. 'It is time, anyhow, for me to go and pasture the mare.'

V

Tarás's imp, being also free that night, came, as agreed, to help his comrades subdue Iván the Fool. He came to the cornfield, looked and looked for his comrades—no one was there. He only found a hole. He went to the meadow, and there he found an imp's tail in the swamp, and another hole in the rye stubble.

'Evidently, some ill-luck has befallen my comrades,' thought he. 'I must take their place and tackle the fool.'

So the imp went to look for Iván, who had already stacked the corn and was cutting trees in the wood. The two brothers had begun to feel crowded, living together, and had told Iván to cut down trees to build new houses for them.

The imp ran to the wood, climbed among the branches, and began to hinder Iván from felling the trees. Iván undercut one tree so that it should fall clear, but in falling it turned askew and caught among some branches. Iván cut a pole with which to lever it aside, and with difficulty contrived to bring it to the ground. He set to work to fell another tree—again the same thing occurred; and with all his efforts he could hardly get the tree clear. He began on a third tree, and again the same thing happened.

Iván had hoped to cut down half a hundred small trees, but had not felled even half a score, and now the night was come and he was tired out. The steam from him spread like a mist through the wood, but still he stuck to his work. He undercut another tree, but his back began to ache so that he could not stand. He drove his axe into the tree and sat down to rest.

The imp, noticing that Iván had stopped work, grew cheerful.

'At last,' thought he, 'he is tired out! He will give it up. Now I can take a rest myself.'

He seated himself astride a branch and chuckled. But soon Iván got up, pulled the axe out, swung it and smote the tree from the opposite side with such force that the tree gave way at once and came crashing down. The imp had not expected this, and had no time to get his feet clear, and the tree in breaking, gripped his paw. Iván began to lop off the branches, when he noticed a live imp hanging in the tree! Iván was surprised.

'What, you nasty thing,' says he, 'so you are here again!'

'I am another one,' says the imp. 'I have been with your brother Tarás.'

'Whoever you are you have met your fate,' said Iván, and swinging his axe he was about to strike him with the haft, but the imp begged for mercy: 'Don't strike me,' said he, 'and I will do anything you tell me to.'

'What can you do?'

'I can make money for you, as much as you want.'

'All right, make some.' So the imp showed him how to do it.

'Take,' said he, 'some leaves from this oak and rub them in your hands, and gold will fall out on the ground.'

Iván took some leaves and rubbed them, and gold ran down from his hands.

'This stuff will do fine,' said he, 'for the fellows to play with on their holidays.'

'Now let me go.' said the imp.

'All right,' said Iván, and taking a lever he set the imp free. 'Now begone! And God be with you,' says he.

And as soon as he mentioned God, the imp plunged into the earth, like a stone into water. Only a hole was left.

VI

So the brothers built houses, and began to live apart; and Iván finished the harvest work, brewed beer, and invited his brothers to spend the next holiday with him. His brothers would not come.

'We don't care about peasant feasts,' said they.

So Iván entertained the peasants and their wives, and drank until he was rather tipsy. Then he went into the street to a ring of dancers; and going up to them he told the women to sing a song in his honour; 'for,' said he, 'I will give you something you never saw in your lives before!'

The women laughed and sang his praises, and when they had finished they said, 'Now let us have your gift.'

'I will bring it directly,' said he.

He took a seed-basket and ran into the woods. The women laughed. 'He is a fool!' said they, and they began to talk of something else.

But soon Iván came running back, carrying the basket full of something heavy.

'Shall I give it you?'

'Yes! give it to us.'

Iván took a handful of gold and threw it to the women. You should have seen them throw themselves upon it to pick it up! And the men around scrambled for it, and snatched it from one another. One old woman was nearly crushed to death. Iván laughed.

'Oh, you fools!' says he. 'Why did you crush the old grandmother? Be quiet, and I will give you some more,' and he threw them some more. The people all crowded round, and Iván threw them all the gold he had. They asked for more, but Iván said,'I have no more just now. Another time I'll give you some more. Now let us dance, and you can sing me your songs.'

The women began to sing.

'Your songs are no good,' says he.

'Where will you find better ones?' say they.

'I'll soon show you,' says he.

He went to the barn, took a sheaf, thrashed it, stood it up, and bumped it on the ground.

'Now,' said he:

> 'O sheaf! my slave
> This order gave:
> Where a straw has been
> Let a soldier be seen!'

And the sheaf fell asunder and became so many soldiers. The drums and trumpets began to play. Iván ordered the soldiers to play and sing. He led them out into the street, and the people were amazed, The soldiers played and sang, and then Iván (forbidding any one to follow him) led them back to the thrashing ground, changed them into a sheaf again, and threw it in its place.

He then went home and lay down in the stables to sleep.

VII

Simon the Soldier heard of all these things next morning, and went to his brother.

'Tell me,' says he, 'where you got those soldiers from, and where you have taken them to?'

'What does it matter to you?' said Iván.

'What does it matter? Why, with soldiers one can do anything. One can win a kingdom.'

Iván wondered.

'Really!' said he; 'Why didn't you say so before? I'll make you as many as you like. It's well the lass and I have thrashed so much straw.'

Iván took his brother to the barn and said:

'Look here; if I make you some soldiers, you must take them away at once, for if we have to feed them, they will eat up the whole village in a day.'

Simon the Soldier promised to lead the soldiers away; and Iván began to make them. He bumped a sheaf on the thrashing floor—a company appeared. He bumped another sheaf, and there was a second company. He made so many that they covered the field.

'Will that do?' he asked.

Simon was overjoyed, and said: 'That will do! Thank you, Iván!'

'All right' said Iván. 'If you want more, come back, and I'll make them. There is plenty of straw this season.'

Simon the Soldier at once took command of his army, collected and organized it, and went off to make war.

Hardly had Simon the Soldier gone, when Tarás the Stout came along. He, too, had heard of yesterday's affair, and he said to his brother:

'Show me where you get gold money! If I only had some to start with, I could make it bring me in money from all over the world.'

Iván was astonished.

'Really!' said he. 'You should have told me sooner. I will make you as much as you like.'

His brother was delighted.

'Give me three baskets-full to begin with.'

'All right,' said Iván. 'Come into the forest; or better still, let us harness the mare, for you won't be able to carry it all.'

They drove to the forest, and Iván began to rub the oak leaves. He made a great heap of gold.

'Will that do?'

Tarás was overjoyed.

'It will do for the present,' said he. 'Thank you, Iván!'

'All right,' says Iván, 'if you want more, come back for it. There are plenty of leaves left.'

Tarás the Stout gathered up a whole cartload of money, and went off to trade.

So the two brothers went away: Simon to fight and Tarás to buy and sell. And Simon the Soldier conquered a kingdom for himself; and Tarás the Stout made much money in trade.

When the two brothers met, each told the other: Simon how he got the soldiers, and Tarás how he got the money. And Simon the Soldier said to his brother, I have conquered a kingdom and live in grand style but I have not money enough to keep my soldiers.'

And Tarás the Stout said, 'And I have made much money, but the trouble is, I have no one to guard it.'

Then said Simon the Soldier, 'Let us go to our brother. I will tell him to make more soldiers, and will give them to you to guard your money, and you can tell him to make money for me to feed my men.

And they drove away to Iván; and Simon said, 'Dear brother, I have not enough soldiers; make me another couple of ricks or so.'

Iván shook his head.

'No!' says he' 'I will not make any more soldiers.'

'But you promised you would.'

'I know I promised, but I won't make any more.'

'But why not, fool?'

'Because your soldiers killed a man. I was ploughing the other day near the road, and I saw a woman taking a coffin along in a cart, and crying. I asked her who was dead. She said, "Simon's soldiers have killed my husband in the war." I thought the soldiers would only play tunes, but they have killed a man. I won't give you any more.'

And he stuck to it, and would not make any more soldiers.

Tarás the Stout, too, began to beg Iván to make him more gold money. But Iván shook his head.

'No, I won't make any more,' said he.

'Didn't you promise?'

'I did, but I'll make no more,' said he.

'Why not, fool?'

'Because your gold coins took away the cow from Michael's daughter.'

'How?'

'Simply took it away! Michael's daughter had a cow. Her children used to drink the milk. But the other day her children came to me to ask for milk. I said, "Where's your cow?" They answered, "The steward of Tarás the Stout came and gave mother three bits of gold, and she gave him the cow, so we have nothing to drink." I thought you were only going to play with the gold pieces, but you have taken the children's cow away. I will not give you any more.'

And Iván stuck to it and would not give him any more. So the brothers went away. And as they went they discussed how they could meet their difficulties. And Simon said:

'Look here, I tell you what to do. You give me money to feed my soldiers, and I will give you half my kingdom with soldiers enough to guard your money.' Tarás agreed. So the brothers divided what they possessed, and both became kings, and both were rich.

VIII

Iván lived at home, supporting his father and mother and working in the fields with his dumb sister. Now it happened that Iván's yard-dog fell sick, grew mangy, and was near dying. Iván, pitying it, got some bread from his sister, put it in his cap, carried it out, and threw it to the dog. But the cap was torn, and together with the bread one of the little roots fell to the ground. The old dog ate it up with the bread, and as soon as she had swallowed it she jumped up and began to play, bark, and wag her tail—in short became quite well again.

The father and mother saw it and were amazed.

'How did you cure the dog?' asked they.

Iván answered: 'I had two little roots to cure any pain, and she swallowed one.'

Now about that time it happened that the King's daughter fell ill, and the King proclaimed in every town and village, that he would reward any one who could heal her, and if any unmarried man could heal the King's daughter he should have her for his wife. This was proclaimed in Ivan's village as well as everywhere else.

His father and mother called Iván, and said to him: 'Have you heard what the King has proclaimed? You said you had a root that would cure any sickness. Go and heal the King's daughter, and you will be made happy for life.'

'All right,' said he.

And Iván prepared to go, and they dressed him in his best. But as he went out of the door he met a beggar woman with a crippled hand.

'I have heard,' said she, 'that you can heal people. I pray you cure my arm, for I cannot even put on my boots myself.'

'All right,' said Iván, and giving the little root to the beggar woman he told her to swallow it. She swallowed it, and was cured. She was at once able to move her arm freely.

His father and mother came out to accompany Iván to the King, but when they heard that he had given away the root, and that he had nothing left to cure the King's daughter with, they began to scold him.

'You pity a beggar woman, but are not sorry for the King's daughter!' said they. But Iván felt sorry for the King's daughter also. So he harnessed the horse, put straw in the cart to sit on, and sat down to drive away.

'Where are you going, fool?'

'To cure the King's daughter.'

'But you've nothing left to cure her with?'

'Never mind,' said he, and drove off.

He drove to the King's palace, and as soon as he stepped on the threshold the King's daughter got well.

The King was delighted, and had Iván brought to him, and had him dressed in fine robes.

'Be my son-in-law,' said he.

'All right,' said Iván.

And Iván married the Princess. Her father died soon after, and Iván became King. So all three brothers were now kings.

IX

The three brothers lived and reigned. The eldest brother, Simon the Soldier, prospered. With his straw soldiers he levied real soldiers. He ordered throughout his whole kingdom a levy of one soldier from every ten houses, and each soldier had to be tall, and clean in body and in face. He gathered many such soldiers and trained them; and when any one opposed him, he sent these soldiers at once, and got his own way, so that every one began to fear him, and his life was a comfortable one. Whatever he cast his eyes on and wished for, was his. He sent soldiers, and they brought him all he desired.

Tarás the Stout also lived comfortably. He did not waste the money he got from Iván, but increased it largely. He introduced law and order into his kingdom. He kept his money in coffers, and taxed the people. He instituted a poll-tax, tolls for walking and driving, and a tax on shoes and stockings and dress trimmings. And whatever he wished for he got. For the sake of money, people brought him everything, and they offered to work for him—for every one wanted money.

Iván the Fool, also, did not live badly. As soon as he had buried his father-in-law, he took off all his royal robes and gave them to his wife to put away in a chest; and he again donned his hempen shirt, his breeches and peasant shoes, and started again to work.

'It's dull for me,' said he. 'I'm getting fat and have lost my appetite and my sleep.' So he brought his father and mother and his dumb sister to live with him, and worked as before.

People said, 'But you are a king!'

'Yes,' said he, 'but even a king must eat.'

One of his ministers came to him and said, 'We have no money to pay salaries.'

'All right,' says he, 'then don't pay them.'

'Then no one will serve.'

'All right; let them not serve. They will have more time to work; let them cart manure. There is plenty of scavenging to be done.'

And people came to Iván to be tried. One said. 'He stole my money.' And Iván said, 'All right, that shows that he wanted it.'

And they all got to know that Iván was a fool. And his wife said to him, 'People say that you are a fool.'

'All right,' said Iván.

His wife thought and thought about it, but she also was a fool.

'Shall I go against my husband? Where the needle goes the thread follows,' said she.

So she took off her royal dress, put it away in a chest, and went to the dumb girl to learn to work. And she learned to work and began to help her husband.

And all the wise men left Iván's kingdom; only the fools remained.

Nobody had money. They lived and worked. They fed themselves; and they fed others.

X

The old Devil waited and waited for news from the imps of their having ruined the three brothers. But no news came. So he went himself to inquire about it. He searched and searched, but instead of finding the three imps he found only the three holes.

'Evidently they have failed,' thought he. 'I shall have to tackle it myself.'

So he went to look for the brothers, but they were no longer in their old places. He found them in three different kingdoms. All three were living and reigning. This annoyed the old Devil very much.

'Well,' said he, 'I must try my own hand at the job.'

First he went to King Simon. He did not go to him in his own shape, but disguised himself as a general, and drove to Simon's palace.

'I hear, King Simon,' said he, 'that you are a great warrior, and as I know that business well, I desire to serve you.'

King Simon questioned him, and seeing that he was a wise man, took him into his service.

The new commander began to teach King Simon how to form a strong army.

'First,' said he, 'we must levy more soldiers, for there are in your kingdom many people unemployed. We must recruit all the young men without exception. Then you will have five times as many soldiers as formerly. Secondly, we must get new rifles and cannons. I will introduce rifles that will fire a hundred balls at once; they will fly out like peas. And I will get cannons that will consume with fire either man, or horse, or wall. They will burn up everything!'

Simon the King listened to the new commander, ordered all young men without exception to be enrolled as soldiers, and had new factories built in which he manufactured large quantities of improved rifles and cannons. Then he made haste to declare war against a neighbouring king. As soon as he met the other army, King Simon ordered his soldiers to rain balls against it and shoot fire from the cannons, and at one blow he burned and crippled half the enemy's army. The neighbouring king was so thoroughly frightened that he gave way and surrendered his kingdom. King Simon was delighted.

'Now,' said he, 'I will conquer the King of India.'

But the Indian King had heard about King Simon and had adopted all his inventions, and added more of his own. The Indian King enlisted not only all the young men, but all the single women also, and got together a greater army even than King Simon's. And he copied all King Simon's rifles and cannons, and invented a way of flying through the air to throw explosive bombs from above.

King Simon set out to fight the Indian King, expecting to beat him as he had beaten the other king; but the scythe that had cut so well had lost its edge. The King of India did not let Simon's army come within gunshot, but sent his women through the air to hurl down explosive bombs on to Simon's army. The women began to rain down bombs on to the army like borax upon cockroaches. The army ran away, and Simon the King was left alone. So the Indian King took Simon's kingdom, and Simon the Soldier fled as best he might.

Having finished with this brother, the old Devil went to King Tarás. Changing himself into a merchant, he settled in Tarás's kingdom, started a house of business, and began spending money. He paid high prices for everything, and everybody hurried to the new merchant's to get money. And so much money spread among the people that they began to pay all their taxes promptly, and paid up all their arrears, and King Tarás rejoiced.

'Thanks to the new merchant,' thought he, 'I shall have more money than ever; and my life will be yet more comfortable.'

And Tarás the King began to form fresh plans, and began to build a new palace. He gave notice that people should bring him wood and stone, and come to work, and he fixed high prices for everything. King Tarás thought people would come in crowds to work as before, but to his surprise all the wood and stone was taken to the merchant's, and all the workmen went there too. King Tarás increased his price, but the merchant bid yet more. King Tarás had much money, but the merchant had still more, and outbid the King at every point.

The King's palace was at a standstill; the building did not get on.

King Tarás planned a garden, and when autumn came he called for the people to come and plant the garden, but nobody came. All the people were engaged digging a pond for the merchant. Winter came, and King Tarás wanted to buy sable furs for a new overcoat. He sent to buy them, but the messengers returned and said, 'There are no sables left. The merchant has all the furs. He gave the best price, and made carpets of the skins.'

King Tarás wanted to buy some stallions. He sent to buy them, but the messengers returned saying, 'The merchant has all the good stallions; they are carrying water to fill his pond.

All the King's affairs came to a standstill. Nobody would work for him, for every one was busy working for the merchant; and they only brought King Tarás the merchant's money to pay their taxes.

And the King collected so much money that he had nowhere to store it, and his life became wretched. He ceased to form plans, and would have been glad enough simply to live, but he was hardly able even to do that. He ran short of everything. One after another his cooks, coachmen, and servants left him to go to the merchant. Soon he lacked even food. When he sent to the market to buy anything, there was nothing to be got—the merchant had bought up everything, and people only brought the King money to pay their taxes.

Tarás the King got angry and banished the merchant from the country. But the merchant settled just across the frontier, and went on as before. For the sake of the merchant's money, people took everything to him instead of to the King.

Things went badly with King Tarás. For days together he had nothing to eat, and a rumour even got about that the merchant was boasting that he would buy up the King himself! King Tarás got frightened, and did not know what to do.

At this time Simon the Soldier came to him, saying, 'Help me, for the King of India has conquered me.'

But King Tarás himself was over head and ears in difficulties. 'I myself,' said he, 'have had nothing to eat for two days.'

XI

Having done with the two brothers, the old Devil went to Iván. He changed himself into a General, and coming to Iván began to persuade him that he ought to have an army.

'It does not become a king,' said he, 'to be without an army. Only give me the order, and I will collect soldiers from among your people, and form one.'

Iván listened to him. 'All right,' said Iván, 'form an army, and teach them to sing songs well. I like to hear them do that.'

So the old Devil went through Ivan's kingdom to enlist men. He told them to go and be entered as soldiers, and each should have a quart of spirits and a fine red cap.

The people laughed.

'We have plenty of spirits,' said they. 'We make it ourselves; and as for caps, the women make all kinds of them, even striped ones with tassels.'

So nobody would enlist.

The old Devil came to Iván and said: 'Your fools won't enlist of their own free will. We shall have to make them.'

'All right,' said Iván, 'you can try.'

So the old Devil gave notice that all the people were to enlist, and that Iván would put to death any one who refused.

The people came to the General and said, 'You say that if we do not go as soldiers the King will put us to death, but you don't say what will happen if we do enlist. We have heard say that soldiers get killed!'

'Yes, that happens sometimes.'

When the people heard this they became obstinate.

'We won't go,' said they. 'Better meet death at home. Either way we must die.'

'Fools! You are fools!' said the old Devil. 'A soldier may be killed or he may not, but if you don't go, King Iván will have you killed for certain.'

The people were puzzled, and went to Iván the Fool to consult him.

'A General has come,' said they, 'who says we must all become soldiers. "If you go as soldiers," says he "you may be killed or you may not, but if you don't go, King Iván will certainly kill you." Is this true?'

Iván laughed and said, 'How can I, alone, put all you to death? If I were not a fool I would explain it to you but as it is, I don't understand it myself.'

'Then' said they, 'we will not serve.'

'All right,' says he, 'don't.'

So the people went to the General and refused to enlist. And the old Devil saw that this game was up, and he went off and ingratiated himself with the King of Tarakán.

'Let us make war,' says he, 'and conquer King Iván's country. It is true there is no money, but there is plenty of corn and cattle and everything else.'

So the King of Tarakán prepared to make war. He mustered a great army, provided rifles and cannons, marched to the frontier, and entered Iván's kingdom.

And people came to Iván and said, 'The King of Tarakán is coming to make war on us.'

'All right,' said Iván, 'let him come.'

Having crossed the frontier, the King of Tarakán sent scouts to look for Iván's army. They looked and looked, but there was no army! They waited and waited for one to appear somewhere, but there were no signs of an army, and nobody to fight with. The King of Tarakán then sent to seize the villages. The soldiers came to a village, and the people, both men and women, rushed out in astonishment to stare at the soldiers. The soldiers began to take their corn and cattle; the people let them have it, and did not resist. The soldiers went on to another village; the same thing happened again. The soldiers went on for one day, and for two days, and everywhere the same thing happened. The people let them have everything, and no one resisted, but only invited the soldiers to live with them.

'Poor fellows,' said they, 'if you have a hard life in your own land, why don't you come and stay with us altogether?'

The soldiers marched and marched: still no army, only people living and feeding themselves and others, and not resisting, but inviting the soldiers to stay and live with them. The soldiers found it dull work, and they came to the King of Tarakán and said, 'We cannot fight here, lead us elsewhere. War is all right, but what is this? It is like cutting pea-soup! We will not make war here any more.'

The King of Tarakán grew angry, and ordered his soldiers to over-run the whole kingdom, to destroy the villages, to burn the grain and the houses, and to slaughter the cattle. 'And if you do not obey my orders,' said he, 'I will execute you all.'

The soldiers were frightened, and began to act according to the King's orders. They began to burn houses and corn, and to kill cattle. But the fools still offered no resistance, and only wept. The old men wept, and the old women wept, and the young people wept.

'Why do you harm us?' they said. 'Why do you waste good things? If you need them, why do you not take them for yourselves?'

At last the soldiers could stand it no longer. They refused to go any further, and the army disbanded and fled.

XII

The old Devil had to give it up. He could not get the better of Iván with soldiers. So he changed himself into a fine gentleman, and settled down in Ivan's kingdom. He meant to overcome him by means of money, as he had overcome Tarás the Stout.

'I wish,' says he, 'to do you a good turn, to teach you sense and reason. I will build a house among you and organize a trade.'

'All right,' said Iván, 'come and live among us if you like.'

Next morning the fine gentleman went out into the public square with a big sack of gold and a sheet of paper, and said, 'You all live like swine. I wish to teach you how to live properly. Build me a house according to this plan. You shall work, I will tell you how, and I will pay you with gold coins.' And he showed them the gold.

The fools were astonished; there was no money in use among them; they bartered their goods, and paid one another with labour. They looked at the gold coins with surprise.

'What nice little things they are!' said they.

And they began to exchange their goods and labour for the gentleman's gold pieces. And the old Devil began, as in Tarás's kingdom, to be free with his gold, and the people began to exchange everything for gold and to do all sorts of work for it.

The old Devil was delighted, and thought he to himself, 'Things are going right this time. Now I shall ruin the Fool as I did Tarás, and I shall buy him up body and soul.'

But as soon as the fools had provided themselves with gold pieces they gave them to the women for necklaces. The lasses plaited them into their tresses, and at last the children in the street began to play with the little pieces. Everybody had plenty of them, and they stopped taking them. But the fine gentleman's mansion was not yet half-built, and the grain and cattle for the year were not yet provided. So he gave notice that he wished people to come and work for him, and that he wanted cattle and grain; for each thing, and for each service, he was ready to give many more pieces of gold.

But nobody came to work and nothing was brought. Only sometimes a boy or a little girl would run up to exchange an egg for a gold coin, but nobody else came, and he had nothing to eat. And being hungry, the fine gentleman went through the village to try and buy something for dinner. He tried at one house, and offered a gold piece for a fowl, but the housewife wouldn't take it.

'I have a lot already,' said she.

He tried at a widow's house to buy a herring, and offered a gold piece.

'I don't want it, my good sir,' said she. 'I have no children to play with it, and I myself already have three coins as curiosities.'

He tried at a peasant's house to get bread, but neither would the peasant take money.

'I don't need it,' said he, 'but if you are begging "for Christ's sake," wait a bit and I'll tell the housewife to cut you a piece of bread.'

At that the Devil spat, and ran away. To hear Christ's name mentioned, let alone receiving anything for Christ's sake, hurt him more than sticking a knife into him.

And so he got no bread. Every one had gold, and no matter where the old Devil went, nobody would give anything for money, but every one said, 'Either bring something else, or come and work, or receive what you want in charity for Christ's sake.'

But the old Devil had nothing but money; for work he had no

liking, and as for taking anything 'for Christ's sake' he could not do that. The old Devil grew very angry.

'What more do you want, when I give you money?' said he. 'You can buy everything with gold, and hire any kind of labourer.' But the fools did not heed him.

'No, we do not want money,' said they. 'We have no payments to make, and no taxes, so what should we do with it?'

The old Devil lay down to sleep—supperless.

The affair was told to Iván the Fool. People came and asked him, 'What are we to do? A fine gentleman has turned up, who likes to eat and drink and dress well, but he does not like to work, does not beg in "Christ's name," but only offers gold pieces to every one. At first people gave him all he wanted until they had plenty of gold pieces, but now no one gives him anything. What's to be done with him? He will die of hunger before long.'

Iván listened.

'All right,' says he, 'we must feed him. Let him live by turn at each house as a shepherd does.'

There was no help for it. The old Devil had to begin making the round.

In due course the turn came for him to go to Ivan's house. The old Devil came in to dinner, and the dumb girl was getting it ready.

She had often been deceived by lazy folk who came early to dinner—without having done their share of work—and ate up all the porridge, so it had occurred to her to find out the sluggards by their hands. Those who had horny hands, she put at the table, but the others got only the scraps that were left over.

The old Devil sat down at the table, but the dumb girl seized him by the hands and looked at them—there were no hard places there: the hands were clean and smooth, with long nails. The dumb girl gave a grunt and pulled the Devil away from the table. And Iván's wife said to him, 'Don't be offended, fine gentleman. My sister-in-law does not allow any one to come to table who hasn't horny hands. But wait awhile, after the folk have eaten you shall have what is left.'

The old Devil was offended that in the King's house they wished him to feed like a pig. He said to Iván, 'It is a foolish law you have in your kingdom that every one must work with his hands. It's your stupidity that invented it. Do people work only with their hands? What do you think wise men work with?'

And Iván said, 'How are we fools to know? We do most of our work with our hands and our backs.'

'That is because you are fools! But I will teach you how to work with the head. Then you will know that it is more profitable to work with the head than with the hands.'

Iván was surprised.

'If that is so' said he, 'then there is some sense in calling us fools!'

And the old Devil went on. 'Only it is not easy to work with one's head. You give me nothing to eat, because I have no hard places on my hands, but you do not know that it is a hundred times more difficult to work with the head. Sometimes one's head quite splits.'

Iván became thoughtful.

'Why, then, friend, do you torture yourself so? Is it pleasant when the head splits? Would it not be better to do easier work with your hands and your back?'

But the Devil said, 'I do it all out of pity for you fools. If I didn't torture myself you would remain fools for ever. But, having worked with my head, I can now teach you.'

Iván was surprised.

'Do teach us!' said he, 'so that when our hands get cramped we may use our heads for a change.'

And the Devil promised to teach the people. So Iván gave notice throughout the kingdom that a fine gentleman had come who would teach everybody how to work with their heads; that with the head more could be done than with the hands; and that the people ought all to come and learn.

Now there was in Ivan's kingdom a high tower, with many steps leading up to a lantern on the top. And Iván took the gentleman up there that every one might see him.

So the gentleman took his place on the top of the tower and began to speak, and the people came together to see him. They thought the gentleman would really show them how to work with the head without using the hands. But the old Devil only taught them in many words how they might live without working. The people could make nothing of it. They looked and considered, and at last went off to attend to their affairs.

The old Devil stood on the tower a whole day, and after that a second day, talking all the time. But standing there so long he grew hungry, and the fools never thought of taking food to him up in the tower. They thought that if he could work with his head better than with his hands, he could at any rate easily provide himself with bread.

The old Devil stood on the top of the tower yet another day, talking away. People came near, looked on for awhile, and then went away.

And Iván asked, 'Well, has the gentleman begun to work with his head yet?'

'Not yet,' said the people; 'he's still spouting away.'

The old Devil stood on the tower one day more, but he began to grow weak, so that he staggered and hit his head against one of the pillars of the lantern. One of the people noticed it and told Ivan's wife, and she ran to her husband, who was in the field.

'Come and look,' said she. 'They say the gentleman is beginning to work with his head.'

Iván was surprised.

'Really?' says he, and he turned his horse round, and went to the tower. And by the time he reached the tower the old Devil was quite exhausted with hunger, and was staggering and knocking his head against the pillars. And just as Iván arrived at the tower, the Devil stumbled, fell, and came bump, bump, bump, straight down the stairs to the bottom, counting each step with a knock of his head!

'Well!' says Iván, 'the fine gentleman told the truth when he said that "sometimes one's head quite splits." This is worse than blisters; after such work there will be swellings on the head.'

The old Devil tumbled out at the foot of the stairs, and struck his head against the ground. Iván was about to go up to him to see how much work he had done—when suddenly the earth opened and the old Devil fell through. Only a hole was left.

Iván scratched his head.

'What a nasty thing,' says he. 'It's one of those devils again! What a whopper! He must be the father of them all.'

Iván is still living, and people crowd to his kingdom. His own brothers have come to live with him, and he feeds them, too. To every one who comes and says 'Give me food!' Iván says, 'All right. You can stay with us; we have plenty of everything.'

Only there is one special custom in his kingdom; whoever has horny hands comes to table, but whoever has not, must eat what the others leave.

1885

PART IV. STORIES WRITTEN TO PICTURES (1885)

EVIL ALLURES, BUT GOOD ENDURES

There lived in olden times a good and kindly man. He had this world's goods in abundance, and many slaves to serve him. And the slaves prided themselves on their master, saying:

'There is no better lord than ours under the sun. He feeds and clothes us well, and gives us work suited to our strength. He bears no malice and never speaks a harsh word to any one. He is not like other masters, who treat their slaves worse than cattle: punishing them whether they deserve it or not, and never giving them a friendly word. He wishes us well, does good, and speaks kindly to us. We do not wish for a better life.'

Thus the slaves praised their lord, and the Devil, seeing it, was vexed that slaves should live in such love and harmony with their master. So getting one of them, whose name was Aleb, into his power, the Devil ordered him to tempt the other slaves. And one day, when they were all sitting together resting and talking of their master's goodness, Aleb raised his voice, and said:

'It is stupid to make so much of our master's goodness. The Devil himself would be kind to you, if you did what he wanted. We serve our master well, and humour him in all things. As soon as he thinks of anything, we do it: foreseeing all his wishes. What can he do but be kind to us? Just try how it will be if, instead of humouring him, we do him some harm instead. He will act like any one else, and will repay evil for evil, as the worst of masters do.

The other slaves began denying what Aleb had said and at last bet with him. Aleb undertook to make their master angry. If he failed, he was to lose his holiday garment; but if he succeeded, the other slaves were to give him theirs. Moreover, they promised to defend him against the master, and to set him free if he should be put in chains or imprisoned. Having arranged this bet, Aleb agreed to make his master angry next morning.

Aleb was a shepherd, and had in his charge a number of valuable, pure-bred sheep, of which his master was very fond. Next morning, when the master brought some visitors into the enclosure to show them the valuable sheep, Aleb winked at his companions, as if to say:

'See, now, how angry I will make him.'

All the other slaves assembled, looking in at the gates or over the fence, and the Devil climbed a tree near by to see how his servant would do his work. The master walked about the enclosure, showing his guests the ewes and lambs, and presently he wished to show them his finest ram.

'All the rams are valuable,' said he, 'but I have one with closely twisted horns, which is priceless. I prize him as the apple of my eye.'

Startled by the strangers, the sheep rushed about the enclosure, so that the visitors could not get a good look at the ram. As soon as it stood still, Aleb startled the sheep as if by accident, and they all got mixed up again. The visitors could not make out which was the priceless ram. At last the master got tired of it.

'Aleb, dear friend,' he said, 'pray catch our best ram for me, the one with the tightly twisted horns. Catch him very carefully, and hold him still for a moment.'

Scarcely had the master said this, when Aleb rushed in among the sheep like a lion, and clutched the priceless ram. Holding him fast by the wool, he seized the left hind leg with one hand, and, before his master's eyes, lifted it and jerked it so that it snapped like a dry branch. He had broken the ram's leg and it fell bleating on to its knees. Then Aleb seized the right hind leg, while the left twisted round and hung quite limp. The visitors and the slaves exclaimed in dismay, and the Devil, sitting up in the tree, rejoiced that Aleb had done his task so cleverly. The master looked as black as thunder, frowned, bent his head, and did not say a word. The visitors and the slaves were silent, too, waiting to see what would follow. After remaining silent for a while, the master shook himself as if to throw off some burden. Then he lifted his head, and raising his eyes heavenward, remained so for a short time. Presently the wrinkles passed from his face, and he looked down at Aleb with a smile saying:

'Oh, Aleb, Aleb! Your master bade you anger me; but my master is stronger than yours. I am not angry with you, but I will make your master angry. You are afraid that I shall punish you, and you have been wishing for your freedom. Know, then, Aleb, that I shall not punish you; but, as you wish to be free, here, before my guests, I set you free. Go where you like, and take your holiday garment with you!'

And the kind master returned with his guests to the house; but the Devil, grinding his teeth, fell down from the tree, and sank through the ground.

1885

LITTLE GIRLS WISER THAN MEN

It was an early Easter. Sledging was only just over; snow still lay in the yards; and water ran in streams down the village street.

Two little girls from different houses happened to meet in a lane between two homesteads, where the dirty water after running through the farm-yards had formed a large puddle. One girl was very small, the other a little bigger. Their mothers had dressed them both in new frocks. The little one wore a blue frock the other a yellow print, and both had red kerchiefs on their heads. They had just come from church when they met, and first they showed each other their finery, and then they began to play. Soon the fancy took them to splash about in the water, and the smaller one was going to step into the puddle, shoes and all, when the elder checked her:

'Don't go in so, Malásha,' said she, 'your mother will scold you. I will take off my shoes and stockings, and you take off yours.'

They did so, and then, picking up their skirts, began walking towards each other through the puddle. The water came up to Malásha's ankles, and she said:

'It is deep, Akoúlya, I'm afraid!'

'Come on,' replied the other. 'Don't be frightened. It won't get any deeper.'

When they got near one another, Akoúlya said:

'Mind, Malásha, don't splash. Walk carefully!'

She had hardly said this, when Malásha plumped down her foot so that the water splashed right on to Akoúlya's frock. The frock was splashed, and so were Akoúlya's eyes and nose. When she saw the stains on her frock, she was angry and ran after Malásha to strike her. Malásha was frightened, and seeing that she had got herself into trouble, she scrambled out of the puddle, and prepared to run home. Just then Akoúlya's mother happened to be passing, and seeing that her daughter's skirt was splashed, and her sleeves dirty, she said:

'You naughty, dirty girl, what have you been doing?'

'Malásha did it on purpose,' replied the girl.

At this Akoúlya's mother seized Malásha, and struck her on the back of her neck. Malásha began to howl so that she could be heard all down the street. Her mother came out.

'What are you beating my girl for?' said she; and began scolding her neighbour. One word led to another and they had an angry quarrel. The men came out and a crowd collected in the street, every one shouting and no one listening. They all went on quarrelling, till one gave another a push, and the affair had very nearly come to blows, when Akoúlya's old grandmother, stepping in among them, tried to calm them.

'What are you thinking of, friends? Is it right to behave so? On a day like this, too! It is a time for rejoicing, and not for such folly as this.'

They would not listen to the old woman and nearly knocked her off her feet. And she would not have been able to quiet the crowd, if it had not been for Akoúlya and Malásha themselves. While the women were abusing each other, Akoúlya had wiped the mud off her frock, and gone back to the puddle. She took a stone and began scraping away the earth in front of the puddle to make a channel through which the water could run out into the street. Presently Malásha joined her, and with a chip of wood helped her dig the channel. Just as the men were beginning to fight, the water from the little girls' channel ran streaming into the street towards the very place where the old woman was trying to pacify the men. The girls followed it; one running each side of the little stream.

'Catch it, Malásha! Catch it!' shouted Akoúlya; while Malásha could not speak for laughing.

Highly delighted, and watching the chip float along on their stream, the little girls ran straight into the group of men; and the old woman, seeing them, said to the men:

'Are you not ashamed of yourselves? To go fighting on account of these lassies, when they themselves have forgotten all about it, and are playing happily together. Dear little souls! They are wiser than you!'

The men looked at the little girls, and were ashamed, and, laughing at themselves, went back each to his own home.

'Except ye turn, and become as little children, ye shall in no wise enter into the kingdom of heaven.'

1885

ILYÁS

There once lived, in the Government of Oufá a Bashkír named Ilyas. His father, who died a year after he had found his son a wife, did not leave him much property. Ilyas then had only seven mares, two cows, and about a score of sheep. He was a good manager, however, and soon began to acquire more. He and his wife worked from morn till night; rising earlier than others and going later to bed; and his possessions increased year by year. Living in this way, Ilyas little by little acquired great wealth. At the end of thirty-five years he had 200 horses, 150 head of cattle, and 1,200 sheep. Hired laborers tended his flocks and herds, and hired women milked his mares and cows, and made kumiss, butter and cheese. Ilyas had abundance of everything, and every one in the district envied him. They said of him:

'Ilyas is a fortunate man: he has plenty of everything. This world must be a pleasant place for him.'

People of position heard of Ilyas and sought his acquaintance. Visitors came to him from afar; and he welcomed every one, and gave them food and drink. Whoever might come, there was always kumiss, tea, sherbet, and mutton to set before them. Whenever visitors arrived a sheep would be killed, or sometimes two; and if many guests came he would even slaughter a mare for them.

Ilyas had three children: two sons and a daughter; and he married them all off. While he was poor, his sons worked with him, and looked after the flocks and herds themselves; but when he grew rich they got spoiled and one of them took to drink. The eldest was killed in a brawl; and the younger, who had married a self-willed woman, ceased to obey his father, and they could not live together any more.

So they parted, and Ilyas gave his son a house and some of the cattle; and this diminished his wealth. Soon after that, a disease broke out among Ilyas's sheep, and many died. Then followed a bad harvest, and the hay crop failed; and many cattle died that winter. Then the Kirghíz captured his best herd of horses; and Ilyas's property dwindled away. It became smaller and smaller, while at the same time his strength grew less; till, by the time he was seventy years old, he had begun to sell his furs, carpets, saddles, and tents. At last he had to part with his remaining cattle, and found himself face to face with want. Before he knew how it had happened, he had lost everything, and in their old age he and his wife had to go into service. Ilyas had nothing left, except the clothes on his back, a fur cloak, a cup, his indoor shoes

and overshoes, and his wife, Sham-Shemagi, who also was old by this
time. The son who had parted from him had gone into a far country,
and his daughter was dead, so that there was no one to help the old
couple.

Their neighbour, Muhammad-Shah, took pity on them.
Muhammad-Shah was neither rich nor poor, but lived comfortably, and
was a good man. He remembered Ilyas's hospitality, and pitying him,
said:

'Come and live with me, Ilyas, you and your old woman. In
summer you can work in my melon-garden as much as your strength
allows, and in winter feed my cattle; and Sham-Shemagi shall milk my
mares and make kumiss. I will feed and clothe you both. When you
need anything, tell me, and you shall have it.'

Ilyas thanked his neighbour, and he and his wife took service with
Muhammad-Shah as laborers. At first the position seemed hard to
them, but they got used to it, and lived on, working as much as their
strength allowed.

Muhammad-Shah found it was to his advantage to keep such
people, because, having been masters themselves, they knew how to
manage and were not lazy, but did all the work they could. Yet it
grieved Muhammad-Shah to see people brought so low who had been
of such high standing.

It happened once that some of Muhammad-Shah's relatives came
from a great distance to visit him, and a Mullah came too. Muhammad-
Shah told Ilyas to catch a sheep and kill it. Ilyas skinned the sheep, and
boiled it, and sent it in to the guests. The guests ate the mutton, had
some tea, and then began drinking kumiss. As they were sitting with
their host on down cushions on a carpet, conversing and sipping kumiss
from their cups, Ilyas, having finished his work passed by the open
door. Muhammad-Shah, seeing him pass, said to one of the guests:

'Did you notice that old man who passed just now?'

'Yes,' said the visitor, 'what is there remarkable about him?'

'Only this—that he was once the richest man among us,' replied
the host. 'His name is Ilyas. You may have heard of him.'

'Of course I have heard of him,' the guest answered 'I never saw
him before, but his fame has spread far and wide.'

'Yes, and now he has nothing left,' said Muhammad-Shah, 'and he
lives with me as my labourer, and his old woman is here too—she
milks the mares.'

The guest was astonished: he clicked with his tongue, shook his
head, and said:

'Fortune turns like a wheel. One man it lifts, another it sets down!
Does not the old man grieve over all he has lost?'

'Who can tell. He lives quietly and peacefully, and works well.'

'May I speak to him?' asked the guest. 'I should like to ask him about his life.'

'Why not?' replied the master, and he called from the kibítka in which they were sitting:

'Babay;' (which in the Bashkir tongue means 'Grandfather ') 'come in and have a cup of kumiss with us, and call your wife here also.'

Ilyas entered with his wife; and after exchanging greetings with his master and the guests, he repeated a prayer, and seated himself near the door. His wife passed in behind the curtain and sat down with her mistress.

A Cap of kumiss was handed to Ilyas; he wished the guests and his master good health, bowed, drank a little, and put down the cup.

'Well, Daddy,' said the guest who had wished to speak to him, 'I suppose you feel rather sad at the sight of us. It must remind you of your former prosperity, and of your present sorrows.'

Ilyas smiled, and said:

'If I were to tell you what is happiness and what is misfortune, you would not believe me. You had better ask my wife. She is a woman, and what is in her heart is on her tongue. She will tell you the whole truth.'

The guest turned towards the curtain.

'Well, Granny,' he cried, 'tell me how your former happiness compares with your present misfortune.'

And Sham-Shemagi answered from behind the curtain:

'This is what I think about it: My old man and I lived for fifty years seeking happiness and not finding it; and it is only now, these last two years, since we had nothing left and have lived as laborers, that we have found real happiness, and we wish for nothing better than our present lot.'

The guests were astonished, and so was the master; he even rose and drew the curtain back, so as to see the old woman's face. There she stood with her arms folded, looking at her old husband, and smiling; and he smiled back at her. The old woman went on:

'I speak the truth and do not jest. For half a century we sought for happiness, and as long as we were rich we never found it. Now that we have nothing left, and have taken service as laborers, we have found such happiness that we want nothing better.'

'But in what does your happiness consist?' asked the guest.

'Why, in this,' she replied, 'when we were rich my husband and I had so many cares that we had no time to talk to one another, or to think of our souls, or to pray to God. Now we had visitors, and had to consider what food to set before them, and what presents to give them, lest they should speak ill of us. When they left, we had to look after our laborers who were always trying to shirk work and get the best food, while we wanted to get all we could out of them. So we sinned. Then we were in fear lest a wolf should kill a foal or a calf, or thieves steal our horses. We lay awake at night, worrying lest the ewes should overlie their lambs, and we got up again and again to see that all was well. One thing attended to, another care would spring up: how, for instance, to get enough fodder for the winter. And besides that, my old man and I used to disagree. He would say we must do so and so, and I would differ from him; and then we disputed—sinning again. So we passed from one trouble to another, from one sin to another, and found no happiness.'

'Well, and now?'

'Now, when my husband and I wake in the morning, we always have a loving word for one another and we live peacefully, having nothing to quarrel about. We have no care but how best to serve our master. We work as much as our strength allows and do it with a will, that our master may not lose but profit by us. When we come in, dinner or supper is ready and there is kumiss to drink. We have fuel to burn when it is cold and we have our fur cloak. And we have time to talk, time to think of our souls, and time to pray. For fifty years we sought happiness, but only now at last have we found it.'

The guests laughed.

But Ilyas said:

'Do not laugh, friends. It is not a matter for jesting—it is the truth of life. We also were foolish at first, and wept at the loss of our wealth; but now God has shown us the truth, and we tell it, not for our own consolation, but for your good.'

And the Mullah said:

'That is a wise speech. Ilyas has spoken the exact truth. The same is said in Holy Writ.'

And the guests ceased laughing and became thoughtful.

1885

PART V. FOLK-TALES RETOLD

THE THREE HERMITS (1886)

An Old Legend Current in the Volga District

'And in praying use not vain repetitions, as the Gentiles do: for they think that they shall be heard for their much speaking. Be not therefore like unto them: for your Father knoweth what things ye have need of, before ye ask Him.'—*Matt. vi. 7, 8*

A Bishop was sailing from Archangel to the Solovétsk Monastery; and on the same vessel were a number of pilgrims on their way to visit the shrines at that place. The voyage was a smooth one. The wind favourable, and the weather fair. The pilgrims lay on deck, eating, or sat in groups talking to one another. The Bishop, too, came on deck, and as he was pacing up and down, he noticed a group of men standing near the prow and listening to a fisherman who was pointing to the sea and telling them something. The Bishop stopped, and looked in the direction in which the man was pointing. He could see nothing however, but the sea glistening in the sunshine. He drew nearer to listen, but when the man saw him, he took off his cap and was silent. The rest of the people also took off their caps, and bowed.

'Do not let me disturb you, friends,' said the Bishop. 'I came to hear what this good man was saying.'

'The fisherman was telling us about the hermits,' replied one, a tradesman, rather bolder than the rest.

'What hermits?' asked the Bishop, going to the side of the vessel and seating himself on a box. 'Tell me about them. I should like to hear. What were you pointing at?'

'Why, that little island you can just see over there,' answered the man, pointing to a spot ahead and a little to the right. 'That is the island where the hermits live for the salvation of their souls.'

'Where is the island?' asked the Bishop. 'I see nothing.'

'There, in the distance, if you will please look along my hand. Do you see that little cloud? Below it and a bit to the left, there is just a faint streak. That is the island.'

The Bishop looked carefully, but his unaccustomed eyes could make out nothing but the water shimmering in the sun.

'I cannot see it,' he said. 'But who are the hermits that live there?'

'They are holy men,' answered the fisherman. 'I had long heard tell of them, but never chanced to see them myself till the year before last.'

And the fisherman related how once, when he was out fishing, he had been stranded at night upon that island, not knowing where he was. In the morning, as he wandered about the island, he came across an earth hut, and met an old man standing near it. Presently two others came out, and after having fed him, and dried his things, they helped him mend his boat.

'And what are they like?' asked the Bishop.

'One is a small man and his back is bent. He wears a priest's cassock and is very old; he must be more than a hundred, I should say. He is so old that the white of his beard is taking a greenish tinge, but he is always smiling, and his face is as bright as an angel's from heaven. The second is taller, but he also is very old. He wears tattered, peasant coat. His beard is broad, and of a yellowish grey colour. He is a strong man. Before I had time to help him, he turned my boat over as if it were only a pail. He too, is kindly and cheerful. The third is tall, and has a beard as white as snow and reaching to his knees. He is stern, with over-hanging eyebrows; and he wears nothing but a mat tied round his waist.'

'And did they speak to you?' asked the Bishop.

'For the most part they did everything in silence and spoke but little even to one another. One of them would just give a glance, and the others would understand him. I asked the tallest whether they had lived there long. He frowned, and muttered something as if he were angry; but the oldest one took his hand and smiled, and then the tall one was quiet. The oldest one only said: "Have mercy upon us," and smiled.'

While the fisherman was talking, the ship had drawn nearer to the island.

'There, now you can see it plainly, if your Grace will please to look,' said the tradesman, pointing with his hand.

The Bishop looked, and now he really saw a dark streak—which was the island. Having looked at it a while, he left the prow of the vessel, and going to the stern, asked the helmsman:

'What island is that?'

'That one,' replied the man, 'has no name. There are many such in this sea.'

'Is it true that there are hermits who live there for the salvation of their souls?'

'So it is said, your Grace, but I don't know if it's true. Fishermen say they have seen them; but of course they may only be spinning yarns.'

'I should like to land on the island and see these men,' said the Bishop. 'How could I manage it?'

'The ship cannot get close to the island,' replied the helmsman, 'but you might be rowed there in a boat. You had better speak to the captain.'

The captain was sent for and came.

'I should like to see these hermits,' said the Bishop. 'Could I not be rowed ashore?'

The captain tried to dissuade him.

'Of course it could be done,' said he, 'but we should lose much time. And if I might venture to say so to your Grace, the old men are not worth your pains. I have heard say that they are foolish old fellows, who understand nothing, and never speak a word, any more than the fish in the sea.'

'I wish to see them,' said the Bishop, 'and I will pay you for your trouble and loss of time. Please let me have a boat.'

There was no help for it; so the order was given. The sailors trimmed the sails, the steersman put up the helm, and the ship's course was set for the island. A chair was placed at the prow for the Bishop, and he sat there, looking ahead. The passengers all collected at the prow, and gazed at the island. Those who had the sharpest eyes could presently make out the rocks on it, and then a mud hut was seen. At last one man saw the hermits themselves. The captain brought a telescope and, after looking through it, handed it to the Bishop.

'It's right enough. There are three men standing on the shore. There, a little to the right of that big rock.'

The Bishop took the telescope, got it into position, and he saw the three men: a tall one, a shorter one, and one very small and bent, standing on the shore and holding each other by the hand.

The captain turned to the Bishop.

'The vessel can get no nearer in than this, your Grace. If you wish to go ashore, we must ask you to go in the boat, while we anchor here.'

The cable was quickly let out, the anchor cast, and the sails furled. There was a jerk, and the vessel shook. Then a boat having been lowered, the oarsmen jumped in, and the Bishop descended the ladder and took his seat. The men pulled at their oars, and the boat moved rapidly towards the island. When they came within a stone's throw they saw three old men: a tall one with only a mat tied round his waist: a shorter one in a tattered peasant coat, and a very old one bent with age and wearing an old cassock—all three standing hand in hand.

The oarsmen pulled in to the shore, and held on with the boathook while the Bishop got out.

The old men bowed to him, and he gave them his benediction, at which they bowed still lower. Then the Bishop began to speak to them.

'I have heard,' he said, 'that you, godly men, live here saving your own souls, and praying to our Lord Christ for your fellow men. I, an unworthy servant of Christ, am called, by God's mercy, to keep and teach His flock. I wished to see you, servants of God, and to do what I can to teach you, also.'

The old men looked at each other smiling, but remained silent.

'Tell me,' said the Bishop, 'what you are doing to save your souls, and how you serve God on this island.'

The second hermit sighed, and looked at the oldest, the very ancient one. The latter smiled, and said:

'We do not know how to serve God. We only serve and support ourselves, servant of God.'

'But how do you pray to God?' asked the Bishop.

'We pray in this way,' replied the hermit. 'Three are ye, three are we, have mercy upon us.'

And when the old man said this, all three raised their eyes to heaven, and repeated:

'Three are ye, three are we, have mercy upon us!'

The Bishop smiled.

'You have evidently heard something about the Holy Trinity,' said he. 'But you do not pray aright. You have won my affection, godly men. I see you wish to please the Lord, but you do not know how to serve Him. That is not the way to pray; but listen to me, and I will teach you. I will teach you, not a way of my own, but the way in which God in the Holy Scriptures has commanded all men to pray to Him.'

And the Bishop began explaining to the hermits how God had revealed Himself to men; telling them of God the Father, and God the Son, and God the Holy Ghost.

'God the Son came down on earth,' said he, 'to save men, and this is how He taught us all to pray. Listen and repeat after me: "Our Father."'

And the first old man repeated after him, 'Our Father,' and the second said, 'Our Father,' and the third said, 'Our Father.'

'Which art in heaven,' continued the Bishop.

The first hermit repeated, 'Which art in heaven,' but the second blundered over the words, and the tall hermit could not say them properly. His hair had grown over his mouth so that he could not speak plainly. The very old hermit, having no teeth, also mumbled indistinctly.

The Bishop repeated the words again, and the old men repeated them after him. The Bishop sat down on a stone, and the old men stood before him, watching his mouth, and repeating the words as he uttered them. And all day long the Bishop laboured, saying a word twenty, thirty, a hundred times over, and the old men repeated it after him. They blundered, and he corrected them, and made them begin again.

The Bishop did not leave off till he had taught them the whole of the Lord's prayer so that they could not only repeat it after him, but could say it by themselves. The middle one was the first to know it, and to repeat the whole of it alone. The Bishop made him say it again and again, and at last the others could say it too.

It was getting dark, and the moon was appearing over the water, before the Bishop rose to return to the vessel. When he took leave of the old men, they all bowed down to the ground before him. He raised them, and kissed each of them, telling them to pray as he had taught them. Then he got into the boat and returned to the ship.

And as he sat in the boat and was rowed to the ship he could hear the three voices of the hermits loudly repeating the Lord's prayer. As the boat drew near the vessel their voices could no longer be heard, but they could still be seen in the moonlight, standing as he had left them on the shore, the shortest in the middle, the tallest on the right, the middle one on the left. As soon as the Bishop had reached the vessel and got on board, the anchor was weighed and the sails unfurled. The wind filled them, and the ship sailed away, and the Bishop took a seat in the stern and watched the island they had left. For a time he could still see the hermits, but presently they disappeared from sight, though the island was still visible. At last it too vanished, and only the sea was to be seen, rippling in the moonlight.

The pilgrims lay down to sleep, and all was quiet on deck. The Bishop did not wish to sleep, but sat alone at the stern, gazing at the sea where the island was no longer visible, and thinking of the good old men. He thought how pleased they had been to learn the Lord's prayer; and he thanked God for having sent him to teach and help such godly men.

So the Bishop sat, thinking, and gazing at the sea where the island had disappeared. And the moonlight flickered before his eyes, sparkling, now here, now there, upon the waves. Suddenly he saw something white and shining, on the bright path which the moon cast across the sea. Was it a seagull, or the little gleaming sail of some small boat? The Bishop fixed his eyes on it, wondering.

'It must be a boat sailing after us,' thought he 'but it is overtaking us very rapidly. It was far, far away a minute ago, but now it is much nearer. It cannot be a boat, for I can see no sail; but whatever it may be, it is following us, and catching us up.'

And he could not make out what it was. Not a boat, nor a bird, nor a fish! It was too large for a man, and besides a man could not be out there in the midst of the sea. The Bishop rose, and said to the helmsman:

'Look there, what is that, my friend? What is it?' the Bishop repeated, though he could now see plainly what it was—the three hermits running upon the water, all gleaming white, their grey beards shining, and approaching the ship as quickly as though it were not morning.

The steersman looked and let go the helm in terror.

'Oh Lord! The hermits are running after us on the water as though it were dry land!'

The passengers hearing him, jumped up, and crowded to the stern. They saw the hermits coming along hand in hand, and the two outer ones beckoning the ship to stop. All three were gliding along upon the water without moving their feet. Before the ship could be stopped, the hermits had reached it, and raising their heads, all three as with one voice, began to say:

'We have forgotten your teaching, servant of God. As long as we kept repeating it we remembered, but when we stopped saying it for a time, a word dropped out, and now it has all gone to pieces. We can remember nothing of it. Teach us again.'

The Bishop crossed himself, and leaning over the ship's side, said:

'Your own prayer will reach the Lord, men of God. It is not for me to teach you. Pray for us sinners.'

And the Bishop bowed low before the old men; and they turned and went back across the sea. And a light shone until daybreak on the spot where they were lost to sight.

1886

THE IMP AND THE CRUST (1886)

A poor peasant set out early one morning to plough, taking with him for his breakfast a crust of bread. He got his plough ready, wrapped the bread in his coat, put it under a bush, and set to work. After a while when his horse was tired and he was hungry, the peasant fixed the plough, let the horse loose to graze and went to get his coat and his breakfast

He lifted the coat, but the bread was gone! He looked and looked, turned the coat over, shook it out—but the bread was gone. The peasant could not make this out at all.

'That's strange,' thought he; 'I saw no one, but all the same some one has been here and has taken the bread!'

It was an imp who had stolen the bread while the peasant was ploughing, and at that moment he was sitting behind the bush, waiting to hear the peasant swear and call on the Devil.

The peasant was sorry to lose his breakfast, but 'It can't be helped,' said he. 'After all, I shan't die of hunger! No doubt whoever took the bread needed it. May it do him good!'

And he went to the well, had a drink of water, and rested a bit. Then he caught his horse, harnessed it, and began ploughing again.

The imp was crestfallen at not having made the peasant sin, and he went to report what had happened to the Devil, his master.

He came to the Devil and told how he had taken the peasant's bread, and how the peasant instead of cursing had said, 'May it do him good!'

The Devil was angry, and replied: 'If the man got the better of you, it was your own fault—you don't understand your business! If the peasants, and their wives after them, take to that sort of thing, it will be all up with us. The matter can't be left like that! Go back at once,' said he, 'and put things right. If in three years you don't get the better of that peasant, I'll have you ducked in holy water!'

The imp was frightened. He scampered back to earth, thinking how he could redeem his fault. He thought and thought, and at last hit upon a good plan.

He turned himself into a labouring man, and went and took service with the poor peasant. The first year he advised the peasant to sow corn in a marshy place. The peasant took his advice, and sowed in the marsh. The year turned out a very dry one, and the crops of the other peasants were all scorched by the sun, but the poor peasant's corn grew thick and tall and full-eared. Not only had he grain enough to last him for the whole year, but he had much left over besides.

The next year the imp advised the peasant to sow on the hill; and it turned out a wet summer. Other people's corn was beaten down and rotted and the ears did not fill; but the peasant's crop, up on the hill, was a fine one. He had more grain left over than before, so that he did not know what to do with it all.

Then the imp showed the peasant how he could mash the grain and distil spirit from it; and the peasant made strong drink, and began to drink it himself and to give it to his friends.

So the imp went to the Devil, his master, and boasted that he had made up for his failure. The Devil said that he would come and see for himself how the case stood.

He came to the peasant's house, and saw that the peasant had invited his well-to-do neighbours and was treating them to drink. His wife was offering the drink to the guests, and as she handed it round she tumbled against the table and spilt a glassful.

The peasant was angry, and scolded his wife: 'What do you mean, you slut? Do you think it's ditchwater, you cripple, that you must go pouring good stuff like that over the floor?'

The imp nudged the Devil, his master, with his elbow: 'See,' said he, 'that's the man who did not grudge his last crust!'

The peasant, still railing at his wife, began to carry the drink round himself. Just then a poor peasant returning from work came in uninvited. He greeted the company, sat down, and saw that they were drinking. Tired with his day's work he felt that he too would like a drop. He sat and sat, and his mouth kept watering, but the host instead of offering him any only muttered: 'I can't find drink for every one who comes along.'

This pleased the Devil; but the imp chuckled and said, 'Wait a bit, there's more to come yet!'

The rich peasants drank, and their host drank too. And they began to make false, oily speeches to one another.

The Devil listened and listened, and praised the imp.

'If,' said he, 'the drink makes them so foxy that they begin to cheat each other, they will soon all be in our hands.'

'Wait for what's coming,' said the imp. 'Let them have another glass all round. Now they are like foxes, wagging their tails and trying to get round one another; but presently you will see them like savage wolves.'

The peasants had another glass each, and their talk became wilder and rougher. Instead of oily speeches they began to abuse and snarl at one another. Soon they took to fighting, and punched one another's noses. And the host joined in the fight, and he too got well beaten.

The Devil looked on and was much pleased at all this.

'This is first-rate!' said he.

But the imp replied: 'Wait a bit—the best is yet to come. Wait till they have had a third glass. Now they are raging like wolves, but let them have one more glass, and they will be like swine.'

The peasants had their third glass, and became quite like brutes. They muttered and shouted, not knowing why, and not listening to one another.

Then the party began to break up. Some went alone, some in twos, and some in threes, all staggering down the street. The host went out to speed his guests, but he fell on his nose into a puddle, smeared himself from top to toe, and lay there grunting like a hog.

This pleased the Devil still more.

'Well,' said he, 'you have hit on a first-rate drink, and have quite made up for your blunder about the bread. But now tell me how this drink is made. You must first have put in fox's blood: that was what made the peasants sly as foxes. Then, I suppose, you added wolf's blood: that is what made them fierce like wolves. And you must have finished off with swine's blood, to make them behave like swine.'

'No,' said the imp, 'that was not the way I did it. All I did was to see that the peasant had more corn than he needed. The blood of the beasts is always in man; but as long as he has only enough corn for his needs, it is kept in bounds. While that was the case, the peasant did not grudge his last crust. But when he had corn left over, he looked for ways of getting pleasure out of it. And I showed him a pleasure—drinking! And when he began to turn God's good gifts into spirits for his own pleasure—the fox's, wolf's and swine's blood in him all came out. If only he goes on drinking, he will always be a beast!'

The Devil praised the imp, forgave him for his former blunder, and advanced him to a post of high honour.

1886

HOW MUCH LAND DOES A MAN NEED? (1886)

I

An elder sister came to visit her younger sister in the country. The elder was married to a tradesman in town, the younger to a peasant in the village. As the sisters sat over their tea talking, the elder began to boast of the advantages of town life: saying how comfortably they lived there, how well they dressed, what fine clothes her children wore what good things they ate and drank, and how she went to the theatre, promenades, and entertainments.

The younger sister was piqued, and in turn disparage the life of a tradesman, and stood up for that of a peasant.

'I would not change my way of life for yours,' said she. We may live roughly, but at least we are free from anxiety. You live in better style than we do but though you often earn more than you need, you are very likely to lose all you have. You know the proverb, "Loss and gain are brothers twain." It often happens that people who are wealthy one day are begging their bread the next. Our way is safer. Though a peasant's life is not a fat one, it is a long one. We shall never grow rich, but we shall always have enough to eat.'

The elder sister said sneeringly:

'Enough? Yes, if you like to share with the pigs and the calves! What do you know of elegance or manners! However much your goodman may slave, you will die as you are living—on a dung heap—and your children the same.'

'Well, what of that?' replied the younger. 'Of course our work is rough and coarse. But, on the other hand, it is sure; and we need not bow to any one. But you, in your towns, are surrounded by temptations; to-day all may be right, but to-morrow the Evil One may tempt your husband with cards, wine, or women, and all will go to ruin. Don't such things happen often enough?'

Pahóm, the master of the house, was lying on the top of the oven, and he listened to the women's chatter.

'It is perfectly true,' thought he. 'Busy as we are from childhood tilling mother earth, we peasants have no time to let any nonsense settle in our heads. Our only trouble is that we haven't land enough. If I had plenty of land, I shouldn't fear the Devil himself!'

The women finished their tea, chatted a while about dress, and then cleared away the tea-things and lay down to sleep.

But the Devil had been sitting behind the oven, and had heard all that was said. He was pleased that the peasant's wife had led her husband into boasting, and that he had said that if he had plenty of land he would not fear the Devil himself.

'All right,' thought the Devil. 'We will have a tussle. I'll give you land enough; and by means of that land I will get you into my power.'

II

Close to the village there lived a lady, a small landowner, who had an estate of about three hundred acres. She had always lived on good terms with the peasants, until she engaged as her steward an old soldier, who took to burdening the people with fines. However careful Pahóm tried to be, it happened again and again that now a horse of his got among the lady's oats, now a cow strayed into her garden, now his calves found their way into her meadows—and he always had to pay a fine.

Pahóm paid up, but grumbled, and, going home in a temper, was rough with his family. All through that summer, Pahóm had much trouble because of this steward; and he was even glad when winter came and the cattle had to be stabled. Though he grudged the fodder when they could no longer graze on the pasture-land, at least he was free from anxiety about them.

In the winter the news got about that the lady was going to sell her land, and that the keeper of the inn on the high road was bargaining for it. When the peasants heard this they were very much alarmed.

'Well', thought they, 'if the innkeeper gets the land, he will worry us with fines worse than the lady's steward. We all depend on that estate.'

So the peasants went on behalf of their Commune and asked the lady not to sell the land to the innkeeper offering her a better price for it themselves. The lady agreed to let them have it. Then the peasants tried to arrange for the Commune to buy the whole estate so that it might be held by them all in common. They met twice to discuss it, but could not settle the matter; the Evil One sowed discord among them, and they could not agree. So they decided to buy the land individually, each according to his means; and the lady agreed to this plan as she had to the other.

Presently Pahóm heard that a neighbour of his was buying fifty acres, and that the lady had consented to accept one half in cash and to wait a year for the other half. Pahóm felt envious

'Look at that,' thought he, 'the land is all being sold, and I shall get none of it.' So he spoke to his wife.

'Other people are buying,' said he, 'and we must also buy twenty acres or so. Life is becoming impossible. That steward is simply crushing us with his fines.'

So they put their heads together and considered how they could manage to buy it. They had one hundred roubles laid by. They sold a colt, and one half of their bees; hired out one of their sons as a labourer, and took his wages in advance; borrowed the rest from a brother-in-law, and so scraped together half the purchase money.

Having done this, Pahóm chose out a farm of forty acres, some of it wooded, and went to the lady to bargain for it. They came to an agreement, and he shook hands with her upon it, and paid her a deposit in advance. Then they went to town and signed the deeds; he paying half the price down, and undertaking to pay the remainder within two years.

So now Pahóm had land of his own. He borrowed seed, and sowed it on the land he had bought. The harvest was a good one, and within a year he had managed to pay off his debts both to the lady and to his brother-in-law. So he became a landowner, ploughing and sowing his own land, making hay on his own land, cutting his own trees, and feeding his cattle on his own pasture. When he went out to plough his fields, or to look at his growing corn, or at his grass-meadows, his heart would fill with joy. The grass that grew and the flowers that bloomed there, seemed to him unlike any that grew elsewhere. Formerly, when he had passed by that land it had appeared the same as any other land, but now it seemed quite different.

III

So Pahóm was well-contented, and everything would have been right if the neighbouring peasants would only not have trespassed on his corn-fields and meadows. He appealed to them most civilly, but they still went on: now the Communal herdsmen would let the village cows stray into his meadows; then horses from the night pasture would get among his corn. Pahóm turned them out again and again, and forgave their owners, and for a long time he forbore from prosecuting any one. But at last he lost patience and complained to the District Court. He knew it was the peasants' want of land, and no evil intent on their part, that caused the trouble; but he thought:

'I cannot go on overlooking it, or they will destroy all I have. They must be taught a lesson.'

So he had them up, gave them one lesson, and then another, and two or three of the peasants were fined. After a time Pahóm's neighbours began to bear him a grudge for this, and would now and then let their cattle on to his land on purpose. One peasant even got into Pahóm's wood at night and cut down five young lime trees for their bark. Pahóm passing through the wood one day noticed something white. He came nearer, and saw the stripped trunks lying on the ground, and close by stood the stumps, where the trees had been. Pahóm was furious.

'If he had only cut one here and there it would have been bad enough,' thought Pahóm, 'but the rascal has actually cut down a whole clump. If I could only find out who did this, I would pay him out.'

He racked his brains as to who it could be. Finally he decided: 'It must be Simon—no one else could have done it.' So he went to Simon's homestead to have a look round, but he found nothing, and only had an angry scene. However, he now felt more certain than ever that Simon had done it, and he lodged a complaint. Simon was summoned. The case was tried, and re-tried, and at the end of it all Simon was acquitted, there being no evidence against him. Pahóm felt still more aggrieved, and let his anger loose upon the Elder and the Judges.

'You let thieves grease your palms,' said he. 'If you were honest folk yourselves, you would not let a thief go free.'

So Pahóm quarrelled with the Judges and with his neighbours.

Threats to burn his building began to be uttered. So though Pahóm had more land, his place in the Commune was much worse than before.

About this time a rumour got about that many people were moving to new parts.

'There's no need for me to leave my land,' thought Pahóm. 'But some of the others might leave our village and then there would be more room for us. I would take over their land myself, and make my estate a bit bigger. I could then live more at ease. As it is, I am still too cramped to be comfortable.

One day Pahóm was sitting at home, when a peasant, passing through the village, happened to call in. He was allowed to stay the night, and supper was given him. Pahóm had a talk with this peasant and asked him where he came from. The stranger answered that he came from beyond the Volga, where he had been working. One word led to another, and the man went on to say that many people were settling in those parts. He told how some people from his village had settled there. They had joined the Commune, and had had twenty-five acres per man granted them. The land was so good, he said, that the rye sown on it grew as high as a horse, and so thick that five cuts of a sickle made a sheaf. One peasant, he said, had brought nothing with him but his bare hands, and now he had six horses and two cows of his own.

Pahóm's heart kindled with desire. He thought:

'Why should I suffer in this narrow hole, if one can live so well elsewhere? I will sell my land and my homestead here, and with the money I will start afresh over there and get everything new. In this crowded place one is always having trouble. But I must first go and find out all about it myself.'

Towards summer he got ready and started. He went down the Volga on a steamer to Samára, then walked another three hundred miles on foot, and at last reached the place. It was just as the stranger had said. The peasants had plenty of land: every man had twenty-five acres of Communal land given him for his use, and any one who had money could buy, besides, at two shillings an acre as much good freehold land as he wanted.

Having found out all he wished to know, Pahóm returned home as autumn came on, and began selling off his belongings. He sold his land at a profit, sold his homestead and all his cattle, and withdrew from membership of the Commune. He only waited till the spring, and then started with his family for the new settlement.

IV

As soon as Pahóm and his family arrived at their new abode, he applied for admission into the Commune of a large village. He stood treat to the Elders, and obtained the necessary documents. Five shares of Communal land were given him for his own and his sons' use: that is to say—125 acres (not all together but in different fields) besides the use of the Communal pasture. Pahóm put up the buildings he needed, and bought cattle. Of the Communal land alone he had three times as much as at his former home, and the land was good corn-land. He was ten times better off than he had been. He had plenty of arable land and pasturage, and could keep as many head of cattle as he liked.

At first, in the bustle of building and settling down, Pahóm was pleased with it all, but when he got used to it he began to think that even here he had not enough land. The first year, he sowed wheat on his share of the Communal land, and had a good crop. He wanted to go on sowing wheat, but had not enough Communal land for the purpose, and what he had already used was not available; for in those parts wheat is only sown on virgin soil or on fallow land. It is sown for one or two years, and then the land lies fallow till it is again overgrown with prairie grass. There were many who wanted such land, and there was not enough for all; so that people quarrelled about it. Those who were better off, wanted it for growing wheat, and those who were poor, wanted it to let to dealers, so that they might raise money to pay their taxes. Pahóm wanted to sow more wheat; so he rented land from a dealer for a year. He sowed much wheat and had a fine crop, but the land was too far from the village—the wheat had to be carted more than ten miles. After a time Pahóm noticed that some peasant-dealers were living on separate farms, and were growing wealthy; and he thought:

'If I were to buy some freehold land, and have a homestead on it, it would be a different thing altogether. Then it would all be nice and compact.'

The question of buying freehold land recurred to him again and again.

He went on in the same way for three years: renting land and sowing wheat. The seasons turned out well and the crops were good, so that he began to lay money by. He might have gone on living contentedly, but he grew tired of having to rent other people's land every year, and having to scramble for it. Wherever there was good land to be had, the peasants would rush for it and it was taken up at once, so that unless you were sharp about it you got none. It happened in the third year that he and a dealer together rented a piece of pasture land from some peasants; and they had already ploughed it up, when there was some dispute, and the peasants went to law about it, and things fell out so that the labour was all lost.

'If it were my own land,' thought Pahóm, 'I should be independent, and there would not be all this unpleasantness.'

So Pahóm began looking out for land which he could buy; and he came across a peasant who had bought thirteen hundred acres, but having got into difficulties was willing to sell again cheap. Pahóm bargained and haggled with him, and at last they settled the price at 1,500 roubles, part in cash and part to be paid later. They had all but clinched the matter, when a passing dealer happened to stop at Pahóm's one day to get a feed for his horses. He drank tea with Pahóm, and they had a talk. The dealer said that he was just returning from the land of the Bashkírs, far away, where he had bought thirteen thousand acres of land, all for 1,000 roubles. Pahóm questioned him further, and the tradesman said:

'All one need do is to make friends with the chiefs. I gave away about one hundred roubles, worth of dressing-gowns and carpets, besides a case of tea, and I gave wine to those who would drink it; and I got the land for less than twopence an acre. And he showed Pahóm the title-deeds, saying:

'The land lies near a river, and the whole prairie is virgin soil.'

Pahóm plied him with questions, and the tradesman said:

'There is more land there than you could cover if you walked a year, and it all belongs to the Bashkírs. They are as simple as sheep, and land can be got almost for nothing.'

'There now,' thought Pahóm, 'with my one thousand roubles, why should I get only thirteen hundred acres, and saddle myself with a debt besides. If I take it out there, I can get more than ten times as much for the money.'

V

Pahóm inquired how to get to the place, and as soon as the tradesman had left him, he prepared to go there himself. He left his wife to look after the homestead, and started on his journey taking his man with him. They stopped at a town on their way, and bought a case of tea, some wine, and other presents, as the tradesman had advised. On and on they went until they had gone more than three hundred miles, and on the seventh day they came to a place where the Bashkírs had pitched their tents. It was all just as the tradesman had said. The people lived on the steppes, by a river, in felt-covered tents. They neither tilled the ground, nor ate bread. Their cattle and horses grazed in herds on the steppe. The colts were tethered behind the tents, and the mares were driven to them twice a day. The mares were milked, and from the milk kumiss was made. It was the women who prepared kumiss, and they also made cheese. As far as the men were concerned, drinking kumiss and tea, eating mutton, and playing on their pipes, was all they cared about. They were all stout and merry, and all the summer long they never thought of doing any work. They were quite ignorant, and knew no Russian, but were good-natured enough.

As soon as they saw Pahóm, they came out of their tents and gathered round their visitor. An interpreter was found, and Pahóm told them he had come about some land. The Bashkírs seemed very glad they took Pahóm and led him into one of the best tents, where they made him sit on some down cushions placed on a carpet, while they sat round him. They gave him tea and kumiss, and had a sheep killed, and gave him mutton to eat. Pahóm took presents out of his cart and distributed them among the Bashkírs, and divided amongst them the tea. The Bashkírs were delighted. They talked a great deal among themselves, and then told the interpreter to translate.

'They wish to tell you,' said the interpreter, 'that they like you, and that it is our custom to do all we can to please a guest and to repay him for his gifts. You have given us presents, now tell us which of the things we possess please you best, that we may present them to you.'

'What pleases me best here,' answered Pahóm 'is your land. Our land is crowded, and the soil is exhausted; but you have plenty of land and it is good land. I never saw the like of it.'

The interpreter translated. The Bashkírs talked among themselves for a while. Pahóm could not understand what they were saying, but saw that they were much amused, and that they shouted and laughed. Then they were silent and looked at Pahóm while the interpreter said:

'They wish me to tell you that in return for your presents they will gladly give you as much land as you want. You have only to point it out with your hand and it is yours.'

The Bashkírs talked again for a while and began to dispute. Pahóm asked what they were disputing about, and the interpreter told him that some of them thought they ought to ask their Chief about the land and not act in his absence, while others thought there was no need to wait for his return.

VI

While the Bashkírs were disputing, a man in a large fox-fur cap appeared on the scene. They all became silent and rose to their feet. The interpreter said, 'This is our Chief himself.'

Pahóm immediately fetched the best dressing-gown and five pounds of tea, and offered these to the Chief. The Chief accepted them, and seated himself in the place of honour. The Bashkírs at once began telling him something. The Chief listened for a while, then made a sign with his head for them to be silent, and addressing himself to Pahóm, said in Russian:

'Well, let it be so. Choose whatever piece of land you like; we have plenty of it.'

'How can I take as much as I like?' thought Pahóm. 'I must get a deed to make it secure, or else they may say, "It is yours," and afterwards may take it away again.'

'Thank you for your kind words,' he said aloud. 'You have much land, and I only want a little. But I should like to be sure which bit is mine. Could it not be measured and made over to me? Life and death are in God's hands. You good people give it to me, but your children might wish to take it away again.'

'You are quite right,' said the Chief. 'We will make it over to you.'

'I heard that a dealer had been here,' continued Pahóm, 'and that you gave him a little land, too, and signed title-deeds to that effect. I should like to have it done in the same way.'

The Chief understood.

'Yes,' replied he, 'that can be done quite easily. We have a scribe, and we will go to town with you and have the deed properly sealed.'

'And what will be the price?' asked Pahóm.

'Our price is always the same: one thousand roubles a day.'

Pahóm did not understand.

'A day? What measure is that? How many acres would that be?'

'We do not know how to reckon it out,' said the Chief. 'We sell it by the day. As much as you can go round on your feet in a day is yours, and the price is one thousand roubles a day.'

Pahóm was surprised.

'But in a day you can get round a large tract of land,' he said.

The Chief laughed.

'It will all be yours!' said he. 'But there is one condition: If you don't return on the same day to the spot whence you started, your money is lost.'

'But how am I to mark the way that I have gone?'

'Why, we shall go to any spot you like, and stay there. You must start from that spot and make your round, taking a spade with you. Wherever you think necessary, make a mark. At every turning, dig a hole and pile up the turf; then afterwards we will go round with a plough from hole to hole. You may make as large a circuit as you please, but before the sun sets you must return to the place you started from. All the land you cover will be yours.'

Pahóm was delighted. It was decided to start early next morning. They talked a while, and after drinking some more kumiss and eating some more mutton, they had tea again, and then the night came on. They gave Pahóm a feather-bed to sleep on, and the Bashkírs dispersed for the night, promising to assemble the next morning at daybreak and ride out before sunrise to the appointed spot.

VII

Pahóm lay on the feather-bed, but could not sleep. He kept thinking about the land.

'What a large tract I will mark off!' thought he. 'I can easily do thirty-five miles in a day. The days are long now, and within a circuit of thirty-five miles what a lot of land there will be! I will sell the poorer land, or let it to peasants, but I'll pick out the best and farm it. I will buy two ox-teams, and hire two more laborers. About a hundred and fifty acres shall be plough-land, and I will pasture cattle on the rest.'

Pahóm lay awake all night, and dozed off only just before dawn. Hardly were his eyes closed when he had a dream. He thought he was lying in that same tent, and heard somebody chuckling outside. He wondered who it could be, and rose and went out and he saw the Bashkír Chief sitting in front of the tent holding his sides and rolling about with laughter. Going nearer to the Chief, Pahóm asked: 'What are you laughing at?' But he saw that it was no longer the Chief, but the dealer who had recently stopped at his house and had told him about the land. Just as Pahóm was going to ask, 'Have you been here long?' he saw that it was not the dealer, but the peasant who had come up from the Volga, long ago, to Pahóm's old home. Then he saw that it was not the peasant either, but the Devil himself with hoofs and horns sitting there and chuckling, and before him lay a man barefoot, prostrate on the ground, with only trousers and a shirt on. And Pahóm dreamt that he looked more attentively to see what sort of a man it was that was lying there, and he saw that the man was dead and that it was himself! He awoke horror-struck.

'What things one does dream,' thought he.

Looking round he saw through the open door that the dawn was breaking.

'It's time to wake them up,' thought he. 'We ought to be starting.'

He got up, roused his man (who was sleeping in his cart), bade him harness; and went to call the Bashkírs.

'It's time to go to the steppe to measure the land,' he said.

The Bashkírs rose and assembled, and the Chief came too. Then they began drinking kumiss again, and offered Pahóm some tea, but he would not wait.

'If we are to go, let us go. It is high time,' said he.

VIII

The Bashkírs got ready and they all started: some mounted on horses, and some in carts. Pahóm drove in his own small cart with his servant, and took a spade with him. When they reached the steppe, the morning red was beginning to kindle. They ascended a hillock (called by the Bashkírs a shikhan) and dismounting from their carts and their horses, gathered in one spot. The Chief came up to Pahóm and stretching out his arm towards the plain:

'See,' said he, 'all this, as far as your eye can reach, is ours. You may have any part of it you like.'

Pahóm's eyes glistened: it was all virgin soil, as flat as the palm of your hand, as black as the seed of a poppy, and in the hollows different kinds of grasses grew breast high.

The Chief took off his fox-fur cap, placed it on the ground and said:

'This will be the mark. Start from here, and return here again. All the land you go round shall be yours.'

Pahóm took out his money and put it on the cap. Then he took off his outer coat, remaining in his sleeveless under-coat. He unfastened his girdle and tied it tight below his stomach, put a little bag of bread into the breast of his coat, and tying a flask of water to his girdle, he drew up the tops of his boots, took the spade from his man, and stood ready to start. He considered for some moments which way he had better go—it was tempting everywhere.

'No matter,' he concluded, 'I will go towards the rising sun.'

He turned his face to the east, stretched himself and waited for the sun to appear above the rim.

'I must lose no time,' he thought, 'and it is easier walking while it is still cool.'

The sun's rays had hardly flashed above the horizon, before Pahóm, carrying the spade over his shoulder went down into the steppe.

Pahóm started walking neither slowly nor quickly. After having gone a thousand yards he stopped, dug a hole, and placed pieces of turf one on another to make it more visible. Then he went on; and now that he had walked off his stiffness he quickened his pace. After a while he dug another hole.

Pahóm looked back. The hillock could be distinctly seen in the sunlight, with the people on it, and the glittering tires of the cart-wheels. At a rough guess Pahóm concluded that he had walked three miles. It was growing warmer; he took off his under-coat, flung it across his shoulder, and went on again. It had grown quite warm now; he looked at the sun, it was time to think of breakfast.

'The first shift is done, but there are four in a day, and it is too soon yet to turn. But I will just take off my boots,' said he to himself.

He sat down, took off his boots, stuck them into his girdle, and went on. It was easy walking now.

'I will go on for another three miles,' thought he, 'and then turn to the left. This spot is so fine, that it would be a pity to lose it. The further one goes, the better the land seems.'

He went straight on for a while, and when he looked round, the hillock was scarcely visible and the people on it looked like black ants, and he could just see something glistening there in the sun.

'Ah,' thought Pahóm, 'I have gone far enough in this direction, it is time to turn. Besides I am in a regular sweat, and very thirsty.'

He stopped, dug a large hole, and heaped up pieces of turf. Next he untied his flask, had a drink, and then turned sharply to the left. He went on and on; the grass was high, and it was very hot.

Pahóm began to grow tired: he looked at the sun and saw that it was noon.

'Well,' he thought, 'I must have a rest.'

He sat down, and ate some bread and drank some water; but he did not lie down, thinking that if he did he might fall asleep. After sitting a little while, he went on again. At first he walked easily: the food had strengthened him; but it had become terribly hot, and he felt sleepy; still he went on, thinking: 'An hour to suffer, a life-time to live.'

He went a long way in this direction also, and was about to turn to the left again, when he perceived a damp hollow: 'It would be a pity to leave that out,' he thought. 'Flax would do well there.' So he went on past the hollow, and dug a hole on the other side of it before he turned the corner. Pahóm looked towards the hillock. The heat made the air hazy: it seemed to be quivering, and through the haze the people on the hillock could scarcely be seen.

'Ah!' thought Pahóm, 'I have made the sides too long; I must make this one shorter.' And he went along the third side stepping faster. He looked at the sun: it was nearly half way to the horizon, and he had not yet done two miles of the third side of the square. He was still ten miles from the goal.

'No,' he thought, 'though it will make my land lop-sided, I must hurry back in a straight line now. I might go too far, and as it is I have a great deal of land.'

So Pahóm hurriedly dug a hole, and turned straight towards the hillock.

IX

Pahóm went straight towards the hillock, but he now walked with difficulty. He was done up with the heat, his bare feet were cut and bruised, and his legs began to fail. He longed to rest, but it was impossible if he meant to get back before sunset. The sun waits for no man, and it was sinking lower and lower.

'Oh dear,' he thought, 'if only I have not blundered trying for too much! What if I am too late?'

He looked towards the hillock and at the sun. He was still far from his goal, and the sun was already near the rim.

Pahóm walked on and on; it was very hard walking, but he went quicker and quicker. He pressed on, but was still far from the place. He began running, threw away his coat, his boots, his flask, and his cap, and kept only the spade which he used as a support.

'What shall I do,' he thought again, 'I have grasped too much, and ruined the whole affair. I can't get there before the sun sets.'

And this fear made him still more breathless. Pahóm went on running, his soaking shirt and trousers stuck to him, and his mouth was parched. His breast was working like a blacksmith's bellows, his heart was beating like a hammer, and his legs were giving way as if they did not belong to him. Pahóm was seized with terror lest he should die of the strain.

Though afraid of death, he could not stop. 'After having run all that way they will call me a fool if I stop now,' thought he. And he ran on and on, and drew near and heard the Bashkírs yelling and shouting to him, and their cries inflamed his heart still more. He gathered his last strength and ran on.

The sun was close to the rim, and cloaked in mist looked large, and red as blood. Now, yes now, it was about to set! The sun was quite low, but he was also quite near his aim. Pahóm could already see the people on the hillock waving their arms to hurry him up. He could see the fox-fur cap on the ground, and the money on it, and the Chief sitting on the ground holding his sides. And Pahóm remembered his dream.

'There is plenty of land,' thought he, 'but will God let me live on it? I have lost my life, I have lost my life! I shall never reach that spot!'

Pahóm looked at the sun, which had reached the earth: one side of it had already disappeared. With all his remaining strength he rushed on, bending his body forward so that his legs could hardly follow fast enough to keep him from falling. Just as he reached the hillock it suddenly grew dark. He looked up—the sun had already set! He gave a cry: 'All my labour has been in vain,' thought he, and was about to stop, but he heard the Bashkírs still shouting, and remembered that though to him, from below, the sun seemed to have set, they on the hillock could still see it. He took a long breath and ran up the hillock. It was still light there. He reached the top and saw the cap. Before it sat the Chief laughing and holding his sides. Again Pahóm remembered his dream, and he uttered a cry: his legs gave way beneath him, he fell forward and reached the cap with his hands.

'Ah, that's a fine fellow!' exclaimed the Chief 'He has gained much land!'

Pahóm's servant came running up and tried to raise him, but he saw that blood was flogging from his mouth. Pahóm was dead!

The Bashkírs clicked their tongues to show their pity.

His servant picked up the spade and dug a grave long enough for Pahóm to he in, and buried him in it. Six feet from his head to his heels was all he needed.

1886

A GRAIN AS BIG AS A HEN'S EGG (1886)

One day some children found, in a ravine, a thing shaped like a grain of corn, with a groove down the middle, but as large as a hen's egg. A traveller passing by saw the thing, bought it from the children for a penny, and taking it to town sold it to the King as a curiosity.

The King called together his wise men, and told them to find out what the thing was. The wise men pondered and pondered and could not make head or tail of it, till one day, when the thing was lying on a window-sill, a hen flew in and pecked at it till she made a hole in it, and then every one saw that it was a grain of corn. The wise men went to the King and said:

'It is a grain of corn.'

At this the King was much surprised; and he ordered the learned men to find out when and where such corn had grown. The learned men pondered again, and searched in their books, but could find nothing about it. So they returned to the King and said:

'We can give you no answer. There is nothing about it in our books. You will have to ask the peasants; perhaps some of them may have heard from their fathers when and where grain grew to such a size.'

So the King gave orders that some very old peasant should be brought before him; and his servants found such a man and brought him to the King. Old and bent, ashy pale and toothless, he just managed with the help of two crutches to totter into the King's presence.

The King showed him the grain, but the old man could hardly see it; he took it, however, and felt it with his hands. The King questioned him, saying:

'Can you tell us, old man, where such grain as this grew? Have you ever bought such corn, or sown such in your fields?'

The old man was so deaf that he could hardly hear what the King said, and only understood with great difficulty.

'No!' he answered at last, 'I never sowed nor reaped any like it in my fields, nor did I ever buy any such. When we bought corn, the grains were always as small as they are now. But you might ask my father. He may have heard where such grain grew.'

So the King sent for the old man's father, and he was found and brought before the King. He came walking with one crutch. The King showed him the grain, and the old peasant, who was still able to see, took a good look at it. And the King asked him:

'Can you not tell us, old man, where corn like this used to grow? Have you ever bought any like it, or sown any in your fields?'

Though the old man was rather hard of hearing, he still heard better than his son had done.

'No,' he said, 'I never sowed nor reaped any grain like this in my field. As to buying, I never bought any, for in my time money was not yet in use. Every one grew his own corn, and when there was any need we shared with one another. I do not know where corn like this grew. Ours was larger and yielded more flour than present-day grain, but I never saw any like this. I have, however, heard my father say that in his time the grain grew larger and yielded more flour than ours. You had better ask him.'

So the King sent for this old man's father, and they found him too, and brought him before the King. He entered walking easily and without crutches: his eye was clear, his hearing good, and he spoke distinctly. The King showed him the grain, and the old grandfather looked at it, and turned it about in his hand.

'It is long since I saw such a fine grain,' said he, and he bit a piece off and tasted it.

'It's the very same kind,' he added.

'Tell me, grandfather,' said the King, 'when and where was such corn grown? Have you ever bought any like it, or sown any in your fields?'

And the old man replied:

'Corn like this used to grow everywhere in my time. I lived on corn like this in my young days, and fed others on it. It was grain like this that we used to sow and reap and thrash.'

And the King asked:

'Tell me, grandfather, did you buy it anywhere, or did you grow it all yourself?'

The old man smiled.

'In my time,' he answered, 'no one ever thought of such a sin as buying or selling bread; and we knew nothing of money. Each man had corn enough of his own.'

'Then tell me, grandfather,' asked the King, 'where was your field, where did you grow corn like this?'

And the grandfather answered:

'My field was God's earth. Wherever I ploughed, there was my field. Land was free. It was a thing no man called his own. Labour was the only thing men called their own.'

'Answer me two more questions,' said the King. 'The first is, Why did the earth bear such grain then and has ceased to do so now? And the second is, Why your grandson walks with two crutches, your son with one, and you yourself with none? Your eyes are bright, your teeth sound, and your speech clear and pleasant to the ear. How have these things come about?'

And the old man answered:

'These things are so, because men have ceased to live by their own labour, and have taken to depending on the labour of others. In the old time, men lived according to God's law. They had what was their own, and coveted not what others had produced.

1886

THE GODSON (1886)

'Ye have heard that it was said, An eye for an eye, and a tooth for a tooth, but I say unto you, Resist not him that is evil.'—*Matt. v. 38, 39*

'Vengeance is mine; I will repay.'—*Rom. xii. 19*

I

A son was born to a poor peasant. He was glad and went to his neighbour to ask him to stand godfather to the boy. The neighbour refused—he did not like standing godfather to a poor man's child. The peasant asked another neighbour, but he too refused, and after that the poor father went to every house in the village, but found no one willing to be godfather to his son. So he set off to another village, and on the way he met a man who stopped and said:

'Good-day, my good man; where are you off to?'

'God has given me a child,' said the peasant, 'to rejoice my eyes in youth, to comfort my old age, and to pray for my soul after death. But I am poor, and no one in our village will stand godfather to him, so I am now on my way to seek a godfather for him elsewhere.'

'Let me be godfather,' said the stranger.

The peasant was glad, and thanked him, but added: 'And whom shall I ask to be godmother?'

'Go to the town,' replied the stranger, 'and, in the square, you will see a stone house with shop-windows in the front. At the entrance you will find the tradesman to whom it belongs. Ask him to let his daughter stand godmother to your child.'

The peasant hesitated.

'How can I ask a rich tradesman?' said he. 'He will despise me, and will not let his daughter come.'

'Don't trouble about that. Go and ask. Get everything ready by to-morrow morning, and I will come to the christening.'

The poor peasant returned home, and then drove to the town to find the tradesman. He had hardly taken his horse into the yard, when the tradesman himself came out.

'What do you want?' said he.

'Why, sir,' said the peasant, 'you see God has given me a son to rejoice my eyes in youth, to comfort my old age, and to pray for my soul after death. Be so kind as to let your daughter stand godmother to him.

'And when is the christening?' said the tradesman.

'To-morrow morning.'

'Very well. Go in peace. She shall be with you at Mass to-morrow morning.'

The next day the godmother came, and the godfather also, and the infant was baptized. Immediately after the christening the godfather went away. They did not know who he was, and never saw him again.

II

The child grew up to be a joy to his parents. He was strong, willing to work, clever and obedient. When he was ten years old his parents sent him to school to learn to read and write. What others learnt in five years, he learnt in one, and soon there was nothing more they could teach him.

Easter came round, and the boy went to see his godmother, to give her his Easter greeting.

'Father and mother,' said he when he got home again, 'where does my godfather live? I should like to give him my Easter greeting, too.'

And his father answered:

'We know nothing about your godfather, dear son. We often regret it ourselves. Since the day you were christened we have never seen him, nor had any news of him. We do not know where he lives, or even whether he is still alive.'

The son bowed to his parents.

'Father and mother,' said he, 'let me go and look for my godfather. I must find him and give him my Easter greeting.

So his father and mother let him go, and the boy set off to find his godfather.

III

The boy left the house and set out along the road. He had been walking for several hours when he met a stranger who stopped him and said:

'Good-day to you, my boy. Where are you going?'

And the boy answered:

'I went to see my godmother and to give her my Easter greeting, and when I got home I asked my parents where my godfather lives, that I might go and greet him also. They told me they did not know. They said he went away as soon as I was christened, and they know nothing about him, not even if he be still alive. But I wished to see my godfather, and so I have set out to look for him.'

Then the stranger said: 'I am your godfather.'

The boy was glad to hear this. After kissing his godfather three times for an Easter greeting, he asked him:

'Which way are you going now, godfather? If you are coming our way, please come to our house; but if you are going home, I will go with you.'

'I have no time now,' replied his godfather, 'to come to your house. I have business in several villages; but I shall return home again to-morrow. Come and see me then.'

'But how shall I find you, godfather?'

'When you leave home, go straight towards the rising sun, and you will come to a forest; going through the forest you will come to a glade. When you reach this glade sit down and rest awhile, and look around you and see what happens. On the further side of the forest you will find a garden, and in it a house with a golden roof. That is my home. Go up to the gate, and I will myself be there to meet you.'

And having said this the godfather disappeared from his godson's sight.

IV

The boy did as his godfather had told him. He walked eastward until he reached a forest, and there he came to a glade, and in the midst of the glade he saw a pine tree to a branch of which was tied a rope supporting a heavy log of oak. Close under this log stood a wooden trough filled with honey. Hardly had the boy had time to wonder why the honey was placed there, and why the log hung above it, when he heard a crackling in the wood, and saw some bears approaching; a she-bear, followed by a yearling and three tiny cubs. The she-bear, sniffing the air, went straight to the trough, the cubs following her. She thrust her muzzle into the honey, and called the cubs to do the same. They scampered up and began to eat. As they did so, the log, which the she-bear had moved aside with her head, swung away a little and, returning, gave the cubs a push. Seeing this the she-bear shoved the log away with her paw. It swung further out and returned more forcibly, striking one cub on the back and another on the head. The cubs ran away howling with pain, and the mother, with a growl, caught the log in her fore paws and, raising it above her head flung it away. The log flew high in the air and the yearling, rushing to the trough, pushed his muzzle into the honey and began to suck noisily. The others also drew near, but they had not reached the trough when the log, flying back, struck the yearling on the head and killed him. The mother growled louder than before and, seizing the log, flung it from her with all her might. It flew higher than the branch it was tied to; so high that the rope slackened; and the she-bear returned to the trough, and the little cubs after her. The log flew higher and higher, then stopped, and began to fall. The nearer it came the faster it swung, and at last, at full speed, it crashed down on her head. The she-bear rolled over, her legs jerked and she died! The cubs ran away into the forest.

V

The boy watched all this in surprise, and then continued his way. Leaving the forest, he came upon a large garden in the midst of which stood a lofty palace with a golden roof. At the gate stood his godfather, smiling. He welcomed his godson, and led him through the gateway into the garden. The boy had never dreamed of such beauty and delight as surrounded him in that place.

Then his godfather led him into the palace, which was even more beautiful inside than outside. The godfather showed the boy through all the rooms: each brighter and finer than the other, but at last they came to one door that was sealed up.

'You see this door,' said he. 'It is not locked, but only sealed. It can be opened, but I forbid you to open it. You may live here, and go where you please and enjoy all the delights of the place. My only command is—do not open that door! But should you ever do so, remember what you saw in the forest.'

Having said this the godfather went away. The godson remained in the palace, and life there was so bright and joyful that he thought he had only been there three hours, when he had really lived there thirty years. When thirty years had gone by, the godson happened to be passing the sealed door one day, and he wondered why his godfather had forbidden him to enter that room.

'I'll just look in and see what is there,' thought he, and he gave the door a push. The seals gave way, the door opened, and the godson entering saw a hall more lofty and beautiful than all the others, and in the midst of it a throne. He wandered about the hall for a while, and then mounted the steps and seated himself upon the throne. As he sat there he noticed a sceptre leaning against the throne, and took it in his hand. Hardly had he done so when the four walls of the hall suddenly disappeared. The godson looked around, and saw the whole world, and all that men were doing in it. He looked in front, and saw the sea with ships sailing on it. He looked to the right, and saw where strange heathen people lived. He looked to the left, and saw where men who were Christians, but not Russians, lived. He looked round, and on the fourth side, he saw Russian people, like himself.

'I will look,' said he, 'and see what is happening at home, and whether the harvest is good.'

He looked towards his father's fields and saw the sheaves standing in stooks. He began counting them to see whether there was much corn, when he noticed a peasant driving in a cart. It was night, and the godson thought it was his father coming to cart the corn by night. But as he looked he recognized Vasíly Koudryashóf, the thief, driving into the field and beginning to load the sheaves on to his cart. This made the godson angry, and he called out:

'Father, the sheaves are being stolen from our field!'

His father, who was out with the horses in the night-pasture, woke up.

'I dreamt the sheaves were being stolen,' said he. 'I will just ride down and see.'

So he got on a horse and rode out to the field. Finding Vasíly there, he called together other peasants to help him, and Vasíly was beaten, bound, and taken to prison.

Then the godson looked at the town, where his godmother lived. He saw that she was now married to a tradesman. She lay asleep, and her husband rose and went to his mistress. The godson shouted to her:

'Get up, get up, your husband has taken to evil ways.'

The godmother jumped up and dressed, and finding out where her husband was, she shamed and beat his mistress, and drove him away.

Then the godson looked for his mother, and saw her lying asleep in her cottage. And a thief crept into the cottage and began to break open the chest in which she kept her things. The mother awoke and screamed, and the robber seizing an axe, swung it over his head to kill her.

The godson could not refrain from hurling the sceptre at the robber. It struck him upon the temple, and killed him on the spot.

VI

As soon as the godson had killed the robber, the walls closed and the hall became just as it had been before.

Then the door opened and the godfather entered, and coming up to his godson he took him by the hand and led him down from the throne.

'You have not obeyed my command,' said he. 'You did one wrong thing, when you opened the forbidden door; another, when you mounted the throne and took my sceptre into your hands; and you have now done a third wrong, which has much increased the evil in the world. Had you sat here an hour longer, you would have ruined half mankind.'

Then the godfather led his godson back to the throne, and took the sceptre in his hand; and again the walls fell asunder and all things became visible. And the godfather said:

'See what you have done to your father. Vasíly has now been a year in prison, and has come out having learnt every kind of wickedness, and has become quite incorrigible. See, he has stolen two of your father's horses, and he is now setting fire to his barn. All this you have brought upon your father.'

The godson saw his father's barn breaking into flames, but his godfather shut off the sight from him, and told him to look another way.

'Here is your godmother's husband,' he said. 'It is a year since he left his wife, and now he goes after other women. His former mistress has sunk to still lower depths. Sorrow has driven his wife to drink. That's what you have done to your godmother.'

The godfather shut off this also, and showed the godson his father's house. There he saw his mother weeping for her sins, repenting, and saying:

'It would have been better had the robber killed me that night. I should not have sinned so heavily.'

'That,' said the godfather, 'is what you have done to your mother.'

He shut this off also, and pointed downwards; and the godson saw two warders holding the robber in front of a prison-house.

And the godfather said:

'This man had murdered ten men. He should have expiated his sins himself, but by killing him you have taken his sins on yourself. Now you must answer for all his sins. That is what you have done to yourself. The she-bear pushed the log aside once, and disturbed her cubs; she pushed it again, and killed her yearling; she pushed it a third time, and was killed herself. You have done the same. Now I give you thirty years to go into the world and atone for the robber's sins. If you do not atone for them, you will have to take his place.'

'How am I to atone for his sins?' asked the godson.

And the godfather answered:

'When you have rid the world of as much evil as you have brought into it, you will have atoned both for your own sins and for those of the robber.'

'How can I destroy evil in the world?' the godson asked.

'Go out,' replied the godfather, 'and walk straight towards the rising sun. After a time you will come to a field with some men in it. Notice what they are doing, and teach them what you know. Then go on and note what you see. On the fourth day you will come to a forest. In the midst of the forest is a cell and in the cell lives a hermit. Tell him all that has happened. He will teach you what to do. When you have done all he tells you, you will have atoned for your own and the robber's sins.'

And, having said this, the godfather led his godson out of the gate.

VII

The godson went his way, and as he went he thought: How am I to destroy evil in the world? Evil is destroyed by banishing evil men, keeping them in prison, or putting them to death. How then am I to destroy evil without taking the sins of others upon myself?'

The godson pondered over it for a long time, but could come to no conclusion. He went on until he came to a field where corn was growing thick and good and ready for the reapers. The godson saw that a little calf had got in among the corn. Some men who were at hand saw it, and mounting their horses they chased it backwards and forwards through the corn. Each time the calf was about to come out of the corn some one rode up and the calf got frightened and turned back again, and they all galloped after it, trampling down the corn. On the road stood a woman crying.

'They will chase my calf to death,' she said.

And the godson said to the peasants:

'What are you doing? Come out of the cornfield all of you, and let the woman call her calf.'

The men did so; and the woman came to the edge of the cornfield and called to the calf. 'Come along, Browney, come along,' said she. The calf pricked up its ears, listened a while, and then ran towards the woman of its own accord, and hid its head in her skirts, almost knocking her over. The men were glad the woman was glad, and so was the little calf.

The godson went on, and he thought:

'Now I see that evil spreads evil. The more people try to drive away evil, the more the evil grows. Evil, it seems, cannot be destroyed by evil; but in what way it can be destroyed, I do not know. The calf obeyed its mistress and so all went well; but if it had not obeyed her, how could we have got it out of the field?'

The godson pondered again, but came to no conclusion, and continued his way.

VIII

He went on until he came to a village. At the furthest end he stopped and asked leave to stay the night. The woman of the house was there alone, house-cleaning, and she let him in. The godson entered, and taking his seat upon the brick oven he watched what the woman was doing. He saw her finish scrubbing the room and begin scrubbing the table. Having done this, she began wiping the table with a dirty cloth. She wiped it from side to side—but it did not come clean. The soiled cloth left streaks of dirt. Then she wiped it the other way. The first streaks disappeared, but others came in their place. Then she wiped it from one end to the other, but again the same thing happened. The soiled cloth messed the table; when one streak was wiped off another was left on. The godson watched for awhile in silence, and then said:

'What are you doing, mistress?'

'Don't you see I'm cleaning up for the holiday. Only I can't manage this table, it won't come clean. I'm quite tired out.'

'You should rinse your cloth,' said the godson, 'before you wipe the table with it.'

The woman did so, and soon had the table clean.

'Thank you for telling me,' said she.

In the morning he took leave of the woman and went on his way. After walking a good while, he came to the edge of a forest. There he saw some peasants who were making wheel-rims of bent wood. Coming nearer, the godson saw that the men were going round and round, but could not bend the wood.

He stood and looked on, and noticed that the block, to which the piece of wood was fastened, was not fixed, but as the men moved round it went round too. Then the godson said:

'What are you doing, friends?'

'Why, don't you see, we are making wheel rims. We have twice steamed the wood, and are quite tired out, but the wood will not bend.'

'You should fix the block, friends,' said the godson, 'or else it goes round when you do.'

The peasants took his advice and fixed the block, and then the work went on merrily.

The godson spent the night with them, and then went on. He walked all day and all night, and just before dawn he came upon some drovers encamped for the night, and lay down beside them. He saw that they had got all their cattle settled, and were trying to light a fire. They had taken dry twigs and lighted them, but before the twigs had time to burn up, they smothered them with damp brushwood. The brushwood hissed and the fire smouldered and went out. Then the drovers brought more dry wood, lit it, and again put on the brushwood—and again the fire went out. They struggled with it for a long time, but could not get the fire to burn. Then the godson said:

'Do not be in such a hurry to put on the brushwood. Let the dry wood burn up properly before you put any on. When the fire is well alight you can put on as much as you please.'

The drovers followed his advice. They let the fire burn up fiercely before adding the brushwood, which then flared up so that they soon had a roaring fire.

The godson remained with them for a while, and then continued his way. He went on, wondering what the three things he had seen might mean; but he could not fathom them.

IX

The godson walked the whole of that day, and in the evening came to another forest. There he found a hermit's cell, at which he knocked.

'Who is there?' asked a voice from within.

'A great sinner,' replied the godson. I must atone for another's sins as well as for my own.

The hermit hearing this came out.

'What sins are those that you have to bear for another?'

The godson told him everything: about his godfather; about the she-bear with the cubs; about the throne in the sealed room; about the commands his godfather had given him, as well as about the peasants he had seen trampling down the corn, and the calf that ran out when its mistress called it.

'I have seen that one cannot destroy evil by evil,' said he, 'but I cannot understand how it is to be destroyed. Teach me how it can be done.

'Tell me,' replied the hermit, 'what else you have seen on your way.'

The godson told him about the woman washing the table, and the men making cart-wheels, and the drovers fighting their fire.

The hermit listened to it all, and then went back to his cell and brought out an old jagged axe.

'Come with me,' said he.

When they had gone some way, the hermit pointed to a tree.

'Cut it down,' he said.

The godson felled the tree.

'Now chop it into three,' said the hermit.

The godson chopped the tree into three pieces. Then the hermit went back to his cell, and brought out some blazing sticks.

'Burn those three logs,' said he.

So the godson made a fire, and burnt the three logs till only three charred stumps remained.

'Now plant them half in the ground, like this.'

The godson did so.

'You see that river at the foot of the hill. Bring water from there in your mouth, and water these stumps. Water this stump, as you taught the woman: this one as you taught the wheel-wrights: and this one, as you taught the drovers. When all three have taken root and from these charred stumps apple-trees have sprung you will know how to destroy evil in men, and will have atoned for all your sins.'

Having said this, the hermit returned to his cell. The godson pondered for a long time, but could not understand what the hermit meant. Nevertheless he set to work to do as he had been told.

X

The godson went down to the river, filled his mouth with water, and returning, emptied it on to one of the charred stumps. This he did again and again, and watered all three-stumps. When he was hungry and quite tired out, he went to the cell to ask the old hermit for some food. He opened the door, and there upon a bench he saw the old man lying dead. The godson looked round for food, and he found some dried bread and ate a little of it. Then he took a spade and set to work to dig the hermit's grave. During the night he carried water and watered the stumps, and in the day he dug the grave. He had hardly finished the grave and was about to bury the corpse, when some people from the village came, bringing food for the old man.

The people heard that the old hermit was dead, and that he had given the godson his blessing, and left him in his place. So they buried the old man, gave the bread they had brought to the godson, and promising to bring him some more, they went away.

The godson remained in the old man's place. There he lived, eating the food people brought him, and doing as he had been told: carrying water from the river in his mouth and watering the charred stumps.

He lived thus for a year, and many people visited him. His fame spread abroad, as a holy man who lived in the forest and brought water from the bottom of a hill in his mouth to water charred stumps for the salvation of his soul. People flocked to see him. Rich merchants drove up bringing him presents, but he kept only the barest necessaries for himself, and gave the rest away to the poor.

And so the godson lived: carrying water in his mouth and watering the stumps half the day, and resting and receiving people the other half. And he began to think that this was the way he had been told to live, in order to destroy evil and atone for his sins.

He spent two years in this manner, not omitting for a single day to water the stumps. But still not one of them sprouted.

One day, as he sat in his cell, he heard a man ride past, singing as he went. The godson came out to see what sort of a man it was. He saw a strong young fellow, well dressed, and mounted on a handsome, well-saddled horse.

The godson stopped him, and asked him who he was, and where he was going.

'I am a robber,' the man answered, drawing rein. 'I ride about the highways killing people; and the more I kill, the merrier are the songs I sing.'

The godson was horror-struck, and thought:

'How can the evil be destroyed in such a man as this? It is easy to speak to those who come to me of their own accord and confess their sins. But this one boasts of the evil he does.'

So he said nothing, and turned away, thinking: 'What am I to do now? This robber may take to riding about here, and he will frighten away the people. They will leave off coming to me. It will be a loss to them, and I shall not know how to live.'

So the godson turned back, and said to the robber:

'People come to me here, not to boast of their sins, but to repent, and to pray for forgiveness. Repent of your sins, if you fear God; but if there is no repentance in your heart, then go away and never come here again. Do not trouble me, and do not frighten people away from me. If you do not hearken, God will punish you.'

The robber laughed:

'I am not afraid of God, and I will not listen to you. You are not my master,' said he. 'You live by your piety, and I by my robbery. We all must live. You may teach the old women who come to you, but you have nothing to teach me. And because you have reminded me of God, I will kill two more men tomorrow. I would kill you, but I do not want to soil my hands just now. See that in future you keep out of my way!'

Having uttered this threat, the robber rode away. He did not come again, and the godson lived in peace, as before, for eight more years.

XI

One night the godson watered his stumps, and, after returning to his cell, he sat down to rest, and watched the footpath, wondering if some one would soon come. But no one came at all that day. He sat alone till evening, feeling lonely and dull, and he thought about his past life. Ho remembered how the robber had reproached him for living by his piety; and he reflected on his way of life. 'I am not living as the hermit commanded me to,' thought he. 'The hermit laid a penance upon me, and I have made both a living and fame out of it; and have been so tempted by it, that now I feel dull when people do not come to me; and when they do come, I only rejoice because they praise my holiness. That is not how one should live. I have been led astray by love of praise. I have not atoned for my past sins, but have added fresh ones. I will go to another part of the forest where people will not find me; and I will live so as to atone for my old sins and commit no fresh ones.'

Having come to this conclusion the godson filled a bag with dried bread and, taking a spade, left the cell and started for a ravine he knew of in a lonely spot, where he could dig himself a cave and hide from the people.

As he was going along with his bag and his spade he saw the robber riding towards him. The godson was frightened, and started to run away, but the robber overtook him.

'Where are you going?' asked the robber.

The godson told him he wished to get away from the people and live somewhere where no one would come to him. This surprised the robber.

'What will you live on, if people do not come to see you?' asked he.

The godson had not even thought of this, but the robber's question reminded him that food would be necessary.

'On what God pleases to give me,' he replied.

The robber said nothing, and rode away.

'Why did I not say anything to him about his way of life?' thought the godson. 'He might repent now. To-day he seems in a gentler mood, and has not threatened to kill me.' And he shouted to the robber:

'You have still to repent of your sins. You cannot escape from God.'

The robber turned his horse, and drawing a knife from his girdle threatened the hermit with it. The latter was alarmed, and ran away further into the forest.

The robber did not follow him, but only shouted:

'Twice I have let you off, old man, but next time you come in my way I will kill you!'

Having said this, he rode away. In the evening when the godson went to water his stumps—one of them was sprouting! A little apple tree was growing out of it.

XII

After hiding himself from everybody, the godson lived all alone. When his supply of bread was exhausted, he thought: 'Now I must go and look for some roots to eat.' He had not gone far, however, before he saw a bag of dried bread hanging on a branch. He took it down, and as long as it lasted he lived upon that.

When he had eaten it all, he found another bagful on the same branch. So he lived on, his only trouble being his fear of the robber. Whenever he heard the robber passing he hid thinking:

'He may kill me before I have had time to atone for my sins.'

In this way he lived for ten more years. The one apple-tree continued to grow, but the other two stumps remained exactly as they were.

One morning the godson rose early and went to his work. By the time he had thoroughly moistened the ground round the stumps, he was tired out and sat down to rest. As he sat there he thought to himself:

'I have sinned, and have become afraid of death. It may be God's will that I should redeem my sins by death.'

Hardly had this thought crossed his mind when he heard the robber riding up, swearing at something. When the godson heard this, he thought:

'No evil and no good can befall me from any one but from God.'

And he went to meet the robber. He saw the robber was not alone, but behind him on the saddle sat another man, gagged, and bound hand and foot. The man was doing nothing, but the robber was abusing him violently. The godson went up and stood in front of the horse.

'Where are you taking this man?' he asked.

'Into the forest,' replied the robber. 'He is a merchant's son, and will not tell me where his father's money is hidden. I am going to flog him till he tells me.'

And the robber spurred on his horse, but the godson caught hold of his bridle, and would not let him pass.

'Let this man go!' he said.

The robber grew angry, and raised his arm to strike.

'Would you like a taste of what I am going to give this man? Have I not promised to kill you? Let go!'

The godson was not afraid.

'You shall not go,' said he. 'I do not fear you. I fear no one but God, and He wills that I should not let you pass. Set this man free!'

The robber frowned, and snatching out his knife, cut the ropes with which the merchant's son was bound, and set him free.

'Get away both of you,' he said, 'and beware hour you cross my path again.'

The merchant's son jumped down and ran away. The robber was about to ride on, but the godson stopped him again, and again spoke to him about giving up his evil life. The robber heard him to the end in silence, and then rode away without a word.

The next morning the godson went to water his stumps and lo! the second stump was sprouting. A second young apple-tree had begun to grow.

XIII

Another ten years had gone by. The godson was sitting quietly one day, desiring nothing, fearing nothing, and with a heart full of joy.

'What blessings God showers on men!' thought he. 'Yet how needlessly they torment themselves. What prevents them from living happily?'

And remembering all the evil in men, and the troubles they bring upon themselves, his heart filled with pity.

'It is wrong of me to live as I do,' he said to himself. 'I must go and teach others what I have myself learnt.'

Hardly had he thought this, when he heard the robber approaching. He let him pass, thinking:

'It is no good talking to him, he will not understand.'

That was his first thought, but ho changed his mind and went out into the road. He saw that the robber was gloomy, and was riding with downcast eyes. The godson looked at him, pitied him, and running up to him laid his hand upon his knee.

'Brother, dear,' said he, 'have some pity on your own soul! In you lives the spirit of God. You suffer, and torment others, and lay up more and more suffering for the future. Yet God loves you, and has prepared such blessings for you. Do not ruin yourself utterly. Change your life!'

The robber frowned and turned away.

'Leave me alone!' said he.

But the godson held the robber still faster, and began to weep.

Then the robber lifted his eyes and looked at the godson. He looked at him for a long time, and alighting from his horse, fell on his knees at the godson's feet.

'You have overcome me, old man,' said he. 'For twenty years I have resisted you, but now you have conquered me. Do what you will with me, for I have no more power over myself. When you first tried to persuade me, it only angered me more. Only when you hid yourself from men did I begin to consider your words: for I saw then that you asked nothing of them for yourself. Since that day I have brought food for you, hanging it upon the tree.'

Then the godson remembered that the woman got her table clean only after she had rinsed her cloth. In the same way, it was only when he ceased caring about himself, and cleansed his own heart, that he was able to cleanse the hearts of others.

The robber went on.

'When I saw that you did not fear death, my heart turned.'

Then the godson remembered that the wheel-wrights could not bend the rims until they had fixed their block. So, not till he had cast away the fear of death and made his life fast in God, could he subdue this man's unruly heart.

'But my heart did not quite melt,' continued the robber, 'until you pitied me and wept for me.'

The godson, full of joy, led the robber to the place where the stumps were. And when they got there, they saw that from the third stump an apple-tree had begun to sprout. And the godson remembered that the drovers had not been able to light the damp wood until the fire had burnt up well. So it was only when his own heart burnt warmly, that another's heart had been kindled by it.

And the godson was full of joy that he had at last atoned for his sins.

He told all this to the robber, and died. The robber buried him, and lived as the godson had commanded him, teaching to others what the godson had taught him.

1886

THE REPENTANT SINNER (1886)

'And he said unto Jesus, Lord, remember me when thou comest into thy Kingdom. And Jesus said unto him, Verily I say unto thee, Today shalt thou be with me in paradise.'—*Luke xxiii. 42, 43*

There was once a man who lived for seventy years in the world, and lived in sin all that time. He fell ill but even then did not repent. Only at the last moment, as he was dying, he wept and said:

'Lord! forgive me, as Thou forgavest the thief upon the cross.'

And as he said these words, his soul left his body. And the soul of the sinner, feeling love towards God and faith in His mercy, went to the gates of heaven and knocked, praying to be let into the heavenly kingdom.

Then a voice spoke from within the gate:

'What man is it that knocks at the gates of Paradise and what deeds did he do during his life?'

And the voice of the Accuser replied, recounting all the man's evil deeds, and not a single good one.

And the voice from within the gates answered:

'Sinners cannot enter into the kingdom of heaven. Go hence!'

Then the man said:

'Lord, I hear thy voice, but cannot see thy face, nor do I know thy name.'

The voice answered:

'I am Peter, the Apostle.'

And the sinner replied:

'Have pity on me, Apostle Peter! Remember man's weakness, and

God's mercy. Wert not thou a disciple of Christ? Didst not thou hear his teaching from his own lips, and hadst thou not his example before thee? Remember then how, when he sorrowed and was grieved in spirit, and three times asked thee to keep awake and pray, thou didst sleep, because thine eyes were heavy, and three times he found thee sleeping. So it was with me. Remember, also, how thou didst promise to be faithful unto death, and yet didst thrice deny him, when he was taken before Caiaphas. So it was with me. And remember, too, how when the cock crowed thou didst go out and didst weep bitterly. So it is with me. Thou canst not refuse to let me in.'

And the voice behind the gates was silent.

Then the sinner stood a little while, and again began to knock, and to ask to be let into the kingdom of heaven.

And he heard another voice behind the gates, which said:

'Who is this man, and how did he live on earth?'

And the voice of the Accuser again repeated all the sinner's evil deeds, and not a single good one.

And the voice from behind the gates replied:

'Go hence! Such sinners cannot live with us in Paradise.' Then the sinner said:

'Lord, I hear thy voice, but I see thee not, nor do I know thy name.'

And the voice answered:

'I am David; king and prophet.'

The sinner did not despair, nor did he leave the gates of Paradise, but said:

Have pity on me, King David! Remember man's weakness, and God's mercy. God loved thee and exalted thee among men. Thou hadst all: a kingdom, and honour, and riches, and wives, and children; but thou sawest from thy house-top the wife of a poor man, and sin entered into thee, and thou tookest the wife of Uriah, and didst slay him with the sword of the Ammonites. Thou, a rich man, didst take from the poor man his one ewe lamb, and didst kill him. I have done likewise. Remember, then, how thou didst repent, and how thou saidst, "I acknowledge my transgressions: my sin is ever before me?" I have done the same. Thou canst not refuse to let me in.'

And the voice from within the gates was silent.

The sinner having stood a little while, began knocking again, and asking to be let into the kingdom of heaven. And a third voice was heard within the gates, saying:

'Who is this man, and how has he spent his life on earth?'

And the voice of the Accuser replied for the third time, recounting the sinner's evil deeds, and not mentioning one good deed.

And the voice within the gates said:

'Depart hence! Sinners cannot enter into the kingdom of heaven.'

And the sinner said:

'Thy voice I hear, but thy face I see not, neither do I know thy name.'

Then the voice replied:

'I am John the Divine, the beloved disciple of Christ.'

And the sinner rejoiced and said:

'Now surely I shall be allowed to enter. Peter and David must let me in, because they know man's weakness and God's mercy; and thou wilt let me in, because thou lovest much. Was it not thou, John the Divine who wrote that God is Love, and that he who loves not, knows not God? And in thine old age didst thou not say unto men: "Brethren, love one another." How, then, canst thou look on me with hatred, and drive me away? Either thou must renounce what thou hast said, or loving me, must let me enter the kingdom of heaven.'

And the gates of Paradise opened, and John embraced the repentant sinner and took him into the kingdom of heaven.

1886

THE EMPTY DRUM (1891)

A Folktale Long Current in the Region of the Volga

Emelyán was a labourer and worked for a master. Crossing the meadows one day on his way to work, he nearly trod on a frog that jumped right in front of him, but he just managed to avoid it. Suddenly he heard some one calling to him from behind.

Emelyán looked round and saw a lovely lassie, who said to him: 'Why don't you get married, Emelyán?'

'How can I marry, my lass?' said he. 'I have but the clothes I stand up in, nothing more, and no one would have me for a husband.'

'Take me for a wife,' said she.

Emelyán liked the maid. 'I should be glad to,' said he, 'but where and how could we live?'

'Why trouble about that?' said the girl. 'One only has to work more and sleep less, and one can clothe and feed oneself anywhere.'

'Very well then, let us marry,' said Emelyán. 'Where shall we go to?'

'Let us go to town.'

So Emelyán and the lass went to town, and she took him to a small hut on the very edge of the town, and they married and began housekeeping.

One day the King, driving through the town, passed by Emelyán's hut. Emelyán's wife came out to see the King. The King noticed her and was quite surprised.

'Where did such a beauty come from?' said he; and stopping his carriage he called Emelyán's wife and asked her: 'Who are you?'

'The peasant Emelyán's wife,' said she.

'Why did you, who are such a beauty, marry a peasant?' said the King. 'You ought to be a queen!'

'Thank you for your kind words,' said she, 'but a peasant husband is good enough for me.'

The King talked to her awhile and then drove on. He returned to the palace, but could not get Emelyán's wife out of his head. All night he did not sleep, but kept thinking how to get her for himself. He could think of no way of doing it, so he called his servants and told them they must find a way.

The King's servants said: 'Command Emelyán to come to the palace to work, and we will work him so hard that he will die. His wife will be left a widow, and then you can take her for yourself.'

The King followed their advice. He sent an order that Emelyán should come to the palace as a workman and that he should live at the palace, and his wife with him.

The messengers came to Emelyán and gave him the King's message. His wife said, 'Go, Emelyán; work all day, but come back home at night.'

So Emelyán went, and when he got to the palace the King's steward asked him, 'Why have you come alone, without your wife?'

'Why should I drag her about?' said Emelyán. 'She has a house to live in.'

At the King's palace they gave Emelyán work enough for two. He began the job not hoping to finish it; but when evening came, lo and behold! it was all done. The steward saw that it was finished, and set him four times as much for next day.

Emelyán went home. Everything there was swept and tidy; the oven was heated, his supper was cooked and ready, and his wife sat by the table sewing and waiting for his return. She greeted him, laid the table, gave him to eat and drink, and then began to ask him about his work.

'Ah!' said he, 'it's a bad business: they give me tasks beyond my strength, and want to kill me with work.'

'Don't fret about the work,' said she, 'don't look either before or behind to see how much you have done or how much there is left to do; only keep on working and all will be right.'

So Emelyán lay down and slept. Next morning he went to work again and worked without once looking round. And, lo and behold! by the evening it was all done, and before dark he came home for the night.

Again and again they increased Emelyán's work, but he always got through it in good time and went back to his hut to sleep. A week passed, and the King's servants saw they could not crush him with rough work so they tried giving him work that required skill. But this, also, was of no avail. Carpentering, and masonry, and roofing, whatever they set him to do, Emelyán had it ready in time, and went home to his wife at night. So a second week passed.

Then the King called his servants and said: 'Do I feed you for nothing? Two weeks have gone, and I don't see that you have done anything. You were going to tire Emelyán out with work, but I see from my windows how he goes home every evening—singing cheerfully! Do you mean to make a fool of me?'

The King's servants began to excuse themselves. 'We tried our best to wear him out with rough work,' they said, 'but nothing was too hard for him; he cleared it all off as though he had swept it away with a broom. There was no tiring him out. Then we set him to tasks needing skill, which we did not think he was clever enough to do, but he managed them all. No matter what one sets him, he does it all, no one knows how. Either he or his wife must know some spell that helps them. We ourselves are sick of him, and wish to find a task he cannot master. We have now thought of setting him to build a cathedral in a single day. Send for Emelyán, and order him to build a cathedral in front of the palace in a single day. Then, if he does not do it, let his head be cut off for disobedience.'

The King sent for Emelyán. 'Listen to my command,' said he: 'build me a new cathedral on the square in front of my palace, and have it ready by to-morrow evening. If you have it ready I will reward you, but if not I will have your head cut off.'

When Emelyán heard the King's command he turned away and went home. 'My end is near,' thought he. And coming to his wife, he said: 'Get ready, wife we must fly from here, or I shall be lost by no fault of my own.'

'What has frightened you so?' said she, 'and why should we run away?'

'How can I help being frightened? The King has ordered me, to-morrow, in a single day, to build him a cathedral. If I fail he will cut my head off. There is only one thing to be done: we must fly while there is yet time.'

But his wife would not hear of it. 'The King has many soldiers,' said she. 'They would catch us anywhere. We cannot escape from him, but must obey him as long as strength holds out.'

'How can I obey him when the task is beyond my strength?'

'Eh, goodman, don't be downhearted. Eat your supper now, and go to sleep. Rise early in the morning and all will get done.'

So Emelyán lay down and slept. His wife roused him early next day. 'Go quickly,' said she, 'and finish the cathedral. Here are nails and a hammer; there is still enough work there for a day.'

Emelyán went into the town, reached the palace square, and there stood a large cathedral not quite finished. Emelyán set to work to do what was needed, and by the evening all was ready.

When the King awoke he looked out from his palace, and saw the cathedral, and Emelyán going about driving in nails here and there. And the King was not pleased to have the cathedral—he was annoyed at not being able to condemn Emelyán and take his wife. Again he called his servants. 'Emelyán has done this task also,' said the King, 'and there is no excuse for putting him to death. Even this work was not too hard for him. You must find a more cunning plan, or I will cut off your heads as well as his.'

So his servants planned that Emelyán should be ordered to make a river round the palace, with ships sailing on it. And the King sent for Emelyán and set him this new task.

'If,' said he, 'you could build a cathedral in one night, you can also do this. To-morrow all must be ready. If not, I will have your head off.'

Emelyán was more downcast than before, and returned to his wife sad at heart.

'Why are you so sad?' said his wife. 'Has the King set you a fresh task?'

Emelyán told her about it. 'We must fly,' said he.

But his wife replied: 'There is no escaping the soldiers; they will catch us wherever we go. There is nothing for it but to obey.'

'How can I do it?' groaned Emelyán.

'Eh! eh! goodman,' said she, 'don't be downhearted. Eat your supper now, and go to sleep. Rise early, and all will get done in good time.'

So Emelyán lay down and slept. In the morning his wife woke him. 'Go,' said she 'to the palace—all is ready. Only, near the wharf in front of the palace, there is a mound left; take a spade and level it.

When the King awoke he saw a river where there had not been one; ships were sailing up and down, and Emelyán was levelling a mound with a spade. The King wondered, but was pleased neither with the river nor with the ships, so vexed was he at not being able to condemn Emelyán. 'There is no task,' thought he, 'that he cannot manage. What is to be done?' And he called his servants and again asked their advice.

'Find some task,' said he, 'which Emelyán cannot compass. For whatever we plan he fulfils, and I cannot take his wife from him.'

The King's servants thought and thought, and at last devised a plan. They came to the King and said: 'Send for Emelyán and say to him: "Go to there, don't know where," and bring back "that, don't know what." Then he will not be able to escape you. No matter where he goes, you can say that he has not gone to the right place, and no matter what he brings, you can say it is not the right thing. Then you can have him beheaded and can take his wife.'

The King was pleased. 'That is well thought of,' said he. So the King sent for Emelyán and said to him: 'Go to "there, don't know where," and bring back "that, don't know what." If you fail to bring it, I will have you beheaded.'

Emelyán returned to his wife and told her what the King had said. His wife became thoughtful.

'Well,' said she, 'they have taught the King how to catch you. Now we must act warily.' So she sat and thought, and at last said to her husband: 'You must go far, to our Grandam—the old peasant woman, the mother of soldiers—and you must ask her aid. If she helps you to anything, go straight to the palace with it, I shall be there: I cannot escape them now. They will take me by force, but it will not be for long. If you do everything as Grandam directs, you will soon save me.'

So the wife got her husband ready for the journey. She gave him a wallet, and also a spindle. 'Give her this,' said she. 'By this token she will know that you are my husband.' And his wife showed him his road.

Emelyán set off. He left the town behind, and came to where some soldiers were being drilled. Emelyán stood and watched them. After drill the soldiers sat down to rest. Then Emelyán went up to them and asked: 'Do you know, brothers, the way to "there, don't know where?" and how I can get "that, don't know what?"'

The soldiers listened to him with surprise. 'Who sent you on this errand?' said they

'The King,' said he.

'"From the day we became soldiers," said they, "we go 'don't know where,' and never yet have we got there; and we seek we "don't know what," and cannot find it. We cannot help you.'

Emelyán sat a while with the soldiers and then went on again. He trudged many a mile, and at last came to a wood. In the wood was a hut, and in the hut sat an old, old woman, the mother of peasant soldiers, spinning flax and weeping. And as she spun she did not put her fingers to her mouth to wet them with spittle, but to her eyes to wet them with tears. When the old woman saw Emelyán she cried out at him: 'Why have you come here?' Then Emelyán gave her the spindle, and said his wife had sent it.

The old woman softened at once, and began to question him. And Emelyán told her his whole life: how he married the lass; how they went to live in the town; how he had worked, and what he had done at the palace; how he built the cathedral, and made a river with ships on it, and how the King had now told him to go to 'there, don't know where, and bring back 'that, don't know what.'

The Grandam listened to the end, and ceased weeping. She muttered to herself: 'The time has surely come,' and said to him: 'All right, my lad. Sit down now, and I will give you something to eat.'

Emelyán ate, and then the Grandam told him what to do. 'Here,' said she, 'is a ball of thread; roll it before you, and follow where it goes. You must go far till you come right to the sea. When you get there you will see a great city. Enter the city and ask for a night's lodging at the furthest house. There look out for what you are seeking.'

'How shall I know it when I see it, Granny?' said he.

'When you see something men obey more than father or mother, that is it. Seize that, and take it to the King. When you bring it to the King, he will say it is not right, and you must answer: "If it is not the right thing it must be smashed," and you must beat it, and carry it to the river, break it in pieces, and throw it into the water. Then you will get your wife back and my tears will be dried.'

Emelyán bade farewell to the Grandam and began rolling his ball before him. It rolled and rolled until at last it reached the sea. By the sea stood a great city, and at the further end of the city was a big house. There Emelyán begged for a night's lodging, and was granted it. He lay down to sleep, and in the morning awoke and heard a father rousing his son to go and cut wood for the fire. But the son did not obey. 'It is too early,' said he, 'there is time enough.' Then Emelyán heard the mother say, 'Go, my son, your father's bones ache; would you have him go himself? It is time to be up!'

But the son only murmured some words and fell asleep again. Hardly was he asleep when something thundered and rattled in the street. Up jumped the son and quickly putting on his clothes ran out into the street. Up jumped Emelyán, too, and ran after him to see what it was that a son obeys more than father or mother. What he saw was a man walking along the street carrying, tied to his stomach, a thing which he beat with sticks, and that it was that rattled and thundered so, and that the son had obeyed. Emelyán ran up and had a look at it. He saw it was round, like a small tub, with a skin stretched over both ends, and he asked what it was called.

He was told, 'A drum.'

'And is it empty?'

'Yes, it is empty.'

Emelyán was surprised. He asked them to give the thing to him, but they would not. So Emelyán left off asking, and followed the drummer. All day he followed, and when the drummer at last lay down to sleep, Emelyán snatched the drum from him and ran away with it.

He ran and ran, till at last he got back to his own town. He went to see his wife, but she was not at home. The day after he went away, the King had taken her. So Emelyán went to the palace, and sent in a message to the King: 'He has returned who went to "there, don't know where," and he has brought with him "that, don't know what."'

They told the King, and the King said he was to come again next day.

But Emelyán said, 'Tell the King I am here to-day, and have brought what the King wanted. Let him come out to me, or I will go in to him!'

The King came out. 'Where have you been?' said he.

Emelyán told him.

'That's not the right place,' said the King. 'What have you brought?'

Emelyán pointed to the drum, but the King did not look at it.

'That is not it.'

'If it is not the right thing,' said Emelyán, 'it must be smashed, and may the devil take it!'

And Emelyán left the palace, carrying the drum and beating it. And as he beat it all the King's army ran out to follow Emelyán, and they saluted him and waited his commands.

The King, from his window, began to shout at his army telling them not to follow Emelyán. They did not listen to what he said, but all followed Emelyán.

When the King saw that, he gave orders that Emelyán's wife should be taken back to him, and he sent to ask Emelyán to give him the drum.

'It can't be done,' said Emelyán. 'I was told to smash it and to throw the splinters into the river.'

So Emelyán went down to the river carrying the drum, and the soldiers followed him. When he reached the river bank Emelyán smashed the drum to splinters, and threw the splinters into the stream. And then all the soldiers ran away.

Emelyán took his wife and went home with her. And after that the King ceased to trouble him; and so they lived happily ever after.

1891

PART VI. ADAPTATIONS FROM THE FRENCH

THE COFFEE-HOUSE OF SURAT (1893)

After Bernardin De Sent-Pierre

In the town of Surat, in India, was a coffee-house where many travellers and foreigners from all parts of the world met and conversed.

One day a learned Persian theologian visited this coffee-house. He was a man who had spent his life studying the nature of the Deity, and reading and writing books upon the subject. He had thought, read, and written so much about God, that eventually he lost his wits became quite confused, and ceased even to believe in the existence of a God.

The Shah, hearing of this, had banished him from Persia.

After having argued all his life about the First Cause, this unfortunate theologian had ended by quite perplexing himself, and instead of understanding that he had lost his own reason, he began to think that there was no higher Reason controlling the universe.

This man had an African slave who followed him everywhere. When the theologian entered the coffeehouse, the slave remained outside, near the door sitting on a stone in the glare of the sun, and driving away the flies that buzzed around him. The Persian having settled down on a divan in the coffee-house, ordered himself a cup of opium. When he had drunk it and the opium had begun to quicken the workings of his brain, he addressed his slave through the open door:

'Tell me, wretched slave,' said he, 'do you think there is a God, or not?'

'Of course there is,' said the slave, and immediately drew from under his girdle a small idol of wood.

'There,' said he, 'that is the God who has guarded me from the day of my birth. Every one in our country worships the fetish tree, from the wood of which this God was made.'

This conversation between the theologian and his slave was listened to with surprise by the other guests in the coffee-house. They were astonished at the master's question, and yet more so at the slave's reply.

One of them, a Brahmin, on hearing the words spoken by the slave, turned to him and said:

'Miserable fool! Is it possible you believe that God can be carried under a man's girdle? There is one God—Brahma, and he is greater than the whole world, for he created it. Brahma is the One, the mighty God, and in His honour are built the temples on the Ganges' banks, where his true priests, the Brahmins, worship him. They know the true God, and none but they. A thousand score of years have passed, and yet through revolution after revolution these priests have held their sway, because Brahma, the one true God, has protected them.'

So spoke the Brahmin, thinking to convince every one; but a Jewish broker who was present replied to him, and said:

'No! the temple of the true God is not in India. Neither does God protect the Brahmin caste. The true God is not the God of the Brahmins, but of Abraham, Isaac, and Jacob. None does He protect but His chosen people, the Israelites. From the commencement of the world, our nation has been beloved of Him, and ours alone. If we are now scattered over the whole earth it is but to try us; for God has promised that He will one day gather His people together in Jerusalem. Then, with the Temple of Jerusalem—the wonder of the ancient world—restored to its splendour, shall Israel be established a ruler over all nations.'

So spoke the Jew, and burst into tears. He wished to say more, but an Italian missionary who was there interrupted him.

'What you are saying is untrue,' said he to the Jew. 'You attribute injustice to God. He cannot love your nation above the rest. Nay rather, even if it be true that of old He favoured the Israelites, it is now nineteen hundred years since they angered Him, and caused Him to destroy their nation and scatter them over the earth, so that their faith makes no converts and has died out except here and there. God shows preference to no nation, but calls all who wish to be saved to the bosom of the Catholic Church of Rome, the one outside whose borders no salvation can be found.'

So spoke the Italian. But a Protestant minister who happened to be present, growing pale, turned to the Catholic missionary and exclaimed:

'How can you say that salvation belongs to your religion? Those only will be saved, who serve God according to the Gospel, in spirit and in truth, as bidden by the word of Christ.'

Then a Turk, an office-holder in the custom-house at Surat, who was sitting in the coffee-house smoking a pipe, turned with an air of superiority to both the Christians.

'Your belief in your Roman religion is vain,' said he. 'It was superseded twelve hundred years ago by the true faith: that of Mohammed! You cannot but observe how the true Mohammedan faith continues to spread both in Europe and Asia, and even in the enlightened country of China. You say yourselves that God has rejected the Jews; and, as a proof, you quote the fact that the Jews are humiliated and their faith does not spread. Confess then the truth of Mohammedanism, for it is triumphant and spreads far and wide. None will be saved but the followers of Mohammed, God's latest prophet; and of them, only the followers of Omar, and not of Ali, for the latter are false to the faith.'

To this the Persian theologian, who was of the sect of Ali, wished to reply; but by this time a great dispute had arisen among all the strangers of different faiths and creeds present. There were Abyssinian Christians, Llamas from Tibet, Ismailians and Fire-worshippers. They all argued about the nature of God, and how He should be worshipped. Each of them asserted that in his country alone was the true God known and rightly worshipped.

Every one argued and shouted, except a Chinaman, a student of Confucius, who sat quietly in one corner of the coffee-house, not joining in the dispute. He sat there drinking tea and listening to what the others said, but did not speak himself.

The Turk noticed him sitting there, and appealed to him, saying:

'You can confirm what I say, my good Chinaman. You hold your peace, but if you spoke I know you would uphold my opinion. Traders from your country, who come to me for assistance, tell me that though many religions have been introduced into China, you Chinese consider Mohammedanism the best of all, and adopt it willingly. Confirm, then, my words, and tell us your opinion of the true God and of His prophet.'

'Yes, yes,' said the rest, turning to the Chinaman, 'let us hear what you think on the subject.'

The Chinaman, the student of Confucius, closed his eyes, and thought a while. Then he opened them again, and drawing his hands out of the wide sleeves of his garment, and folding them on his breast, he spoke as follows, in a calm and quiet voice.

Sirs, it seems to me that it is chiefly pride that prevents men agreeing with one another on matters of faith. If you care to listen to me, I will tell you a story which will explain this by an example.

I came here from China on an English steamer which had been round the world. We stopped for fresh water, and landed on the east coast of the island of Sumatra. It was mid-day, and some of us, having landed, sat in the shade of some coconut palms by the seashore, not far from a native village. We were a party of men of different nationalities.

As we sat there, a blind man approached us. We learnt afterwards that he had gone blind from gazing too long and too persistently at the sun, trying to find out what it is, in order to seize its light.

He strove a long time to accomplish this, constantly looking at the sun; but the only result was that his eyes were injured by its brightness, and he became blind.

Then he said to himself:

'The light of the sun is not a liquid; for if it were a liquid it would be possible to pour it from one vessel into another, and it would be moved, like water, by the wind. Neither is it fire; for if it were fire, water would extinguish it. Neither is light a spirit, for it is seen by the eye, nor is it matter, for it cannot be moved. Therefore, as the light of the sun is neither liquid, nor fire, nor spirit, nor matter, it is—nothing!'

So he argued, and, as a result of always looking at the sun and always thinking about it, he lost both his sight and his reason. And when he went quite blind, he became fully convinced that the sun did not exist.

With this blind man came a slave, who after placing his master in the shade of a coconut tree, picked up a coconut from the ground, and began making it into a night-light. He twisted a wick from the fibre of the coconut: squeezed oil from the nut into the shell, and soaked the wick in it.

As the slave sat doing this, the blind man sighed and said to him:

'Well, slave, was I not right when I told you there is no sun? Do you not see how dark it is? Yet people say there is a sun... But if so, what is it?'

'I do not know what the sun is,' said the slave 'That is no business of mine. But I know what light is. Here, I have made a night-light, by the help of which I can serve you and find anything I want in the hut.'

And the slave picked up the coconut shell, saying:

'This is my sun.'

A lame man with crutches, who was sitting near by heard these words, and laughed:

'You have evidently been blind all your life,' said he to the blind man, 'not to know what the sun is, I will tell you what it is. The sun is a ball of fire, which rises every morning out of the sea and goes down again among the mountains of our island each evening. We have all seen this, and if you had had your eyesight you too would have seen it.'

A fisherman, who had been listening to the conversation, said:

'It is plain enough that you have never been beyond your own island. If you were not lame, and if you had been out as I have in a fishing-boat, you would know that the sun does not set among the mountains of our island, but as it rises from the ocean every morning so it sets again in the sea every night. What I am telling you is true, for I see it every day with my own eyes.'

Then an Indian who was of our party, interrupted him by saying:

'I am astonished that a reasonable man should talk such nonsense. How can a ball of fire possibly descend into the water and not be extinguished? The sun is not a ball of fire at all, it is the Deity named Deva who rides for ever in a chariot round the golden mountain, Meru. Sometimes the evil serpents Ragu and Ketu attack Deva and swallow him: and then the earth is dark. But our priests pray that the Deity may be released, and then he is set free. Only such ignorant men as you, who have never been beyond their own island, can imagine that the sun shines for their country alone.'

Then the master of an Egyptian vessel, who was present, spoke in his turn.

'No,' said he, 'you also are wrong. The sun is not a Deity, and does not only round India and its golden mountain. I have sailed much on the Black Sea, and along the coasts of Arabia, and have been to Madagascar and to the Philippines. The sun lights the whole earth, and not India alone. It does not circle round one mountain, but rises far in the east, beyond the Isles of Japan, and sets far, far away in the west, beyond the islands of England. That is why the Japanese call their country "Nippon," that is "the birth of the sun." I know this well, for I have myself seen much, and heard more from my grandfather, who sailed to the very ends of the sea.'

He would have gone on, but an English sailor from our ship interrupted him.

'There is no country,' he said, 'where people know so much about the sun's movements as in England. The sun, as every one in England knows, rises nowhere and sets nowhere. It is always moving round the earth. We can be sure of this for we have just been round the world ourselves, and nowhere knocked up against the sun. Wherever we went, the sun showed itself in the morning and hid itself at night, just as it does here.'

And the Englishman took a stick and, drawing circles on the sand, tried to explain how the sun moves in the heavens and goes round the world. But he was unable to explain it clearly, and pointing to the ship's pilot said:

'This man knows more about it than I do. He can explain it properly.'

The pilot, who was an intelligent man, had listened in silence to the talk till he was asked to speak. Now every one turned to him, and he said:

'You are all misleading one another, and are yourselves deceived. The sun does not go round the earth, but the earth goes round the sun, revolving as it goes and turning towards the sun in the course of each twenty-four hours, not only Japan, and the Philippines and Sumatra where we now are, but Africa, and Europe and America, and many lands besides. The sun does not shine for some one mountain, or for some one island, or for some one sea, nor even for one earth alone, but for other planets as well as our earth. If you would only look up at the heavens, instead of at the ground beneath your own feet, you might all understand this, and would then no longer suppose that the sun shines for you, or for your country alone.'

Thus spoke the wise pilot, who had voyaged much about the world, and had gazed much upon the heavens above.

'So on matters of faith,' continued the Chinaman the student of Confucius, 'it is pride that causes error and discord among men. As with the sun, so it is with God. Each man wants to have a special God of his own, or at least a special God for his native land. Each nation wishes to confine in its own temples Him, whom the world cannot contain.

'Can any temple compare with that which God Himself has built to unite all men in one faith and one religion?

'All human temples are built on the model of this temple, which is God's own world. Every temple has its fonts, its vaulted roof, its lamps, its pictures or sculptures, its inscriptions, its books of the law, its offerings, its altars and its priests. But in what temple is there such a font as the ocean; such a vault as that of the heavens; such lamps as the sun, moon, and stars; or any figures to be compared with living, loving, mutually-helpful men? Where are there any records of God's goodness so easy to understand as the blessings which God has strewn abroad for man's happiness? Where is there any book of the law so clear to each man as that written in his heart? What sacrifices equal the self-denials which loving men and women make for one another? And what altar can be compared with the heart of a good man, on which God Himself accepts the sacrifice?

'The higher a man's conception of God, the better will he know Him. And the better he knows God the nearer will he draw to Him, imitating His goodness, His mercy, and His love of man.

'Therefore, let him who sees the sun's whole light filling the world, refrain from blaming or despising the superstitious man, who in his own idol sees one ray of that same light. Let him not despise even the unbeliever who is blind and cannot see the sun at all.'

So spoke the Chinaman, the student of Confucius; and all who were present in the coffee-house were silent, and disputed no more as to whose faith was the best.

1893

TOO DEAR! (1897)

Tolstoy's Adaptation of a Story by Guy de Maupassant

Near the borders of France and Italy, on the shore of the Mediterranean Sea, lies a tiny little kingdom called Monaco. Many a small country town can boast more inhabitants than this kingdom, for there are only about seven thousand of them all told, and if all the land in the kingdom were divided there would not be an acre for each inhabitant. But in this toy kingdom there is a real kinglet; and he has a palace, and courtiers, and ministers, and a bishop, and generals, and an army.

It is not a large army, only sixty men in all, but still it is an army. There were also taxes in this kingdom as elsewhere: a tax on tobacco, and on wine and spirits and a poll-tax. But though the people there drink and smoke as people do in other countries, there are so few of them that the King would have been hard put to it to feed his courtiers and officials and to keep himself, if he had not found a new and special source of revenue. This special revenue comes from a gaming house, where people play roulette. People play, and whether they win or lose the keeper always gets a percentage on the turnover; and out of his profits he pays a large sum to the King. The reason he pays so much is that it is the only such gambling establishment left in Europe. Some of the little German Sovereigns used to keep gaming houses of the same kind, but some years ago they were forbidden to do so. The reason they were stopped was because these gaming houses did so much harm. A man would come and try his luck, then he would risk all he had and lose it, then he would even risk money that did not belong to him and lose that too, and then, in despair, he would drown or shoot himself. So the Germans forbade their rulers to make money in this way; but there was no one to stop the King of Monaco, and he remained with a monopoly of the business.

So now every one who wants to gamble goes to Monaco. Whether they win or lose, the King gains by it. 'You can't earn stone palaces by honest labour,' as the proverb says; and the Kinglet of Monaco knows it is a dirty business, but what is he to do? He has to live; and to draw a revenue from drink and from tobacco is also not a nice thing. So he lives and reigns, and rakes in the money, and holds his court with all the ceremony of a real king.

He has his coronation, his levees; he rewards, sentences, and pardons, and he also has his reviews, councils, laws, and courts of justice: just like other kings, only all on a smaller scale.

Now it happened a few years ago that a murder was committed in this toy King's domains. The people of that kingdom are peaceable, and such a thing had not happened before. The judges assembled with much ceremony and tried the case in the most judicial manner. There were judges, and prosecutors, and jurymen, and barristers. They argued and judged, and at last they condemned the criminal to have his head cut off as the law directs. So far so good. Next they submitted the sentence to the King. The King read the sentence and confirmed it. 'If the fellow must be executed, execute him.'

There was only one hitch in the matter; and that was that they had neither a guillotine for cutting heads off, nor an executioner. The Ministers considered the matter, and decided to address an inquiry to the French Government, asking whether the French could not lend them a machine and an expert to cut off the criminal's head; and if so, would the French kindly inform them what the cost would be. The letter was sent. A week later the reply came: a machine and an expert could be supplied, and the cost would be 16,000 francs. This was laid before the King. He thought it over. Sixteen thousand francs! 'The wretch is not worth the money,' said he. 'Can't it be done, somehow, cheaper? Why 16,000 francs is more than two francs a head on the whole population. The people won't stand it, and it may cause a riot!'

So a Council was called to consider what could be done; and it was decided to send a similar inquiry to the King of Italy. The French Government is republican, and has no proper respect for kings; but the King of Italy was a brother monarch, and might be induced to do the thing cheaper. So the letter was written, and a prompt reply was received.

The Italian Government wrote that they would have pleasure in supplying both a machine and an expert; and the whole cost would be 12,000 francs, including travelling expenses. This was cheaper, but still it seemed too much. The rascal was really not worth the money. It would still mean nearly two francs more per head on the taxes. Another

Council was called. They discussed and considered how it could be done with less expense. Could not one of the soldiers perhaps be got to do it in a rough and homely fashion? The General was called and was asked: 'Can't you find us a soldier who would cut the man's head off? In war they don't mind killing people. In fact, that is what they are trained for.' So the General talked it over with the soldiers to see whether one of them would not undertake the job. But none of the soldiers would do it. 'No,' they said, 'we don't know how to do it; it is not a thing we have been taught.'

What was to be done? Again the Ministers considered and reconsidered. They assembled a Commission, and a Committee, and a Sub-Committee, and at last they decided that the best thing would be to alter the death sentence to one of imprisonment for life. This would enable the King to show his mercy, and it would come cheaper.

The King agreed to this, and so the matter was arranged. The only hitch now was that there was no suitable prison for a man sentenced for life. There was a small lock-up where people were sometimes kept temporarily, but there was no strong prison fit for permanent use. However, they managed to find a place that would do, and they put the young fellow there and placed a guard over him. The guard had to watch the criminal, and had also to fetch his food from the palace kitchen.

The prisoner remained there month after month till a year had passed. But when a year had passed, the Kinglet, looking over the account of his income and expenditure one day, noticed a new item of expenditure. This was for the keep of the criminal; nor was it a small item either. There was a special guard, and there was also the man's food. It came to more than 600 francs a year. And the worst of it was that the fellow was still young and healthy, and might live for fifty years. When one came to reckon it up, the matter was serious. It would never do. So the King summoned his Ministers and said to them:

'You must find some cheaper way of dealing with this rascal. The present plan is too expensive.' And the Ministers met and considered and reconsidered, till one of them said: 'Gentlemen, in my opinion we must dismiss the guard.' 'But then,' rejoined another Minister, 'the fellow will run away.' 'Well,' said the first speaker, 'let him run away, and be hanged to him!' So they reported the result of their deliberations to the Kinglet, and he agreed with them. The guard was dismissed, and they waited to see what would happen. All that happened was that at dinner-time the criminal came out, and, not finding his guard, he went to the King's kitchen to fetch his own dinner. He took what was given him, returned to the prison, shut the door on himself, and stayed inside. Next day the same thing occurred. He went for his food at the proper time; but as for running away, he did not show the least sign of it! What was to be done? They considered the matter again.

'We shall have to tell him straight out,' said they 'that we do not want to keep him.' So the Minister of Justice had him brought before him.

'Why do you not run away?' said the Minister. 'There is no guard to keep you. You can go where you like, and the King will not mind.'

'I daresay the King would not mind,' replied the man, 'but I have nowhere to go. What can I do? You have ruined my character by your sentence, and people will turn their backs on me. Besides, I have got out of the way of working. You have treated me badly. It is not fair. In the first place, when once you sentenced me to death you ought to have executed me; but you did not do it. That is one thing. I did not complain about that. Then you sentenced me to imprisonment for life and put a guard to bring me my food; but after a time you took him away again and I had to fetch my own food. Again I did not complain. But now you actually want me to go away! I can't agree to that. You may do as you like, but I won't go away!'

What was to be done? Once more the Council was summoned. What course could they adopt? The man would not go. They reflected and considered. The only way to get rid of him was to offer him a pension. And so they reported to the King. 'There is nothing else for it,' said they; 'we must get rid of him somehow.' The sum fixed was 600 francs, and this was announced to the prisoner.

'Well,' said he, 'I don't mind, so long as you undertake to pay it regularly. On that condition I am willing to go.'

So the matter was settled. He received one-third of his annuity in advance, and left the King's dominions. It was only a quarter of an hour by rail; and he emigrated, and settled just across the frontier, where he bought a bit of land, started market-gardening, and now lives comfortably. He always goes at the proper time to draw his pension. Having received it, he goes to the gaming tables, stakes two or three francs, sometimes wins and sometimes loses, and then returns home. He lives peaceably and well.

It is a good thing that he did not commit his crime in a country where they do not grudge expense to cut a man's head off, or to keeping him in prison for life.

1897

PART VII. STORIES GIVEN TO AID THE PERSECUTED JEWS

ESARHADDON, KING OF ASSYRIA

The Assyrian King, Esarhaddon, had conquered the kingdom of King Lailie, had destroyed and burnt the towns, taken all the inhabitants captive to his own country, slaughtered the warriors, beheaded some chieftains and impaled or flayed others, and had confined King Lailie himself in a cage.

As he lay on his bed one night, King Esarhaddon was thinking how he should execute Lailie, when suddenly he heard a rustling near his bed, and opening his eyes saw an old man with a long grey bead and mild eyes.

'You wish to execute Lailie?' asked the old man.

'Yes,' answered the King. 'But I cannot make up my mind how to do it.'

'But you are Lailie,' said the old man.

'That's not true,' replied the King. 'Lailie is Lailie, and I am I.'

'You and Lailie are one,' said the old man. 'You only imagine you are not Lailie, and that Lailie is not you.'

'What do you mean by that?' said the King. 'Here am I, lying on a soft bed; around me are obedient men-slaves and women-slaves, and to-morrow I shall feast with my friends as I did to-day; whereas Lailie is sitting like a bird in a cage, and to-morrow he will be impaled, and with his tongue hanging out will struggle till he dies, and his body will be torn in pieces by dogs.'

'You cannot destroy his life,' said the old man.

'And how about the fourteen thousand warriors I killed, with whose bodies I built a mound?' said the King. 'I am alive, but they no longer exist. Does not that prove that I can destroy life?'

'How do you know they no longer exist?'

'Because I no longer see them. And, above all, they were tormented, but I was not. It was ill for them, but well for me.'

'That, also, only seems so to you. You tortured yourself, but not them.'

'I do not understand,' said the King.

'Do you wish to understand?'

'Yes, I do.'

'Then come here,' said the old man, pointing to a large font full of water.

The King rose and approached the font.

'Strip, and enter the font.'

Esarhaddon did as the old man bade him.

'As soon as I begin to pour this water over you,' said the old man, filling a pitcher with the water, 'dip down your head.'

The old man tilted the pitcher over the King's head and the King bent his head till it was under water.

And as soon as King Esarhaddon was under the water he felt that he was no longer Esarhaddon, but some one else. And, feeling himself to be that other man, he saw himself lying on a rich bed, beside a beautiful woman. He had never seen her before, but he knew she was his wife. The woman raised herself and said to him:

'Dear husband, Lailie! You were wearied by yesterday's work and have slept longer than usual, and I have guarded your rest, and have not roused you. But now the Princes await you in the Great Hall. Dress and go out to them.'

And Esarhaddon—understanding from these words that he was Lailie, and not feeling at all surprised at this, but only wondering that he did not know it before—rose, dressed, and went into the Great Hall where the Princes awaited him.

The Princes greeted Lailie, their King, bowing to the ground, and then they rose, and at his word sat down before him; and the eldest of the Princes began to speak, saying that it was impossible longer to endure the insults of the wicked King Esarhaddon, and that they must make war on him. But Lailie disagreed, and gave orders that envoys shall be sent to remonstrate with King Esarhaddon; and he dismissed the Princes from the audience. Afterwards he appointed men of note to act as ambassadors, and impressed on them what they were to say to King Esarhaddon. Having finished this business, Esarhaddon—feeling himself to be Lailie—rode out to hunt wild asses. The hunt was successful. He killed two wild asses himself, and having returned home, feasted with his friends, and witnessed a dance of slave girls. The next day he went to the Court, where he was awaited by petitioners suitors, and prisoners brought for trial; and there as usual he decided the cases submitted to him. Having finished this business, he again rode out to his favourite amusement: the hunt. And again he was successful: this time killing with his own hand an old lioness, and capturing her two cubs. After the hunt he again feasted with his friends, and was entertained with music and dances, and the night he spent with the wife whom he loved.

So, dividing his time between kingly duties and pleasures, he lived for days and weeks, awaiting the return of the ambassadors he had sent to that King Esarhaddon who used to be himself. Not till a month had passed did the ambassadors return, and they returned with their noses and ears cut off.

King Esarhaddon had ordered them to tell Lailie that what had been done to them—the ambassadors—would be done to King Lailie himself also, unless he sent immediately a tribute of silver, gold, and cypress-wood, and came himself to pay homage to King Esarhaddon.

Lailie, formerly Esarhaddon, again assembled the Princes, and took counsel with them as to what he should do. They all with one accord said that war must be made against Esarhaddon, without waiting for him to attack them. The King agreed; and taking his place at the head of the army, started on the campaign. The campaign lasts seven days. Each day the King rode round the army to rouse the courage of his warriors. On the eighth day his army met that of Esarhaddon in a broad valley through which a river flowed. Lailie's army fought bravely, but Lailie, formerly Esarhaddon, saw the enemy swarming down from the mountains like ants, over-running the valley and overwhelming his army; and, in his chariot, he flung himself into the midst of the battle, hewing and felling the enemy. But the warriors of Lailie were but as hundreds, while those of Esarhaddon were as thousands; and Lailie felt himself wounded and taken prisoner. Nine days he journeyed with other captives, bound, and guarded by the warriors of Esarhaddon. On the tenth day he reached Nineveh, and was placed in a cage. Lailie suffered not so much from hunger and from his wound as from shame and impotent rage. He felt how powerless he was to avenge himself on his enemy for all he was suffering. All he could do was to deprive his enemies of the pleasure of seeing his sufferings; and he firmly resolved to endure courageously without a murmur, all they could do to him. For twenty days he sat in his cage, awaiting execution. He saw his relatives and friends led out to death; he heard the groans of those who were executed: some had their hands and feet cut off, others were flayed alive, but he showed neither disquietude, nor pity, nor fear. He saw the wife he loved, bound, and led by two black eunuchs. He knew she was being taken as a slave to Esarhaddon. That, too, he bore without a murmur. But one of the guards placed to watch him said, 'I pity you, Lailie; you were a king, but what are you now?' And hearing these words, Lailie remembered all he had lost. He clutched the bars of his cage, and, wishing to kill himself, beat his head against them. But he had not the strength to do so and, groaning in despair, he fell upon the floor of his cage.

At last two executioners opened his cage door, and having strapped his arms tight behind him, led him to the place of execution, which was soaked with blood. Lailie saw a sharp stake dripping with blood, from which the corpse of one of his friends had just been torn, and he understood that this had been done that the stake might serve for his own execution. They stripped Lailie of his clothes. He was startled at the leanness of his once strong, handsome body. The two executioners seized that body by its lean thighs; they lifted him up and were about to let him fall upon the stake.

'This is death, destruction!' thought Lailie, and, forgetful of his resolve to remain bravely calm to the end, he sobbed and prayed for mercy. But no one listened to him.

'But this cannot be,' thought he. 'Surely I am asleep. It is a dream.' And he made an effort to rouse himself, and did indeed awake, to find himself neither Esarhaddon nor Lailie—but some kind of an animal. He was astonished that he was an animal, and astonished, also, at not having known this before.

He was grazing in a valley, tearing the tender grass with his teeth, and brushing away flies with his long tail. Around him was frolicking a long-legged, dark-gray ass-colt, striped down its back. Kicking up its hind legs, the colt galloped full speed to Esarhaddon, and poking him under the stomach with its smooth little muzzle, searched for the teat, and, finding it, quieted down, swallowing regularly. Esarhaddon understood that he was a she-ass, the colt's mother, and this neither surprised nor grieved him, but rather gave him pleasure. He experienced a glad feeling of simultaneous life in himself and in his offspring.

But suddenly something flew near with a whistling sound and hit him in the side, and with its sharp point entered his skin and flesh. Feeling a burning pain, Esarhaddon—who was at the same time the ass—tore the udder from the colt's teeth, and laying back his ears galloped to the herd from which he had strayed. The colt kept up with him, galloping by his side. They had already nearly reached the herd, which had started off, when another arrow in full flight struck the colt's neck. It pierced the skin and quivered in its flesh. The colt sobbed piteously and fell upon its knees. Esarhaddon could not abandon it, and remained standing over it. The colt rose, tottered on its long, thin legs, and again fell. A fearful two-legged being—a man—ran up and cut its throat.

'This cannot be; it is still a dream! thought Esarhaddon, and made a last effort to awake. 'Surely I am not Lailie, nor the ass, but Esarhaddon!'

He cried out, and at the same instant lifted his head out of the font... The old man was standing by him, pouring over his head the last drops from the pitcher.

'Oh, how terribly I have suffered! And for how long!' said Esarhaddon.

'Long?' replied the old man, 'you have only dipped your head under water and lifted it again; see, the water is not yet all out of the pitcher. Do you now understand?'

Esarhaddon did not reply, but only looked at the old man with terror.

'Do you now understand,' continued the old man, 'that Lailie is you, and the warriors you put to death were you also? And not the warriors only, but the animals which you slew when hunting and ate at your feasts were also you. You thought life dwelt in you alone but I have drawn aside the veil of delusion, and have let you see that by doing evil to others you have done it to yourself also. Life is one in them all, and yours is but a portion of this same common life. And only in that one part of life that is yours, can you make life better or worse—increasing or decreasing it. You can only improve life in yourself by destroying the barriers that divide your life from that of others, and by considering others as yourself, and loving them. By so doing you increase your share of life. You injure your life when you think of it as the only life, and try to add to its welfare at the expense of other lives. By so doing you only lessen it. To destroy the life that dwells in others is beyond your power. The life of those you have slain has vanished from your eyes, but is not destroyed. You thought to lengthen your own life and to shorten theirs, but you cannot do this. Life knows neither time nor space. The life of a moment, and the life of a thousand years: your life and the life of all the visible and invisible beings in the world, are equal. To destroy life, or to alter it, is impossible; for life is the one thing that exists. All else, but seems to us to be.'

Having said this the old man vanished.

Next morning King Esarhaddon gave orders that Lailie and all the prisoners should be set at liberty and that the executions should cease.

On the third day he called his son Assur-bani-pal, and gave the kingdom over into his hands; and he himself went into the desert to think over all he had learnt. Afterwards he went about as a wanderer through the towns and villages, preaching to the people that all life is one, and that when men wish to harm others, they really do evil to themselves.

1903

WORK, DEATH AND SICKNESS

A LEGEND

A legend from the South American Indians

God, say they, at first made men so that they had no need to work: they needed neither houses, nor clothes, nor food, and they all lived till they were a hundred, and did not know what illness was.

When, after some time, God looked to see how people were living, he saw that instead of being happy in their life, they had quarrelled with one another, and, each caring for himself, had brought matters to such a pass that far from enjoying life, they cursed it.

Then God said to himself: 'This comes of their living separately, each for himself.' And to change this state of things, God so arranged matters that it became impossible for people to live without working.

To avoid suffering from cold and hunger, they were now obliged to build dwellings, and to dig the ground, and to grow and gather fruits and grain.

'Work will bring them together,' thought God. 'They cannot make their tools, prepare and transport their timber, build their houses, sow and gather their harvests, spin and weave, and make their clothes, each one alone by himself.'

'It will make them understand that the more heartily they work together, the more they will have and the better they will live; and this will unite them.'

Time passed on, and again God came to see how men were living, and whether they were now happy.

But he found them living worse than before. They worked together (that they could not help doing), but not all together, being broken up into little groups. And each group tried to snatch work from other groups, and they hindered one another, wasting time and strength in their struggles, so that things went ill with them all.

Having seen that this, too, was not well, God decided so as to arrange things that man should not know the time of his death, but might die at any moment; and he announced this to them.

'Knowing that each of them may die at any moment,' thought God, 'they will not, by grasping at gains that may last so short a time, spoil the hours of life allotted to them.'

But it turned out otherwise. When God returned to see how people were living, he saw that their life was as bad as ever.

Those who were strongest, availing themselves of the fact that men might die at any time, subdued those who were weaker, killing some and threatening others with death. And it came about that the strongest and their descendants did no work, and suffered from the weariness of idleness, while those who were weaker had to work beyond their strength, and suffered from lack of rest. Each set of men feared and hated the other. And the life of man became yet more unhappy.

Having seen all this, God, to mend matters, decided to make use of one last means; he sent all kinds of sickness among men. God thought that when all men were exposed to sickness they would understand that those who are well should have pity on those who are sick, and should help them, that when they themselves fall ill those who are well might in turn help them.

And again God went away, but when He came back to see how men lived now that they were subject to sicknesses, he saw that their life was worse even than before. The very sickness that in God's purpose should have united men, had divided them more than ever. Those men who were strong enough to make others work, forced them also to wait on them in times of sickness; but they did not, in their turn, look after others who were ill. And those who were forced to work for others and to look after them when sick, were so worn with work that they had no time to look after their own sick, but left them without attendance. That the sight of sick folk might not disturb the pleasures of the wealthy, houses were arranged in which these poor people suffered and died, far from those whose sympathy might have cheered them, and in the arms of hired people who nursed them without compassion, or even with disgust. Moreover, people considered many of the illnesses infectious, and, fearing to catch them, not only avoided the sick, but even separated themselves from those who attended the sick.

Then God said to Himself: 'If even this means will not bring men to understand wherein their happiness lies, let them be taught by suffering.' And God left men to themselves.

And, left to themselves, men lived long before they understood that they all ought to, and might be, happy. Only in the very latest times have a few of them begun to understand that work ought not to be a bugbear to some and like galley-slavery for others, but should be a common and happy occupation, uniting all men. They have begun to understand that with death constantly threatening each of us, the only reasonable business of every man is to spend the years, months, hours, and minutes, allotted him—in unity and love. They have begun to understand that sickness, far from dividing men, should, on the contrary, give opportunity for loving union with one another.

1903

THREE QUESTIONS

It once occurred to a certain king, that if he always knew the right time to begin everything; if he knew who were the right people to listen to, and whom to avoid, and, above all, if he always knew what was the most important thing to do, he would never fail in anything he might undertake.

And this thought having occurred to him, he had it proclaimed throughout his kingdom that he would give a great reward to any one who would teach him what was the right time for every action, and who were the most necessary people, and how he might know what was the most important thing to do.

And learned men came to the King, but they all answered his questions differently.

In reply to the first question, some said that to know the right time for every action, one must draw up in advance, a table of days, months and years, and must live strictly according to it. Only thus, said they, could everything be done at its proper time. Others declared that it was impossible to decide beforehand the right time for every action; but that, not letting oneself be absorbed in idle pastimes, one should always attend to all that was going on, and then do what was most needful. Others, again, said that however attentive the King might be to what was going on, it was impossible for one man to decide correctly the right time for every action, but that he should have a Council of wise men, who would help him to fix the proper time for everything.

But then again others said there were some things which could not wait to be laid before a Council, but about which one had at once to decide whether to undertake them or not. But in order to decide that one must know beforehand what was going to happen. It is only magicians who know that; and, therefore in order to know the right time for every action, one must consult magicians.

Equally various were the answers to the second question. Some said, the people the King most needed were his councillors; others, the priests; others, the doctors; while some said the warriors were the most necessary.

To the third question, as to what was the most important occupation: some replied that the most important thing in the world was science. Others said it was skill in warfare; and others, again, that it was religious worship.

All the answers being different, the King agreed with none of them, and gave the reward to none. But still wishing to find the right answers to his questions, he decided to consult a hermit, widely renowned for his wisdom.

The hermit lived in a wood which he never quitted and he received none but common folk. So the King put on simple clothes, and before reaching the hermit's cell dismounted from his horse, and, leaving his bodyguard behind, went on alone.

When the King approached, the hermit was digging the ground in front of his hut. Seeing the King, he greeted him and went on digging. The hermit was frail and weak, and each time he stuck his spade into the ground and turned a little earth, he breathed heavily.

The King went up to him and said: 'I have come to you, wise hermit, to ask you to answer three questions: How can I learn to do the right thing at the right time? Who are the people I most need, and to whom should I, therefore, pay more attention than to the rest? And, what affairs are the most important and need my first attention?'

The hermit listened to the King, but answered nothing. He just spat on his hand and recommenced digging.

'You are tired,' said the King, 'let me take the spade and work awhile for you.'

'Thanks!' said the hermit, and, giving the spade to the King, he sat down on the ground.

When he had dug two beds, the King stopped and repeated his questions. The hermit again gave no answer, but rose, stretched out his hand for the spade, and said:

'Now rest awhile—and let me work a bit.'

But the King did not give him the spade, and continued to dig. One hour passed, and another. The sun began to sink behind the trees, and the King at last stuck the spade into the ground, and said:

'I came to you, wise man, for an answer to my questions. If you can give me none, tell me so, and I will return home.'

'Here comes some one running,' said the hermit, 'let us see who it is.'

The King turned round, and saw a bearded man come running out of the wood. The man held his hands pressed against his stomach, and blood was flowing from under them. When he reached the King, he fell fainting on the ground moaning feebly. The King and the hermit unfastened the man's clothing. There was a large wound in his stomach. The King washed it as best he could, and bandaged it with his handkerchief and with a towel the hermit had. But the blood would not stop flowing, and the King again and again removed the bandage soaked with warm blood, and washed and rebandaged the wound. When at last the blood ceased flowing, the man revived and asked for something to drink. The King brought fresh water and gave it to him. Meanwhile the sun had set, and it had become cool. So the King, with the hermit's help, carried the wounded man into the hut and laid him on the bed. Lying on the bed the man closed his eyes and was quiet; but the King was so tired with his walk and with the work he had done, that he crouched down on the threshold, and also fell asleep—so soundly that he slept all through the short summer night. When he awoke in the morning, it was long before he could remember where he was, or who was the strange bearded man lying on the bed and gazing intently at him with shining eyes.

'Forgive me!' said the bearded man in a weak voice, when he saw that the King was awake and was looking at him.

'I do not know you, and have nothing to forgive you for,' said the King.

'You do not know me, but I know you. I am that enemy of yours who swore to revenge himself on you, because you executed his brother and seized his property. I knew you had gone alone to see the hermit, and I resolved to kill you on your way back. But the day passed and you did not return. So I came out from my ambush to find you, and I came upon your bodyguard, and they recognized me, and wounded me. I escaped from them, but should have bled to death had you not dressed my wound. I wished to kill you, and you have saved my life. Now, if I live, and if you wish it, I will serve you as your most faithful slave, and will bid my sons do the same. Forgive me!'

The King was very glad to have made peace with his enemy so easily, and to have gained him for a friend, and he not only forgave him, but said he would send his servants and his own physician to attend him, and promised to restore his property.

Having taken leave of the wounded man, the King went out into the porch and looked around for the hermit. Before going away he wished once more to beg an answer to the questions he had put. The hermit was outside, on his knees, sowing seeds in the beds that had been dug the day before.

The King approached him, and said:

'For the last time, I pray you to answer my questions, wise man.'

'You have already been answered!' said the hermit still crouching on his thin legs, and looking up at the King, who stood before him.

'How answered? What do you mean?' asked the King.

'Do you not see,' replied the hermit. 'If you had not pitied my weakness yesterday, and had not dug these beds for me, but had gone your way, that man would have attacked you, and you would have repented of not having stayed with me. So the most important time was when you were digging the beds; and I was the most important man; and to do me good was your most important business. Afterwards, when that man ran to us, the most important time was when you were attending to him, for if you had not bound up his wounds he would have died without having made peace with you. So he was the most important man, and what you did for him was your most important business. Remember then: there is only one time that is important— Now! It is the most important time because it is the only time when we have any power. The most necessary man is he with whom you are, for no man knows whether he will ever have dealings with any one else: and the most important affair is, to do him good, because for that purpose alone was man sent into this life!'

1903

THE END

Printed in Great Britain
by Amazon

45895606R00131